THE GRAY PROPHECY

THE ELEMENTAL REALM SERIES

BOOK ONE

MARIA A. EDEN

For all those who have felt alone
and found a friend in magic.

PART ONE
MOON IN LIBRA

"New beginnings are always best when the moon is in Libra.
Libra accepts us for what we are."
-The Essential Guide to Celestial Magic

CORI

The winter solstice was 102 days away. Cori's tattered journal was stained with coffee rings and creased in the corners from being repeatedly pushed into her purse. She picked it up from the passenger seat and ran her thumb over the cover illustration of the Golden Gate Bridge before turning to the first page.

Dear Starlight,
I hope this diary will remind you of home.
-Mama

Beneath her mother's twirly script, Cori had started her countdown from 3,401.

She turned to the back cover, where a photograph was tucked neatly behind a paper clip. A man in a leather jacket stood hand in hand with a small boy on the steps of a trolley.

His mouth was curled up slightly, as though he were about to tell a witty joke. Beside him, the little boy beamed so brightly at the camera, the word *cheese* practically echoed off the glossy paper.

It was late afternoon when she finally pulled into the gravel parking lot. She loathed being late, and being late on her first day made her want to vomit. Her mother's handwriting was a reassuring hand on her shoulder, smeared ink on the page whispering in soothing tones from three thousand miles away.

Puffing out a resigned breath that freed the wavy wisps of stray hair from her forehead, she carefully tucked the notebook back into her purse.

Three tattered canvas duffel bags were shoved into the back of her woebegone Volkswagen Golf, containing all her worldly possessions. She straightened her spine and righted herself, attempting to balance a bag full of her research binders and ocean gear on her shoulder without falling face first onto the pavement.

An impressive building stood at the edge of the parking lot, an amalgam of a barn and a factory. Beyond it, a narrow strip of sand was lined with neat rows of brightly colored houses.

As the shore curved to the north, a haphazard collection of flat, steep cliffs sparked with light, like candles dancing in the salty mist.

Small town. Remote location. Perfect place to hide.

She tightened the laces of her duck boots and rearranged the bag over her shoulder once more before treading to the entrance. A foghorn sounded in the distance, and a nostalgic ache echoed through her chest.

Thick air laced with salt, gasoline, and sea-washed sweat wrapped around her as she entered the building, where busy crews hauled nets and motor parts through a bustling, open-air wharf.

"There she is," a familiar raspy voice echoed from the bottom of the stairs.

"Anne!" Cori threw down her bags and pulled her former professor into a hug. "I'm so sorry I'm late. When I left New Haven this morning, the map said it would take seven hours, but—"

Anne dismissively waved her hand before grabbing one of her bags. "Don't worry. The drive up here can be rough on a Friday afternoon."

Cori hastily smoothed her hair into a ponytail before following Anne up the stairs where modern glass office windows on the second floor struck a pleasing contrast to the worn plank walls below.

"I'm so glad you're finally joining us, Cori," Anne said as they reached the end of the hallway. Her bracelets jangled together as she opened the door with a flourish. "The office is a bit basic compared to the ecology labs at Yale, but it's got its own charm."

A desk near the front entrance held a steaming cup of black coffee and a tackle box labeled with Cori's name. Ceramic cats, like the ones she used to see in Chinatown, bobbed kinetic paws behind a tidy pile of notebooks.

"Jordan's been working all day putting together some gear for you," Anne said.

On cue, a stunning man with ripped jeans, a black T-shirt, and nails painted in an iridescent violet hue strode around the corner. "Anne, I swear. If those assholes in the governor's office send me one more angry email, I'm going to hike into Augusta, just so I can shove my boot—This must be Dr. Evans." His hand rose to cover his mouth. "I'm sorry you had to see me on a tirade. Your first impression of me is probably ruined forever."

"Jordan runs this place. He's the operations manager I told you about," Anne said.

Cori nodded, fidgeting with the hem of her sweatshirt. Jordan smiled at her expectantly, his posture tall and confident. In this tiny office, something told her she wouldn't get away with hiding behind a microscope all day. Suddenly her throat dried, like clay left in the sun.

"It's nice to meet you," she said, her voice cracking. "I'm so sorry I'm late."

Jordan shrugged. "You didn't miss much. We've spent all day dealing with a broken boat. Maybe you can take a look at it. Anne mentioned you had a mechanical mind. Unlike your predecessor," he paused with an eye roll, "who barely knew how to put the key in the engine."

Anne pursed her lips at him. "You were always so hard on Adam. He was just a bit—"

"...chamomile?" Jordan finished for her.

Cori laughed awkwardly at their exchange. Adam may have been inept at his job, but acting like a bland cup of decaffeinated tea in a world of caramel macchiato happened to be Cori's go-to move. She swallowed the dry lump in her throat as her fingers drifted habitually to the charm bracelet on her wrist.

"I'll show you the lab," Anne said.

The three of them picked up her things and turned a corner to a tidy little room around the back of Jordan's work area.

A large picture window looked out to sea, bathing the room with the warm amber glow of the sun dipping behind the trees. The picturesque cliffs she had noticed on her arrival loomed majestically over a sparkling little town. Waves glimmered like constellations of stars, crashing on the rocks.

"Not a bad view," Anne mused. "Better than the dumpsters behind the engineering building in New Haven."

Cori nodded in agreement as she took in the vista. The window faced north, an ideal position for viewing the night sky. Something deep in her gut stirred.

She clenched her jaw, pushing down the rising sensation in the chest. *Not here. Not now.*

She was far too close to the solstice to let that part of herself resurface.

"If you're finished staring out the window, I can show you the boat." Jordan said.

Heat flooded her cheeks. "Absolutely," she said with a determined nod of her head. She set off after him, shaking off the feeling of unease.

"This building used to be a boat-servicing wharf," Jordan explained as they strode down the stairs. "That's why it gives off such industrial vibes. A few years ago, the town got some funds with a research grant from the state to remodel. There was a contingency that allowed environmental scientists to set up shop here if the crews in residence agreed to share their marina." Jordan raised his eyebrows at her.

"I expect that probably went over with mixed levels of enthusiasm."

He smirked. "That's one way to say it."

The men on the lower level were dressed in layers of flannel under their coveralls. Anne had already warned Cori that there was always a bite of cold in Maine, even in early September. Farley was on the northern coast, just south of Acadia on north Penobscot Bay. The tide map and the location made it the perfect spot to be an ecologist and an even better spot to blend into the shadows for the next three months.

"The town was struggling with revenue when the government issued the grant," Jordan explained. "It was the only thing that could get them out of the bind. A lot of the locals are still a little sore about it, but to be honest, most of the sentiment was welcoming. This is the type of town where people grow up and never leave. The community's close," he explained.

"What was it like moving up here?" Cori asked, trying to keep up with his long strides as they walked toward the dock.

His hand drifted to his chest. "How can you tell I'm not a local?" he asked with mock ostentation.

Cori cringed, cursing her unfortunate predisposition to make every situation just a little awkward.

"Your accent," she said, fidgeting with her charm bracelet again.

Jordan shrugged. "The accent always gives it away. This isn't New York. Moving up here took some adjustment. There aren't too many gay Black men in northern Maine, as you may have guessed. I met Anne in Manhattan. She was trying to get donations from the PR firm I was working for at the time."

He stopped walking as they approached the dock, gesturing towards a small, neat vessel bobbing silently in the water.

"Do you ever get out on the boat?" Cori asked.

He returned a serious look. "I don't do boats, Dr. Evans."

"Noted," she said, squaring her shoulders as she stepped aboard. "I can take a look. This is a sterndrive?"

Jordan cocked his head and crossed his arms.

"Right," she said, flushing. She hoped she could be useful for something today besides being a walking stereotype of a socially awkward scientist. As she set to work examining the gears, Jordan eyed her skeptically from the dock.

Luckily, the problem stemmed from a simple jam on the throttle. She released the lever in tandem with a sigh of relief and reset the position. When she turned the key, the engine sputtered before growling to life.

Jordan raised his eyebrows. "Well-done, Dr. Evans."

She smiled tentatively at him as some of the tension in her shoulders loosened. "Please, call me Cori."

Gooseflesh prickled on her skin as the wind picked up, her gaze sweeping reflexively skyward. It wasn't even dusk but the stars blinked through a cobalt sky. Weary energy drummed through her veins, cresting in tandem to the beat of her heart.

Cori hastily pushed it away. *I said not now.*

She tore her gaze away from the glittering canopy above her. It was going to be hard to turn off her senses in a place like this. In New Haven, sound and light from campus blared with near constant distraction.

Until this moment, Cori had purposely avoided places like this. Her Eye had been closed for the past nine years, and she preferred it stay that way.

The hum of a distant engine grew with ferocious intensity offshore. As it neared, the composition of the air thickened. An electric tingle spread from the outermost layer of her skin down to the marrow of her bone. Her hair stood on edge and sparks of energy danced on her tongue.

It could only mean one thing. There was another witch nearby.

Dread rose in her chest. This was the last place on Earth she expected to confront a witch. The pesky magic of her Eye fluttered in response to the charge in the air.

She turned back to Jordan, perhaps a little too sharply. He jumped in response.

"You know what, I'm exhausted from the drive and I would love to unpack," she said briskly.

Jordan gaped at her as she leaped from the deck of the boat. If Cori Evans was good at one thing, it was running away.

ADRIAN

As dusk settled on the marina, the water surged around him. Adrian could always sense the tide. The rhythm of the water was within his blood, and the urgency rose and fell in his chest. As he gripped the rudder of the ship, water particles in the air clung to him, begging to do his bidding. The boat slid over the waves, like an extension of his body.

This was his favorite time of the day to be on the boat. Every wave crested with a golden kiss of sun, covering the marina like a shimmering blanket. The water was deepening, becoming dark and cold underneath him, like the coming of a winter's day.

He imagined this is what it felt like for all fishermen to some extent, but his connection to the water was different. As he tightened down the nets, he glanced at Seth, now at the rudder. His older brother shivered. Adrian knew he felt it, too.

They were sweaty and exhausted, and the end of the day beckoned to them with the promise of something warm to eat and a cold IPA. After baking in the heat of the sun all afternoon, the cool depths of the water seemed just right.

"Dad's going to lose it when he realizes we're officially down this week," Seth shouted at him through the wind.

Adrian frowned. His father was hard on his sons, but he was

even harder on himself. One terrible investment after the other had led them down a dangerous path.

Adrian had not realized how deeply in debt they were until several years earlier, when he had come home from college, freshly minted with a degree in business management.

David was out collecting traps today while his sons manned the rig. Even the most experienced and gifted fisherman could catch only so much if the waters were empty.

This had been an awful summer for sea bugs, and Adrian had spent every free moment of his time trying to adjust their prices to squeak out a profit. They had lost a few customers along the way, and it seemed like he was caught in a never-ending battle with his father about the price hikes.

Sure, every lobstering family in town was feeling it. But the Huxleys were different. Special. More in tune. David believed that they, of all people, should be able to overcome a poor season. A poor investment. Multiple misguided choices. Empty waters.

It made situations like this sting even deeper.

As they sped to the marina, Adrian noticed Seth growing inpatient. "This motor sure needs a tune-up," he grumbled. Seth placed his hand on the wheel, and the boat surged with renewed speed. The dock was growing larger now.

Adrian rolled his eyes as he shouted back over the roar of the water. "If you crash into the dock again, Dad is going to have two things to lecture us about," he warned. He cringed at the thought of another costly repair to their aging rig.

It never made sense to Adrian to rush to the shore. Especially at this time of day. He closed his eyes as the water washed over his face in microscopic droplets of cool mist. He breathed it in, and the spray of the ocean fed him a renewed energy.

As they slowed down to the marina and neared their docking at the mouth of the enormous building ahead of them, the cool freshness of the air changed instantly. The brothers looked at each other in confusion.

They both felt it.

The air had turned all at once electric and magnetic. The hair on the back of Adrian's neck prickled with intensity, and he knew.

There was another witch on the dock.

CORI

C ori sat down heavily at her new desk, her possessions scattered around her in her feeble attempt at unpacking. A vibration of nervous energy shook her hands as she carefully unpacked a box of slides. She knew that her magic would eventually break through again, no matter how hard she tried to lock it away.

Why now?

She had successfully pushed away her Eye since she left for Yale at seventeen, the year all witches come of age. When she sent in her college acceptance letter, she didn't tell her family about it.

She couldn't.

This part of her life would be safer for everyone if they didn't know where she was going. After years of plotting, they had no better alternative. It was safer for her, and it was safer for the coven.

She closed her eyes, bracing herself, as her magic twitched to life. A vision was coming. It had been so long since she had received one, but she immediately recognized the visceral dread as her Eye broke its way to the forefront of her mind.

. . .

The row home in San Francisco always smelled a bit like sandalwood incense. *Astrid lit candles and sprinkled lavender under a whimsically painted sign, the plait of her blond hair cascading down her back.*

Happy 9th Birthday, Cordelia.

"Can you light the rest of those candles?" *her mother called back to her. Giggles echoed from the other side of the room where two other girls from the coven were at work setting up the ritual circle.*

"Do you think Cori knows how to light candles?" *Josephine whispered to her friend.*

"I know how to do it," *Cori muttered indignantly. She hastily whispered the incantation, but the wicks merely sparked pathetically.*

"Girls, don't tease Cordelia," *her mother said sternly.*

The girls exchanged a serious look. Astrid Mangianelli was the coven leader, and getting scolded by her was not something to take lightly.

"Sorry, Priestess," *they said in unison.*

"Cordelia's a Celestial witch. It's not easy for her to live in a coven of Charms witches." *Cori's cheeks heated at her mother's rebuke.* "Every witch—Celestial, Charms, Gray or Elemental—can do basic charms. She just needs to use the incantation." *Her mother smiled encouragingly at her.* "We've been practicing."

Astrid's cool, blue eyes flashed as she nodded at her misfit daughter. Cori puffed out a deep breath and wrinkled her forehead as she methodically whispered the incantation, lighting the candle ablaze with her magic.

"I knew you could do it, Starlight." *Astrid squeezed her daughter's shoulders before crossing the room to finish hanging the sign.*

"Why are you a Celestial witch?" *asked Josephine, the priestess now comfortably out of earshot.*

Cori's shoulder tipped up. "Because my father was a Celestial witch."

"Why don't you go live with him, then?" *Josephine asked scathingly.* "Then he can be the one to teach you magic."

Red heat flared in her cheeks. "Because my father's dead."

Josephine's face paled as Alexandra nudged her in the ribs.

"Well, I think it's pretty cool that you're Celestial," Alexandra said quickly. "Where do you keep your Eye?"

Cori's eyebrows rose into her hair. "I don't keep it anywhere. It's in my head. Sometimes it takes over my sense of sight, and I get a vision—like I'm watching a movie—from the past, present or future."

"My mother says you can see ghosts," Josephine said ominously, raising her hands as though she were a zombie.

Cori wasn't sure if she wanted to punch Josephine in the jaw or run up to her room and bury her face in her pillow. She opened her mouth to respond when a serious voice interrupted them.

"Cori can see spirits, as a matter of fact. And if you girls don't stop teasing her, I'll make sure she sends some mean, bloody ones to your house to wake you up in the middle of the night."

Enzo to the rescue. As usual.

Her brother sauntered into the room, escorted by his best friend, Calvin. The girls blushed a deep crimson. She bit back the urge to give her brother the biggest hug of her life but instead arranged her face into a cool, satisfied smirk.

"I could do it, you know," Cori said, finding her courage. She squinted at Josephine. Sure, she could see spirits, but she couldn't make them do her bidding. Josephine didn't need to know that part.

Calvin laughed heartily as he mussed Cori's hair. "Don't mess around with this girl. She can see spirits, but she can also see auras. That means she can sense what you're thinking about—almost like she can read your mind."

"No, she can't," Josephine retorted.

"Oh yes, I can," Cori shot back. "And right now, I can sense that you think Calvin's hot." Josephine's face paled. "And that you're holding in a fart."

The boys let out a thunderous laugh as Josephine stormed from the room, either to find her mother or let out the gas she was accused of holding in. Cori could see auras. All Celestials could.

She couldn't detect people's stomach discomfort, but her first accusation was all truth. Enzo and Calvin were popular and good-looking. Any time the other girls saw them, the haze of energy around them turned a smoky red.

"Come on, Cor," Enzo said, hooking his arm around hers. "I have a birthday gift for you."

Cori followed him into the kitchen, where he presented her with a neatly gift-wrapped parcel.

She smiled up at her brother as she tore through the paper, revealing a double paned picture frame. On one side, a man stood on the steps of a trolley, holding a little boy's hand. The man had neatly combed brown hair and dark eyes that sparkled with flecks of gold.

Her eyes.

She bit her lip hard enough to dull the ache rising in her chest. On the other side of the frame, her name was written in calligraphy.

"I found this picture of Papa and got it framed. Did you know he named you? Right before he died, he told me he was going to name you Cordelia because of a vision he had about you." He pointed to the description etched in fine writing under her name.

"Cordelia," she read aloud. "Latin; meaning: heart, star of the sea."

She sucked in a breath, returning to the present. It made sense that this place would bring her back to a time when she missed her father most. It was funny that you could miss someone that you had never even met.

Mourn something you never even knew.

But as she took in the view of the ocean from her office window, she felt her father there with her in a way. His prediction had come true. She had dedicated her life to the ocean, and now she was taking on her first big endeavor toward trying to save it.

The charm bracelet on her arm jangled as she twirled it through her fingers.

It had been so long since she had received a vision. Locking her Eye away in the bustle of Yale's campus had been easy. Occasionally, she had run into another witch, the tingle of magic bristling on her skin in an inopportune moment. She would usually flee the scene, but in rare instances, she ended up small-talking with another witch, pretending she was a Charms witch with little to no magical ability.

She had gotten an invitation to the coven on campus, but she shoved it in a drawer. The only person she allowed herself to get close to at Yale was Anne, and Anne only knew one side of her—the boring scientist, not the cursed witch. Committing all her energy into her research turned out to be a highly effective way to tamp down her magic.

Over the years, she continued to have shadows of her visions in her sleep, the only time she couldn't consciously control her Eye. Dreams were different for Cori, like a vivid extension of reality. Every night, she replayed scenes from her childhood, saw glimpses of her mother and brother in the present, and received messages of the future. Some of her regular dreams were still a mystery to her.

A blue flame, rapidly engulfing a piece of folded paper. The sound of a little girl giggling in a faraway voice, perfumed by the smell of cotton candy. Two electric blue eyes haloed in a constellation of freckles that perfectly mirrored the constellation of Cetus.

She jumped when she heard a soft knock on the door. Anne popped her head in, her eyebrows raised. "Were you burning incense in here?"

Cori felt her cheeks flush. "No..." she stammered. "It must be coming from one of my bags."

Anne shrugged. "Well, we should probably get going. I know you have a lot of settling in to do. I was thinking...you should stay with Geoff and me. For as long as you want."

"Don't worry about me." Cori waved her hand in the air. "I made a reservation at the Collins Inn for the next few days until I can find an apartment."

Anne shook her head with a sigh. "The Collins Inn is just a

spare bedroom in Greg Collins's basement. I'll call him and tell him you made a mistake."

Cori rubbed her forehead. "I don't want to impose," she said.

"Stop it," Anne returned, scooping up Cori's duffel bag and leading the way to the door before she could argue any more about the topic.

Adrian

Adrian heaved his metal lunchbox onto the dented and stained kitchen table with a heavy clunk of resignation. His muscles ached and his stomach had been rumbling for the past hour, but stepping into the warm kitchen settled him and immediately put him at ease.

Something amazing was brewing on the stove, which dulled the sting of his disappointing day. Rosemary and sage.

Rubbing his hand over his aching shoulder, he inhaled deeply over the heavy stew pot, chipped and dented and bubbling on a slow simmer. At least it must have been a good harvest day.

Hannah Huxley rarely had a poor harvest. The residents in town liked to joke that Hannah could grow a pepper out of a rock. Only her family knew the true reason.

Hannah was a Ground Elemental witch, and if she put her mind to it, she probably could coax almost anything to grow anywhere. With the right blend of soil, salts, and a few well-placed potions, she had brought in a successful crop again this summer. If it wasn't for his mother, Adrian was sure they would be bankrupt by now.

Hannah opened the screen door with her hip, covered as usual in dirt and grasses, humming to herself. She held a bounty of root vegetables, their stems tumbling over the side of her wicker basket.

"Let me grab that, Ma."

"Thanks, honey." She sighed, wiping her hands on her apron. "Can you wash those for me?"

He grabbed a handful of celery out of the basket as she clamored through the cabinet, pulling out a cutting board. Adrian waited until her back was turned before he snuck a spoon out of the drawer.

The spoon was halfway to the stew when Hannah pivoted toward him, her face stern. "Adrian Huxley, get your grubby hands away from that pot." He froze. She always had a supernatural way of knowing when he was trying to sneak food. He put down the spoon with a shrug.

"I'm sorry. But I'm starving, and this smells so damn good..." He pouted at her pleadingly.

"Don't pull that flattery bullshit with me." She narrowed her eyes at him, fighting a smile. Reluctantly, she pulled out a small bowl and scooped a few bites out with her ladle.

He pumped his fist triumphantly as he sat down at the table. "You're the best, Ma."

She rolled her eyes as she pulled a knife from the block. "I may be a pushover, but your father is not. Goddess knows. Do not even *think* about bringing up the catch at dinner tonight. I have enough of my special—erm—recipe in that stew. David should have a very peaceful and contented night." She tied her apron with a vigorous knot as she turned to the stove.

He stretched his arms up, the tension in his shoulders loosening as heaviness settled into his limbs. Adrian sure as hell didn't want to bring up the catch. It had been weighing on him all week. After this evening, however, something new was on his mind.

Hannah pointed a wooden spoon at her son. "When you take over the business, promise me you'll make your father retire. He's going to have a heart attack if he keeps staring at those books all day."

His jaw tightened. David Huxley might look over the books, like a good business owner, but Adrian was sure his dad had no clue what he was looking at.

Unfortunately, his father's lack of knowledge about business had never stopped him from criticizing his son's every move. If anything, his ignorance fueled his disapproval.

"In other news," he said, changing the subject. She turned to him with eyebrows raised. "Seth and I sensed another witch in town today at the dock." He held his breath, testing her response.

It was exceedingly rare to meet other witches in Farley. The idea of another Water Elemental in town nauseated him. The last thing they needed was more competition out on the water.

They lived in the kind of town that people never visited. The kind that people never left.

You were born in Farley, grew up in Farley, met a nice girl at the high school, married her, had a few kids who would someday learn to fish and trap, and then you retired in Farley, drinking as many craft beers as you desired until you eventually died in Farley.

Hannah looked thoughtful for a moment, but she turned back to her strew, nonplussed. "It was probably some environmentalist passing through town," she reasoned. "Did you get a look at them?"

The Huxleys had never belonged to a coven. Most Elementals didn't, as a matter of practice, preferring to use their talents within the human communities. Water Elementals, like himself, usually gravitated toward the ocean or river. He knew of a few other fishing families in Maine like theirs, but they lived down the coast.

Ground Elementals, like his mother, usually farmed, built, or worked for quarries. Most of the time, a coven was not needed and actually impeded the witches' successes or talents in their community.

He tried to think of the last time he had met another witch in town, and his mind came up blank. Besides the occasional visits from his grandparents in his childhood, Adrian was quite sure that he had never crossed paths with another witch in town before today.

"What are you two talking about?" A tall young woman with auburn hair and stylishly ripped jeans strode into the room.

At sixteen, Ariel was about to become of age, which worried his mother. His little sister had shocked everyone when she came into her powers as a Fire Elemental. If Adrian had a dollar for every time his sister burned him through the years, he would never have to worry about the family's finances again.

His parents half expected Ariel to set the house aflame during her angst-ridden teenage temper tantrums. Sure, Seth used to flood the bathroom sometimes in his adolescent years, and there was more than one occasion where Adrian had made it rain on a planting day, but Ariel was on her third set of singed bedsheets.

"Adrian and Seth sensed another witch at the dock today," Hannah explained.

Ariel shrugged dismissively. "It was probably someone passing through," she similarly reasoned. She stuck her finger directly into the bubbling hot pot of stew, extracting a carrot and popping it into her mouth.

"Ariel, please!" Hannah begged. The stove burner flared with a teasing gust of flame as Ariel sat down with her prize. "I was just telling Adrian that your father is in a mood, so we all need to have a nice, mellow dinner tonight."

"Well, with the calming tonic you slipped in here, we should all be asleep by nine," Ariel said, her mouth full of stew.

Hannah's anger faltered as she fought a guilty smile. "Is it that obvious?" She clapped her hands. "I know! Two more licorice roots, and he should never know the difference."

Ariel and Adrian shared a look. Their mother tried to make sure everyone was always at their best and happiest. A household full of Elementals could be a messy—sometimes dangerous— place to live if someone was off temper.

Sure, they stayed mostly to themselves. Their little farmhouse was cleverly situated atop one of Farley's seaside cliffs. It was surrounded by acres of lush vegetable fields, gorgeous pollinator plants, busy hives of bees, and several ponds that Hannah and David had coaxed out of the ground.

They had an idyllic little oasis in an otherwise sleepy and, admittedly, drab town.

Adrian stared into the glow of the stovetop flames. They surged under the pot, licking between the grates with a sizzle as a bead of condensation met the heat. He couldn't push back the sense of uneasiness despite his mother's cleverly brewed tonic.

CORI

Anne opened the door to the guest cottage with a flourish. "Ta-da!"

Cori strolled through the doors as Anne clicked on the entryway light. She had never seen a house so cozy. The door opened to a tidy little room with whitewashed walls. There was a kitchen carved into the corner, defined by a butcher-block table.

Against the wall was a farmhouse sink, flanked with a solitary cherrywood cabinet that was charmingly worn and weathered. An ancient-looking icebox refrigerator was tucked in between the cabinet and the half wall that seemed to lead to a bedroom.

There was an old rotary phone on the wall, resting atop an antique bracket. The wall was adorned by mismatched shelves in the kitchen and a window of wavy glass that looked out to a small garden and the ocean beyond it.

A quaint sitting area housed two couches that, despite their aged appearance, looked warm and comfortable. The jute rug on the floor was tattered and torn.

Through the front bay window, she could see the ocean beyond the rocky drive that had led up to the cliffside cottage.

"I hope you don't mind the rug," Anne said. "This is our cat's favorite place to bathe in the sun...and sharpen her claws. We never find her in the main house. It might have something to do with the nice, warm sun patches that come through the skylights," Anne laughed.

Cori smiled widely as she looked up at the skylights. It was getting dark now, and she could practically feel the moon orbiting around her, pulling her gaze toward the sky with its gravity.

Just then, something softly rubbed against her leg.

"There you are, Turtle, speak of the devil," Anne laughed.

"Funny, she looks more like a cat to me." Cori bent down to scratch a fuzzy ear. "But I can see why you named her Turtle." The calico cat had beautiful markings of white, cream, and brown that distinctly looked like a tortoise shell.

The connection between witches and cats was one of those old fables that happened to be true. She closed her eyes and remembered fondly how many strays they used to attract to their town house in San Francisco. The neighbors had issued a few complaints through the years.

"Are we going to be roommates, pretty girl?" Turtle craned her neck as Cori scratched under her ear. She purred deeply as she leaned in.

"I hope this will be comfortable enough," Anne went on. "Farley really doesn't have a booming rental market, after all. Geoff and I would be more than happy to have you stay here as long as you like."

Cori opened her mouth with a question on her lips when Anne interrupted, raising her hand. "And don't even ask me what the rent is. You can make it up to me by working hard. God knows I'm not going to pay you what you really deserve. Oh, and you can spend part of the day entertaining Jordan for me. I love him to death, but he truly never shuts up."

Cori laughed at this, unsure just how entertained Jordan would be by her fumbling attempts at small talk. Her shoulder tipped up. "We can argue about this again another time."

"You can consider us even, then. Besides, if you don't live here, then nobody would. Except Turtle. And what would it say about me if I had a guesthouse just for my cat?"

After assuring the hot water heater was working, Anne bid

her a good-night. Cori huffed a deep breath, taking in her new home.

The cottage was small, dark, and starkly cold. After walking the perimeter and muttering a few of her mother's finest protective spells, she piled some of the wood from the basket into a dirty cast-iron stove, setting it alight with magic.

The bed, she found, was covered with crisp white sheets and a sky blue flannel coverlet. She walked around her bed, whispering her mother's spells into the air.

A spell to protect her from bad dreams and one to prevent her from oversleeping. It was not until the familiar electric crackle of her mother's magic settled into the atmosphere of the room that she really felt at home.

It took her less than ten minutes to unpack her few worldly possessions. Then she set out on the most important task at hand. While all witches could do basic spells, Charms witches could weave their own, and her mother had invented quite a few ingenious spells through the years.

Her note-sending spell was Cori's favorite.

Dear Mama,

How was the summer solstice? I didn't have time to celebrate much myself because I was preparing to move. After what seemed like a hundred years of school, I finally got a full-time job. I wish I could tell you all about it. Of course, I won't be able to tell you where I am, but I will say that the views are beautiful. And Papa's vision continues to be stronger and stronger each day. Love you and miss you terribly.

102 days.

Love, Starlight

She touched the paper to her heart, folded it three times to fit into her palm, and said the incantation. The paper melted into her hand, and she knew at that moment, three thousand miles away, the note would materialize in her mother's palm right now.

She stared into the fire, eagerly expecting her reply. Cori could think of no better feeling in the world than that little piece of paper, crisp in her hand, smelling no doubt of lavender and sandalwood. A special charm her mother made, just for them. A bridge between them in time and space.

As soon as she received her response, she eagerly unfolded the violet paper. Her mother usually tucked a newspaper clipping into the notes. *Peanuts* was her favorite, but this time the clipping appeared to be a from a pamphlet.

Dearest Starlight,

Congratulations on your new job! I'm beyond proud of you and hope you're doing something you love. I asked your brother to send you a letter, so expect one soon. He's been under a lot of pressure lately. I found this pamphlet in his apartment. Stay vigilant, of course, but I hope you're making friends. I miss you every minute of every day.

Mama

Cori let out a ragged sigh. How could her mother expect her to stay vigilant and also make friends? It had been hard for her to make friends even before she had a target on her back. Her mother couldn't be so delusional to think that her misfit daughter had developed social skills, even after all these years.

She unfurled the clipping from the pamphlet that had been tucked into the note.

Her prophecy—the one that would come to be in 102 days. Nausea bubbled up into her throat as she read and reread the words on the page. What exactly did they mean by *mitigation efforts?*

She considered sending a letter to Enzo right away but cast the thought out of her mind. Mama had said he was under a lot of pressure. She was certain he was working out a way to stop this meeting from happening.

She pulled out her laptop and connected to the Wi-Fi with the password Anne had scrawled on a sticky note for her.

She typed "Los Angeles Reform Coven" into the search bar, and the results smacked her in the face with the first image that she saw.

Calvin Hanson, her brother's handsome best friend, was all grown up, but his face still had the same boy-next-door guise that she remembered from when she was a teenager.

She clicked on the image of Calvin, bedecked in an expensive-looking suit, and it redirected her to the page.

28

She gaped at the screen with horror. Using dark magic was strictly forbidden by the Covenant, but this coven challenged that and openly defied it to prey on feeble witches that wanted to bolster their power.

She clicked through the website, shaking her head in disbelief as she read the description of the courses and workshops that the coven offered. She scrolled through the "about me" section where Calvin gushed about their methods—a manifesto to allow all witches to come to their full potential.

The more research she did, the more her Eye started to blink and hum a warning in her mind. It was early in the morning, with the first golden beams of day, that she finally fell asleep, her laptop open on the pillow next to her.

ADRIAN

The humidity in the air was coupled with a great heaviness. He had woken from a deep sleep this morning, knowing it would rain before he even opened his eyes.

Another day off the boat. Another day with a negative net gain.

"Obviously not a morning to get on the water," David said at breakfast, peering through the darkness out the window. The wind whipped through the trees, howling through the branches of the pines. "The rain should start by nine. We still have plenty of time to get some traps up onshore."

"I bet it starts at eight," Seth said with a teasing smile, hiding behind his coffee mug.

David took pride in his weather predictions, and Seth's favorite game in the morning was pushing his dad's buttons. In truth, it was his favorite game at any time of the day.

"Oh yeah, asshole?" David smiled back at him triumphantly. "For your unnecessary cheek and constant mockery of my superior talents, you get to be the one to accompany me."

He took a large swig of his coffee and returned his mug to the table with authority. On his way to the stove, he patted his oldest son on the back so hard that a breakfast sausage he was chewing on launched halfway across the table.

Adrian couldn't help but snigger as Seth leered at him.

David retrieved a sausage of his own from the pan. "If you clowns wake up your sister, I am going to make both of you come with me, and we can work until the rain stops," he said as he crossed the kitchen to the back mudroom. "The last thing I need to deal with on a rainy day is a house that smells like a burnt match."

Adrian took the rare opportunity for freedom to take a jog along the cliffside. Clearing his head was never easy, and the only way he knew how was to run. The pounding of his feet on the gravel of the road was the only thing that drowned out the nagging worry in his mind.

He laced up his shoes and set out for the path at the edge of their yard that led down to the small side street shared with other houses that faced the sea.

The dank impending rain in the air clung to his skin, but the breaths that filled his lungs were diametrically cool and light. The final few days of summer were melting away into autumn.

In the next few weeks, the currents of the water would turn icy while the misty humidity would fade into the empty crispness of the autumn air.

The sun was fully up now, but the light was muted by the heavy gray clouds that tore across the sky in the gales of wind. He took a turn around the large fir tree that lined the path when he felt it—the same electric energy he had sensed on the dock the day before.

He stopped in his tracks, his magic humming with curiosity, and maybe a bit of trepidation.

Not all witches were the type you wanted to run into with your guard down. He searched the coast, squinting as his eyes dropped to the shore below.

Standing at the edge of the water, near the rocks in the sandy cove, a woman looked out to sea. He couldn't see her face from the height of the cliff, but she appeared to be frozen in time. Could she feel the same electric energy in the air?

He watched her wavy brown hair billow behind her in the

wind of the impending storm, and after several moments of staring, he, too, seemed to be frozen.

After a few heartbeats, he realized the waves beyond her swelled to greater heights as the tide approached. Pretty soon, the small cove would be covered in water. Something about her posture gave him pause, but he needed to go down there and warn her. He couldn't very well let her drown.

Adrian climbed down the stone steps that led to the shore, as though being guided by an invisible tether.

CORI

The first night in the cottage was disrupted by vivid dreams. She stirred as a piece of yellow legal paper materialized in her hand.

C, Mama wanted me to write to you. She said congratulations were in order, but she didn't tell me why. I'm sure you're doing well—wherever you are. Things are escalating here, but I've been handling it. Keep your head down.

All my love, E

P.S. 101 days

It must have been a late night for Enzo if he was writing to her at this time of the morning in western time.

Keep your head down. He had underlined it.

She got out of bed and paced the cold floor. Turtle watched her with an amused tilt to her furry head as she tried to drown out the magic that had surged to life in her blood.

The only other Celestial witch she had ever known was her grandmother. Nonna lived across the world, in the same village in

Italy where her father had grown up, which made learning Celestial magic from her a special challenge.

Her grandmother lived with them for a full summer when Cori was a teenager, and they had crammed in as many lessons as they could. She had died a year later.

"The worst thing for your Eye is noise, *Stellina*," Nonna had said. "You can't turn it off. You can only push it away."

Cori pulled on her thickest pair of socks and warmest sweater, a feeble attempt to warm the chill that had settled on her skin.

She could really use a little advice right now. It had been easy to push away her magic until she stood on that dock yesterday and felt electricity crawling straight to the marrow of her bones.

Through the bay window, rain clouds loomed sinisterly over the horizon of the ocean, giving her an idea. She hoped the roar of the waves and the rumble of thunder would be loud enough to tamp her Eye back down in the depths of her abdomen where it belonged.

The wind off the ocean was brisk, whipping the long waves of her hair around her head as she descended a set of stone steps hewn from the rock that led down to the cove below.

She pulled the salty air into her lungs, pulling back her magic along with it. Despite her attempt, the waves crashing on the shore only amplified the steady blink of her Eye. Her stomach lurched as she tumbled into another vision.

Enzo sat slumped in a hotel room chair, his shirt unbuttoned and his tie loosened as he scrolled through his phone. He scrubbed his hands through his hair, the dark brown now peppered with occasional grays.

A soft knock rapping on the door made him stand up quickly. After peering through the peephole, he opened it, revealing a handsome, broad-shouldered man leaning on the door frame.

"Was that a party, or what?" Calvin asked, clapping his friend on the shoulder.

Enzo nodded. "Another one for the books," he said wearily. "Cal, I'm not going to the after-party."

Calvin winked back at him, tipping out his hands in defeat. "Not surprised."

"I'm exhausted, and I'm getting too old to drink like this. If I don't go to bed now, I'm going to be toast in the morning."

"Enz, come on. We're only thirty-two years old. You have a great thing going at the restaurant. Take the rest of the weekend off. This party in the Valley is going to be unforgettable."

"I'll take a rain check," Enzo said firmly. "My flight back is in four hours. If I get a nap now, I'll make it in time for the end of the lunch rush."

"Suit yourself, old man," Calvin said teasingly as he pulled away into the hall.

As the door of the hotel room swung closed, Enzo sighed a slew of expletives to himself before collapsing into bed, fully clothed.

Cori squinted against the wind as she came back to herself, the roar of the waves growing in her ears. As she slowed her breathing, the rumble of the water crashing over the worn rocks vibrated in her chest. The ocean wasn't quieting her Eye. It was feeding it.

She pulled the note from her brother out of her pocket, blinking back tears. The yellow paper turned over in her fingers, the very fibers within it linking her to Enzo.

The vision seemed to be from the present, and if that were the case, Enzo could be with Calvin right now. He would stop this *mitigation effort* at the LARC, or at the very least throw them off her trail and assure that whatever they were plotting didn't involve her death.

Cal mentioned a restaurant. It had always been his dream. Cori smiled to herself at the memory of Enzo looking through Papa's old recipe books. There were so many things she had missed. So many moments and milestones she could never get back. What would it have felt like to be with her brother for the grand opening?

She turned around to go back to the house when she felt it. Electric heat in the air, buzzing through her as it had on the dock the day before. The silhouette of a tall man was outlined through the mist on the rocky steps she had just descended.

Her feet betrayed her, anchoring her to the sand as she watched him materialize through the heavy air. Waves grew louder behind her, and it was as though she was stuck in time, connected and magnetized to each grain of sand beneath her shoes, trapped by rock and turbulent water.

He treaded toward her with one arm out to brace the wind. "Are you okay?" he called.

The man stepped through the mist, the hair on her arms prickling with the intensity of his magic. As he neared, she locked eyes with him—dazzling blue eyes that were haloed with a constellation of freckles over the left eyebrow.

Her breath was stuck in the wind, suffocating her with her own shock. It wasn't the first time she had seen those eyes. The pulse of her magic drowned out the quickening of her heart.

"Yes, I'm OK." She pushed out the words. "I was taking a walk." An overwhelming urge to run away consumed her. Her rational brain cried out to her limbs.

Run past him, climb up those steps. She could leave a note for Anne explaining that she had made a terrible mistake and needed to leave. Despite the instinct tugging at her, her body remained rooted to the spot as she gaped at him.

It seemed like an eternity had passed before he spoke again. "It's about to rain. And see how high the surf's getting? In about five minutes, this whole cove is going to be under water," he explained.

"Oh. I didn't know," she answered back over the roar of the water. The tide had pushed in between the worn rocks, curling toward the cliff.

"Follow me," he said.

Cori walked after the stranger whose eyes she had seen hundreds of times in her dreams. The mysterious witch strode up the steps carved into the cliffside, sometimes taking two at a time. His tall, muscular frame maneuvered over the rocks like a cat.

Thick raindrops were coming down by the time they were up the stairs. She glanced back over her shoulder toward the cove and noted the spot she had been standing less than several minutes ago was now getting pummeled by waves that were lapping up against the nearby rocks.

"Thanks," she said, turning to him and raising the hood on her coat. "I should really run home before I get..." She stopped mid-sentence as an umbrella opened above her head, shielding her from the storm. "Soaked."

But there wasn't an umbrella.

A canopy above her was made of water itself, she and her companion tucked neatly underneath. In the same instant, she transformed from uncomfortably sodden to completely dry. It was as though the water simply materialized off her. When she blinked up at him again, he winked at her.

An Elemental.

Elementals were the most elusive and solitary types in the magical community, so it was little wonder someone like him would live in such an isolated place.

"Let me walk you home. I'm Adrian, by the way," he said.

Thunder roared over her head, drowning out the pounding of her heart. Damn it, he was good-looking, too. The deep blue pools of his eyes stood out against his tanned and freckled skin, and his dark chestnut hair had subtle highlights, as though he were touched by the rays of the sun.

The firm line of his jaw was punctuated by a cleft in his chin and speckled with a dusting of stubble. His heavily muscled arms, adorned with a tattoo that peeked out of his right shirtsleeve, glistened with a subtle sheen of sweat. Instead of moving her feet toward the cottage, she stared up at him blankly.

Earlier that very morning, she had received a warning from her brother.

Keep you head down. He had underlined it. It was foolish to walk under an enchanted water canopy with a stranger—a stranger who happened to be a witch. Enzo would be furious.

But this man wasn't really a stranger. How could he be? She had seen him before, hundreds, maybe thousands of times. Sensing his magic around her, she opened her senses, allowing herself to get a good look at his aura.

She hadn't looked at anyone's aura in years but her magic surged responsively, as though it was relieved to be free. Her Eye widened, like a lion stretching his jaw in preparation of a roar, allowing her to see the wisps of energy rolling off him. His aura emitted a kind, genuine warmth.

For as long as she could remember, she had woken from the dream feeling heavy and warm, and the heat radiating from him reminded her of the weight of those dreams.

"Thanks," she said reluctantly.

"You were at the dock yesterday, weren't you?" he asked.

She nodded in affirmation. As they approached the guest-house, she again considered running away from him abruptly and slamming the door behind her.

The notion that another witch now knew where she lived was nauseating. Despite the approving hum of her magic, she couldn't shake the nagging feeling of her rational brain.

Maybe you dreamed about him because he was destined to murder you, she cautioned herself. But they were only about five steps away from the front gate that led to her door.

"Erm, well, thanks again," she said, gesturing to the guest cottage.

"You're staying with Anne?" he asked with interest. "I didn't know she had family coming to visit."

"Oh, I'm not family. I just joined her lab at the marina." She fought the urge to smack herself in the forehead.

Stop talking to him.

"You're a scientist?" he asked, raising a brow.

She nodded, noting a healthy dose of relief radiating from his aura now. She had locked the gate with a protective spell, and she shot him an anxious glance before she waved her hand over the latch and whispered the incantation to open it.

More relief radiated from him. "Are you a Charms witch?"

"Yes," she said quickly, falling easily into the familiar lie. "But I don't know much magic. Thanks for saving me from a monsoon on my morning walk," she continued briskly as she stepped into the dry safety of the portico over her door. *Monsoon?* She kicked herself.

He shrugged. "Happy to be of service. Sorry. I didn't catch your name."

"Oh, right. I'm Cori. Maybe I'll see you around sometime, Adrian."

A wry grin spread on his face that made her heart leap into her throat. "Cori, that's not a maybe," he laughed as he jogged out into the rain. "See you at the marina."

As he ran up the street toward the top of the cliff, he angled his head up to the sky, allowing the rain to fall freely on his face. Cori watched him disappear into the mist, thinking that Farley might not be such a good place to hide, after all.

CORI

Cori knocked softly on Anne's door later that day after the rain had settled down and the sun was peeking through the trees. The main house had an expansive front porch, adorned with glittering wind chimes singing an eerie song in the breeze.

A crude statue of a gnome urinating into a rock garden flanked the wooden steps. There were two red rocking chairs on either side of the door, still wet with beads of condensation from the earlier deluge.

Her attention shifted to the sky, watching the clouds dissipate. She closed her eyes and felt the stars spinning above her. Sagittarius, Pisces, Pegasus, *Cetus*. The sea monster in the sky. Fifteen stars, highlighted by three bright giants. She tried to shake the image out of her head as she climbed the front steps.

She desperately needed to get to the lab, to focus on organizing her research and getting her new gear ready. Immersing herself in science had always been an effective way to push away her magic before. It was certainly worth a try.

Anne's husband, Geoff, came to the door, opening it a crack. "No solicitors!" he yelled menacingly from behind the chain.

"Geoff," she laughed while rubbing her temples. "It's Cori."

"Oh, thank goodness," he said, flinging open the door. He pushed aside a slobbering bullmastiff trying to force past him.

The enormous dog was panting heavily in his pursuit of the intruder at the door as Geoff used his whole body's weight to keep him at bay. "Moses, for God's sake, go lie down!" The massive creature bounded to his nearby dog bed, and Geoff threw him a biscuit. "Sorry about the chain. If one more old lady knocks on my door asking me if I found Jesus, I'm going to lose my mind. Do you think I should put a few gargoyles on the porch?"

Cori snorted. "That would probably only provoke them. Is Anne around? I was going to head to the office, but I never got the entry code to the door."

"Ah yes," he said, putting on his glasses. He wore a stained white polo shirt and sweatpants, and a sloppily folded *Wall Street Journal* was tucked under his arm. "Anne is at the farmers market, but before she left, she said, 'Geoff, here's the office door code for when Cori inevitably knocks on the door trying to work on a Saturday.'"

She twisted her face and scrunched her eyes in embarrassment. "Well, I guess I'm nothing if not predictable," she shrugged. If only they knew just how unpredictable she truly was. She took the piece of paper from him. "The code to the door is 1111?" she asked dryly.

Geoff shrugged. "I guess so."

"And you had to write that down?" she teased.

He pointed at her. "Enough of that or I am going to sic one of my gargoyles on you." Moses barked deeply in response to his master's raised voice. She jaunted down the steps, laughing as she strolled toward her car. "I'm serious, I'm going to raise the rent by 100 percent."

"One hundred percent of zero dollars is still zero dollars," she reminded him, opening the car door.

"To think I used to be an economist," he grumbled.

She heard the chain slide into place behind her. Did people in Maine routinely install chain locks on their doors? she wondered. You can take the man out of the city, but you can't take the city out the man, she supposed.

She was about to put her key to the ignition when her Eye snapped to attention again, this time without warning.

She looked down at her hands, smeared with markers and glue. Her body was trembling, and her skin was all at once flushed and cold. In the coven assembly room, there were about a dozen elders sitting in a circle, gaping at her. Her blurry eyes found her mother's face, pale with shock.

"Mama?" she asked breathlessly. She attempted to stand up but faltered immediately, nausea bubbling in her abdomen.

"Do you realize what just happened, young lady?" one of the stern-looking elders asked her.

"No." She needed to breathe. In and out. "One minute I was making solstice signs with you, then all I could see was color. I felt my mouth moving, but nothing was coming out but a scream. All the color faded to black." She watched what was left of the blood drain from her mother's face.

"Cordelia, let's lie down. You need to rest—you aren't well."

In an instant she was back in her car, hands clutching the steering wheel with white knuckles. She pried her hands off the wheel and relaxed them, noting the marks that she inflicted with her fingernails during her flashback.

The bombardment of visions and the sudden prodding from her Eye had been bothersome before. But now—reliving that moment—she was thrust into terror. Her breaths quickened, burning her chest with each inhalation.

Adrenaline flooded her senses. She used to keep a paper bag in the car to breathe into when this happened, but it had been so long since she had a panic attack.

The prophecy she had delivered that day had defined who she would need to become for the rest of her life.

Breathe in. Hold. Breath out.

Such a big part of how Cori coped with the prophecy was to

continue to run. The doomed twelve-year-old girl from her vision would go down in infamy. She didn't go by Cordelia anymore. That girl had disappeared. In fact, she doubted she would even look up if someone called out her full name.

Inhale one. Exhale two.

Her own family didn't know where she lived, or even what she looked like, and she missed them with every ounce of her soul. She wasn't a witch anymore, certainly not a Celestial witch. She was a harmless Charms witch to anyone who noticed but that was the smallest part of her. A part that had been tamed, groomed, and locked away. Until yesterday.

You're okay. You're safe. You're alone.

But you can't run from the natural orbit of the Earth, or the convergence of the stars. And no matter how delusional she had become, she knew she could not run from the fact that she had made a prophecy that would change magic forever. And she certainly couldn't change the fact that there were many witches out there who wanted her dead because of it.

ADRIAN

Adrian stepped out of the storm over the threshold of the farmhouse where he was immediately greeted with the sound of roaring laughter.

Turning the corner into the family room, his father was hovering over an irate version of his brother. Ariel was also there, trying to catch her breath, laughing with such vigor that steam was bellowing out of her head like a chimney.

"What kind of father has this reaction when their eldest son nearly gets killed?" Seth asked indignantly.

David whooped a laugh. "Killed!" he bellowed. "That's one way to describe it, I guess." He spotted Adrian's form in the doorway. "Care to enlighten your brother?" David asked, his eyebrows arched in amusement.

"Please, have a seat. You're going to need it," Ariel explained, out of breath.

Adrian sat heavily on the couch next to her.

"I was almost run over by a freaking boat, Adrian. Are you happy now? That's what happened. The only thing that matters is—I nearly died. I could have drowned after the impact," he said darkly.

This really made David lose it. He started laughing so hard, he could barely speak. "Seth, I swear to God. If you—of all people—

die by drowning, I'll pretend you were adopted. I'll ask the coroner to omit me from your death certificate. The newspaper won't print my name in your obituary."

"There has to be more to the story than that," Adrian prodded him. "You didn't see Jess on the dock again and rev the boat motor, did you?" At this, David and Ariel nearly fell on the floor.

"Wait, stop it!" Ariel laughed. "Has he done this before? I can't breathe. What an idiot!"

"I didn't see the other guy coming, OK? I was simply picking up speed. Yes, I saw her and that might have been why, but I was distracted. Damn, you make it sound like you've never been distracted before." Seth sulked, tenderly placing a bag of frozen peas on his head.

"Sure, I've been distracted before. But I've never been so distracted that my belt loop got caught in Auggie Stewart's hook, causing my body to be flung into the ocean between two colliding boats," David reasoned in between laughs.

Adrian's mouth dropped open. "You crashed into Auggie? Holy shit. Did he beat you to a pulp?" He couldn't help but laugh now at the image.

Auggie Stewart was sixty-seven years old, but in his youth, he was a marine and one of the best semiprofessional boxers in Maine. The guy looked like he was made of leather and smelled of tobacco and dried blood. Adrian recalled one time he had accidentally loaded one of Auggie's crates onto their boat at the dock. The look he had received in response could have turned a man to stone. The thought of it still sent shivers down his spine.

"We were trying to beat the storm after pulling in traps. Yes, I collided with him, but then I fell in the water and got pulled under the boat. I'm lucky I have control over the water, or the propeller would have juiced me to death. Like I said, I almost died, so I think he took pity on me. I scratched his gunwale, so I have to go over there tomorrow and fix it. I think he might murder me, so I'm bringing you along as an eyewitness."

Seth gave his brother a pleading look, and Adrian rolled his eyes. He ran his hand through his hair. "Please tell me you didn't damage our rig?" The thought of coming up with that kind of money made his stomach turn sour.

"Nothing a coat of paint won't fix," David said, his tone hardening. "Another close call."

A close call. Is that what they were calling their financial setbacks now? Adrian could think of about a hundred things he would rather do on his day off than get stared down by Auggie at the marina.

He had planned to balance the books in the morning, and he slumped into the chair when he realized he would end up staying up late tomorrow night, all because his brother had been distracted by a woman.

A pang of sympathy cut through his chest. To be completely fair, he had also been distracted by a woman this morning. Adrian ran his hand through his rain-dampened hair again. "I met the new witch in town on my run," he said, snapping everyone's attention away from Seth.

"In town?" David asked. "That's odd. Usually people pass through, but none of the locals have ever brought around witches before."

"Well, I ran into her on the beach." He left out the part about saving her from being swallowed by the high tide. And the part about how she might have been the most beautiful thing he had ever seen in his life. And how she had looked at him like he was a serial killer. "Looks like she's taking a job at the marina," he explained. He saw a sudden worry flash in his dad's eyes. "Charms witch, science-type person," he quickly continued.

David breathed out a ragged sigh of relief. "We've never had another one of our kind around here before," he mused. "I guess if she's hanging out with the scientist crowd, we probably won't see much of her anyway," he reasoned, "But it might be nice to have a Charms witch around. I hear they're good at fixing all sorts of odd problems."

Adrian groaned. He could see David now, asking for a net mending spell for a pound of fresh lobster.

"Dad, are you delusional?" Ariel asked. "In this town, you see everyone all the time no matter what crowd they associate with. For Goddess's sake, there are maybe ten people who live here that are even worth talking to. Are you telling me that another witch moved close by, and you don't want to get to know her?"

She stood from her chair with a shake of her head. "I'm going to find Mom," she continued. Adrian heard her mumbling as she walked toward the front door. "Men. Another witch moves to town, and they don't even have the decency to invite her over for dinner."

CORI

G olden hues of the midday sun poured into the large picture window of her office, illuminating the gadgets from the tackle box. She inspected a bright red floatation buoy, about the size of a doughnut. At the bottom of each float, a long, insulated collection of wire dangled at various lengths.

Each box was triple-insulated and waterproofed. A timer and plastic-ensconced GPS device was affixed to each side the box. Cori pushed the timer to its end, at which time the door of the box sprang open and resealed again. She smiled, shaking her head in awe. Anne was brilliant. What an ingenious way to collect water samples at specific times of the day and at specific depths and locations.

She opened the closet door and found the centrifuge machine, a set of micropipettes, and a rudimentary microscope setup along with slides and stain. It would be difficult to analyze the size of the plastic particulates without an electron micro-scope, and she had certainly taken for granted how much equip-ment was available to her in the lab at Yale, but she had also never been privy to such a clever and creative way to collect data before.

She peered into the microscope at the slides she had found in a box on Jordan's desk. The brightly colored plastic granules peppered her view, colored spots in a murky mix of otherwise organic material.

She zoomed in, hopeful to get lost in the microscopic world of the ocean, but her Eye snapped open instead.

Pressing her ear to the wall of her bedroom, she strained to hear her mother's voice, hushed as she spoke to the other priestesses in the adjacent living room. Enzo walked in with a pile of laundry cascading over his arms. He shot her a reproachful look.

"You know you aren't supposed to be eavesdropping," he said, throwing the laundry on her bed.

"I just don't understand," she said indignantly. "I don't know why suddenly the coven is so concerned about me and what I can and cannot do. Mama said I can't go to camp this summer. It makes no sense." Cordelia felt hot tears stinging her eyes.

Enzo looked up at the ceiling with a serious gaze. "You really don't know why they're worried?" he asked incredulously.

"I don't."

"Cor, you made a prediction that's going to change magic as we know it forever."

An exasperated sigh escaped her chest. "I know that! I don't even care about what I predicted, Enz. It won't affect you, and it won't affect me."

His brow furrowed. "There are a lot of witches out there who don't want this prophecy to come true," he explained with calculated seriousness. "You can understand that, right?"

"Who cares what they think?" She crossed her arms around her body, hugging her favorite blanket.

"Cor, I don't know if I'm the one who should tell you this." He swallowed hard, his throat bobbing. He was silent for a few moments, as though considering his words with care. "It's fabled that if you kill the witch who makes a prophecy, then it will not come to be," he said, the power of his words washing over the room.

Cordelia dropped her blanket and gaped at him. Her mother had always warned her that there were many witches out there abusing the dark element. How many of those witches knew about her prophecy? Knew about her? She stood up and walked to the window, the stars above her turning on their axis, plunging her forward along with them.

Enzo's voice was serious and sad when he broke the heavy silence in the room. "This is why you're in danger. This is why you will someday need to disappear."

Cori's gaze shifted back to focus on the microscopic world in front of her, the drumbeat of her magic pulsing in lockstep to the pounding of her heart.

After years of silence from her Eye, the visions were consuming her. She cursed at herself. It had always been so easy for her to trap her Eye out of the way.

Why now? Why here?

Despite her anger, she allowed her mind to linger on the sweet nostalgia of the vision. Being back in her bedroom in San Francisco for a moment—only to be thrust back to the lonely isolation of her reality—was a sickening kind of torture.

Did her mother still live in the same house? She shoved her curiosity away. The more information she knew about her family, the more it could be used against them. The more they didn't know about her, the more protected they all were.

Witches could take that information and use dark magic to find her. If they wanted to end her life to nullify her prophecy, they would go to great measures to find her family.

Cori Evans is an engineer. A PhD. Someone like her should be blissfully ignorant about a prophecy that a twelve-year-old Celestial witch made in California fourteen years ago.

She was hidden, but now that the time was near, inevitably, they would look for her. They were hunting for Cordelia Mangianelli, not Cori Evans. Would the trail of lies and secrecy be enough?

She thought this remote, anonymous town would be the perfect place to hide, but she had been here less than twenty-four hours and she had already revealed pieces of herself to a complete stranger.

Her head was heavy, and her eyes stung as she walked toward the window and watched the boats bobbing innocently in the water. Each vessel was like an island to itself, serenely drifting on the waves in solitude.

What if she set sail on a boat with enough rations to last her until the solstice? Would it look suspicious to Anne and Jordan if she left suddenly before even starting the job?

Yes, that would certainly be out of character. It would probably prompt a police investigation. Perhaps even a news story. She could see the headlines of the evening news now: Young, Single Scientist-Woman Disappears from Middle of Nowhere. Ship Missing in the Harbor. The last thing she needed was a media frenzy, especially when the investigators of her murder discovered she had been using a fake identity for the past nine years. It was best to keep her head down and simply make it through the next 101 days.

Cori loaded up her car with the tackle box and several binders of last year's data. She shrugged off her sweatshirt as she buckled her seat belt, enjoying the warmth of the sun as it shone on her bare shoulders.

Her hair, wavy from the humidity of the car, stuck to her as she swept it into a bun. Gulls called to each other on the bay as the light dipped low in the sky. Just as they sounded on another bay—three thousand miles away.

She pulled her dented Volkswagen Golf onto the side road that led to where Anne's house was perched on the grassy hillside. As she turned into the rock driveway, the intensity of electric energy crawled over her skin once more.

Only this time, it was accompanied by an intense heat. Her stomach dipped as she grabbed for her keys to make a quick rush into the cottage.

Before she could duck low and pivot herself behind her car, she turned to find two witches locked arm in arm, staring curiously at her with wide eyes.

The younger woman, a teenager with flaming auburn hair and an athletic frame, was dressed stylishly in a crop top and high-waisted jeans. She wore a pair of boots that were extensively scuffed on the heels.

Beside her, a middle-aged woman with gentle waves of dark brown hair offered a tentative smile. Her arms cradled a basket of wildflowers of the most colorful array Cori had ever seen. The wind picked up, and she felt a pang of homesickness once more as the scent of lavender incense wafted to her on the breeze.

"Holy Mother, it's true," the young witch said, awestruck.

"Stop staring," her companion scolded as she elbowed her in the side. "I'm Hannah Huxley. We live on the top of the hill," she continued, her voice like warm honey.

Something about this woman reminded her so intensely of her own mother—so intensely of home. "This is my daughter, Ariel. I think you may have met my son Adrian this morning?" she asked expectantly.

For the second time in one day, Cori felt like she was a deer caught in the headlights of a tractor trailer. Heat rose to her cheeks as her mouth opened and a garble of incoherent sound came out.

Hannah waved her hand sheepishly, "Goddess, help me. It was rude of us to catch you off guard like this. Here come the nosy neighbors, out of the woodwork! Come on, Ariel, let's head home."

"Wait!" she stammered, finding her words. Adrenaline surged through her. *What's wrong with you?* Her feet remained traitorously rooted to the gravel. "I was just surprised," she said, managing a crooked smile.

"Are you really a scientist?" Ariel asked, crossing her arms. "That's pretty cool."

Cori's encounter with Adrian this morning was rushed and awkward, and she could barely remember what she said to him.

He had gone home and told his family about her. Something welled up inside her stomach that made her all at once sick and elated.

"Um, yes," she stammered. "I'm an engineer in marine ecology." Cori's words tumbled out like awkward gravel.

Stop talking to them, you idiot.

She cleared her throat, pushing away her fear. Sure, every fiber of her being was telling her she should run all the way back to New Haven, but her own mother had even suggested that she should make some friends. The homesickness elicited by the visions had ripped open an old wound, tapping into the void of her loneliness.

"I'm Cori. I just moved here to take a job at the marina." She had just met these strangers on the street—if you could call this a street—and divulged multiple important pieces of information about herself. And for the first time in almost a decade, it felt *right*. There was no going back now.

This family of local Elemental witches did not feel like a threat. She widened her Eye to their auras. The two women had warm, open energy.

"When my brother told us about you, I thought he was lying," Ariel continued with a sly smile.

Cori's stomach turned over. Adrian really had told his whole family about her. She supposed that another witch showing up in a town like this was worth mentioning, after all. Did he also mention that she almost got swept away to sea that morning? Her cheeks heated again.

"Nonsense," Hannah fussed. "Cori, it's a pleasure to meet you. Actually, this is wonderful timing. Would you like to come over tonight for dinner? Ariel and I were just at my hive, and we collected fresh honeycomb for my biscuits."

The wildflowers must belong to the bees, Cori realized.

She bit her lip, grappling with herself. "I wouldn't want to impose."

"Impose?" Ariel squeaked. "The only other witches I've ever known *in my life* are my parents and my smelly brothers—and my grandparents, but they're dead—so it would literally offend me if you didn't accept my mother's invitation."

Cori looked to Hannah, who was massaging her jaw with her

fingertips. She let out a heavy sigh. "My daughter is right, I'm afraid."

Every ounce of her tried to come up with an excuse. An explanation for why she couldn't have dinner with them. Not tonight or ever. But instead, she said one word.

"Sure."

ADRIAN

Three binders were spread open on the Huxleys' kitchen table, each one overflowing with stained papers and crumpled ledgers. Adrian had pledged to digitize their books when he graduated from college three years ago, but he regretted making that promise.

Truth be told, David couldn't care less if the data was housed in an Excel spreadsheet or on the coffee-stained sheets of the binders. Adrian shook his head and puffed out an exasperated sigh.

Until recently, David had kept records in half-legible pencil smudges, making it almost impossible to track trends and productivity. Adrian had finished meticulously logging the summer's data, which meant it was time to move on to the monumental task of entering the numbers from the previous years.

David had over twenty years' worth of information in those binders, but Adrian guessed he needed at least five years' worth of data to get a good handle on the trends—and an idea about what his father's mistakes had cost them.

Part of the reason he had selected accounting as a major in college was rooted in his desire to take over this aspect of the business. Seth had majored in business but left college after just one year. Their parents had grown increasingly concerned with Seth's disinterest in academics only halfway into his first semester.

Everyone knew that Adrian, always the more academic of the two, would fare better at school.

While Seth had spent most of his time in school partying and playing rugby—Hannah was particularly upset with his choice in recreational sports—Adrian had kept to himself and studied hard.

Even though he was encouraged by his mother to live on campus, he had commuted to class and took as many online classes as he could. He approached the entire experience with a one-track mind.

Finish school so you can fix this mess.

He sighed and drained the last few dregs of his beer. Seth was snoring from the couch in the next room. Adrian laughed to himself as he recalled the events of the morning that had led to his inevitable fatigue. He probably had a wicked concussion after the boat collision. Ariel was out with their mom, and David was mending nets in the back shed.

The house was rarely this quiet.

The serenity was fractured by the squeak of the screen door and the build of chattering voices in the foyer.

He heard his sister laughing in response to something his mother said in a stern tone, but the next voice he heard was softer, with a musical quality that certainly did not belong to one of the Huxley women. He looked up from the glare of the monitor to find Cori nodding to him from the hallway.

His heart leaped so far into his throat, he thought he would choke on it. "I knew my mom and sister would hunt you down soon enough."

The flush in her cheeks evaporated into her skin. "They found me on the side of the road and invited me to dinner." She fidgeted with the hem of her sleeve. "Apparently, there aren't too many stray witches around here. They were nice enough to rescue me from cereal for dinner."

He took off his baseball hat and ran his fingers self-consciously through his messy hair. She wore leggings that hugged

56

the curves of her hips and a flannel shirt that she had tied in the front. Her wavy brown hair fell over her shoulders when she tucked a strand behind her ear.

Even though she seemed more relaxed than she had been in the storm this morning, there was still an edge of desperation in her face. Her eyes smoldered with intensity as she bit her lip.

He leaned back in his chair, twisting his face in mock disapproval. "You may regret leaving your cereal behind. My dad grills on Saturdays, and the brisket has been in the smoker about two hours too long."

"Who dares to insult my brisket?" A deep voice boomed from the kitchen with the intensity of a crashing wave.

Adrian sucked in a deep breath and rolled his eyes. "Can you cool it with the *Lord of the Rings* impressions? We have a guest."

David walked into the room with enormous presence, looking insulted. "First, that was not a *Lord of the Rings* impression, it was a *Wizard of Oz* impression. Second, the last time I checked, you don't pay rent here, and you have never cooked me a meal. Until you do, you will happily eat my dry brisket without complaint."

"Well, if I remember correctly," countered Adrian with a playful roll of his eyes, "You owe me approximately ten years of salary compensation for a job I've been doing for free since I was in high school."

"Excellent, I'll inform the IRS you'll start paying taxes effective immediately," David shot back as he punched his son hard on the shoulder. Adrian winced. David was almost as tall as his son—and much rounder around the middle—but the man was still strong.

His father turned his attention to the mysterious new witch in town. "I'm David," he said warmly. "I'm sorry you had to witness my son being a wiseass. He's the smart one in the family, but he rarely wins arguments."

Adrian shook his head at his father, who was dressed like a fictional fisherman featured on a box of fish sticks. His face was canvased with an unruly salt-and-pepper beard, and he wore stained denim overalls with a thick flannel shirt. His front pocket, missing a button, was comically held together by a fishhook. Adrian crossed his arms and raised his eyebrows as his father held out a bait-stained hand to Cori.

She shook it, her forehead wrinkling as she surveyed him. Despite his gritty exterior, David had a warm twinkle in his eye and the corners of his mouth were curled up in what appeared to be permanent amusement.

"I'm Cori," she said, "I just moved into the guest cottage at Anne and Geoff Calhoun's place. I just joined her research team."

"Ah, Anne and Geoff are good friends of ours," he returned with a smile. "She's the only scientist I know at the marina who gets out on the boat before dawn. Every once in a while, I throw some of her fancy red doughnuts into the bay for her. No idea what she does with them, but my boat can get into some of the more remote sites." He winked at her with a knowing nod.

Hannah bustled past, tying a blue linen apron that was smudged with flour around her waist. "Ariel, are you going to help with these biscuits, or what?" she shouted up the stairs.

Moments later, Ariel came clomping down the steps, texting feverishly on her phone as she marched into the kitchen with Hannah and David.

Adrian found himself in the room alone with Cori, and as he met her gaze, her cheeks paled.

"I bet you're used to having other witches around you all the time," he said apologetically. "For us, this is a rare event. My mom will probably bring out the fancy salad bowls." Apart from his grandparents, Adrian could not remember them ever having another witch in their house.

Cori laughed, her posture relaxing a bit. "Well, less than ten minutes ago, I was getting ready to eat cereal out of a paper bowl, so fancy salad bowls would be a major upgrade. So is dry brisket, come to think of it." She looked out the window, fidgeting with a delicate gold charm bracelet that had slid down her wrist.

"That's a pretty bracelet," he said awkwardly, grasping at the air for something to talk about besides his crazy family. The shimmering golden bangle was adorned with three jeweled charms. A sun, a moon, and a star.

She looked down at her wrist, her mouth twisting into a sideways smile. "Thanks." She turned the charms over in her fingers. "My grandmother gave it to me before she died. One of the elders in her village blessed it with a luck charm. I never take it off."

Cori breathed deeply and closed her eyes for a moment. When her large almond-shaped eyes opened again, sadness flashed within them.

"Does it bring you luck?" he asked.

She angled her face toward him. Her thick brown hair had a subtle golden sheen that highlighted her eyes. Her eyes reminded him of honey that had been left in the jar, solidifying into a gold caramel. He tried not to stare as light sparkled within them, like stars in the night sky.

She spoke after a pause. "Today it did. I was almost swallowed by the ocean this morning," she reminded him.

The corner of his lip curled up as he held back a laugh. "Hmm, that was lucky," he said mockingly.

Ariel swept into the room, shoving a pile of napkins into his hands. "Is my brother boring you to death with his endless math homework?" Ariel asked Cori, gesturing to the pile of binders.

"No," she returned, tipping her shoulder up. "He wasn't. But math doesn't bore me."

Ariel arched a brow. "That's too bad. Come with me, Cori. Mom asked me to set the table on the deck."

Cori followed Ariel through the kitchen door, and he couldn't help his gaze from traveling down the soft curves of her hips as they swayed. When she glanced back at him and caught him staring, he could have sworn her eyes flared with gold before they widened.

CORI

On the back deck of Huxley Farm, Cori softly gasped at the expansive vistas of the sea beyond the idyllic garden before her. Stretching miles ahead of her from the top of the cliff, the view was spectacular. A charming red lighthouse off in the distance beckoned with a warm, slow blink of light.

This was what she pictured when she envisioned the Maine landscape—only far better.

The garden was dotted with expertly placed ornamental grasses that lined beds of lush wildflowers. Their stems swayed in the breeze, and the petals fluttered, greeting her with an array of floral aromas. A path of sandy rock wound through the beds with an organic easiness that could only have been conjured with magic. The sea below them thundered against the rocks and sent mist into the air that caught the light of the setting sun.

Her Eye fluttered open, this time gently.

Two boys played in the garden. Their pants were stained with grass and mud, and their hair was caked with sand and sweat, freckled skin shining in the sun. The smaller boy grabbed a shovel and started eagerly digging. Excitedly, he leaped to his feet, clutching an orange plastic dinosaur. "Ma, I found another one!"

Rain dripped from the sky, summoned by his triumph. The boys tipped back their heads with wide smiles, greeting the cool drops as a woman laughed warmly in the distance.

Cori recognized the little boy with the chestnut brown hair and dirty sneakers as she snapped back into reality and saw Adrian's head bowed over the table. Despite the happiness in the memory, sorrow welled within her. This glimpse into the past shadows of this garden made her yearn deeper for the times that she had spent with her own family.

Seeing the Huxleys interact in such an easy, warm way left a hollow ache within her. It had been that way with her family once, but it was so long ago it felt like that piece of her had gone cold.

Ariel shivered, wrapping herself in a thick, colorful sweater. "It's not even October yet, and it's already cold," she complained. She sat in front of the stone fire pit, and the wood erupted into flame.

Cori's sucked in a breath. *A Fire Elemental.* Her mother had told her stories of how the Fire Elementals were the only survivors of the burnings that led to the formation of the Covenant against dark magic. According to the legends, the Fire Elementals passed down a desire for vengeance to their descendants.

Cori saw Adrian roll his eyes. "Show-off," he muttered under his breath.

"What was that?" Ariel asked, reaching her hand directly into the fire to adjust the wood. "If you weren't enjoying the warm fire, I'll make it go away."

In an instant, the flames extinguished in the fire pit as the napkin Adrian was folding started to smolder and smoke in his hands.

"Holy shit, Ariel," Adrian scolded as he dropped the steaming napkin on the worn wooden table. Suddenly, the water from a nearby glass pitcher leaped into the air and neatly extinguished the flame. Cori watched Adrian shake the napkin, and it was bone-dry again immediately. "You could have burned me that time." He frowned at her and slowly shook his head with annoyance.

Her face lit up with playful teasing that only a little sister could muster. She cocked her head at him, fire in her eyes. "I light a fire pit, and I'm a show-off, but you make water soar through the air, and that's OK?" She shot back. She turned back to the fire pit, and it was alight once more. She nodded her head toward the table as a dozen tea lights flickered to life.

"Yeah, because I was simply reacting to your insanity. It was instinct. Completely different," he calmly reasoned as he continued to fold the napkins.

Cori noted that the water had rematerialized in the pitcher. "How did you refill the pitcher?" she asked curiously.

"Oh, I just summoned it from the air," he explained nonchalantly. "Easy in the summer, when the air is so humid. Harder to do it in the winter when the air is dry, but there's always vapor in the air."

Cori suddenly became acutely aware of the humidity all around her. A cool mist brushed by her cheek as Adrian looked up from his task and smiled. "So, you aren't all Water Elementals, then?" she asked.

Adrian shook his head. "Pop, my brother, Seth, and I are Water. Ariel is Fire. Mom is Ground."

Just then, another broad-shouldered man stood in the doorway. He leaned on its frame, massaging a bag of frozen peas to his neck. He groaned when the sunlight struck him, and he stepped tentatively onto the deck like a linebacker that had just been tackled, retreating to the sidelines.

Just as tall as his brother but with cropped hair, a full beard, and rougher features, Seth waddled into his chair, eyes squinting in pain. Cori noticed a large intricate tattoo of what appeared to be a whale tail peeking out of the neck of his white T-shirt onto his thick neck. Ariel rolled her eyes as she lounged back in her chair, scrolling through her phone.

"Ah, here comes our gallant hero, licking his wounds as he

recovers from the most impressive array of masculinity the folks Down East have ever witnessed," David teased from the porch.

"Don't ask." Adrian shook his head at Cori's inquisitive look. "Seth got himself into quite the pickle today, and in doing so completely ruined my weekend."

He looked at his brother who gave a guilty shrug in reply before settling into his chair with a grunt. He kicked up his feet on the empty seat next to him.

"One good thing came of it, though," Seth smirked at Adrian. "Jess just texted asking if I was OK." He raised his eyebrows. "Then she asked if there was anything she could do to make me feel better," he added with a wicked grin.

Ariel pretended to gag.

Hannah appeared out of nowhere and smacked her oldest son on the back of the head, hard.

"Damn it, Ma! What is wrong with you?" Seth winced, looking wounded.

"What is wrong with *you*? We have a guest over, and this is the first impression you're giving her. She probably thinks you're a macho loon."

"Sorry, Cori," Seth said in his smoothest retort. "I didn't realize I was being so uncouth in the pleasure of your company."

Cori hid her amused smile behind her water glass as she stifled a laugh. David chuckled outright at his son's series of misfortunes.

As David stepped in to give Seth some tips on how to respond to the text message, much to Hannah's chagrin, Cori took in the scene in front of her. Ariel happily dipped her biscuit in the brisket's juice, while Hannah dressed one of the most colorful salads she had ever seen.

Cori looked up from the table and locked eyes with Adrian as he took a sip from his bottle of beer. She inhaled sharply at the sight of his eyes and the constellation of freckles in perfect alignment above them. She glanced up at the sky, Saturn growing brighter over the ocean as the sun set behind her back.

"What time are the two of you headed over to fix Auggie's boat?" David asked Seth.

"I told him we would be there early, eight at the latest," Seth explained. At this Adrian groaned. "I don't want the whole day to be ruined. With the size of that dent, I'm guessing it will take at least two hours. I am probably going to need to take off at least half of the wood on the port side and replace it. Do you have any spare planks in the shed?"

At that moment, Cori felt her stomach lurch, as her Eye snapped to attention.

The morning air was cool and brisk. Adrian and Seth sat on the dock, sidled up next to a large white boat. An old man sat on a crate nearby, detangling a net and muttering under his breath.

A drill plugged into a frayed extension cord snaked through the work area emitting a warmth that was heavy and electric. Adrian picked up the drill, dragging the cord into a puddle near the crate with an unnatural, ethereal shimmer. His finger depressed the trigger on the drill as a spark arced from the cord, setting the floor around the old man into a heavy blaze.

She gasped as she snapped back to the reality of the dinner table, her Eye retreating deep into her gut, bile rising in her throat in its wake. The smell of electric heat and singed flesh hung in her nose, so real she almost coughed on the smell. She was breathing fast, her skin was clammy, and her heart was pounding with panic.

She clenched the table with white knuckles, cursing her Eye.

Adrian's eyes were fixed on her.

Hannah had gone pale. "Cori, honey...are you OK?" she asked softly.

Cori tipped up her chin and looked toward Adrian, still recovering from her vision. "You can't fix that boat tomorrow morning."

Seth dipped his head low and raised his eyebrows. "What do you mean we can't fix the boat tomorrow?" he asked incredulously. "I promised Auggie I would fix it. To be honest, I want to fix it, I need to, after everything that happened today. It would be the only fair thing to do." He cocked his head at Cori in anticipation.

Across the table, David's fork was frozen halfway en route to his mouth, and Ariel was peering at her over the blue light of her cell phone. Hannah stared back at Cori, a look of maternal concern etched into her brow.

Cori forced her breaths to slow. How was she going to explain this? She tried to reel in the panic attack that was blooming in her gut. Nonna had always said she couldn't control these visions, but she had quieted her magic in New Haven.

Ever since she had stepped foot in this town, her Eye was a beast she could no longer control. Here of all places, eating dinner with a family of strangers, witches no less.

She really wanted these people to like her, and that was a new sentiment for her. Being alone was safer. It was easier—until the moment this family invited her into their home. Until the moment she got a taste of what she had been yearning for. She was sick of being lonely, but she was not about to reveal another colossal piece of information about herself. This part of her was out-of-bounds, vowed into silence, and locked away.

Cori paused, overwhelmed, as she tried to figure out a way to get herself out of this mess. She opened her mouth to muddle through a response when Adrian's voice broke the silence.

"I had promised Cori I was going to take her out on Anne's boat in the morning," he said coolly, the lie gliding effortlessly from his lips. Cori attempted to conceal her shock as she slowly turned her head toward him, mouth slightly agape. "She needs to get a feel for the embankment, and she said she'd never operated a sterndrive before." He took a sip from his water glass casually as he gestured toward Seth. "I had no idea you had volunteered my services," he continued, rolling his eyes.

David eyed him shrewdly. "That was very nice of you to offer, son." There was a barely detectable teasing lilt to his voice.

Seth smirked at this as Hannah's eyes shot daggers at him.

"I'm not familiar with the sterndrive at all," she lied, hiding her shaking hands under the table. "Adrian suggested I get the hang of it before my first run on Monday morning. The drop-off seems to be more irregular here. I don't want to scrape the bottom on my first trip out." The hammering of her heart slowed down as she built on the lie, tension easing from her chest. "Anne has been so generous to me. I'm staying in her guest cottage rent-free."

She watched the furrow on Hannah's face relax, replaced with a look of commiserate understanding as she nodded her head in reply. The rest of the family was busy with the last bites of their pie, seemingly nonplussed by her irrational outburst.

Seth shoved an entire biscuit in his mouth as he finally nodded at her. "Nice. Cori, we'll pick you up at seven thirty, sharp. You can help us with Auggie. Maybe he'll be kinder to us in the presence of a lady."

A sigh of relief broke through her lips as she sipped the last few drops of her wine. She exchanged a look with Adrian. Cori opened herself up to his aura. *Suspicion and a hint of resentment.*

"Anne probably doesn't mind you living in the guest cottage," Ariel said matter-of-factly. "It puts another human barrier between her and Richard's house."

David smacked the table as he let out a thunderous laugh.

"You've got a point there." Hannah chuckled in return as the rest of the family nodded in unanimous agreement and amusement.

"Who's Richard?" Cori asked, emptying her glass. At this, Hannah refilled Cori's wine.

They spent the last hour of their meal regaling her with tale after ridiculous tale of their neighbor Richard. He and his wife lived in the house between Anne's property and the Huxleys' farmhouse.

Richard was an artist, and he had a habit of collecting odd objects from around the neighborhood and fashioning them into sculptures. One summer, he had stolen a perfectly good hubcap from Seth's new truck. Weeks later they discovered it as the centerpiece of a new water feature Richard had crafted in his garden.

Ariel told a story of how Richard had tried to kidnap Anne's cat after she had developed a habit of taking naps in his window boxes. Turtle, to nobody's surprise, did not come quietly. She had marked him with so many scratches, Richard tried to sue Anne for assault.

Geoff had retaliated with a phony court summons, leaving it on Richard's doorstep in an official-looking envelope, citing "cat napping" and "endangering the welfare of a feline."

At this point in the story, Hannah was laughing so hard she was crying. "So, the next week, he tried to kidnap her again."

Cori belly-laughed in disbelief. The second bottle of wine was empty now. "How was that supposed to help the situation?"

"The bastard sent back the envelope with a lock of the cat's hair tucked into it," David roared.

Cori nearly spit out her wine. "Oh, poor Turtle!" she laughed.

"You're acquainted with the cat?" David asked.

"Oh, I'm not just acquainted with her, she's my roommate," Cori explained.

"Ah, the stereotype of the witch as the wacky cat lady lives strong in you," Ariel laughed. "Be careful, Richard might try to kidnap you next."

Cori shivered. "How did they rescue her?"

"Well, if I remember correctly, Geoff and Moses barged into the house, yelling something about a warrant," David said, draining his beer. "Don't worry. If Crazy Richard tries to kidnap you, you could always hit him with a nice curse."

"I'll have to work on that," she said with a content sigh. She had not laughed this hard in a very long time. She closed her eyes as the wine, the fire, and the sound of laughter filled her with a feeling of contentment she hadn't experienced in years.

Seth eventually stood up with a stretch of his arms, rubbing the muscles on the back of his neck. "Better call it a night if we are going to be fixing boats on a Sunday morning," he explained. He nodded at Cori, and said, "See you bright and early, then?"

Cori nodded as she stood. "I should get home as well—still lots of unpacking to do," she lied.

Adrian stood automatically in response. "I'll walk you home," he stated, looking at her with a stare that penetrated her skin. It wasn't posed as a request or a question, and Cori had the feeling he wouldn't accept "no" as an answer.

ADRIAN

Rocks and broken shells crunched under Adrian's sneakers as he walked down the sandy garden path to the side gate, Cori at his heels. It was difficult to see now in the darkness, but the fullness of the moon provided an eerie glow that guided him toward the path along the cliffside. Cori walked beside him on the grass-lined walkway.

Her delicate heart-shaped face was angled toward the sky as she strode along, her eyebrows furrowed and her lips pursed. Her eyes asked an unsaid question, the golden flecks becoming even more illuminated in the moonglow.

They reached the driveway that led to Anne's cottage as her voice broke through the rhythm of the waves. "You didn't have to lie for me, you know," she said. She had stopped in her tracks, inquisitive eyes now focused intently on him.

He didn't know why he had lied for her.

When she had snapped out of whatever trancelike state she had slipped into at dinner, he could tell she was on the verge of panic. If he hadn't been studying her so closely to begin with, perhaps he wouldn't have noticed the change in her at all. It lasted only for a moment. Her eyes had become opaque, and the golden hue seemed to be sucked from them for an instant.

It felt like only a few heartbeats had elapsed, but he could sense something was wrong. That she had *left*.

He had been studying her closely because, well, he couldn't help himself. When he had sensed her presence on the dock the day before, the electrical tingle seemed to stay on his skin and linger there. After meeting her on the beach this morning, it felt like a piece of her was embedded within his skin.

"Not that big of a deal. It was only the second time today I saved you from something unpleasant," he reasoned. He smiled easily at her, remembering how she had almost gotten washed away by the tide this morning.

There were many things he would rather do than help Seth fix Auggie's boat, but the thought of spending the morning with Cori alone on the water seemed like more than an adequate excuse. "What happened to you at dinner?" he asked.

Cori's face turned ghostly white. She hesitated, her mouth opening and closing with half-formed words. *What exactly was she holding back from him?*

She released a breath and squared her shoulders. "Sometimes that happens to me," she said carefully and slowly. "I had a feeling like if you went to work on that boat something bad was going to happen to you. In my head, I saw a fire." She breathed out a sigh as she looked up at him. "I know it sounds strange. I just didn't want you to get hurt. That's all."

He pursed his lips together in thought. "I'm a Water Elemental, Cori," he reminded her. "Usually, fire isn't a problem for me..." he trailed off in thought, "Unless it was an electrical fire."

Cori's eyes widened at this statement, but Adrian shrugged, nonplussed. They continued walking down the side street. She craned her neck to see into Richard's front yard, her interest kindled by the dinnertime storytelling. He smiled secretly at her as she stood on tiptoes to get a look over the fence, fidgeting nervously again with the dainty bracelet on her wrist. She wasn't nearly tall enough to see over to the other side.

"Need a boost?" he teased her.

The tension in her brow fractured as she laughed. "No

thanks. I'll just have to imagine what it looks like over there until I can investigate in the daylight hours."

She seemed more relaxed as they walked along the path to the gate. Adrian had always been naturally empathic, but he couldn't remember a time he seemed so in tune to another person.

He let her walk a few steps ahead of him and watched the way the moonlight traced lines over her shoulders. She tipped her hand out slightly, grazing the tips of the boxwoods with her fingers as she walked along the path.

She turned toward him, a soft smile playing on her lips. "Good night, Adrian. Thanks again for walking me home..." Her words trailed off, contemplating. "And thanks for offering to show me the boat tomorrow."

He opened his mouth to say something, but no words came to him at that moment. She waved her hand over the gate, her lips gently whispering an incantation as the latch clicked open. It swung open with a melodic creak.

She waved her hand over the door in the same fashion, and the door opened with her magic. She looked back at him one more time, her golden eyes twinkling at him as she disappeared like vapor into the darkness of the cottage.

He walked back up the path, only this time he was the one who felt like he was removed from himself. The lights were still on in the main house, and he could see his mother bent over the kitchen sink, no doubt canning something she had harvested earlier. Ariel's light was on, too, but the light in his parents' room was out. David always fell asleep earlier than anyone else in the family, especially when Hannah slipped him a tonic.

He continued into the garden, taking long strides toward the barn. He took the steps two by two up to the side deck that led to the apartment he shared with Seth. His brother's light was also out, so he sat down at their small round kitchen table, resting his head in his hands, feeling the electric energy that seemed to weave over his skin wash over him in waves until he was too tired to continue blinking.

He let the undulation lull him into a deep, undisturbed sleep.

CORI

The pillow was too soft. It deflated under her head like a marshmallow. Cori stared up at the cracked plaster ceiling of her bedroom for what seemed like hours, in limbo between thoughts and dreams as she relived the events of the past two days. She wholeheartedly blamed her substandard pillow for her insomnia but replaying dinner at the farmhouse over in her mind wasn't helping, either.

The Huxleys had welcomed her into their quaint little farmhouse. She hadn't felt like she was a part of a family for so many years, and dragging these unwilling people into the occupational hazards of her existence made her head hurt.

Pulling *Adrian* into the danger that loomed over her pierced through her like a needle laced with guilt.

In the morning she would play it cool. She would accompany the Huxley brothers down to the dock and throw that frayed extension cord into the trash before either of them noticed. The idea of Adrian getting hurt overshadowed any doubt she had in getting involved.

She couldn't get him out of her head, and she was furious with herself. The clock next to the bed flipped to midnight. *One hundred days.*

This was not a time to befriend an Elemental witch, even if she had dreamed about him for her entire life. Even if he was an infuriatingly gorgeous man who had saved her from being washed away in the ocean. She tried closing her eyes, but all she could see was the curve of his mouth tipping up in that playful smile.

"Mama, did Papa ever dream about you before you met?" She was sitting on the cedar chest at the foot of her bed as her mother braided her hair, like she did every night. Her mother's fingers stilled, tangled in the strands.

"I don't know. I never asked him," she said. Her voice was calm, but a bitter sorrow wafted from her aura.

"I dream about people I don't know every day," she said, tipping up her shoulder.

"Hmm, we can call Nonna tomorrow and ask her about it."

"You were fated to Papa." Cori didn't like to pry, but her childhood brain was brimming with so many questions. "Enzo told me."

Her mother didn't answer right away. "Yes, we were fated." She stilled. "—are fated."

Cordelia's throat stung with her mother's grief, and she immediately regretted bringing it up. "Maybe you can meet someone else and fall in love." She had seen it happen in the movies and on TV all the time.

Astrid puffed out a breath, her fingers moving methodically through the ends of her daughter's hair. "I'm afraid it doesn't work that way."

"Sure, it does," Cordelia reassured her, making her voice soft the same way her mother did for her when she was sad or unsure.

Astrid squeezed her daughter's shoulder before she replied, "When you're bonded by fate through magic, you can't love anyone except the person you're bonded to."

Cordelia shook her head. "But Papa's dead. How can you be bonded to him?"

"The magic that bonds you doesn't go away when one of you

moves into the spirit realm." Her mother wrapped an elastic around the end of her long braid. "Your magic is intertwined when you bond with someone you're fated to. I used to be able to feel what he felt, and one day when I move into the spirit realm, I'll feel him again."

"You felt his emotions? Like I feel auras?" Cordelia's head was spinning.

"Almost. When your father took his first flying lesson, I was pregnant with your brother. I was planting bulbs in the garden that morning. Suddenly I felt like my body was floating off the ground."

Cordelia's eyes widened. "You flew, Mama?"

"No, but I marked the time. When he got home, I asked him what time he started his lesson. It was the same. Fated witches can feel emotions and surges in their partner's magic through their bond. That bond is unbreakable. It's an ancient magic that we don't have control over."

She swung around in her seat and faced her mother, looking her in the eye, her forehead scrunched in thought. "But he's gone, so you can never love again?"

"No. But it was worth it," she replied. All the sorrow was gone, replaced with the crispness of certainty. "It was out of my control from the beginning, and as soon as we fell in love, it completed the bond."

Cordelia wrinkled her nose. "What if I'm fated to someone who smells bad."

Her mother's aura lightened, her laugher breaking through the wisps of sorrow wafting around her. "Not everyone has a fated partner, and the Giver won't bind you by fate to someone you won't like. You need to fall in love to complete the bond." She tossed her daughter a playful wink. "Besides, even a smelly person will smell good to someone who loves them."

Cordelia had written a list of questions for her grandmother, and the following morning, her fingers danced over the complex trail of numbers on the kitchen phone that lead to her Nonna.

"Through us, the Mother voices us as a harbinger of important news. She will never let you know something you aren't supposed to *know, and she will never give you knowledge you are too weak to handle. Every day you must pray to the Mother, the Giver, and the Other, and they will give you the knowledge to guide your Eye, Cordelia."*

"What about my dreams, Nonna?"

"We only dream about what we're supposed to know, Stellina."

When she was released from the grip of her vision and her eyes adjusted to the dim light of the room, she unleashed an array of expletives into the darkness as she punched her pathetic excuse for a pillow.

She was angry with herself—she was angry with her Eye—for reminding her of this conversation with her mother. The blinking extension of her magic flared in defiance before settling into her chest in retreat of her anger.

She twirled the charm bracelet around her wrist as she finally drifted to sleep, her past and her future tangled within her mind, leading to dreams that were both reminiscent and diametrically uncertain.

———

She awoke on her own with the first rays of dawn. Although she had set her phone alarm, she had stirred from sleep with an innate desire to gaze into the sky before the sun washed out the stars with light.

She pulled on her frayed jeans, layering her favorite Yoda T-shirt and a Yale hoodie under her fleece jacket. She tamed the thick strands of her hair into a braid, taking her coffee out to the back garden. The lights were still out at Anne and Geoff's house.

Something nudged her leg in the darkness.

"Good morning, Turtle." She softly petted the calico head of her new roommate. "I'm sorry, friend. I don't know where Anne stores the Fancy Feast."

Turtle mewled in offense, stalking off toward the main house.

Cori faced the west at the last depths of the night sky, soaking in the light from the constellations. Like always, they seemed to feed her, energizing her spirit. She had shrouded herself from them for so long, it felt good to bask in their light again, like reconnecting with old friends.

It felt right, despite the voice in her head that told her to go back to bed and pull the blankets over her head.

The whir of an engine broke the silence, as a pickup truck turned into the drive. The truck slowed to a stop in front of the cottage as Seth rolled down the window.

"Good morning!" Seth greeted her with unnatural enthusiasm for this time of day. Adrian, bleary-eyed in the passenger seat, looked less well rested. His coffee mug was balanced on his lap, head resting on the seat back.

"You seem chipper for someone who sustained a concussion yesterday," she greeted as she climbed into the back seat. "Thanks again for the ride to the marina."

"Concussion or no, some people are morning people." He smiled ruggedly at her. "Some people are not." Adrian rolled his eyes at him and took another sip of his coffee. "I got a solid seven hours of sleep, woke up feeling like a million, and snuck in a quick morning jog, all before my brother poured his coffee."

"I was hoping the concussion would make your mouth run less," Adrian countered.

"Not a chance," Seth said cheerfully. "I won't be taken down by a head injury, young Adrian."

"Young Adrian," he scoffed. "Please. I'm thirteen months younger than you, Seth."

"Thirteen months is enough, young man." Seth was enjoying himself. Cori could tell that he was playing off his audience.

"Think of all the things that could happen in thirteenth months," Cori reasoned.

"Exactly. I knew I liked you, Cori. Thirteen months is an eternity. The Constitution was written in a mere three months, you know." Seth was practically giddy with early morning zeal, the radiance of his aura bouncing off the steering wheel, extroverted and energetic. From the passenger seat, she sensed nothing but annoyance and reluctance.

They pulled into the center of town, stopping at the one traffic light in Farley. There were several other trucks at the marina, no doubt getting an early start and an extra day for the catch as lobster season was slowing. At this time of the summer, most of the lobsters would have migrated farther offshore for the onset of the winter months, growing into their hard shells.

Cori had heard that the summer months had been low yield this year, and many local crews were bracing for extended offshore time this autumn and winter. She noticed Adrian's brow furrow in the rearview mirror as he scanned the parked trucks.

"Do you ever fish on weekends?" she asked.

"Depends," Adrian responded, the muscle in his jaw ticked with tension as he surveyed the parked cars. "The law has restricted times. You can't pull traps on Sundays, starting at four o'clock Saturday afternoon until one hour before dawn on Monday morning. Anyone here now must be working on the coast."

"Dad and I were out for a brief time yesterday morning before the storm," Seth explained. "We were rushing back when the storm came in, and so was Auggie—the wrinkled bastard." He rubbed the back of his head with a scowl.

"Do you think the boat is already docked and ready for repair?" Dread washed over Cori.

How much guilt would Seth carry if someone became injured on account of his foolishness? It was nothing compared to the guilt she would feel if she didn't stop it from happening. She cursed her Eye for burdening her with this information, but one glance at Adrian made her simultaneously thank the Mother.

Despite Seth's teasing demeanor, she could tell his heart was in the right place. She sensed a desperation from him to right a wrong. Seth may be brash and loud, but at his heart, she could tell he was righteous and loyal to the core.

Seth slung a heavy bag of tools over his shoulder. "I'll happily show you the enormous dent my head made in Auggie's boat. He should be waiting down here, no doubt tapping his foot and staring at his watch. Even though we're ten minutes early." He started down the wooden steps toward the dock as Cori glanced back at the truck.

Adrian scanned her face and crossed his arms. "Maybe you can help us replace the planks."

ADRIAN

H e couldn't read her. Why was she so willing to accompany them this morning, so early and for such an unpleasant chore? Despite her willingness, she fidgeted with her bag, her eyebrows knitted together as her eyes scanned the dock.

"Maybe you can distract Auggie, and I can fix the boat with a charm," she said with a nervous laugh.

Seth stopped in his tracks. "Could you really do that?" He narrowed his eyes and cocked his head skeptically.

"Well..." she trailed off with a shrug of her shoulder. "I have a spell for fixing broken glass. I have one for ripped paper. Come to think of it, I don't have one for mending splintered wood or metal. I'm not very skilled with magic, so I try not to use it at all, to be honest." With a resigned sigh, she fiddled with her bracelet. Her eyes darted to Adrian for a fleeting moment. "I guess we're going to have to fix it the old-fashioned way."

We. She really intended to fix this boat with them.

Clearly, she was a more patient and forgiving person than he was. He wondered if her scientific background gave her a strange desire to do something that, by his measure, was one of the most tedious and back-breaking tasks imaginable. He was dreading this with every fiber of his being, mostly because of the owner of the busted boat. Auggie had given him the creeps ever since he was a little boy.

Adrian had known that he had an innate power over the water from a very young age. It was embedded into his blood. He could swim before he could speak. Before he could even formulate words, he learned how to ask the water for what he needed. *Will you hold me up? Will you swell around my feet? Will you come together and fall from the sky?*

He could make a wave splash his mother and father when they gave him a bath. One early morning, his father had brought him to the boat. Seth was learning how to tie rope to the cleat, and Adrian was along for the ride, only six or seven years old.

He had been staring absent-mindedly at the water, swirling a stick around with the power of his magic. It was second nature, like twirling a pencil around your finger or tapping your foot. He had sleepily watched the driftwood trace patterns in the water, but when he had looked up, he saw Auggie, aged even all those years ago.

The old man had been staring at him, stone straight, and stuck to the deck like a grizzled statue. Adrian had been caught in the act. He was doing something he was not supposed to do—using his magic out in the open. The old man had pursed his lips and whistled. Sailors were superstitious, probably more than most. Some had luck for the sea—well, many called it luck, but others called it magic.

Water Elementals were part of the folklore, like mermaids or giant squid. All fishermen heard tales of that one family or sailor that seemed to have an uncanny knack, having a way with the water that was more than what was "natural."

He had seen a flash of realization in Auggie's eye that day, but he never told his father or Seth what had happened. From that moment on, Auggie seemed to watch them more carefully. It was as if he were waiting for a moment to reveal them for what they were. His family was respected. Hannah's farm employed more people than any business in town. He couldn't blame Auggie, though, for being weary and bitter toward them. They had an unfair advantage, and if anyone found out they used that advantage in an already competitive market, it would jeopardize everything.

Lobster is money, and money is easier to come by when you can feel the water speaking to you. At least it used to be.

The old man sat on the stern of a boat ahead, perched on an overturned milk crate.

Seth marched up to Auggie and shook his hand firmly, setting his own toolbox down next to a puddle of glossy liquid on the dock. Adrian hung back a few paces, studying Cori's face despite himself. She stilled when she saw the toolbox, and for a fleeting moment, her eyes had darkened before golden embers of light surged back into them.

"Hey—" She broke the tense silence, and Adrian jumped at her voice. "Do you think we'll need to pull the boat onto the lift?" She nodded at the winch and line, connected to the bow.

"No, I don't think so," he said, scrutinizing the damage. "Most of the broken planks are above the waterline."

"Well, I can move this old toolbox out of the way, just in case." She bent down, throwing him a forced smile.

"That's heavy. Let me get it," he offered.

They grabbed for the handle simultaneously, and he found his hand clasped over hers, sending a jolt of electric energy up his arm.

Her eyes widened as her hand gripped tighter around the handle. "It's nothing," she said briskly as she yanked the toolbox away from him.

As she grappled with the full weight of the box, it dropped to the ground, spilling its contents. Cori's face paled when a tattered extension cord fell to her feet.

"Well, that looks dangerous," she said, her voice in a slightly higher register. "I have a new one up in the office. I'll just grab it." She locked eyes with him for a moment, before running briskly toward the building like a scared mouse, the cord clenched in her fist.

As he stood alone on the dock, he inspected the pool of gaso-

81

line on the decking, gleaming with iridescent mischief under the stern. He bit back the feeling of suspicion that rose within him, but he couldn't shake the memory of Cori's eerie behavior from the night before.

They set out on the task at hand, methodically removing the boards from the damaged portion of the boat. Cori returned shortly, gaining a few gruff nods of thanks from Auggie as she presented him with a new extension cord.

It wasn't long before the men were dripping in sweat over the miter saw, Cori handing them new boards from the dock that she had carefully measured up against the damaged ones. Adrian pulled his polo shirt off as the sun blared down on them, and he couldn't help but notice Cori's cheeks flush as she diverted her eyes away.

Something primal flared inside him at her response, but he pushed it aside.

She watched and worked alongside them with bright-eyed attention, asking how they were intending to overlap the boards to assure weatherproofing. She made a clever suggestion about the water seal that made Auggie raise his eyebrows. The old man smiled at her, growling out an approval.

After they applied the first coat of paint, Cori grabbed her bag. "Well, I should probably take off and get some work done," she blurted.

"I thought my brother had promised to show you how to steer the sterndrive," Seth returned. Adrian glared at him, but his brother flashed him an impish smile.

"Oh, right. I'll gather my stuff, then," she said. Another flush rose on her cheeks as she left them to retrieve the keys for Anne's boat. Auggie whistled softly into the air as he watched her walk toward the office.

"Not too often you meet someone who looks like that who has half a brain for boat building," the old man chuckled.

Adrian felt his hand clench on the saw, his knuckles whitening with tension.

"Well, she's a scientist," he ground out. "It's not a shock that she knows how to do something as simple as nailing boards together."

Seth cleared his throat as Auggie chuckled some more, handing Seth a beer from his faded cooler.

Adrian watched Seth plug the new extension cord into the outlet and head toward the boat. Auggie sat down on the milk crate and cracked open the beer, one foot in the pool of gasoline. The cord dragged into the pool as Seth trailed it back to the boat. As it powered on, a sense of dread rose in Adrian's chest, but his brother worked on. Unfazed and unharmed.

As Auggie and Seth worked on, Adrian stared at them, a chill sweeping over his skin. If Seth had used Auggie's extension cord, they may have set a fire. An electrical fire. Cori's hunch and her strange obsession with the extension cord didn't make any sense at all. Unless it wasn't a hunch. Unless it was more than that.

He patted himself dry with a towel and pulled the pale blue cotton polo back over his head as he made his way along the dock toward Anne's boat.

Cori was there, head bent over her tackle box, assembling one of the electronic trackers Anne used. He and his family helped Anne frequently. It took only moments for Adrian to guide the tracker to just the right depth in the water.

It looked as though Cori had taken the gadget apart and put it back together again. Her laptop was open to a spreadsheet, as she cross-referenced a map of the harbor. The midday sun was high in the sky, and Cori's sweatshirt was tied around her waist, her hair cascading over her sun-kissed shoulders as she bent over her work.

She was so distracted she didn't notice his approach. She startled, a nervous smile on her lips. "Fixing the boat is taking a little longer than Seth expected?"

"He underestimated how much damage his massive skull could inflict." He shrugged, rolling his eyes. The air around him was lighter, energized even, at the prospect of getting out on the water, but something inside him felt heavy.

She was hiding something.

"The sterndrive doesn't seem too different now that I am

looking at it up close," she said. "I know the in-drive is more contained, but this shouldn't be too difficult to get a hang of, right?"

He approached the tiny boat and stepped onto the deck of the vessel with heavy boots. "You turn it the same way." He showed her, steadying the gears as he held the key in the ignition. The motor sputtered to life beneath their feet, the water surging around them. "Why don't we pull out of the harbor?" he suggested. The breeze kicked up around them as the tiny yet powerful boat crept through the water.

She carefully steered the boat though the maze of docked and moored vessels, gauging the response between the steering column and the speed of the motor.

He scrutinized the way her fingers easily grazed the switch, knowing just when to flip the gear. "You know exactly how to sail a sterndrive, don't you?"

Her eyes flared with golden flecks of light as a guilty smile played at her lips. "No. I've always had a natural way with boats, I guess."

He swallowed a lump in his throat. *Another lie.*

The coast snaked upward to the east just north of town as he pointed out landmarks that he liked to use to guide his boat home.

"You don't have an onboard GPS?" she asked him, as she tracked her position on the screen.

"We've never really needed one," he said with a shrug. Other teams had used them, but the more experienced families, especially the ones who had been fishing off the coast of Farley for generations, usually relied on the tried and true landmarks. The lighthouse to the north, the markers on the marina at the Farley Center, and the rocky island to the south made an almost perfect equilateral triangle.

"What's on the island?" she asked. Goose bumps dotted her bare arms as she pulled her sweatshirt up around her shoulders, the crisp wind intensifying the farther offshore they traveled.

"Mostly brush, one small cave, a few abandoned fishing cabins at the cove, and rock on the periphery," he explained. "Seth and I go out there every once in a while to camp, but it's too windy most of the year. We don't go as much as we used to."

He smiled to himself at the memories of camping with his brother as teenagers and the times they had stolen beers from his dad's cooler.

"You can only dock on the north side, the rest of the island has too steep of an embankment. It only takes about twenty minutes to hike it, end to end." He saw her shiver as her gaze swept over the desolate island. "Mainers call it Cetus Island," he continued. At this, her gaze shifted to his face, amusement playing on her lips. "What's so funny?" he asked.

"Nothing's funny," she said, biting her lip. "That's just an interesting name for an island, that's all." She pursed her lips together, crossing her arms, a laugh breaking free.

"The island's shaped like a whale if you look on the map." He spread the map out, smoothing the corners. "It's named for the constellation of Cetus, the sea monster. Have you heard of it?" Now he was laughing, and he didn't know why. Nothing about the island, or its name, had seemed amusing to him before.

She smiled, scrunching her nose as though she had told herself a secret joke. "I've heard of it."

"Damn it," he thought. She was adorable.

The late afternoon light dipped over the coast, the warm rays reflecting in sharp angles over the tops of the towering evergreens onshore as they swayed. The motor quieted as they bobbed on the water.

Despite the water growing colder underneath, every droplet around them drank in the golden warmth from the sun, swelling with heat and magic.

The light glinted off the golden bracelet around her wrist, and before he could stop himself, he reached for it, turning the little sun over in his fingers.

Her hand stilled, but she didn't move away.

He traced a slow line toward the moon and the star that circled her hand, stopping over the delicate skin of her wrist, memorizing the lines of her palm as he turned her hand over on his own.

"You said the bracelet was blessed with a charm for luck?" he asked.

She nodded, her lips parting as his fingers grazed her wrist. The wind picked up, tossing a wavy strand of hair over her eyes.

He lifted his other hand automatically to brush away the strand of windswept hair, and he ran his fingers softly through it as he tucked it behind her ear. The boat was almost still now, as he traced the line of her jaw. She didn't move. Didn't pull away.

He wanted to etch into his brain the way her face looked in the golden light. Even though he had seen her for the first time only yesterday, he felt like he had spent a lifetime looking at that face. Every curve seemed familiar, as if it was part of a dream he had only just now remembered.

The electric energy within him surged to life as the boat swelled underneath them, the water rising and bending to his will. She leaned forward, the shift under the boat narrowing the distance between them, as the golden embers in her eyes flared to life.

CORI

His hand was still touching her wrist, lingering there. She allowed her magic to surface, finding his aura—full of heavy, smoky need.

His gaze, deep and blue as the water swirling around them, dipped down to her mouth, and the heaviness between them grew, wrapping around her in a way that made her want to simultaneously lunge for him and dive into the water to escape.

When a vision of his eyes had wafted into her dreams, she would awaken breathless and warm as though something inside her had been stirred. The heaviness of his aura pierced through her, cracking something open that felt familiar yet new, waiting to take root.

She had always been in tune to the people around her, sensing their emotions, even their intentions like whispers on the wind. Most of the time, this power felt like a burden, but at this moment, she was fed by his energy. It flowed out of him with an intensity that she couldn't help but drink in. He angled his head toward her, his lips dangerously close to hers. The water surged again under the boat, the dizzying force of his magic surrounding her.

But this—this was like nothing she had felt before. She couldn't just sense his *aura*, she could sense his *magic*, and for a fleeting moment, the weight of the tide itself rose in her blood. She realized she had been holding her breath as panic gripped her and she broke the physical connection between them, pulling her wrist from his hand as she pulled back in her seat.

He shivered as the tether between them broke, and her heart nearly stopped. *Holy Mother, did he feel it, too?*

His lips parted, trying to formulate his words. "We should head back," he said after a moment. The sun had dipped below the trees, the sky pink and streaked with clouds, as it gave in to the late afternoon.

She nodded quickly, but a part of her, the part that was connected to her instinct and her heart, wanted to float there on the water with him forever, leaving all the uncertainty of the past three thousand days behind her.

She smoothed her hair hastily into a ponytail and pulled her sweatshirt around her shoulders.

He gripped the steering wheel, his knuckles white. "Do you mind if I drive?" he asked.

She nodded again, her voice betraying her with the inability to make a sound.

He pulled the key from the ignition and handed it to her. The boat surged under them, the power of the water propelling them toward the shore.

———

Auggie and Seth were perched on the crates in front of a portable television, beer cans strewn at their feet, as they watched the Red Sox game.

Auggie's filthy shirt was wrapped around his neck, his wrinkled skin browned and withering over what probably used to be very muscular shoulders. A cigar dangled from his mouth as he slammed his open hand onto the side of the boat. "That was a strike," he grunted.

"Mind the paint, old man," Seth said absent-mindedly, as he stood up to get a better look at the replay. Auggie glowered at

88

him. "How were the driving lessons?" He cocked his head toward Adrian.

"Good. She didn't need me at all," Adrian said smoothly, rubbing a hand through his hair.

She swallowed a lump in her throat. Maybe she needed him, but not in the way he meant.

"Well, even though my brother's a dumbass, I'm glad you came to help us," Seth laughed. "If it wasn't for you, it would've taken us twice as long to weatherproof the boards."

"Yeah, we appreciate it," Adrian said slowly. His eyes connected to her for a moment before he gazed down at the electrical cord still draped in the pool of gasoline. *Fire isn't usually a problem for me—unless it's an electrical fire.*

The pit of her stomach tightened and turned over. The heat of Adrian's aura had cooled now, replaced by something she couldn't quite place.

"Ayuh' we do appreciate yer," Auggie said gruffly. "The young lady came out here today to help you out—hard tellin' not knowin' why," he continued. "Least you can do is take her out to a drink, ya ungrateful bastards."

CORI

The brothers led Cori to the aged boardwalk that connected the Farley Center to the road. They walked past the parking lot, now emptied of cars and trucks at the day's end. The sun had lowered, and in the late afternoon light, the early glow of the moon broke through the pale blue sky.

She tipped her head up as the moon tumbled onward on its orbit, the venerating movement above humming with soft reassurance.

Her mother's head, highlighted with silvery gray, bowed over a teacup as a kettle whistled on the stove. The cord of the phone dangled behind her as she twirled it in her fingers. "Enzo, we've been through this before." Her voice was tinged with exasperation. "You're making a difficult situation even worse. If things are so bad at the restaurant..."

Her voice broke off as her brother's muffled voice argued through the receiver. She turned off the stove and poured the steamy water over a sachet of tea leaves as a sigh huffed out of her.

"I'll try my best," she said, her shoulders slumping. "Pick me up at ten o'clock." Then her mother—her always serene mother—slammed the phone back onto the wall.

Her pounding heart slowed as her Eye released its grip. The brothers were a few paces ahead of her now, thankfully oblivious to the pause in her steps while receiving the vision. She had never seen her mother get angry before. While many things may have changed during her absence, it seemed incredibly out of character for her mother to hang up on Enzo like that.

Enzo had been with Calvin yesterday.

It was possible that Astrid didn't like the idea of Enzo putting himself in harm's way. Her stomach turned as she wondered if the meeting about the prophecy was still taking place. Hopefully Enzo had convinced him to call the whole thing off by now. He had been worried about the restaurant while he was at the hotel with Calvin, but now he was arguing about it on the phone with his mother.

She chewed on her lip, overwhelmed knowing that there was no comfort she could give him from three thousand miles away. No encouraging words she could share with him.

In one hundred days, she would be back where she belonged. Anne would understand. The project she had been hired to oversee could easily be wrapped up in a few months, maybe a year at the most. It was normal for academics to travel from one project to the next, and she had already researched ecology groups out in California. As soon as the solstice was behind her, she would send out her résumé.

Ahead of her, Seth laughed at something Adrian said, and he punched his brother playfully on the arm. A small sliver of hope cracked from her heart, deflating it. She shoved her hands deep into the front pocket of her sweatshirt, pushing the thought aside.

They led her to a small walking path that connected the marina to the shops. She wondered that there may be a viable social scene in Farley, after all.

They strode past an open-air seafood restaurant looking out onto the water, bustling with customers dining alfresco. Next door, a coffee shop was nestled into a building bedecked with cedar shingles. Spying the extensive pastry cases inside, she made a mental note to stop there the next day.

Across the cobbled pathway, there was a florist and a yoga studio on a side street that was dotted with charming little lamp-posts and benches. At the end of the path, a lively brick building was flooded by the sounds of music and laughter.

"Probably not as nice as the bars you're used to," Seth said as he ushered her in the door. "Carl keeps most of the good Mainer breweries on tap, though, and he makes wicked good nachos."

Cori had not been inside a bar in a very long time. Defending her thesis was full-time and lonely work, and she had made it a point to keep away from social situations throughout her time at Yale. Most of the other students had family and friends come out to celebrate after the doctoral awards, but Cori had celebrated alone with a bottle of wine in her apartment. The fewer people she knew, the less suspicion there would be.

A wave of anxiety rose within her. It had never been easy for her to meet new people, and yet here she was at a bar with two new friends.

Friends who were witches.

She breathed in the air, laced with the oil of fried food and the sweet tang of fermented hops, as they made their way past the bar toward an empty booth.

"Well, look what the tall, handsome fisherman brothers dragged in," a familiar voice called out. Jordan turned the corner, beer in hand wearing designer jeans and a Bob Dylan T-shirt. His other arm was locked elbow to elbow with one of the most stunning women Cori had ever seen.

"Cori, this is Jess." He turned toward the beautiful girl on his arm with purpose. "This is who I was telling you about from the office. The new scientist." He winked at Cori, and she gave them an awkward wave coupled with a tentative smile.

Seth shifted on his feet next to her. His laid-back and playful essence had hardened, and his aura was now teeming with heated tension. This was who had distracted him before he crashed the boat, and now she could see why.

Jess had blond hair braided into two perfect plaits that cascaded over her shoulder from under a baseball cap. She wore an ironically simple white T-shirt that was tucked into a pair of faded jeans, but she oozed glamor and sexy confidence. Jess eyed Cori up and down and gave Jordan a nod.

Jess was every girl who used to effortlessly flirt with boys and go to parties in high school. Every girl that Cori looked at with longing and self-deprecation in her heart from behind the pages of a science textbook.

"Agreed, she looks normal to me. Well, as normal as someone who would choose to move to this godforsaken place." She nudged Jordan playfully on the arm. "It's so nice to finally meet you, Cori. Jordan has been gushing about how you fixed Anne's boat all weekend," she said, winking.

Seth shot Cori a confused look, and heat rose in her chest. Luckily, Jess distracted him with a playful touch on his arm.

"How did it go with Auggie today?" she asked him with a concerned pout.

Jess's other hand reached for the tip of her braid, twirling it in a casually seductive way. Seth's aura exuded sexual tension. Jess's aura, on the other hand, dripped with power. She had him wrapped around her finger and she knew it.

Cori slid into the booth between Adrian and Jordan, sending Jess an invisible message that she was not a threat to her conquest. Not that a girl like her would stand a chance in a contest for affection with someone like Jess.

"Boat is good as new, but my brain may be permanently damaged," Seth said with a smirk, rubbing his hand through his hair.

"It was already in a relatively damaged state, even before yesterday," Adrian teased him.

A short, stocky man adorned with an impressive collection of tattoos approached their table. Adrian raised his hands in relief. "Carl, you're a sight for sore eyes. I'm in desperate need of a round, maybe a pitcher. I spent the whole day with Seth and Auggie fixing a fucking boat."

"Well, shit. Sounds like a pitcher to me." Carl turned a curious eye down the table. "Ah, an out-of-towner!"

Jordan nudged Cori with his shoulder, making his introductions between the barkeep and the new scientist in town. She could feel Adrian's gaze on her in silent appraisal as she struck up small talk with Carl about what she liked to drink.

Carl seemed like the type of barkeep who liked to know the preferences of every customer, so he could have your drink of choice at the ready the moment you darkened his door.

"So, let me get this straight." Seth stared at Cori incredulously. "You don't like *beer*?"

"It's not that I don't like beer," she argued, trying to defend herself. "It's just that I would prefer to drink wine, if I'm given the choice."

"Why would you even move to Maine if you don't like beer?" Seth shook his head.

"I do like beer!" She huffed, "I'm from California, we drink a lot of wine, OK?"

Her heart stilled. She had never—not once—revealed something so personal about herself to a stranger before. Sitting in a bar, in close distance to a dozen people she didn't know, no less. Sure, she could tell that she and Seth and Adrian were the only witches in the bar, but witches regularly employed, or even bewitched, humans to do their will. Now they all knew she was from California.

She shrank into the booth.

When people had asked where she was from in the past, her response was always swift and easy. *Oh, from the West Coast*, she would reply airily. If someone tried to pry, she employed a very handy charm her mother had written for her. After murmuring the incantation, people would change the subject and simply forget that she had told them anything at all.

But it was too late, and too risky, to bewitch anyone at this table. Adrian and Seth would sense it, and she had already noticed on more than one occasion the brothers were suspicious of her. She tried to reel in her panic and lighten the tone in her voice as Adrian and Seth argued about what was the best brewery in Portland.

Seth and Jess made their way to a private booth, where she gently inspected the wound on Seth's head with careful and delicate hands. He said something to her and smiled wickedly. She laughed and pushed him hard on the shoulder. They finished their pints, Jess whispering something into his ear that made his eyes widen.

"Oh, she's going in for the kill." Jordan leaned back, surveying them. He nodded to Jess with admiration. "This on-again, off-again bullshit those two have is exhausting. I feel like I'm watching an episode of *Dawson's Creek*."

Cori snorted into her wineglass. "Wow, you just really dated yourself there." Jordan glowered at her. "So, they did date?" she asked.

Adrian rolled his eyes. "She broke things off when she went to college, but she ended up moving back home. Everyone always does." He drained his glass, and she noticed his words were coming more easily, a smooth buzz on his lips. "He was devastated when she left," he explained with sincerity. "She's been back for a few months. She worked in Boston for a while after school. Sounds like she broke up with her fiancé"—he raised his eyebrows—"and now she's about to make up for lost time."

Jess was leaning in close, her hand on Seth's forearm. The sexual energy oozed off them, making Cori want to shove her nosy Eye deep down into her gut where it belonged. This was the part of her power that troubled her the most.

She had forgotten how difficult it was to be in larger crowds, sensing everyone's feelings. It was exhausting, overwhelming, and sucked the energy from her.

Adrian told Jordan all about their day with Auggie, and when Cori's wineglass was emptied, a new one arrived moments later at the table. Carl was rapidly becoming her favorite resident of Farley. Two booths away, her attention shifted to a middle-aged man who sat with a friend. The crushing heaviness of sadness and mourning rolled off him.

She was not surprised when the spirit of a woman materialized behind him. Her passing seemed recent, and it was common in the early days of grief that people would be visited. It's easier for the spirit when a soul has only recently crossed over into the realm.

Cori watched the woman, a mere wisp of light and breath only she could see, put a hand on the man's shoulder as a tear rolled from his eye. She kissed him softly on the cheek before making her way over to his companion, thanking him, too, with a kiss for being a good friend on a dark day. The man's hand drifted absent-mindedly to his cheek, completely unaware, but aware all the same.

The spirit saw Cori from across the room and nodded before dematerializing back to the spirit realm. She let go of a ragged breath, relieved that the spirit had not tried to interact with her. Even when her Eye had been locked away during her time at Yale, there was nothing she could do to stop herself from seeing spirits.

She came out of her haze as Jordan nudged her sharply in the ribs.

He cocked his head to Seth and Jess as they headed toward the door together. "And there they go," he said approvingly.

"Well, there goes our ride," Adrian puffed out an annoyed sigh as he drained his third beer. "Come on, Cori. I guess we're walking home."

"Okay, I'll just ask Carl for my check," she said, craning her neck toward the bar.

He raised a brow at her. "Nope. Your money's no good here. Our tab is always open at Carl's."

Jordan cocked his head at her as they rose from the table. "You watch out for those Huxley boys, Dr. Evans." He patted Adrian hard on the back before they made their way to the door and into the cool, dark night.

ADRIAN

The crunch of gravel under their feet scraped in his ear against the gentle hum of the ocean as they walked the steeply sloped path that led to the cliffs. The houses were spaced far apart, and the only light on the street came from their windows and the warmth of the moonglow overhead.

"You're a doctor?" he asked her.

"Oh, yeah. I have a PhD in marine ecology."

"Is that how you met Anne?" he asked her.

She paused. "She was my professor at Yale."

Damn. He could tell she was smart after admiring her problem-solving skills with the boat today, but that was a whole other level of intelligence. He would tell her about his bachelor degree in business some other time.

The starlight danced on Cori's face, etching lines of introspection into her delicate features. She nearly tripped several times, her eyes focused upward, poised with an unspoken question as she looked at the stars.

It had happened again but this time she had been staring at a man at the bar. Doug Jenson, poor guy. He had just lost his wife to cancer, leaving him a widower with two young boys. He hadn't been out on the water all summer because she was too ill. Adrian knew it probably meant thousands, likely tens of thousands of dollars, had been lost during the summer season.

When she had seen Doug from across the crowded bar, for a moment all the light had been sucked out of her eyes—just like the night before at dinner. Only this time, she seemed sad instead of panicked.

Adrian had never paid attention to anyone so aptly in his entire life, and he couldn't figure out why. He replayed what happened on the boat in his mind for what seemed like the hundredth time. When he had touched her hand, the sky spun over his head, and he swore he felt not only the swell of the tide but the pull of the moon. He rubbed his hand over the back of his neck.

He broke the silence with a heavy sigh. "Seth and I share an apartment over the barn. I think I'll sleep in my old bedroom in the farmhouse tonight."

Cori twisted her face, trying not to laugh. "You don't want to risk it, huh?"

"Risk hearing my brother groaning like an animal through the thin wall in between our bedrooms? Nah, I'll take my chances. Ariel might set me on fire in her sleep, and Dad might have a bad dream and flood the bathroom but both scenarios are preferable."

Cori laughed softly at all the unfortunate possibilities of the night. "Sounds like a lose-lose-lose situation," she teased.

She looked back at him over her shoulder, an amused smirk dancing on the corners of her mouth, and he caught himself before his hand instinctively reached out to grab hers.

What was wrong with him? He had almost touched her multiple times today, as if his body was being pulled on an invisible line at the end of her reel.

As they turned the bend, an urgent *meow* greeted them at the path. Turtle rubbed her face and whiskers urgently on Cori's legs and sprinted with purpose to the house. They turned toward the cottage, and dread stung the back of his throat. He put out his hand, this time with no hesitation, catching Cori on the wrist. She stopped in her tracks, and he knew she felt the same heaviness in the air. Magic, like electric fear, pushed down on them.

The door of the cottage was cracked open, illuminated ominously by the moon in stark contrast to the darkness of the rooms within.

CORI

Her heart pounded in her ears as her mind shifted into defensive mode. She whispered her mother's incantation, and all the light and electricity inside the house clicked on simultaneously. The hair dryer, which she must have accidentally left plugged in, whirred to life from the bathroom.

At her side, Adrian jumped in surprise. Cori murmured the next incantation as all the doors sprang open at once. She turned to him urgently, the power of her magic pulsing through her as raw instinct took hold.

"Someone was here."

He nodded, following her through the doorway. They began searching every crevice in the two small rooms, but there was no sign of anyone despite the electric heaviness of magic that hung in the air.

"We need to retrace their steps," she explained to him, her voice trembling.

The next incantation left her lips almost silently as she fixed her attention to the door, her magic surging to life once more. The worn floorboards shimmered as ghostly footprints materialized. Adrian gasped, his eyes wide. This charm, one of her mother's finest and most clever spells, showed you the path an intruder had taken in your home.

She had many spells like this in her arsenal, as Astrid had woven many protective charms before Cori's departure, planning for the inevitable dangers to come.

She followed two sets of shimmering footprints through the door. One set, big and thick, most likely made by a pair of boots, diverged into the kitchen. A second set, dainty and curved, like women's flats, trailed into the bedroom.

She looked up at Adrian, an expression of shock on his face. "There were two of them?" he asked her.

"Looks that way," she agreed. "You follow the boots, and I'll follow these little ones."

He nodded.

As Cori traced the steps into her bedroom, she let her Eye bubble to the surface, pulling on the lingering magic of the intruders.

The air in the house buzzed, full of magic and curiosity. A small woman holding a heavy flashlight stalked through the bedroom door. Her black hair fringed her forehead with wispy bangs, and her lips were painted with bloodred lip stain that accentuated the upward curve in the corners.

The intruder paused at the bedside table where two small folded notes were tucked into a drawer. She grasped the yellow note, and her eyes flared in triumph as she read Enzo's angular scrawl.

Cori came back to herself to find Adrian in the doorway, his breaths coming quickly with earnest fear as his stare held on to her.

This time, though, she didn't hesitate. Unfettered adrenaline coursed through her body, blood rising and falling in her heart like the tide. "I followed the spell," she explained. She opened the bedside table drawer, but it was difficult to make out the words and crisp pen strokes now. She held up the note from Enzo, marked with a pentagram, painted in blood.

ADRIAN

When Adrian walked into Cori's bedroom, he found her in a dreamlike haze, standing as still as a statue. Her eyes were out of focus and opaquely black. Only this time, it was not subtle or fleeting. There was no question in his mind. She had left her body. When she snapped back to herself this time, however, she moved with purpose.

She held a note in her trembling hand, defiled with a pentagram etched in bright red blood—a mark of dark magic. The symbol of the devil himself, some said. As he stood alone in the room with her, uneasiness surged within him.

How could I be so stupid?

All this time, he had fought a feeling that she was hiding something from him. She appeared out of nowhere in town with a seemingly simple story. She's a witch, but she is also a scientist. Charms witch, but she says her spells aloud. A witch whose home had been targeted, broken into.

When he had touched her on the boat, the influence of her magic had overcome him, and now she was holding a bloody pentagram.

His chest swelled with realization. He had sensed lies and secrecy in her from the moment he met her. She opened her mouth to speak, but his words came out first. "You're a Gray witch," he said sharply.

His words seemed to cut through her. "Adrian..."

"I had this feeling," he admitted, rubbing his hand through his thick hair. "I don't know what you're doing to me. I wanted to be near you. I was pulled to you." His chest twisted with the sting of betrayal. "I had never felt something like that before. On the boat. You were leading me, using dark magic."

Her face paled. "Adrian, please let me..."

"You could have told me you were a Gray witch. You didn't have to lie." Bitterness rose in his throat. It was one thing to lie to him, but she had lied to his entire family. Heavy humidity rose in the air, summoned by his anger. "As soon as I told you we were Elemental, you wanted a piece of us, didn't you?"

She gaped at him. "What the hell are you talking about?" It was her turn to get angry.

"Please, Cori, it makes perfect sense now. We met a group of Gray witches once, and they wanted my sister's hair. What are you trying to get from us? A vial of a Water Elemental's tears, or a Ground Elemental's fingernails for some dark magic ritual?"

Her jaw tightened, the golden embers in her eyes flaring at his words. Her mouth opened, words hanging on her lips but no sounds came out. He could practically see the wheels turning in her mind.

Her throat bobbed, and she stared at him for a hard minute before she spoke, "I'm not a Gray witch." Her lips turned down in a hard line, her eyes wide. She took a deep breath and steadied herself through her trembling breath. "But you're right. I'm not a Charms witch, either. I lied to you. I'm sorry."

"Then tell me the truth," he said earnestly.

She fixed her gaze at his eyes, golden with intensity, and took a deep breath. "I'm Celestial."

The weight of her words hit him, permeating the heavy humidity between them. The tension in his shoulders lightened, and he willed the vapor in the room to dissipate. Despite willing the water away, heavy tears trailed down her cheeks.

"Why would you keep something like that from me?" he asked, his voice softening. "From anyone?"

"Because the minute you learn the truth, you're in just as much danger as I am."

Part Two

Moon in Scorpio

"Scorpio keeps our secrets. To have the moon within her is like living within a shadow."
-The Mangianelli Grimoire

CORI

She was going to vomit. Her brain was screaming as her Eye nudged her impatiently in the ribs. Revealing herself to him felt so dangerous, yet the idea of him knowing gave her the strangest sense of strength. She reluctantly allowed her Eye into her mind. *He's supposed to know.*

"I'm the teller of the Gray Prophecy," she blurted out. She stilled for a moment, gauging his response, but his expression remained blank. "My name is Cori, but it's a nickname," she continued slowly, her hands trembling as her mouth fought against the words that had been forbidden for so long.

"Actually, my full name is Cordelia Mangianelli. My last name isn't Evans." She lowered her head and raised her eyebrows expectantly.

"Cori, um, Cordelia..."

"Please, don't call me Cordelia. I've always preferred Cori." She sighed, thinking of Enzo. "Or Cor. My brother...he always called me Cor."

"OK. Listen. I'm an Elemental witch. We don't belong to a coven. Never have. My family and I are the only witches in this town. I think we're the only witches in the whole county. I've never heard of this prophecy." His eyebrows came together. "We never get news of things like this. Maybe my parents have heard of it. But if they did, they never shared it with me."

She was surprised that he had never heard of the infamous prophecy, but she was most grateful that he had never heard of *her*.

Panic settled into her chest. She could not believe she just told him the truth, but the accusation he had thrown at her was too much for her to bear. *A Gray witch*. To think that she, of all people, would use dark magic. She kicked herself. It was too late for a memory charm.

"I think moving here was a mistake," she said.

She started to gather her belongings, piling them into her duffel bags.

"What are you doing?" he asked in disbelief.

"I need to leave," she said simply. "I haven't known you that long, but I hope I can trust you. I'll tell Anne that there was a family emergency back home. If anyone asks about me, please just tell them you never saw me." Guilt stung her throat at the thought of him being interrogated—or worse.

Adrian gaped at her. "Why would you leave? Are you in trouble?" He grabbed her forearm, and a shock wave of heavy heat surged into her chest. "Maybe I can help you. Please. I just want to understand."

She stilled. "You really never heard of the Gray Prophecy?"

He shook his head desperately. "I just want to understand."

She let out a sigh. "I can show you." She sat down heavily and patted the bed next to her, urging him to sit. He slowly lowered himself to a seat next to her, his eyebrows knitted together. "Give me your hand?"

His large calloused hands were difficult to encircle with her own. "This might feel a little strange. I don't know any other way to explain this to you," she said apologetically.

"OK." His answer was a whisper.

She closed her eyes and freed her Eye, reaching out for him. A shiver went through her as her magic collided with his. He let out a breath as they were pulled forward, connected by what seemed like a thousand invisible strands of electric energy. She turned back the pages of her past, her Eye eager to show the truth of the memories locked within.

Cori relished for a moment in his magic. She had connected her Eye to other witches like this before, but it had been a long time since she was this vulnerable—this intimate—with someone. Her skin flushed as if she was swimming in a bubbling hot spring, the hairs on her skin prickling.

A velvet smoke hung in the air. As she settled into the feeling, she was overwhelmed by the scent of pine trees and salt, and her skin felt damp. As if she was watching the waves crash off the rocks of the coast, scattering a dense, salty mist.

A young Cordelia sat in her bed, peering out the window. The scent of incense was thick in the air. Her mother smoothed her hair into a neat braid.

"Mama, when are you going to tell me what I said last night?"

"You've been crying and sleeping all day." The woman's voice was full of remorse. "When you give a prophecy, it can drain you for a little while. I wanted to wait until you were strong enough to hear it."

"I'm strong enough now," she said, wiping away a tear. "I need to know."

The woman sighed, smoothing the sheets. She handed her a piece of thick paper, adorned with a curvy script.

The Gray Covenant has been betrayed, weakening the Giver, as was foretold by those whose oath was made. When the great conjunction of Saturn and Jupiter occurs on the winter solstice, the Mother will collect the debt of three hundred years of stolen darkness. All those who have betrayed the Covenant will receive no more, and all those who have borrowed from the betrayal will weaken through the Other.

She turned the paper over and over in her hand. The words felt foreign to her, as though spoken by a ghost.

"I don't remember saying any of that," she said with dismay, turning the words over in her mind.

Her mother's brows came down into a concerned furrow. "Cordelia, there are many witches in the world who practice dark magic," she started to say.

"Not us." She sat up straight, intensity illuminating the golden hues of her eyes.

Her mother dipped her chin and closed her eyes tight as she rubbed her forehead. "Well—many witches do. Despite the Covenant. What you predicted will mean that those who do"—her voice cracked—"will lose their magic on a future solstice."

"So, they'll have no more magic?" she asked with wide eyes, clutching her blanket close to her.

"No, baby. Their magic will fade, as will the magic that we all share through the Other."

"So, all the bad witches will be done with magic." Her mother winced at her words. "That's a good thing, right?"

Her mother stood up and walked toward the window. "Cordelia, witches gain their power from three sources. The Mother, the Giver, and the Other."

"I remember from coven." Cordelia tilted her head, distracted by the light of the moon tumbling into the room.

"We all gain power from each other. When those who have violated the Covenant lose their power, based on your prediction, we will all lose some of our magic. We will all weaken." Her mother bit her lip, studying her daughter's face.

"All of us?"

"All of us," her mother replied with sad eyes.

"Mama," careful words followed a long silence. "Papa was Celestial. Right? Did he ever make a prophecy?"

Her mother's eyes widened at the question. "Never," she rasped.

———

As the room shifted out of focus. An older Cordelia sat in the same spot. Her brother, Enzo, stood near the doorway.

"Cor, I don't know if I'm the one who should tell you this." He swallowed hard. *"It's fabled that if you kill the witch who makes a prophecy, then it will not come to be,"* he said slowly. *He remained silent for a moment as the power of his words washed over the room. "This is why you're in danger, and why you will someday need to disappear."*

———

Cordelia, now the age of a teenager, sat with her mother on the front stoop of a grand town house making flower chains.

She pursed her lips. "When should I hear about the college acceptances?"

Her mother squinted her eyes in a hopeful smile. She gripped her daughter's hand, her eyes dancing with light. "Soon, Starlight. I know you will get in somewhere, even though you're only a sophomore. A perfect SAT score, flawless AP tests, a publication in a renowned scientific journal..."

Cordelia's head dipped down as she twirled the bracelet on her arm.

"I will miss you every minute you're away, honey." Her mother threaded the flower crowns through her fingers, finally choosing one to gingerly place on her daughter's head. *"When the day of the prophecy is behind us, we'll reunite. Until then, you need to stay hidden."*

She listened to the gulls on the bay, dipping low on the hill. "What if they come for you?" Cordelia's question hung in the air.

Her mother's eyes closed gently, as though in silent prayer. She swallowed hard, pivoting her head back and forth in protest. "I'll have nothing to tell them."

———

"Enzo, I need your help," Cordelia called down the hallway. *Her belongings were packed into a large trunk, the remaining items strewn about on the floral bedsheets.*

Her brother's frame appeared in the doorway, now dressed in the business casual clothing of a young professional.

"I don't have a spell to help you pack, Cor." His teasing tone was laced with remorse. "For a smart person, you sure are dumb when it comes to fitting things into a trunk."

She attempted to throw a book at him, but he dodged it narrowly. "I know you don't have a packing spell, but you do have one to alter an ID card." She raised her eyebrows at him with a devilish grin as she waved her driver's license at him.

He sighed. "Fine. Please, just don't tell Ma." He winked as he sat next to her, holding out his hand for the card expectantly. "Just think about your new name, as I turn the card over in my hand."

He held the driver's license in his hand as he wordlessly willed the enchantment through his silent incantation. "Don't you dare tell anyone your new name, not even me." He handed her the magically altered card and stood to leave. "Cor, promise me something, OK? Trust nobody until after the solstice."

Cori looked down at her new name, perfectly altered beyond human detection on her license. "Enz," she said sadly. "See you in 3,285 days."

He took a deep breath, tears stinging his eyes as he crossed the threshold, pulling his sister into a hug.

ADRIAN

Adrian choked as the wind whipped out of his lungs. The connection between them broke. One moment he was inhaling the cool, dry air of the California coast, the next he was falling away from the warmth and comfort of the connection to her, back to the cool humidity of the little cottage.

He braced his arm on the bed, trying to catch his breath as his head spun.

Cori had collapsed into a heap next to him. He couldn't imagine how much magic she had just expended, or how much emotional energy. As he watched her, the slow rising and falling of her chest, the gentle fluttering of her eyelids, he was overcome with an intense desire to scoop her up in his arms and tell her she was safe.

A single tear fell from her eye, tracing a path to the wave of hair at her temple.

"When..." he stammered, not knowing how to organize the questions that were fluttering around his mind.

"I gave the prophecy when I was twelve years old," she answered, rubbing her temples. "I was seventeen when I left home for Yale. My family knew I had gotten into a college, but I couldn't tell them which one."

"They don't know you're here, do they?"

She shook her head. The totality of her isolation and the weight that she carried hit him. She squeezed her eyes tight. "The coven priestesses decided that the safest thing for me, and for my family, was to create a new identity when I came of age, focusing on my studies until the prophecy came to pass."

She sat up slowly, putting her head in her hands. "Nobody ever suspected that a quiet Charms witch would have a mysterious past. I had ways of checking in, always with my mom's magic. Separating from them has kept us all safe." Her eyes dipped down to the floor, the bloody pentagram at her feet. "Until right now."

Adrian's chest tightened. "You must've been so lonely."

She shrugged. "It wasn't so bad. I had my studies to distract me. And there's Anne," she said, her face warming. "Anne was the only person that I ever felt comfortable getting close to. She even invited me to Christmas a few times."

She sighed deeply, her eyes still pale and dark. "I don't even know what their life is like now. I don't know if my brother ever married. Maybe I could be an aunt," she mused with a sad laugh.

Adrian's stomach hollowed at the thought of Cori spending holidays alone in New Haven, wondering about the welfare of her family across the country, being completely in the dark about their happiness and sadness. The expansive darkness of her eyes was regaining the golden hue as she took one restorative breath after another.

He imagined what it would be like to be away from his family for that long. Hell, he had never been away for more than a week. He bit his lip, chewing on his thoughts. There is no way his parents would have sent him away, no matter the risk. He hadn't been there, or lived through it, but he wondered how sending her away—forcing her into exile—was the best choice.

Resentment filled the hollow of his gut.

She shook her head, gulping deeply. "The whole time I was at Yale, I didn't use my Eye. I pushed it away, and I didn't have a single vision until I arrived here. For some reason, my Eye has become unhinged the past few days, and I've been bombarded with one vision after the other," she said bitterly. "You're the first person I've told about any of this since I left California."

"Do you think whoever left the pentagram was here to..." He stilled again, a shiver running through him.

"I think whoever it was knows who I am." She squared her shoulders. "If I'm killed, then the prophecy will die with me. It won't come to be."

He cocked his head. "Are you sure about that?" His eyebrows rose with incredulity. "It sounds like a superstition."

This made her smile. "It doesn't matter if it's true or not. If witches out there believe it to be true, that's all that matters."

He stood at this, nervous energy bouncing through him as he ran his fingers through his hair. "Do you think there are Gray witches out there who would believe that kind of thing?" He was suddenly struck with guilt—just moments ago, he had been accusing her of being a Gray witch.

"It's not just the Gray witches, though," she sighed, resting her head in her hands. "It's the second part of the prophecy that's problematic. If some witches are weakened, then we all are."

He froze. "What do you mean?"

"It's like the prophecy says. 'All those who have betrayed the Covenant will receive no more, and all those who have borrowed from the betrayal will weaken through the Other.'"

He looked down at her, his brow knotted in confusion. "I get the part about the Mother and the Giver," he turned over his words slowly, trying to decode them. "But how would all of us weaken through the Other if a bunch of witches lost their magic?"

Cori raised her eyebrows. "That's what the Other is. The collective magic we all have as a community of witches." She seemed surprised to be explaining something so simple to him.

The Mother, the Goddess that provides the magical being with guidance and comfort. All witches prayed to the Mother when they are in need, when a spell has failed them, or they have lost something. The Giver bestows magic to a being. Nobody knew why the Giver gave to some and held from others, but it seemed to run in families.

"The Other is how magic stays alive," she said thoughtfully. "We all pull energy from each other, and when one witch is weakened, it weakens all of us."

He twisted his face at this, and he let out a relieved laugh. "That's not the Other, Cori."

Her eyes widened in disbelief. "Yes, it is. It's one of the first things they teach you in coven as a kid."

"Well, that's not what we learned as kids. The Other is the magic that's embedded into the fabric of the Earth and sky," he said it with conviction. "The Other is what an Elemental witch pulls their energy from. It's the magic within the water that gives me my power. It's the magic in the heat of the core of the Earth that gives Ariel her power." Cori shivered. "There are no Air Elementals in my family, but those who can, control the wind and the sky through the air that holds magic all around us. The Other has nothing to do with other witches. Think about it, Cori, you're Celestial. I don't know, I've never met a Celestial before you, but don't you get your magic from the stars?"

She shook her head at a loss for words, her mouth agape. "That's not what I was taught in the coven at all."

He didn't know there could be such a different way of thinking of the Other, but what he said rang true in his heart.

She shifted her gaze toward the window, squinting her eyes as though listening for something as she stood up to look at the sky.

"That's not all, though," she said, deep in thought. "I can feel the Other. Auras. I can feel and sense other people's deepest emotions when I open my Eye to them." Now she was the one pacing. "And I can see spirits. Just tonight at the bar, there was a man there with a friend. A woman his age came into the room and kissed him on the cheek." She instinctively moved her hand to her face. "I always assumed my ability to do this came from the Other."

Adrian swallowed hard. "You saw his wife come into the bar?" It all made sense now—the blank looks, the electrical cord on the dock. His heart pulsed with the realization that she had seen an electrical fire sparked by the frayed cord in her vision at dinner last night. That's why she wanted to accompany them this morning. That's why she had known exactly where to look for the cord.

She nodded simply, sitting heavily next to him on the bed. "Did you know her?"

"I told you before, everyone knows everyone in this town. His wife died of cancer a few months ago." He looked at her, fidgeting with the hem of her sweatshirt as she gazed out the window, still deep in thought. She was clearly at odds with herself for being so vulnerable with him.

But she had told him. Nobody else but him. *Why*? He had known her for only a few days. Hell, he barely knew her at all, but he couldn't stop the sensation rising in his chest as he let the reality of her secret sink in. Knowing felt...it felt right. Like he was *supposed* to know.

The idea that there were witches out there that wanted her dead made something inside him—something raw and primitive —crack wide open. She looked back at him, her eyes now fully aglow with her magic, and he knew she could sense his emotions twisting and turning between anguish and anger.

"You said you can read people's emotions?" he asked in a low voice, not shifting his gaze from hers. She nodded. The golden flecks in her eyes were like starlight reflecting in the brightest sky. "What did you sense from me on the boat today?" She flushed at the brashness of his question, and she tore her gaze away. He knew what she had felt from him. The weight of her magic still clung to him, lingering in his blood.

"I felt—warm." She bit her lip.

"What else?" His voice was a deep whisper, and he suddenly realized how close his hand was to her thigh. She was holding back. And he never wanted her to hold anything back from him again.

She dipped her head. "I don't know what it was. It was like the tide rising and falling."

The corner of his mouth ticked up, and he paused for a

moment. She had felt his magic, and now he knew he had sensed hers when the sky started spinning above him on the boat. "Why?" He prodded her.

She looked up to meet his gaze again, and something frantic flashed in her eyes. "I don't know." He hesitated for a moment as his hand rose to graze her cheek, brushing away what was left of the tear that had fallen there.

She leaned into his touch, and his hand drifted back to her hair, lacing his fingers into the loose waves. Although the press of her cheek against his hand was light, there was a heaviness to it that made his skin catch fire. He leaned closer, bringing his lips closer to her ear.

"And what," he whispered as the electric energy of their magic connected again, "are you sensing from me now?" His lips were now barely grazing her cheek as he became consumed by waves of her magic.

She turned toward him and pressed her lips to his, and Adrian plunged into the energy of the sky, liquid heat coursing through his veins.

His touch and his movements became more urgent as he wrapped his hand in her hair, pulling her closer. She abruptly pushed against his chest, letting go of a frantic breath as she withdrew.

Cori's eyes were wide as she stared at him, fear flashing in golden flecks of light. But she didn't look away. Her hand traced the curve of his collarbone, and he released a soft groan as his muscles strained against her touch.

Her head tipped back at the sound, and his lips instinctively moved to her throat, outlining the swell of her jaw, trailing softly along her neck. He could barely breathe. The intensity of his mouth on her hastened the heat as their magic combined, and he became completely lost in the eternity of the sky.

CORI

She froze as the cold realization of what she was doing struck her. Her mind suddenly was clear, drawing her magic in, causing her Eye to snap shut, retreating to that deep place within her gut.

His body froze, his hand gripping her waist, the other wrapped around her shoulder. He pulled himself back, too, pulling air into his lungs.

What am I doing?

Dark witches knew where she was, who she was, and they could use dark magic on anyone she cared about. She had heard stories of witches being tortured, compelled, *killed*. The thought of Adrian being put through that just to get to her—thinking of his family going through that—it was too much for her to bear.

His rough whisper broke the silence, the muscle in his jaw twitching. "I'm sorry." He sighed, holding his eyes closed. "I've never felt something like that before. It was like—" His eyes fluttered opened now, her face still dangerously close to his. "It was like my magic became combined with yours."

Heat drained from her skin and gooseflesh erupted all over her. She had felt the intensity of a kiss before, felt the aura and the essence of the person she was kissing. She had always been able to open her Eye, reading the feelings of need and passion, but she had never been able to sense someone's magic before.

This was something more.

She had dreamed about him her whole life, and from the moment she sensed his magic on the dock, her magic had come alive. It was because of him. When they had kissed, she wasn't just feeling his aura, their magic was fusing.

It was *bonding* them together.

Sudden panic built inside her. "You're not safe with me, Adrian." She stood, building space between them. "This is the whole reason I created this life. So that, until the solstice, nobody would get hurt in pursuit of me."

He cocked his head. "I'm not going to walk away from you just because there's a risk."

But he couldn't possibly realize the weight of that risk. If they were truly fated, and they allowed the bond to fully take root— bile rose in her throat. If she were to be killed in pursuit of nullifying the prophecy, then he could never love again. She remembered the sadness in her mother's eyes when she spoke of her father. How could she do that to Adrian? "Well, you really should walk away." She angled her head up defiantly. "At least until this is all behind me."

A tense silence passed between them. "I'm not leaving you alone here after what happened tonight. What if they come back?"

"I'll ward the house with protective spells."

"I'm staying."

They locked glares with each other in a standoff, stubborn pride flashing in his aura. There was no way he was taking no for an answer.

"Fine," she conceded. "But you're sleeping on the couch." She didn't for one moment consider inviting him into her bed after what had just happened. There was no way she'd be able to control herself.

"Of course." His stare pierced her, a muscle in his jaw twitching. "I just realized something," he said, turning his gaze to the window. "Do you know when the planets will join, on the solstice? Can you predict it based on—I don't know—some astrophysical or celestial chart?"

She nodded, the skin on her arms prickling as her hairs stood on end. "One hundred more days."

CORI

When Cori woke the next morning, Adrian was gone, but there was hot coffee and a plate of over-easy eggs waiting for her on the table. She pulled out her laptop as she munched on her eggs, typing "Los Angeles Reform Coven, news" into the search bar.

Nothing had been updated since the last time she checked the website. She was also disappointed to see the meeting about the prophecy was still posted on the website's calendar page.

She had not told Adrian about the LARC the previous night, but a part of her wondered if he would heed her warning and keep his distance from her if he knew the full extent of the threat. She typed into the search bar again, "The Mother, the Giver, and the Other."

Although she had memorized the words of her prophecy by heart, she had never questioned its meaning. Not until last night. Through all the years of her schooling in the coven, the Other had always been referenced as the collective magic of *witches*.

That's what made her prophecy particularly threatening, not just to those who practiced dark magic. She had never considered that there could be nuances to the meaning of the Other.

According to Adrian's version—what she could only surmise to be the version held true to all Elemental witches—the Other was separate from witches completely but within the fabric of the universe. She scanned through Elemental magic websites, and what he said seemed to be standard thinking.

She tapped her finger on the trackpad of her computer for a few moments before clicking on the search bar again. This time, she keyed in "Adrian Huxley, Farley, Maine." A few newspaper articles popped up on the top of the search engine.

Adrian had apparently been a track star in high school. She found his name on the commencement page for the business school website for the University of Maine. To her relief, nothing incriminating came up as she scrolled.

She pulled the laptop closed, eager to pack up her tackle box and head to the office to focus on the real reason she had come to this town and push Adrian out of her mind. How could she be so reckless with him?

He knew about the prophecy now, but last night had proved that distancing herself from him was going to be a special kind of agony. She could still sense the ghost of his lips on hers, and his magic clung to her like static.

Goddess, he was stubborn, too. She had asked him to leave for a reason. Her brain had been too anxious to allow her to fall asleep right away, and his presence in the living room was like torture. How was she supposed to avoid him?

There isn't a choice, she said to herself. Deep in her gut, her Eye flared in protest.

She smoothed the sheets, tidying the duvet cover over her bed before sitting heavily on its edge, easing open the bedside table. Enzo's letter was the only object within the drawer, the thin, angular lines of his script tainted with the bloody pentagram. Her skin prickled at the thought that her new home had been broken into, and after she had been there for such a brief time.

How had they found her?

She opened her Eye, recalling the look of triumph that had erupted on the witch's face as she found Enzo's note. It was almost as though the note was the thing she was seeking, not Cori herself. She knew of some spells that used an object to locate a person, but the object always had to have some imprint. What kind of magical imprint could Cori have left on a piece of paper that had been in her possession so briefly?

She spent a few moments securing the cottage with her mother's protective charms, proofing the locks and windows, and making them impervious to magic or any type of forced entry.

She knelt next to Turtle, whispering an incantation as she stroked her fur. The feline's ears perked up as though she understood what was happening to her. "Stay out of trouble, you," Cori said, scratching Turtle's fuzzy neck, making sure the protective spell didn't frighten the poor thing. At least she wouldn't be kidnapped by any neighbors now.

She slipped her charm bracelet farther up into the sleeve of her shirt before gathering her belongings, feeling much more prepared for the day now that she had been adequately caffeinated.

Even though there were barely any parking spots left at the Farley Center, she was the first one in the office. She looked out to the sea beyond her window, dotted now with fishing boats of various sizes. The moon was fully set, cloaked by the blue of the sky and the brightness of the sun. She had spent the first hour at her desk setting up her computer and responding to a few emails when she heard the door click open.

Jordan's voice was drenched in annoyance. "Let me tell you something, Anne. I am done with these people at the EPA. Did I tell you I had connections at the Department of the Interior? One of my fraternity brothers from NYU works there, and he's pretty high up." Bags clattered onto the desk. "I am sick of the hoops that I have to jump through to get this data."

"You were in a fraternity?" Anne said incredulously.

"Is that seriously the only thing you just heard me say?" A briefcase snapped open, papers shuffling.

Cori leaned into the room cautiously, a second cup of hot coffee steaming in her hand.

"What data inquiry are you doing with the EPA?"

Jordan gestured with both hands outstretched to Anne, prompting her to explain, still seething in his anger.

"The EPA did a metals study on the coastal waters in the early 2000s," Anne explained. "I need the data to compare it to what we have collected with the buoys to see if there was any positive impact from the no dumping laws."

Cori raised a curious eyebrow. "Have you submitted it as a data inquiry?"

"Yes, and the statistics department is impossible to get a hold of," Jordan griped. "Every time I email them, I get some excuse, or it gets forwarded to some other person who doesn't know what to do."

She nodded with understanding. "I've always hated working with them." She leaned on the wall, crossing her arms in thought. "There was probably a publication associated with it, though, right?"

"I think there was." Anne shuffled onto the couch, her kombucha sloshing around in the glass mason jar she drank it from.

"Well, we can always try to get the paper from the research department instead," Cori reasoned. "That way we can extrapolate the data directly from the paper."

Jordan perked up in his chair, cocking his head. A slow smile spread on his face. "Dr. Evans, you just made my morning."

She snorted, rolling her eyes as she plopped herself down next to Anne. "Please stop calling me Dr. Evans, especially in public. People are going to think I'm asking you to be so formal."

Jordan's grin turned sultry. "And what, may I ask, is making you so concerned about what other people think about you? Could it have something to do with your little trip to Carl's last night?" He crossed his arms and leaned back in his chair as she tried to fight the flush rising in her face.

"What are you talking about?" Anne asked, mouth bursting with a large piece of bagel.

Cori shook her head dismissively. "Yeah, what are you talking about, Jordan?"

"Everyone saw you leave Carl's with Adrian Huxley last night," Jordan said coyly.

Anne choked on her bagel. After nearly aspirating and coughing for a full minute, she laughed. "Hannah's son?"

"Erm..." Cori started twisting the ends of her hair around her fingers. "Yeah, our neighbors. I met them when I was unpacking over the weekend."

"Cori, how much unpacking did you even do this weekend? You have—what—five bags with you?" Anne rose her eyebrows expectantly.

"You've already worn that sweatshirt twice," Jordan said, arching a brow.

Cori glared at him.

"Adrian is the younger one, right?" Anne asked.

"I like to think of him as the dark, brooding, sarcastic one with the nice ass," Jordan corrected her, leaning forward in his chair.

Damn, everyone in this town really did know everyone else's business.

"Wow." Anne raised her eyebrows. "Most of the single women in Farley have been trying to get his attention for years, but you leave a bar with him on your first weekend here." She sat back on the sofa, crossing her arms with a wry smile.

Cori felt the heat intensifying in her cheeks again.

"I heard he has nipple rings," Jordan said smoothly from behind his coffee mug. At this, Anne roared with laughter, nearly spilling what was left of her bagel.

"He does not," Cori said quickly, biting back a laugh. She immediately regretted it, burying her head in her hands.

"So, you admit you've become well enough acquainted with his nipples to know this information?" Jordan mused like a lawyer questioning his witness, a devilish grin playing on his mouth.

Anne was shaking uncontrollably with laughter now on the sofa next to her.

Cori remembered how she had tried not to stare at Adrian when he took his shirt off to work on the boat. Yes, she would have remembered nipple rings, but she had to admit she was rather distracted by the sweat dripping down his sculpted chest. She stood abruptly, trying to hold on to whatever shred of dignity she had left. She pursed her lips and shook her head as she spun on her heel to return to the office.

She could hear Anne's dwindling laughter turn into a chastising tone, as she gathered up her equipment, grabbing the keys to the boat.

ADRIAN

The water churned under the boat as Seth and David pulled to a stop over the traps. As David steadied the rudder and prepared the cranks, Adrian tightened the ropes. When they took to the water that morning, he had succumbed to the waves of intermittent anxiety that gripped him.

The humid air stuck to his lungs as they pulled farther away from the shore.

He breathed deeply, closing his eyes. All around him, he felt the surge and the power of the water. It was always the most intense on the ocean, as they bobbed on top of an expanse of an energy so massive it made him feel like a speck of dust. *This was the Other.* The swell of the water, the hum of the Earth, the crackle of the fire, and the speed of the wind.

The light of the stars.

Seth pulled up the first trap, and Adrian knew before they surveyed it that it wouldn't amount to anything. He exchanged a look with his brother before their father stepped up next to the trap, his hands on his hips. Adrian released the hatch and counted.

One with eggs. *Throw her back.* One too small, *throw him back.*

He cursed at his calipers as each lobster measured just out of range to keep. He shook his head, adding the keepers to the pile, and it went up by only fifteen pounds.

His father kicked the side of the boat with frustration. Disappointment flooded his blood as Seth pulled the motor into gear and they made their way to the next set of traps. In times like this, Hannah would tell them to send out a prayer to the Mother. At least, that's what she had always believed. He remembered lying in bed at night as a young boy, as his mother said his bedtime prayer.

We pray to the Mother, to guide our hand. We give thanks to the Giver for what we command. We bow to the Other, the soul of the land.

The Other had never been described to him as the collective magic of all other witches—until last night. Perhaps that's what the prayer meant by the *soul of the land*.

If the prophecy meant the Other would weaken, would the magic in the water weaken as well? How could something that was infinitely older than humans and witches, something so indeterminable, be weakened?

If Cori was Celestial, then she pulled her energy from the stars. He had never considered that the entire universe itself had a magical energy, but then again, he had never met a Celestial witch before. His head was pounding as he considered the magic embedded in the universe.

Cori could see spirits. He shivered. She could feel people's emotions. Adrian had held her hand and been transported to a different time and place.

If the universe we live in expanded all around us through time, was Cori able to take that energy and bend time and life itself with her magic? His chest tightened, and a lump settled in his throat as he stared out at the vastness of the water.

The heavy clopping of boots announced Seth's presence beside him on the deck. "Those ropes aren't going to tie themselves," his brother grunted as he slapped him on the back.

He shook his head, tying the rope to the chain with determined perfectionism, immersing himself in the monotony of the task at hand as he cranked the chain.

CORI

The midday sun warmed the freckled skin of Cori's shoulders as she steered the little boat toward the dock. She had collected water samples all morning, welcoming the solitude of the waves as she bobbed up and down, alone with her thoughts.

She packed up her samples into small vials of chemical stabilizer using her micropipette, lingering for a moment as she watched ominous gray clouds gathering to the east. The air grew cooler as clouds shrouded the warmth of the sun.

Anne approached the boat, her hands in her pockets. "Let me help you with that box," she offered.

Cori nodded appreciatively, noting that Anne had pulled a pushcart out to the dock to meet her. "Thanks, you're a lifesaver," she said, smiling up at her.

"Cori," Anne said gently. "I hope you didn't take what Jordan said to heart this morning."

"Oh, not at all. I knew he was just teasing." She pushed a strand of hair behind her ear. "It was all in good fun."

Anne pursed her lips. "I just wanted to let you know that it makes me really happy to see you making friends."

Cori let her eyes dart to the floor. "What do you mean? I have plenty of friends."

"Come on, Cori, I used to see you purposefully sit by yourself in the lab. Some of the other grad students would go out for drinks. They always invited you, but you never joined them." Anne considered her with soft eyes. "The Huxleys are nice people. I've only been here for two years, but you get to know everyone in this town quickly. They're a nice family."

Guilt washed over her. A nice family that was now in danger.

"They seem nice," she managed to say.

She and Anne pulled her belongings together before Anne got back on the boat on an expedition to collect kelp samples.

Cori made her way back to the office, pulling the cart full of her gear as large droplets of water splashed onto her head. She had just made it to the garage door when she noted a large gathering huddled around the woodstove in the corner.

In the center, David Huxley was standing among them, telling an animated story as several of his buddies laughed heartily. Some of them held frosty cans of beer, resigned to the end of their day, cut short by the burgeoning storm. Seth sat nearby, baiting hooks as he listened on, chuckling to himself as his father told a story that was probably all too familiar. She allowed herself to be a voyeur, watching the way David's eyes sparkled as he gained another wave of laughter from his friends.

Cori scanned the crowd for Adrian, but he was notably missing. She sighed heavily, sucking in the sticky air. *Good*, she said to herself, vowing to avoid him at all costs for the next ninety-nine days.

Every moment that she stayed here, she was at risk, especially now that she had been discovered. Cori kicked herself for what seemed like the hundredth time for pulling Adrian into this mess. Seth nodded at her from his perch on the milk crate. She winced as she nodded back before turning on her heel and making her way toward the staircase.

She could walk away from this town right now. Anne would understand. Make up a story about another opportunity, perhaps abroad. Pack up her few items and be on a plane from Bar Harbor tomorrow. Her Eye fluttered open as she kicked the idea around in her mind.

You know that's not what you are supposed to do. You are supposed to be here, her Eye chastised her, and she let the message swirl around behind her eyes and settle down heavily in her chest.

Jordan was bent over his laptop, a pencil dancing between his index finger and thumb as he twirled it absent-mindedly in his hand. He barely looked up as he nodded his head toward the couch and sipped the hot beverage in his mug.

"Sit, friend," he said softly as he continued to type feverishly. A satisfied smile uncurled on his lips as he bit the eraser end of the pencil. "I owe you one, you know," he said, finally looking up at her.

"Oh yeah?" She squinted at him dubiously, trying to decide if she forgave him for teasing her this morning.

"I finally got that data from the archives, like you suggested." He leaned back, closing his eyes and rubbing his temples. "I've been transferring it manually into my spreadsheet all morning, but it saved me a ton of time." He tipped his mug at her in a toast.

She crossed her arms and raised her eyebrows at him.

He sighed, "I'm sorry I teased you this morning, Cori." He pursed his lips in an apologetic pout. "You made it too easy, but I'm still sorry." She tried to hide the smile that crept onto her lips as she processed his words. "I went to the bakery and bought you a slice of pound cake."

She sat up straight as he tossed a brown paper bag toward her. Cori dove into the bag as the sweet smell of baked sugar danced around her. "Apology accepted," she said quickly, popping a bite of cake into her mouth.

Jordan's smile twisted with amusement as a shadow darkened the door. He pushed his glasses up on the bridge of his nose and straightened his spine. "Adrian, what brings you upstairs on this stormy afternoon?"

Cori froze, a mouthful of cake protruding awkwardly to the side of her cheek.

Adrian stood at the doorway, leaning into the office nonchalantly. His backward hat sat lopsided on his head as a few stray hairs popped through the front. Rainwater half soaked his T-shirt, but it clung to his heavily muscled chest in a way that made her feel like jelly. He locked his gaze on to her, and she tried to regain conscious control of her mouth.

"Hey, Jordan," he said, taking off his hat to run his hand through dampened hair. "I was just looking for Cori."

She continued to stare at him, dumbfounded—silenced by cake.

Jordan cleared his throat. "Well, here she is," he said expectantly, rapping his fingers on the desk.

She raised her eyebrows, swallowing down the massive lump of buttery sugar that sank in her throat like a brick.

Adrian narrowed his eyes at Jordan and sighed before turning to her. "I was wondering if you were hungry. Do you want to grab an early dinner? We had to call it a day because of the storm."

Jordan slowly turned his head toward Cori, raising his eyebrows so high she thought his eyes might pop out of his head.

This was not part of the plan. She coughed, attempting to dislodge the heavy mound of cake that had settled under her sternum. "No, thanks. I'm all set," she said, gesturing to the bakery bag. "Jordan bought me cake."

Jordan brought his index finger to his brow and closed his eyes with consternation. "Do you intend to eat this cake for dinner?" he asked her as though he could not believe what was unfolding before him.

"Well, I could..." she stammered, but before she knew what was happening, Jordan's hand reached out and grabbed the bag from her with catlike speed.

"That would not be a healthy choice," he scolded her as if she was a toddler. He stared at her expectantly as her eyes shot angry daggers at him.

Cori sheepishly looked up at Adrian's face, which was now adorned with an infuriatingly handsome smirk. She sighed and let out a forced smile. "Sure, I could eat something, I guess."

Jordan shook his head heavily and took an angry sip from his mug.

"You know, too much caffeine can give you high blood pressure," she said, standing to retrieve her pastry bag.

He shot her a dirty look. "I will have you know this is a chai." He took another aggressive sip. "There is barely any caffeine in this beverage." He clicked his laptop shut. "I can surmise for myself what will and will not give me high blood pressure, and it's not a cup of spiced tea," he muttered under his breath as he straightened the papers on his desk. "That is for certain."

She glanced at Adrian, who was now trying with difficulty to hold in a laugh, his arms crossed across his chest.

"Let me grab my stuff." Cori turned away from them and retreated into her office. She lingered a bit longer than she should have, putting away her gear and considering the possibility of escaping out the window. By the time she came out, Adrian and Jordan were laughing heartily together.

"She looked like a hot mess when she got home this morning." Jordan was sitting on his desk now, leaning forward, eager for an audience. Adrian was shaking his head.

"What's so funny?" she asked them curiously.

"Jordan and Jess are roommates. He was just telling me all kinds of things I didn't want to hear about."

She nodded slowly in understanding as she arranged her bags on her shoulders. Another flush rose to her cheeks when Adrian reached out automatically to grab the heaviest one, slinging it on his own back with ease.

"Make sure she eats something with vitamins in it," Jordan called after them. "Maybe a salad."

"Jordan, can you let Anne know I'm going to be collecting samples on the shore tomorrow morning? I need to drive a little north of here to get what I need, so I won't be in the office until later."

"Anne leaves for New York in the morning, and I doubt she'll be back until Thursday at the earliest." He stood up and started straightening his papers. "I'm leaving with her tomorrow," he said stiffly. "The grant money was reappropriated."

Cori watched anger rolling off Jordan's aura. She didn't want to consider the possibility of funds being cut from the project. As much as she hated to see Anne's project derailed or scaled back, it might be the easy out she was looking for.

Jordan sighed. "I completely forgot to tell you. She said to let you know Geoff is coming with her, and she said something about cat food in the garage."

After taking a few notes about some visitors they were expecting to get in the next few days, she felt confident that she could keep things running while they were gone. She reassured Jordan the best she could. If anyone could strong-arm more funding from an academic donor, it was him.

———

The bell on the door jingled with finality as they made their way toward the staircase.

"You don't have to carry my bags, you know." She followed along behind Adrian, taking two steps for every one of his easy, long strides.

"I want to carry it," he said simply with a shrug of his shoulder.

"People are going to think you're trying to impress me or something."

He looked back at her with a frustratingly charming grin and a wink, as he adjusted the weight of the bag on his shoulder. "Maybe I am trying to impress you," he said smoothly.

Her stomach turned inside out, and blood rose to her cheeks. Whatever he was trying to do was working. "I told you last night, it's not a good idea to spend time with me. Especially now."

The rain had stopped, and the light glowed through the lingering humidity in the hot afternoon. The salty scent of the air was accented by wet dew that clung to the grass from the storm.

He walked on toward a scratched and dented blue truck at the edge of the lot. "And I told you last night that I don't care," he shot back at her, a protective edge to his voice. "Is it better for you to walk around town by yourself? Or starve? Because I'm quite sure you wouldn't make it long on a cake-only diet."

"Maybe the cake diet is the new hot thing. Like keto." She didn't know what to think. As much as she worried for Adrian, having him nearby put her strangely at ease, and he seemed to fall easily into the role of her protector. She climbed into the truck next to him. "Where are we going for dinner?" she asked.

She had skipped lunch on the boat that afternoon, and her few bites of pound cake were not nearly enough to hold her over after the manual labor of her morning boat expedition.

"I'm taking you to the grocery store," he said simply, turning over the engine.

"A grocery store?" she asked in disbelief. "I thought you were trying to impress me." She settled back into the seat of the truck as she buckled the hot metal clip.

"I noticed you had no food at your place this morning. I had to run down the road and steal those eggs from my mom's henhouse before I left."

She winced with embarrassment. "That was very nice of you, but I'm afraid you're wasting your time. I don't know how to cook. I would have just stopped at the bakery on the way to work. No big deal."

"Let me give you a little tip. This is not New Haven. We don't have food establishments open at all hours of the day to cater to your every whim. The bakery isn't even open every day. Joanna teaches her yoga classes three days a week. She can't be in two places at once."

"Well, shit." She crossed her arms in anger. In San Francisco, she could have any type of food delivered to her doorstep in a matter of minutes. Her mother never cooked, but Enzo knew how to make all her favorites.

Enzo. Goddess knew he would be furious with her if he knew she was allowing an Elemental witch to drive her to an undisclosed location in his tattered pickup truck. Enzo had always been the one who looked out for her, but she needed to be honest with herself. Adrian filled that void effortlessly.

"I thought you were Italian. Isn't cooking part of your genetic makeup or something?"

"That's a stereotype," she scoffed. "Although my brother, Enzo, was always an excellent cook. He just naturally knew how to do it, you know? Like what spices complement chicken, and how not to burn things." Her heart ached for Enzo's Sunday sauce. It had been so long since she had experienced the sweet smell of tomatoes permeating through their town house on a cool, lazy Sunday afternoon. "My dad was supposedly a great cook," she mused.

Enzo used to memorize their dad's recipe cards, kept in a wooden box by the stove. They were stained and creased in a million places, and Cori could still see the tight, neat, angular scrawl of his notes. Papa's handwriting was just like Enzo's. "Or so I'm told. I think that's where my brother must have gotten his talent from."

Her chest seized up with grief. Memories of her father were not even hers, but Cori knew better than anyone that it was possible to miss someone you had never even known. Even before she had left California, he rarely was mentioned in casual conversation.

Cori had learned from a young age that every time her father's memory was conjured up, her mother's countenance would twist into tormented sorrow. Cori could feel the grief roll off her as if he had just died. Some wounds never heal.

"You never met him, did you?" Adrian asked softly.

She shook her head, the taste of her grief still lingering on her tongue.

"He died in a plane crash before I was born," she responded heavily. A breeze drifted past her cheek, and she wondered for a moment if her father was watching her, guiding her. Telling Adrian about him seemed natural and right. "He was Celestial, like me. My brother is a Charms witch, just like my mom."

After years of bottling up the truth of who she was, letting him in on the secrets of her past felt like a relief, despite the inner struggle between her rational brain and her Eye.

His knuckles had tightened on the steering wheel, and the muscle in his jaw flickered. His aura had turned a bruised purple with waves of iridescent green. She recognized the emotion immediately—pity.

"How far away is this grocery store, anyway?" she asked, to lighten the mood and change the conversation.

"Ayuh, should be to Hannaford's in about thirty minutes," he replied in his thickest Mainer accent.

"Thirty minutes?!"

"Yassah, I keep forgettin' yer from away. Don't worry, Hannaford's the finest kinda store there is in the county."

She laughed as she sank deeper into her seat, her mind wandering to a mental grocery list as she gazed out the window.

———

The store was surprisingly large and well equipped, despite the remote town they had to drive to. Cori stocked up on instant ramen, snacks, and bagels. Adrian advised her not to bother buying any of the produce, not when they had anything she could need at the farm.

An hour later, they were sitting in the back of his truck bed, watching the sunset as they shared pasta salad from a plastic container.

"Is this the romantic dinner you were hoping for when I asked you out earlier?" he asked teasingly.

Romantic. She shoved a forkful of pasta into her mouth, her skin heating. "Yep," she teased back. "For the record, I did not expect you to take me to some fancy restaurant. I also didn't consider the possibility that we would be eating dinner on the back of your truck."

Cori sipped the blueberry wine they had bought and passed it to him. She had been amazed at the sheer number of blueberry-themed foods and drinks she had encountered in the store, and had no idea until today that you could even make a blueberry wine.

"It is a pretty nice view, though, you must admit."

"I'll give you that," she agreed. She tilted her head back, drinking in the light of the first stars in the sky.

"So, do you know the names of all of those stars?"

She nodded. "Most of what you see in the early night sky are planets. They're the brightest in the sky before the sun sets. That's Jupiter." She pointed up. "See how it almost looks blue? That smaller, dimmer light is Saturn. It's part of Capricorn if you trace it up and to the right."

"Did you have to study any of this stuff when you were a kid?"

She shrugged. "Yes and no. I never had to study which stars were which. I was born knowing them. And they talk to me. The moon is passing through the horn of Capricorn." She closed her eyes and sucked in a breath. "That means there will be a fulfillment of something that has been long anticipated," she said in an ethereal voice.

He scanned her face as she leaned her head back. "You just know that?"

She smirked. "Kind of like how you just know when it's going to rain, or when the tide is coming in," she quipped at him. "It's just something that comes naturally to me. When I lived in San Francisco, or even in New Haven, there was so much light pollution, I couldn't see them. I could always feel them spinning up there, but I couldn't see. Moving up here, it's been intense. Like an awakening."

Her stomach clenched, wondering how much of that awakening had to do with *him*. She retreated deep in thought, absent-mindedly twirling between her fingers the dark brown hair that had fallen from her braid as she continued to look up at the sky, questions in her eyes.

He looked up again expectantly, too, as though the sky was inclined to answer her back.

Cori

She woke naturally at dawn the next morning after another restless night. Adrian had dropped her off after the trip to the grocery store before nine, his eyes lingering on her mouth as she unclipped her seat belt. Despite her temptation to kiss him again, she had jumped out of the car and practically ran into the cottage.

She laid in bed for a while when she awoke the next morning, watching the final beams of moonglow dissipate as they were overcome by the sun's rays.

She popped a bagel in the toaster and filled her mug with hot coffee as Turtle rubbed against her legs, mewling to be let outside. As she opened the door, Turtle ran into the garden, and the spray of the sea bouncing off the rocks below inspired her to take a walk. Before she went outside, she retrieved her old notebook and marked the date.

Ninety-eight days.

She carefully climbed the rock path down to the beach, her coffee sloshing out of her mug as she balanced on the smooth rocks that lead to the soft gray sand.

After carefully perching herself on a large piece of driftwood, she watched the ocean waves dance and curl between the rocks. Each breath of salt air fueled her as she savored each sip of her morning pick-me-up. Closing her eyes, she allowed her mind to wander to what it felt like to sit on the bay at home watching the sailboats drift under the bridge.

She became so lost in the memory she didn't notice that someone had been approaching behind her until she saw a long slender shadow appear to her side.

Cori turned her head and squinted into the light, her eyes focusing on the frame of a tiny woman, her dark hair fashioned into a stylish bob with a neat fringe of bangs. Her mouth was twisted into a smile of pure delight, accentuated eerily by the dark red lipstick she wore. She sported a neat little red dress with large shiny buttons that made her look almost comical standing on the rustic beach.

Cori's heart pounded as she recognized the intruder from her vision. She stood quickly, her heart practically leaping out of her chest. There was nowhere to run. The beach was surrounded by the tide, and the only exit, the stone steps, now appeared to be guarded by a tall man wearing a black trench coat.

He wore boots, certainly the same large shoes of the accomplice that broke into her cottage. The mysterious man looked almost bored as he stood on the steps, his arms crossed loosely, as if he was waiting on the platform for a train.

The woman opened her mouth to speak but seemed at a loss for words. She put her hand up to her heart and squeezed her eyes shut before blurting out, "Cordelia?"

Cori's mouth fell open with shock. This woman certainly knew who she was. *Who she really was.* She was so taken aback by the sound of her full name, she took a step toward the water. "Who are you?" she asked as her foot slipped on a seaweed-laden rock below her.

She rehearsed in her mind what she was supposed to do if she was ever cornered by a kidnapper. There was charm to send furniture flying at her attacker, but that would do her no good out on the beach. A charm that would whistle loudly, but she doubted anyone would hear it over the roar of the ocean.

Her mind suddenly was blank, filled only with the shock of finding herself in this predicament.

The woman in front of her stopped smiling now as she narrowed the distance between them, "I'm sensing you might be a little freaked-out right now," she said quickly raising her hands in front of her. "I have a million things I need to tell you, and something about you is giving me major fight-or-flight vibes. I really didn't want to have to do it this way, so I'm sorry about this."

She took a highly embellished pouch out of her pocket and slowly dipped her hand in. When she removed her hand, it was covered in a shimmering powder. She moved her fingers to her lips and softly blew the powder into the wind, where it settled on Cori's face.

Her eyes grew full of a gloomy sensation of exhaustion. She felt the muscles in her arms and legs get heavy as she slowly slumped to the sandy rocks below.

———

When Cori woke, she was lying in the back seat of a small compact car that smelled strongly of patchouli and burnt matches. The big man in the trench coat drove as the woman in the red dress sat in the passenger's seat, her arm propped up on the window as she looked out to the road.

"Oh, I love this song!" she squealed, making the man jump.

"Pru, for God's sake, do you want me to crash this car?" He had a thick English accent and a deep timbre to his voice. "I'm struggling enough with driving on the wrong side of the road in this godforsaken country."

The woman in the passenger seat began to sing along to the radio, her voice happily off-key.

"I'm going to kill my uncle for making me come here," the man said under his breath.

"Come on, Alfie, my dad asked you to come out here because he thinks you're a tough and clever witch, and you would be the perfect person to help me. You should be honored. Plus, this is a gorgeous little town, even you must admit that." She leaned on the window again.

"It's perfectly acceptable," Alfie grumbled.

"It's much more charming than New Haven. I know you hated that place."

Alfie gagged. "New Haven is what would happen to Cambridge if a bunch of hippies moved in."

Cori nearly choked. Just how long had they been following her?

"Oh, Cordelia, you're awake!"

Cori attempted to speak, but only garbled noise came out.

"Oh, yeah. Sorry. I had to tongue-tie you." Her kidnapper scrunched up her spritelike face apologetically. "Couldn't risk you using a spell on us," she explained with a shrug.

Although she couldn't speak, her hands and legs were free. Cori looked down at the floor of the car and spotted a pen and a few crumbled pieces of paper. She had never been more jealous of a Charms witch. It would come in handy to use silent incantations at a time like this. She covered the pen with her foot, developing a plan in her mind.

"Oh, how rude of me! I didn't even introduce myself," her kidnapper said. "I'm Prudence, but you can call me Pru. This is Alfie. He's my cousin from across the pond," she said with an exaggerated English accent and a flourish. Alfie rolled his eyes in the rearview mirror. "Don't mind him, he has that dry English charm and sense of humor that all the gents go nuts over."

Cori raised her eyebrows at Prudence. For a kidnapper, she was extraordinarily polite. She had a million questions tied to her lips that she couldn't make into words, with her tongue glued to the roof of her mouth. Out the window, she recognized the road that led to the south side of town. Alfie pulled to a side road toward a small abandoned dock that looked like it had not been used in years.

With horror she realized that there was a small boat tied to the side. The car pulled to a stop, and she seized the opportunity to scoop the ballpoint pen into her pocket along with a few scraps of paper from the floor.

"Cordelia, be a dear and walk over to that little boat for us?" Prudence asked her sweetly from the front seat. "Alfie thinks we should use more sleeping powder on you, but I would prefer not to carry you at this point. I nearly threw my back out getting you into the car." She rubbed her back as she made a pitiful, pleading face toward her.

She walked obediently to the boat as she had time to fully survey her captors. She opened her Eye to Prudence first. Her aura was pink and pulsing with almost girlish excitement. Although her emotions were intense, Cori didn't sense malicious intent, despite her actions.

There was something else there that was harder to read, something that was almost sad. She sensed Prudence had walls up, most likely expecting that Cori would use her Celestial powers to gain an advantage. Alfie was easier to read—dingy annoyance.

She boarded the boat as instructed, heart hammering in her chest, wondering how they intended to kill her. Would they throw her overboard after inflicting some deadly spell? She could see the coroner's report now—*likely death of natural causes, fell into the water after losing consciousness.*

Death by magic never left a trace or a sign of a struggle on the victim. She wondered how many mysterious deaths that were reported as natural causes were because of dark magic.

Her skin prickled, her breath quickening as hot tears stung her cheeks. Prudence turned from the stern of the ship and wilted a bit when she saw the tears streaming down her face.

"Cordelia, why are you crying?" she asked with apparent genuine concern.

"She can't answer you, remember?" Alfie responded to her. "But if I had to guess, she's probably crying because she was put to sleep with magic and captured by two strangers who are about to take her to a bloody deserted island."

Cori sucked in a deep breath through her nose, squinting into the light as Alfie shoved a few more objects into his duffel. Cetus

Island was just beyond the shoreline, only a short, ten-minute boat ride away.

She tried to remember everything Adrian had told her about the island—something about steep rocks and only being able to dock in a certain spot. The sun was high in the sky, and the air had heated. How long had she been asleep?

"Alfie, please, we've gone through this."

"I know. We have gone through this. Ad nauseam, in fact. But it still doesn't change the fact that there had to be a better way to do this."

"I told you a hundred times," Prudence snapped at him. "We knew she would never come with us willingly. She was raised by Charms witches, for Goddess's sake!" Prudence paused, looking back at her with sorrow in her eyes. "She was never going to trust us."

Alfie rolled his eyes. "Sure, Pru. Because kidnapping someone is always the best way to gain their trust." He shook his head and muttered something under his breath.

Prudence stomped to the stern of the little boat and turned over the engine.

They sailed onward toward the south side of the island and circled until they found a reasonable place to dock. Alfie tied the boat, rather sloppily Cori noted, to an ancient-looking chain that was welded to a shabby mooring. The island was overgrown and wild sea grasses had claimed the beach. There was more rock than sand.

"Welcome to our little slice of paradise," Prudence said. She made her way up the hill to a clearing in the brush.

Cori was getting the feeling that Prudence and Alfie knew exactly where they were going. "Now that you're all safe and sound, I'll be happy to release your tongue." Prudence smiled at her as she twisted her hand, spinning an amulet that swung from a long chain around her neck in her fingertips. Cori felt her mouth relax, and she reflexively stretched her out jaw.

"Pru, I left my pack in the boat! I'll be right up," Alfie called back to her.

Cori seized her chance, liberating the pen and piece of paper from her pocket. She scribbled a word behind her back the best she could and folded the little scrap of paper the way her mother had taught her. She closed her eyes and concentrated on Adrian, whispering the spell as the little piece of paper melted into her hand.

ADRIAN

He heard Seth's voice before he even opened his eyes. "It's our early day, youngblood. Rise and shine."

He sighed into his pillow, realizing that it was well before dawn. Seth was always energetic and happy, no matter the time of day, and this was extremely irritating. Adrian groaned and rubbed his eyes as he rose from the comfort of his pillow.

He had been deeply asleep, dreaming of something warm and soft. He groaned at the hardness that was coupled with an uncomfortable fullness below his waist as the cool air beyond his bedsheets hit him with an unpleasant chill.

His shoulders and arms were sore, having volunteered to man the chain all day yesterday. Seth had offered to take over, and David had warned him he would pay for it, but he had needed to do it. To think less and work more. To pour the frustrations and uncertainties of the past several days into the manual labor of the task at hand. He had pulled in at least a hundred traps single-handedly yesterday.

Sure, he had willed the water to help him. No human could have done it, but it took a physical and mental toll. It was cathartic to work that hard, to pull the energy away from his racing thoughts, and siphon it into the water.

Today he would pay, but it was worth it.

"Shower," he grumbled, walking out to the kitchen where Seth was scrolling through his phone as he drank his cold-pressed juice.

Not only was Seth an insufferable morning person, but he also didn't even require coffee to achieve his unnatural level of morning vigor. Adrian wondered if there was any espresso in the pantry.

He lingered in the shower just long enough to make Seth impatient with him. Once a week they would aim to be finished before noon. David called it their "early day," and the purpose of the endeavor was to get home early enough to help Hannah on the farm. It was always easier to get a few hours of work under their belts before the sun set in the summer, but the days were slowly getting shorter now, yielding to the fast approach of the cold autumn.

If they could empty enough traps before noon, David would consider it a success. There were few things that bothered David more than a late start on the early day, and as much as it brought him joy to watch Seth pace, Adrian didn't feel like dealing with his father's temper.

As they made their way downstairs, the headlights of the truck were waiting for them, casting an eerie cone of light through the morning fog.

"Took you long enough," David muttered from the front seat. He was scrolling through emails on his tablet as Fleetwood Mac played softly on the radio.

Adrian climbed carefully into the back seat, trying not to wince at the stiffness in his shoulders as he straightened his seat belt. He saw his father's eyes on him in the rearview mirror.

"Morning, Pop," he said, feigning energy.

"We're late because Adrian was jerking off in the shower," Seth griped.

Adrian swiftly smacked the baseball cap off his brother's head.

David's eyes narrowed. "Are you going to need to ice your wounds after you refused anyone's help to haul those traps yesterday?" David's words were stern, but there was an edge of pride within them.

Seth scoffed from the front seat, and it took all his restraint not to reach forward and knock off his brother's baseball cap a second time in retaliation for his mockery.

At their core, despite their teasing, they understood. The week Seth had dropped out of college, he refused help with the traps. Eventually he separated his shoulder. Poor Hannah had to deal with him sulking around the farm for two whole days before she pleaded with David to let him come back to the rig.

"I'm good," he said, eliciting a dubious sound from the front seat. Even though David and Seth could tell something was on Adrian's mind, they would never pry.

"Humph." David raised his eyebrows in the rearview, clearing his throat. "Looks like you boys are on your own this morning. I'll drop you off at the dock, but I need to head down to Rockland first thing. We might get a new contract with a restaurant chain down there. Up-and-coming, farm-to-table place. If I play my cards right, we might get a double deal."

Anytime a restaurant or market picked up a contract with their fishing company and the farm simultaneously, David called it a "double deal." The last time David had negotiated a "double deal" it was paired to an investment in a new fishing company. A 50 percent stake in a new rig in Portland. It had taken them months to recoup from the losses when the inexperienced crew eventually went bankrupt. Unease settled down in Adrian's stomach, but Seth clapped David on the shoulder.

"Good news, Pop. We can try to get done by noon and help Mom. Rain last night probably drove the fish down, but we might get a few good bugs out there with this weather."

Adrian nodded. "We got it."

As David pulled the truck away from the dock, Adrian's eyes immediately scanned the parking lot. There was only one other car, Auggie's truck, and one delivery van. No silver hatchback in sight. He didn't expect her to be out here this early, but his eyes scanned for her car nonetheless.

They made it to the first buoy one hour before sunrise, the legal time you can start pulling up the lobster lines. Adrian again insisted on doing the pulling and hauling as Seth sorted through the catch, measured them, and baited the empty traps to go back on the line.

They made their way to the rest of the buoys, and found themselves with a decent haul, all before noon. Seth was measuring the last trap, methodically throwing back the lobster that were too big or two small to harvest. Adrian finished rebaiting the last trap and squinted through the sun to the south.

"Does it feel like rain to you?" he called out to his brother.

"Not at all, why?" Seth put down his calipers and walked down the stern of the ship where Adrian was slumped down, gazing over the horizon. "You alright?" No teasing or mockery colored his tone now.

"I don't think so." He shook his head as his eyes grazed over the water. "You know that feeling of heaviness you get when it's about to rain?" Seth nodded knowingly. "I feel that way now, but it doesn't feel connected to the water."

Seth said nothing, but he walked toward the cooler. He turned off the engine and handed his brother a sandwich and a beer. "You've seemed a little off these past couple of days. Don't look too much into it."

Adrian pulled a deep sigh. "I am off my game. I don't feel like myself." He shook his head. "I'm probably just overthinking it."

Seth chuckled softly as he unwrapped his sandwich.

The delivery truck was waiting for them at the dock when they pulled up. After the weigh-in, they felt good about what they had accomplished in a short period. They were securing the boat to the dock, wrapping elaborate knots to the hooks when Adrian felt it.

A piece of crumpled paper materialized in his hand, scraping up against the rough calluses of his fingers.

Shocked, he unfurled the piece of crumpled, stained paper and saw a shaky scrawl of a blue ballpoint pen. One word.

Cetus.

He stood straight up and clenched his jaw, unexplained fury rising in his chest. Without stopping or questioning, without one breath of hesitation, he untied the knots and felt a surge of water roar to life under them.

"What are you doing?" Seth yelled over the roar of the engine. He didn't answer. Once they were out of range of the curious onlookers on the dock, Adrian killed the motor and willed the boat forward with his magic.

The crest behind the boat was high and wide as they barreled toward the island, turning sharply toward the south past the rocks of the inlet. He could sail there with his eyes closed, but even at this speed, it would take them at least fifteen minutes to get there.

A nervous tension rippled over his skin. *She was in trouble.* He had no idea how he knew this based on one word on a crumpled-up piece of scrap paper, but a fire in his blood urged him forward.

Seth staggered to him, unsteady with the rush of wind and water that surrounded the boat and propelled it to an unnatural speed. He approached carefully; concern etched on his brow.

"Adrian, listen to me!" he called over the wind. "Slow down; you're going to wreck the boat."

Adrian unclenched his fist and slowed the rush of the water under them, but he didn't change his course.

He didn't know how to explain this to Seth. He opened his mouth, but no sound came, as though the connection between his brain and his tongue had been severed. "Cori's in trouble," he said shakily. "She sent me this." He handed his brother the ominous paper message.

Seth blinked down at the scrap of paper, dumbfounded. "Is she trying to tell you she's at Cetus Island?" he asked with confusion. "She sent this to you? How?" He turned the stained paper over in his hands. "Why would she be out there? This is one word on a piece of paper. How do you know she's even in trouble?"

"I just know," Adrian snapped back at him. He had kept nothing from his brother, and if what he expected was correct, now was not the moment to keep secrets. "She sent me the paper with magic." Seth blinked down at the paper. "There's more. Cori isn't a Charms witch."

Seth's eyes widened. "What are we talking about? Why would she send you this? What makes you so sure this is even from her, or some kind of cry for help?"

"I just know!" He shot back at him, fire burning his icy blue eyes. Seth stepped back, crossing his arms patiently in anticipation.

"Cori is a Celestial witch," Adrian said hastily. "She made some kind of crazy prophecy years ago, and she has been living life undercover as a Charms witch because there are a bunch of bad-guy witches out there who want to murder her so the prophecy doesn't come true." Bitter dread rose in his throat as he realized she might already be dead. "Someone broke into her house Saturday night and left a pentagram. We found it when I walked her home after the bar."

Seth was at a loss for words as he processed this unexpected information. He paced up and down the deck several times. Adrian had never seen him speechless before. "So—so you think someone is trying to kill her right now?"

"Yes," he said through clenched teeth, trying to restrain the speed of the water. "I don't know what's going on, Seth." He was breathing hard. "I just have this sense about her. When she sent me the message, I felt like something was wrong. I could feel her fear. I just knew."

He closed his eyes, remembering the way he felt the essence of her magic course through his blood the moment he touched her on the boat and the intensity of their kiss.

Seth raised his eyebrows at him. "Wow." He shook his head, trying to wrap his mind around his brother's response to a little piece of paper with one word scrawled on it. "I mean do you think... Do you think you guys are—?"

"I don't know." Adrian ran his hand through his hair and closed his eyes tight. He had never expected he would meet another witch in this small town and always anticipated that he would find a nice human and settle down. Until this week, it had never been in the cards to have the same connection with another witch that his parents had with each other.

It had never bothered him before.

Even in the magical community, fated witches were the exception, not the rule. He had never considered what it would be like if it happened to him. But from the first moment he sensed her magic, even before he knew who she was, he wasn't the same.

There was a restlessness that kept him awake at night. From the first moment he saw her on the beach, staring out at the water, something in him had shifted. When he looked at that note, he had seen her handwriting and knew it was from her, even though he had never seen her handwriting before.

Despite the lack of words on the page, he knew there was panic in the letters.

Adrian looked up at his brother, desperation etched into his face. Seth's own expression changed. "Let's get there as fast as we can," he said. Adrian let out a relieved sigh as he sped up slightly, only this time he wasn't propelling the boat alone.

CORI

Her mouth was dry, like sand mixed with glue, and her words came out garbled. "Who are you?"

Cori racked her brain for defensive spells now that she could speak again, but none of them applied to being on a deserted island. Prudence glanced back at her; her mouth twisted in a delighted smile as if she held back a delicious secret.

"Cordelia, I have so much to tell you," her kidnapper said. They walked at a brisk pace along the shore before coming to a small sandy cove where a quaint little fishing shelter was perched atop a rocky plateau.

It looked like it had been there for a century. The foundation of worn rock was juxtaposed with neat rows of siding. A thin tendril of smoke rose from the tidy stack of stones that made up the chimney.

Outside, there were camp chairs and various supplies propped up on simple wooden benches. Towels and T-shirts hung from a clothesline, and a little propane stove smoldered nearby. Prudence and Alfie were clearly not alone.

"How many of you are there?" she asked, her voice cracking like gravel under the strain of her fear and her partially numb tongue.

"Here on the island, or in general?" Prudence asked airily. She spun a ring around her finger as she peered out past the cove toward the beach.

"Maybe you should start explaining to me who you are and why you brought me here," Cori snapped at her. "Unless you just want to get down to business and kill me now."

Prudence's eyes widened and her face went pale. "Cordelia, we aren't here to kill you. We're here to save you."

Cori was thunderstruck. "What do you mean you're here to save me?" Her heart drummed harder in her chest. Perhaps a witch like her would have a twisted perception on what it meant to save a Celestial witch who had made an Earth-altering prophecy.

Didn't the prosecutors of the witch trials that led to the Covenant believe they were "saving" witches from the devil as they burned them on a stake?

Prudence walked to a set of camp chairs and motioned for Cori to sit. Her kidnapper stared back at her as though she were some sort of oddity in a glass jar. She offered her a little canteen of water, and she reluctantly drank from it. The lingering effect of the powder seemed to dry out her entire body. She drank deeply.

"The tongue-tie powder can make you super thirsty," Prudence mused. "One of the other kids in our coven used it on me once right before school. My mom had to pick me up that day because the school nurse thought I was having a psychotic break." She twisted her mouth into a reminiscent, playful smile.

Cori looked at her expectantly. She scanned her aura again, and there was no sign of anger, ill will, or malicious intent.

"We've been camping here ever since you drove up from New Haven. A few people came out ahead of time and scouted the place out, setting up camp. We had to stay close, yet considerably far away. When you were in New Haven it was so much easier to guard you."

Cori's head twitched with astonishment. *Guard me?*

Prudence continued, leaning forward in her chair, and playing with the red buttons on her dress. "But it's so much harder to melt into the shadows in a place like this. I mean, all along the northeast, you can't even go into a grocery store without getting the tingle, ya know? There are always a few witches around. But up here? Completely different ball game."

Cori couldn't help but smile despite her confusion and fear. There was something about this woman that was insufferably likable. Her Eye winked at her, filling her with a sense of trust, cooling her nerves.

"Exactly how long have you been following me?" Cori lowered her eyes and crossed her arms as she continued to scan Prudence for any signs of trickery.

"Oh me?" she asked, placing her hand on her heart. "Just since you left for college." Cori's mouth dropped open. "You're only six months younger than me, but I begged to be on your guard as soon as I came of age. Being the coven leader's daughter has its perks sometimes. Dad let me leave San Francisco as soon as I finished high school." Prudence spoke excitedly, as if gossiping with an old friend. She sipped from her canteen and shoved a handful of trail mix in her mouth causally.

Cori's mouth remained fixed open, and her heart clenched. Prudence had been following her? *On a guard?* "Excuse me," she blurted out. "You're from San Francisco?"

"Of course," Prudence said nodding, crunching on some almonds. "From the Bay Area Gray Coven."

Her skin prickled, and her blood ran cold as the air suddenly thickened. The sun, minutes ago intensely orange and high in the sky, was suddenly shrouded with gray clouds. Thunder rumbled in the distance.

Prudence shrugged, looking up. "Well shit, I don't remember seeing rain in the forecast."

Cori stood up. "You're a Gray witch?"

"Yeah, of course."

"Well, excuse me if I'm a little confused." Cori's voice rose. "Just a moment ago you were telling me all about how you've been trying to protect me."

"Exactly." Prudence raised an eyebrow. She heard the crunching of boots on the sand behind her. Cori reeled around and saw Alfie approaching her from the direction of the shack. Prudence leaped up from her chair.

"Let me guess, Pru. You haven't gotten past introductions yet, have you?" Alfie drawled.

"No," she said with confusion in her voice. "But she's freaking out."

Alfie let out a tired sigh. "Pru, she was raised by Charms witches to think that Gray witches practice dark magic."

"I know that," Prudence snapped.

"Well, did you start with the bit that you're a Gray, or did you start with the bit that Grays don't practice dark magic?"

Prudence looked crestfallen. Cori opened her Eye to disappointment and resignation permeating her aura. "Maybe a part of me hoped I wouldn't have to explain it." She sank back down in her camp chair, eyes to the ground.

Alfie cautiously put out his hands toward Cori. "Please hear me out, OK?"

She took a steadying breath and nodded. Prudence looked up at her, dejected yet hopeful. A large raindrop grazed her shoulder before gliding down her arm as the sky continued to darken.

Alfie continued, "When our coven in London heard about your prophecy, we had a party that lasted a whole week." Cori opened her Eye to him. He emulated earnest sincerity. "Ever since the Covenant, Gray witches have carried a burden. When the Covenant banned dark magic, we didn't continue to practice it. At least most of us didn't. We were charged with protecting it. When you predicted that those who have abused dark magic would be punished, it was as if the weight of the world was lifted off our shoulders."

"I don't understand," she said, prodding them to continue.

Prudence rested her chin in her hands. "Imagine being a little girl, learning how to use magic. Gray witches have dark and light magic in their blood. In coven, I learned to push back the dark and recognize it. By the time I was ten, I knew how to pull dark magic from a spell or a potion. How to hold it in my heart and send it back to the Giver." Large, cold raindrops were beating down on them. "But we also learn, very early on, that there are witches who use dark magic willingly. Because everyone knows how powerful a spell can be when there is both a light and dark element within it." The rain was coming down faster as Prudence looked with pleading eyes to her cousin.

"Gray witches are the protectors of the Covenant, Cordelia," he explained. "When we learn of a witch practicing with the dark element, it is our job to seek that witch out and reclaim the dark magic. We must return it to the Giver. Any dark magic that becomes a part of the Other weakens all of us." Alfie sighed as he tipped his head back to regard the incoming storm. "That's why you've offered us a respite. If your prophecy comes to be, we will be free of this burden, once and for all."

Prudence looked up at the sky, crossing her arms around her as a heavy crack of thunder echoed over them. "Cordelia, without you, the Gray witches will be tied to an eternity of policing dark magic. Of course, we want to keep you safe," she explained.

The rain fell in heavy torrents now as Cori turned toward her captors.

"Please, Prudence, call me Cori."

"Only if you call me Pru." Her painted red lips turned up in a smile.

ADRIAN

The boat barreled toward the island with eerie silence as Adrian guided the stern over the waves. As he squinted through the mist that was gathering in the air, he could see a thin plume of smoke curling up from the cove.

He had camped in the fishing cabin at the cove so many times, he could probably navigate the rig to the small dock with his eyes closed.

His brother looked back at him expectantly, noticing it, too. They watched the smoke waft into the clouds, mixing with a heavy electric energy. He and Seth locked gazes again as they simultaneously sensed the expanse of magic in the air.

They had her. Adrian felt his fear materialize above him, as thunder rumbled in the distance and the air heated with the density of his emotions.

Seth shot him a look of warning. "Try to reel that back if you can. It's going to make it a lot harder to rescue her if you unleash a hurricane over us."

He was right. Adrian reined in his emotions the best he could but droplets of water splashed against the skin of his neck as they were beckoned from the sky.

The boat slowed, gliding with unnatural ease on the choppy water. Fire burned under his skin as they guided the boat like a ghost up to the dock. The rig eased to a stop and Seth dropped the rear anchor.

"Well, brother," he asked as he turned the crank, "It's your rescue mission. Shall we go by land or by sea?"

The tension within him cracked for a moment, and he felt a smile tug at his lips. The answer was obvious. They would make it to the cove much faster if they swam. They left their shirts on the dock and dove into the choppy water. No splash, no sound, not a ripple in the water to suggest their presence.

The Huxley brothers couldn't breathe underwater, but they could create a bubble of air around their heads that allowed them to swim under the surface for a prolonged period. Adrian and Seth swam with ease through the waves as the storm intensified over them. The sand sloped toward him as they approached the shore.

Dread washed over his senses. *What if we're too late?*

Even though he had only just met her, he felt as though he had been connected to her for his entire life. Every moment that came before her was tied to her arrival. Every breath and every action he took was in anticipation of the moment that he saw her on that beach, about to be swallowed by the tide. The notion that he might need to realize a future without her—the woman he was fated to—terrified him.

The shore sloped toward them, and they swam upward peering over the surface. He spotted her immediately, standing close to the shore, her long wavy hair swirling loose and wild around her shoulders in the wind.

He let out a breath. She was alive, but she wasn't alone. Two strangers were standing close by, speaking to her with animated and exaggerated gestures. An enormous blond man put up his hands as a tiny woman, who was dressed like she was on her way to an art exhibition, stood nearby with her arms crossed.

Cori's posture appeared tense as she backed away. The large blond man approached her, his hands outstretched as though to stop her.

Adrian and Seth crept out of the water, inching up the large worn rocks toward the cabin. As they got closer, he could not hold back.

The sky opened in torrents as he and Seth now raced toward them, unfazed by the deluge of watery aggression that Adrian unleashed from the sky. Deep puddles formed in between the rocks, called there by his will.

He furrowed his brow, lightning crashing above him, as he willed the water out of the shallow pools around the cove. Water heeded to him, becoming a large orb, revolving in the air like a liquid tornado. The sphere of water levitated off the ground and collided rapidly with the large man in front of him, encapsulating him within it.

The water swirled all around the man as rage, fear, and desperation materialized into a violent whirlpool. Spinning and twisting with the water, the expression on the man's face was gripped by dumbfounded shock.

Adrian held the water there for several moments, completely enraptured by the drive of his magic. So driven by instinct, he couldn't hear or see anything except the prison of water that he controlled.

Darkness crept around him as the man in the water went limp. His concentration was broken as someone tried to pull him down to the ground. He fought them off until he realized with a shock that it was his brother.

Someone was desperately yelling his name. "Adrian! Adrian, let him go!" Her voice was muffled as though he were listening underwater, but the sound of it snapped him back to reality. As he broke concentration on the water, it came crashing down to the sand and rock with an enormous splash.

The man who had been trapped inside the watery prison came crashing down with it, coughing and sputtering as he struggled to his hands and knees on the rocky sand. Adrian turned and saw her, eyes wide with fear, her hand clasped to her chest.

She was frozen for a moment before she ran to him, throwing her arms around his neck. As she buried her head under his chin, the clenching in his chest eased. He put his arms around her, letting his chin rest on the top of her head.

She was alive.

The dark heaviness of the storm dissipated around them as the raindrops became smaller and a breeze broke through the humidity like a sigh of relief.

CORI

They sat beside a small campfire as Prudence and Alfie huddled over the dry heat, attempting to warm up from the sudden assault of the storm. Adrian had dried Cori off with magic but did not afford the same courtesy to her kidnappers.

They sat on a makeshift bench of worn, splintered driftwood planks. The rest of the Gray witches that had been camped in the shack had emerged now, and they stood in a huddle behind Prudence and Alfie, exchanging looks of curiosity, as though they were watching the events of a daytime talk show unfold in real time.

Adrian and Seth flanked her like bookends on the bench, glaring at the other witches around the fire as they explained their intentions. The heat of anger and suspicion pulsed from their auras, but it was countered by the cold desperation and pleading coming from Prudence.

"So, let me get this straight," Seth said after patiently listening to their story. "You claim that you've been protecting her all these years. You also claim that you want to continue to protect her, because apparently, she's famous and made a prophecy that will change the world."

Cori sighed, letting her head fall in her hands. At this rate, there wouldn't be a witch in all New England who didn't know the truth. Her location would be common knowledge within a few days.

Seth continued, "And you revealed this to her by kidnapping her and bringing her to a remote, deserted island?"

"Well, we didn't expect that two maniacs would set siege to the island and try to drown us to death," Alfie drawled.

Out of the corner of her eye, Cori saw Adrian's knuckles grow white.

"We knew Cori wouldn't trust us. She was raised to fear Gray witches, and she had also been conditioned to be secretive. We wanted to be able to properly explain who we were and why we should be trusted." Alfie rolled his eyes. "We had just been getting somewhere when you two stormed in."

Seth snorted at the pun.

Adrian stood now, his suspicion and anger intensifying. "That's a great story, but I still don't get how you think *anyone* would trust you after what you did. You kidnapped her, for fuck's sake! That's not how you treat someone you're trying to protect."

Alfie scoffed, crossing his arms. "You talk a big game, but we don't know much about *you* at all. How are we supposed to know *you* can be trusted?"

Adrian's shoulders tightened, and the muscle in his jaw twitched. "Excuse me?"

"We've been trailing you and your family since Cordelia arrived at this goddess-forsaken place," Alfie continued. Now Seth was standing, too. "You all seemed to take an instant liking to her. Why?"

Cori's blood ran cold. How could she not sense them when they were following her so closely? All this time?

"It's very unlike Cordelia to allow herself to get so close to people this quickly. It took her almost a year to accept an invitation to Anne's house." Another truth. "By then we had enough intelligence on Anne to know that she was a harmless human with no magical connections. But you..." he trailed off, as Adrian lunged for him. Seth caught him by the shoulder before he could raise his fist.

"Cori can clearly tell that we don't intend to harm her," Adrian said through gritted teeth.

Alfie smirked back at him, unafraid even though Adrian had almost drowned him moments ago. "And exactly what is your intention, then?"

Adrian flushed. "I think that's obvious. Cori called me to help her after she was *kidnapped*, and I came. Actions speak louder than words, asshole."

With that, Prudence spoke up, trembling in the shadow of the large man in front of her who had nearly just killed someone with powerful Elemental magic. "Cori should be the one to decide who she should and shouldn't trust," she said, making herself as tall as her petite frame would allow. "After all, she's Celestial. You literally cannot lie or fake your way through anything with her. She can read our emotions and see into our past and future with her Eye. Right?"

Cori nodded, her throat still dry and her head heavy with the weight of the emotions that continued to bombard her from the group of magically charged witches before her.

"Can you really do all that?" Seth asked in awe.

She nodded.

"It's true." Adrian nodded. "I've seen her do it." He locked gazes with her, and her skin prickled. "What do you sense from these people, Cori?"

She stood up and put her hand out to Prudence, who was still trembling a bit. Adrian stepped toward her, his icy blue eyes flashing with worry. Cori nodded to him, and he retreated, threading his hand through his hair.

"May I?" Cori asked, taking a few careful steps toward the frightened witch before her, as though approaching a wounded bird.

Prudence nodded, extending her hand.

Cori's hand connected with Prudence, and her Eye rose from her heart, jumping to attention within her own mind. She allowed herself to plunge into Prudence's magic, and Prudence opened her mind immediately.

There were no walls, no sour taste of resignation, just a minty, cool breeze of eagerness.

A young girl sat on a bench with a smartly dressed man who looked remarkably like her. They had the same upturned lips and smooth black hair. The young girl sported a neat plaid skirt and crisp white button-up blouse, her ebony hair plaited into two neat braids as she swung her Mary Jane-bedecked feet on the bench. Electric energy buzzed as a group of familiar witches strode by them.

Astrid gossiped with a few other women from coven as they set out their yoga mats facing north. The women aligned crystals at the ends of their mats, pulling energy from the sun.

The man leaned down to the girl. "That's the coven, right there." She nodded in response, discreetly. "They come here every Wednesday, and sometimes Cordelia comes with them. Today she must've stayed at home. That's her mother, the pretty one with very blond hair. Astrid Mangianelli. Powerful witch. High priestess. Intelligence on her is that she's very protective. She doesn't trust a few of the elder members at all."

"Why would she not trust them, Daddy?" Prudence whispered.

"Pudding, remember when I told you there are Charm witches out there that see the value of dark magic?" Prudence nodded, her eyes fixed on the group of witches before them. "Every coven has a few bad seeds. I am sure there are more than a few in a coven this size. You know what will happen to these witches after the prophecy comes to be."

Prudence nodded. "They will weaken."

"Some of them could lose their magic altogether," he said seriously, his eyes ominous. "Depending on how dark they've become."

Astrid shot a sideways glance toward the witches at the far end of the group.

Prudence took a deep, steady breath. "Well, they deserve it," she said, pressing her lips into a line.

Her father raised an eyebrow at her. "Honey, I agree with you. But that's why we need to know as much about these people as possi-

ble. Cordelia is our future, and this prophecy will give us peace. If something happens to her, we'll be damned forever. Dark magic has gotten out of control."

Pru's cheeks flushed. "I can't believe anyone would want to kill her. She's just a kid."

Her father let out a ragged breath. "Just a kid who made a prophecy that rocked the world."

Cori's Eye snapped closed, breaking the connection between them. She nearly collapsed on the bench as her vision swam in a flood of blurry colors. A hand rested on her shoulder, and without looking up she knew it was Adrian. His touch reinvigorated her, and she blinked hard, her body adjusting to the jump from the past.

As she regained her strength, Prudence came into focus before her, eyes wide. Cori's mouth felt dry again as she tried to formulate her words.

"I trust them," she whispered.

ADRIAN

The sun was setting by the time Cori boarded the boat with Adrian and Seth. It had taken a significant amount of arguing to allow Cori to leave the island.

Prudence had suggested that Cori go into hiding and permanently move to their headquarters in the cove. They had taken up residence in the little fishing cabin, and Adrian had been surprised to find that the inside of the dwelling was much more charming and cozy than he remembered.

Apparently, the Gray witches had no shortage of spells to fix up the dilapidated old shack.

There were eight of them altogether. A witch named Zion explained to them that Gray witches were known for buying the most haunted-looking house in a neighborhood, banishing all the dark magic and lingering spirits, and using Gray magic to restore the house to its former glory. A heavily tattooed witch named Fern with a nose ring stared at them from the periphery as they spoke.

In the end, it was Cori who convinced the Grays to move to the mainland now that she was aware of their presence. There was no point in trying to remain hidden now that she knew the full truth. She concocted a plan for their cover story.

They were friends from Yale, eager to visit her new home and meet her new friends. Lionel, a witch from the Boston Gray Coven, suggested camping out in his dad's RV. All of them could boondock near the beach together comfortably. At least until the weather turned.

Seth had suggested camping out on the clearing just north of the farm. He had assured them his parents wouldn't mind.

What his parents would mind was their disappearing act today. Adrian rested his elbows on the rail at the stern of the ship, watching the thin shoreline expand into view as they sped toward it. He felt her arm brush against his own as she settled onto the rail next to him.

"Are you OK?" he asked through the wind. She nodded softly in return, looking up at him.

"Thank you for coming to my rescue," she said.

Adrian shrugged. "I'm sorry you had to see me almost kill someone because of it." He was embarrassed, but he knew that he would do it again. Cori pulled her arms around herself as the chill of the ocean grazed the gooseflesh on her arms. He pulled one of his sweatshirts out of his backpack and draped it over her shoulders.

She looked up at him, her lips twisting into a fleeting smile before her eyes glowed. He knew instantly that she was reading him, and he allowed his emotions to intensify. He fed her the sense of relief that had overcome him the moment he felt her embrace on the beach.

As his gaze traced over the curve of her cheek, down to the angle of her jaw, he imagined what it would be like to kiss her neck. He allowed himself to crave what his lips would feel like brushing against her skin, and her eyes widened.

His lip curled up mischievously, a flush rising in her cheeks despite the cool mist in the air. "What's wrong?" he asked.

"Nothing," she responded, allowing the glow to dim in her eyes as she turned her gaze back to the growing shoreline. He could hear Seth on the phone now that they were in cell service range offshore.

"Ma, I'm sorry we didn't make it to the farm this afternoon. I know it was our day to help—No, that storm wasn't in the forecast. Listen, Ma something big happened, and everyone is OK, but we have a lot to explain to you—Is Pop back?—OK, well listen, I should be home in less than thirty minutes. I'll give you the full update, but when Dad gets home, we can come up with a game plan."

Cori's shoulders tightened under the thick cotton of the sweatshirt. Of course, they needed to tell his parents, probably even Ariel. Cori knew the involvement of the Huxley family was a big part of the plan, allowing the Grays to keep a closer watch on her.

"You know what, Cor, the best part of this day is that you don't have to be alone anymore," Adrian assured her. Even though he was skeptical of this mysterious group of witches that appeared out of nowhere, he was relieved that she wouldn't need to do this alone.

Her eyes met his, wild with fear and worry. "But that was never the plan."

"Well, to be honest with you, the original plan was kind of shitty."

Her brow furrowed. "What do you mean?"

"I could never imagine someone I love being sent out into the world to face this burden alone. I know your mom had no choice, but don't you think she would be happy and relieved that you have people here on your side? Especially since there's—what—less than three months until the solstice?"

Her shoulders relaxed slightly. "December 21st." Cori tilted her head to the sky as the first few stars peeked out from behind the dissipating clouds. She looked up at them with a pleading expression on her furrowed brow. "That's Venus, low on the horizon."

"What do you hear?"

She shook her head heavily. "Nothing."

Cori

The waves crashing on the rocky beach below the path drowned out the chaos of her mind. Wind whipped through her hair as she breathed the salty breeze deeply into her lungs. The sky was dark now, and the moon reflected off the wisps of stratus clouds that broke up the dark canvas above them.

The sky was peppered with constellations, turning slowly over the horizon. The gravitational pull of the moon on the Earth's axis tugged at the blood in her veins. Adrian's hand grazed her forearm, and she stopped at the walkway, a few steps from her doorstep.

"Are you really alright?" His soft voice carried over the sound of the crashing waves and the chirp of crickets.

She nodded. "I'm OK. A bit shocked. Completely conflicted over the fact that my identity is out..." she trailed off, collecting her thoughts. The whole day had felt like a nightmare. Her head throbbed. After years of being comfortable in the shadows, her secret had been exposed—a secret that had never been a secret at all, apparently. She let his hand drift down her forearm and his fingers curled around her own. "Are you OK?" she asked him back.

He sighed, pausing for a moment. "No." He ran his free hand

through his hair, searching for words. "I almost killed someone today, and do you know what?"

"What?" She arched a brow as she opened her senses to him. Fear and desperation rolled off his aura, inky black and shimmering in the night's darkness.

"I would do it again. I would do it a hundred times, if I knew you were in trouble." His words sucked the breath from her lungs. "There is something about you I can't understand, Cori. From the moment I saw you standing down there on the beach, I've felt pulled to you. When I kissed you, it felt like the world cracked open. You sent me that note today, and something inside me was unleashed. I'd never felt that kind of fury. I knew you were in trouble. I couldn't control the storm. Seth told me to reel it in but physically I couldn't."

She let out a shaking breath. "I know."

"You *know*?" His voice was strained.

She nodded, biting her lip. *The bond.* She should never have asked him to the island today. Never should have been so selfish, but it had already taken hold of them. "The first time I looked at your face, it was like looking into a dream. Did you know you have fifteen freckles around your left eye?"

He raised a skeptical eyebrow. "I never counted."

"Why would you?" Her hand shook as she lifted her fingers to his face and traced the outline. "This one is Mira, Deneb, Tau..."

His lip curled up in a smile as the tension in his face fractured. "Are you speaking another language?"

She tilted her head toward him. "Kind of. These freckles are perfectly arranged in the constellation of Cetus."

His smile spread. "Are you telling me I have a giant whale on my face?"

"I like it." She ran her fingers over his cheek where the constellation swooped down. "For years, I would see your face in my sleep. I would dream of these stars and wake up just as two blue eyes opened in the middle of them. I recognized you immediately the first time I met you in real life."

He pursed his lips together, and the muscle in his jaw

twitched. "In real life?" He broke away, lifting his touch from her arm.

Her lips parted as she nodded up at him, her magic reaching out for him in tendrils. The speed of the stars collided with the weight of the water in her blood, and he stilled. She knew he felt it too—something ancient, primitive, and raw that couldn't be pushed away or ignored.

The roar of the tide pulsed in her blood. As though pulled by the gravity of the moon, he closed the distance between them, their lips meeting as he pulled her in.

She plunged into the warm, wet heat of his magic the moment they touched. Her breaths quickened and her pulse hammered like thunder in her chest as his hands wrapped around her hair. He grazed over her back, and her spine arched toward him. Her feet lifted off the floor, her legs instinctively wrapping around his waist as she waved her hand over the lock on the door.

Muttering the incantation into his lips, the door flew open with the urgency of her magic. His chest was heaving fast against her as he carried her to the couch.

He sat back on the sofa, and her body fell on top of him as she impatiently tugged at his shirt, feeling his muscles tighten in response to her touch. A moan escaped his lips as her thighs strad-dled him and their mouths connected again. His magic was delicious, and she let herself drink it in.

She slid her hand over his chest, relishing the feeling of his muscles twitching as she grazed them. When she had finally pulled his shirt over his head, she stared down at him for a moment. Bronze, freckled skin pulled taut over muscles that had been honed by years of hard labor.

She slowed her breathing, eyes wide and set to his gaze as she slowly pulled off her own shirt and unclipped her bra. His frozen stare lingered for a heartbeat before he pulled her in for another kiss, this time less frantic. The controlled softness of his lips played over hers slowly and purposefully. His bare skin against hers was almost more than she could stand.

She arched her head back as his kisses trailed down her neck, and she gasped as his powerful hands slid down her thighs, continuing to undress her. His thick, rough fingers parted her flesh in slow careful strokes.

The air thickened with dense humidity as her skin grew hot and slick, and when his fingers slid inside her, she was undone.

Lost to reality. Lost to everything that might happen if she let him in.

She needed more of him.

Bowing her head, she kissed his chest as her hand slid down below his waist, his breath quickening and his heart pounding faster at her approach. She gasped as she found him, enormously hard and eager for her.

She arched her mouth to his ear. "I want all of you."

He let out a pleading breath as her hand encircled him slowly up and down. It wasn't enough. His hands braced her hips as she lowered herself onto him. The force of his magic pulsed through her like lightning as their bodies connected, stunning her into silence as he filled her.

Her body swayed forward as his hands guided her hips up and down, propelling her. She leaned forward again, deepening his thrusts as she ran her fingers through his hair. Air escaped her lungs with moans and gasps as his body met hers like waves crashing powerfully against the shore.

He gripped her hips harder, pulling her down onto him as his mouth closed over the peak of her breast. She could not hold back, crying out in pleasure as release tore through her, tensing her muscles around every inch of him.

He let go a moment later, a second wave rippling through her.

As she collapsed onto him, shimmering beads of water ran down his skin, and she kissed them away, licking the salt from his skin, as they fell down his neck. He pulled her closer to him and curled his arms around her, burying his head in her hair as she settled her head onto his shoulder.

They said nothing for a while, catching their breath as their hearts slowed back to normal. A few more beads of water fell over the curve of his shoulder, and as Cori looked around, she noted condensation on the windows and furniture.

"Cori, I..." he stammered. "That was—"

"I know," she said. She knew what he was trying to say. There were no words to describe the intensity of what they had just shared.

It was not just their bodies that were joined—she could feel the power of his magic as if it was living inside her. Each touch, each breath, and each heartbeat were magnified by it.

"Does this happen every time you—?" She gestured to the water dripping down his body and clinging to the windows.

He laughed. "Yeah, pretty much. I can make it go away when I get my energy back."

"And when might that be?" She ducked under his arm as water dripped from the skylight above them.

"After what you just did to me?" He pulled her closer. "Might be a few hours."

She raised her eyebrows at him.

"Fine," he said, playfully. All the vapor in the room melted away, cooling her skin with the sudden empty dryness. He grabbed the blanket from the back of the sofa and wrapped it around her as he led her to the bed.

CORI

It was dark outside when Cori awoke from sleep with a jolt. She didn't remember the dream, but she knew it was a nightmare. Cold sweat clung to her skin. Adrian didn't stir as she slipped out of bed.

The floor was shockingly cold under her feet, and despite being inside the house, she could see her breath. She walked to the kitchen to quench the parched fear in her throat with a cup of water.

Her eyes focused through the dim light in the aftershocks of her nightmare, when she noted a soft glow from outside the window. Her Eye snapped to attention. *Go to it.*

She pulled on boots and a coat, her gaze fixed on the light. Soft amber gleamed from the garden, emitting a peacefulness and familiarity that she couldn't place. The charm bracelet on her wrist felt heavy and hot with magical energy.

That's odd.

She had worn the bracelet every day since Nonna died, but she had noticed nothing magical about it before.

Wrapping her coat around her, she ventured outside. In the silence of the night, the door hinge let out a creaky sigh. The air was too cold, even for a September night in Maine. The door clicked heavily behind her when she saw it in the garden.

A spirit.

She could tell it was a spirit's aura, and the true source of the light she had seen. A living soul had an aura that was inky and breezy, like watercolor on canvas. Spirits shimmered like an ethereal mist, and as she slowly approached the man, his body was a wisp of light, cast upon a shadow.

Despite the ghostlike appearance of the man, she was struck by how his form was nearly solid. Most spirits could not fully manifest, but this man seemed nearly *there.*

He didn't seem to notice her as she slowly approached him. She was nervous that she would scare him away. Not all spirits were interested in talking to her, but why else would this man be here? She took slow, careful steps toward him, casting his features into her view.

His dark hair was tidy, streaked with gold. As he turned toward her, she was struck by the strong angle of his jaw and the large, familiar eyes. He smiled kindly up at her from his perch on the garden bench, and she gasped.

"Enzo?" she said in disbelief. She reached out as if to touch him, the cold sheen of his aura chilling her skin.

"No, Stellina. I admit I'm not nearly as handsome as your brother turned out to be," the man replied with a warm laugh. His accent was thick and rich like Nonna's.

Cori's heart leaped and her lungs constricted, stealing her breath. "Papa?" she asked in disbelief. The man stood and strode toward her with a warm, deep smile. His arms reached out to hug her, and he wrapped them around her shoulders.

Despite the thick fabric of her coat, *she could feel him.* She didn't know that a spirit could manifest enough to have a solid sense of touch, but her father had seemed to manage it. Warm energy of his magic washed over her. It felt crisp and bright and familiar, like a déjà vu of something that had since been woven into her subconscious.

This man—*this spirit*—who she had never met on this Earth, felt familiar and right, as if she had known him for eternity. She pulled back and stared at his face, her mouth agape, words escaping her. "I just can't believe you're here," she finally said.

His aura flickered as he looked at the ground with sad eyes. "I should have come to you a long time ago, Cordelia." He gripped her hand. "I'm sorry. I was such a coward."

Cori's brow knotted together in confusion. "Coward? Papa, it's OK. I know this must be hard. Manifesting like this. It must take an enormous amount of energy."

He waved his hand dismissively, and she forced back a smile. His gestures were so similar to Nonna's, it was laughable. "*Mia cara*, it would have been easy. Celestial witches are very gifted at manifesting in the spirit form."

Confusion melted away into disappointment. Despite the apparent ease with which it could be done, he and Nonna had never visited her. She had always assumed that the soul could be fatigued from a visit to the living realm.

"Not that I didn't want to," he continued, reading her aura. "I was selfish. I didn't feel like I could answer the inevitable questions I knew you would have, and that weighed on me."

"I do have questions," Cori admitted. "So many." She raked her brain as they all flooded to the surface.

Did he know about her before she was born? Did he have any visions about what she would be like? What was it like when he met Mama? Did he know right away that they were fated? Had he dreamed about Mama when he was a child, the way she had dreamed of Adrian? She shook her head, mulling over which one of these questions would be hard for him to answer.

For her whole life, she had some comfort in knowing that perhaps her father had seen her in visions before he died. The hope that he had known *her* in some way dulled the sting of never knowing *him*.

"But, Cordelia, I have no choice. I come to you now because of your brother." Her lungs sucked in a breath at the words, and the air became lodged in her chest as a ball of guilt. She knew that Enzo would have been furious with her carelessness these past few days. All this time, he was risking his life to protect her, and she had been so reckless—exposing her secret.

She managed to speak. "How?"

His hand squeezed her shoulder. "Your brother has gotten involved in dark magic, Cordelia," he said. The glow around him morphed into an iridescent, sad blue. "Heavily involved. I knew it would happen one day. It was the last prophecy I ever delivered."

Her mouth parted in shock. The surrounding air sucked into a void, pulling with it all the sound. There had to be some kind of mistake. She shook her head numbly.

"I know this is hard to believe," her father continued. "I've been watching Enzo get more and more involved. Just like I predicted he would."

"You made a prophecy about Enzo? You knew he would turn to dark magic?" Her father looked up at her with sad eyes and nodded. "Did Mama know?"

He nodded again, sighing heavily. The sting of betrayal echoed through her chest.

"She knew. I delivered the prophecy to your mother and Nonna a few weeks before you were born."

Cori's head spun. All these years, they had known Enzo would go down this path. Was this the true reason her mother sent her away?

"For hours, your mother refused to tell me what I said. I was in agony. You know what it's like to make a prophecy. We're pulled out of our body. We don't hear what we say, but I could tell when I returned that whatever I had said was devastating." He paced, staring out to the sky as he moved, tipping his head back the same way Cori did when she searched for guidance from the stars.

"When did she tell you?" Cori asked. "It was hours before she told me what I said, but I had a much bigger audience."

"She never told me, but your nonna did. After your mother went to bed that night. It was the most horrible moment of my life."

The air had become supernaturally cold, and a few flakes of

snow danced around her. Cori held in tears, fearing they would turn to ice on her face. "Papa, what was your prophecy?" she whispered.

The lines on his face were etched with sorrow as he closed his eyes. He sat back down on the bench, thinking hard for a few moments before he spoke. "*Son of darkness and light, daughter of sea and sky. The darkness of one will extinguish the light of the other. He will end her life to seal his own fate, banishing the light into eternal darkness.*"

Her chest was heaving now as the tears stung her cheeks. "He will end her life to seal his own fate?" She couldn't believe what she was hearing.

"I predicted your brother would kill you." He clenched his fists. "Not only that he would try, but that he would succeed."

Cori buried her head in her hands as she sat heavily on the bench beside her father. His arms embraced her again as she sobbed silently. Her heart cracked open as she cried for the burden that he carried.

She thought her own prophecy was bad. Cori couldn't imagine being the messenger of one child's eventual demise at the hand of the other.

She sobbed for her mother, knowing the truth now about why she was sent away. It wasn't to protect her from dark witches. She was sent away to protect her from—*Enzo*—someone she loved and trusted.

She grieved for her brother, someone she remembered as kind and good. Was there any part of him left, or was he consumed by darkness in her absence?

"Oh, Papa. I'm so sorry," she said through broken breaths.

"I'm the one who is sorry, Cordelia," he said, choking on his own tears. "Sorry that I had to end my own life to give you a chance at yours."

Shock gripped her, freezing the air in her lungs as she looked up at him.

His face contorted with tortured grief. "That I never got to take you on the trolley. I never got to see you in your school plays and treat you to ramen and ice cream. When I nose-dived my plane into the Pacific Ocean that day, I did it with every intention of saving you from your brother. And that's how I know you are safe from him. You needed to know this. He cannot harm you, and the darkness inside him will not win. Because I wouldn't let it."

He grabbed her hands. Through her tears, she held his stare, his eyes flashing with specks of gold. "That's why I have come here tonight, Cordelia. Your brother has joined a reform coven, and as we speak, they're working out a plan to kill you. Enzo does not know about my prophecy, Cordelia."

"What are they planning to do?" she asked frantically.

"They plan to lure you to Salem, Massachusetts on the solstice by kidnapping your mother. The birthplace of the Covenant. You need to know the truth because..." he paused, gazing up at the sky. "You need to know that they cannot touch you." He paused again, wiping a tear from her cheek, his touch like ice on her skin. "You are the only person who can free your brother from the grip of the darkness."

"What are you saying? Can't I just warn Mama not to go near them?"

He shook his head. "Your mother will go with them willingly. She won't leave your brother's side. Astrid knows the reason I ended my life, and she would rather die herself than stand by and know that I died in vain."

The icy air chilled her skin, sending a shiver through her. "I can leave the country. I'll go to Europe—make sure he won't find me."

Paolo shook his head. "If you are not present on the solstice, Calvin will kill Enzo—and your mother."

The light surrounding him flickered and dimmed as he looked to the sky, beams of moonlight shimmering over the most distant parts of the sea.

She stood and wrapped her arms around the man who had died for her. He felt less solid now, and she knew he was fading back into the spirit realm. "Papa, I'll try. I hope I can be half as strong as you are."

"Stellina, I have watched you for your whole life. I don't think you realize how powerful you truly are. Let the power inside you be free. Stop hiding, and you will find yourself." He planted a soft kiss on your forehead. "Your brother is not the only soul you are capable of saving."

His hands were clasped around hers as he faded away. Just before he left her, panic rose in her heart as she said one last thing to him. "Papa, please come back and visit me again."

He smiled down at her. "Promise," he said. "Cordelia, I'm so proud of you, my star. I love you more than life."

"I love you, too," she whispered, as the snow swirled around them. As if riding the wind, he returned to the sky.

ADRIAN

When Adrian left Cori's cottage the next morning, she was still asleep, her head buried in the pillow. He had conflicted feelings about leaving her, but he knew Seth and David would head to the dock with or without him.

Cori had plans to meet up with Prudence and Alfie later. Even though their intentions had been good, and Cori trusted them, the whole kidnapping thing left a sour taste in his mouth. Pru had apologized to Cori for the way they handled the situation, but Adrian had to admit—there was no other way to inform her.

If Cori had found out they knew who she was, she would have done everything in her power to escape. He smirked himself, realizing that drowning might have been preferable to some spells that Cori likely had in her back pocket.

He walked home, savoring the feeling of the rain falling on his neck and shoulders. Although he could have shielded himself from the storm, he embraced it instead.

By the time he made his way up the drive to the farmhouse, the last rays of moonlight were breaking through the clouds. His father's truck was parked in the driveway. He puffed out his cheeks, blowing out a tired sigh.

Seth would have filled his parents in on what happened last

night. He bit his lip, preparing for the lecture about responsibility.

He dried himself off on the front porch, the cheerful chatter of his parents and Seth echoing from the kitchen. "Damn, all three of them are awake," he muttered to himself. There was no chance Ariel was up this early, but Hannah was often an early riser.

He slunk into the kitchen as his father finished his story.

"...and then I really knew that this guy didn't know what he was talking about when he asked me about the leeks."

Seth sat forward in his chair as he shoveled some hash browns in his mouth. "What does the guy have against leeks?"

"Maybe he has good taste and realizes that leeks are disgusting," Adrian reasoned.

"My leeks are delicious, and you know it," Hannah chuckled.

David snorted. "Well, this guy has a thing for leeks. He wants them bad. Kept asking me if it was possible for us to add them to our crop." He shook his head. "Asked me over and over if it was too cold to grow them in Maine."

"Some chef he is. Doesn't he know they grow best in cold, sandy soil?" Hannah rolled her eyes.

David held up his hand. "Listen up, boys, because this is where your old man really came through. I said to the guy—listen, leeks are a rough trade up here. It takes a lot of energy to grow those bad boys. If you want them, we might have to add some increased irrigation. For the price you're offering..."

"Oh David, you manipulated the poor man." Hannah put her head in her hands.

"So, he goes...*OK, I'll give you an extra thirty-K...should that cover it?*"

Adrian pursed his lips as Seth pumped his fist in the air. "Thirty-K? Like thirty thousand dollars?"

"Ma, you could build the most advanced leek-growing facility in the country," Adrian chimed in. She smiled up at him, a knowing gleam in her eye. If they really got a thirty-thousand-dollar investment from this restaurant owner, it would be just enough to get them out of the hole they were in. He waited for the other shoe to drop. What risky reciprocal plan did David work out this time?

"You could make a leek grow out of this kitchen table," Seth reasoned. "These better be the best damn leeks in the world."

David sat back, cradling his coffee mug in his crossed arms. "Apparently this guy has a signature dish. He's coming up here with New York money. Obviously, he picked the right farm, so he must have some brains in his head."

Seth stood up purposefully, stretching his arms. "When Ariel wakes up can you ask her to come by the apartment later. The pilot light in the water heater is broken, and I need her to light it for me."

"Adrian, if your apartment is in a pile of ash later tonight, you can thank your brother," Hannah warned him.

Adrian settled into his chair, filling his mug with coffee. "Ma, go easy. She's going to be seventeen in less than six months, give her some credit. She can control it—mostly."

David arched an eyebrow at him. "Like you could control the hurricane that you unleashed on a bunch of Gray witches yesterday?"

Here it comes. Adrian scrubbed his hand through his hair and took a large sip from his mug. "So, you heard about that, Pop?"

David leaned back in his chair, studying him.

"Honey, your father got home late last night. When Seth got back, he filled us in on what happened on the island," Hannah said softly from behind her teacup.

Adrian nodded, steadying himself.

"Hannah, Seth, I think I want to have a little talk with my son," David said in a low voice.

Seth sulked out of the room, exchanging a pitying look with his younger brother as he went to pack the truck.

Hannah rose from her seat, failing to hide the amused grin on her face. "I knew you would, dear." She winked at Adrian as she gathered a few gardening tools into her basket and hastily pulled on her boots at the back door.

As the back door creaked closed, Adrian was alone in the kitchen with his father. David, who was never at want for words, sat in his chair for a little while in silence. He sipped his coffee, eyeing him from above the rim of his mug.

Adrian broke the heavy silence. "I don't know how much of the story Seth told you..."

"He told me the whole story."

"Before you tell me how irresponsible I was yesterday, let me just explain."

David was stoic. "There isn't much to explain. Is there? You were supposed to help your mother yesterday, but..."

Adrian slammed his hand onto the table. "She was threatened." He stood from his chair and paced the room. "Pop, she was in trouble. I didn't have a choice." He gripped the back of his chair. "If something happened to her, and I didn't stop it—"

He raised his hands to his head, trying to drown out the memory of what it felt like to have that note appear in his hand. It wasn't until his father's hand landed heavily on his shoulder that he realized he was shaking.

David was regarding his youngest son sympathetically as a proud smile crept onto his lips.

"Adrian, if anyone had threatened your mother how Cori was threatened yesterday, I would have stormed that island, too. You're much more patient and calculating than I am. I wouldn't have snuck up on the assholes. I would have delivered a tidal wave so big it would wash them all away."

Adrian sunk into his chair, his head in his hands. The chair next to him scraped across the floor as his father settled into it. "I don't know what came over me."

The grandfather clock chimed in the living room, as his father sat back in his seat and took a sip of coffee. "I do."

"You do?"

"Of course, I do. You're fated to her." Adrian's heart leaped as

David spoke the words aloud, alighting a truth within him. He looked up at his father, at a loss.

David grinned back at him, proud tears welling up in his eyes.

"My boy," he said, patting his son hard on the shoulder.

CORI

When Adrian left, well before dawn, she had pretended she was still asleep. The pounding in her heart took hours to slow after her father's visit. The skylight over the bed was glowing with early sun as beds of rainwater traced lines over the glass. She watched them fall for a long time, her body cranking with tidal waves of nausea.

She considered writing a letter to her mother, but she pushed the thought away.

No.

Astrid had kept this secret from her. For her whole life. Her father's discussion with her last night was now *her secret*. A secret she wanted to lock in her heart and never let go.

She rolled over in her bed and the smell of pine trees and salt water wafted from the bedsheets. Adrian Huxley was like a drug, and she attempted to get high on the smell of him as she buried her face in the pillow.

Adrian. Goddess, how was she going to tell him?

It was nearly seven when she finally rolled out of bed, her head pounding. Two over-easy eggs were waiting for her on the kitchen table along with some buttered toast and cold coffee. Her heart swelled in her chest at the kind gesture, and she savored every bite. Nobody had cooked breakfast for her in years.

Not since *Enzo*.

She cradled her head in her hands and raked her fingers over her scalp. The notebook was next to her purse. Paper crinkled under her fingers as she opened to the page where she kept track of the days, staring at it for what seemed like forever as she tapped her pen on the table beside her. Finally, she scrawled the latest countdown. *Ninety-seven days.*

What did this countdown even mean to her anymore? *Ninety-seven days until what?* Until the day her brother would try to kill her. The day she could confront her mother about the truth. Ninety-seven days until she could stop living a lie.

Buzzing from her phone snapped her away from the notebook. A text message from Pru.

> Where should we get lunch and talk about the solstice?

———

Carl's was already buzzing with the beginning of the lunch crowd. Cori nodded at the barman as they entered, and he winked at her in greeting as she ushered Pru and Alfie into a secluded booth behind the bar.

Pru shimmied into the seat, excitement on her face as she peered around her and opened her menu. "Wow, this is so charming! Alfie, does it remind you of the pubs back *across the pond*?"

"Stop saying that." He rolled his eyes, scanning the room suspiciously. "I doubt there are this many people wearing flip-flops in all the pubs in the UK combined right now." He examined his menu. "Please tell me this place has decent food, Cori. At least the beer selection looks acceptable."

"Adrian and Seth claim Carl has the best on-tap list in Maine," Cori said with a shrug.

Carl approached them with a warm, welcoming smile as he wiped off the tabletop. Pru beamed up at him while Alfie gave him a scrutinizing look. After pleasantries and introductions, they put their orders in. "We got a new California chardonnay yesterday, Cori," Carl suggested, winking at her as he finished setting out their cutlery.

She let out a breath and some of her tension melted away. "That sounds perfect, thank you."

Even Alfie had to admit the food was good. Heavenly even. Cori closed her eyes, savoring the perfectly crisp french fries that came with her sandwich.

"Delicious, although I will never understand the American tendency to garnish everything with pickles," Alfie mused as he sipped his German ale.

"Just as I will never understand how you Brits eat blood pudding," Pru shot back.

Cori hid her laugh behind her wineglass.

Alfie shrugged. "Before we talk about the important matters, I need to protect the table."

Pru nodded back at him. He opened his backpack and placed a stone on the tabletop. He positioned it in the center of the table and arranged three small gems in a large triangle around each of them on the back of the booth.

The stones gave off a dull energy at first, but when Alfie set down the final gem, the magic buzzed in a circular pattern around them. Cori could not place her finger on how it made her feel, but the magic had an unfettered heaviness to it. "What is that?" she asked. The tone of her voice sounded muted, almost as though she were underwater.

"It's a veiling stone," Pru explained. "Our voices won't carry beyond the perimeter of the gems." She whispered an incantation as she held her hand over the stone. "A minimizing spell," she explained. "Makes everyone around us ignore our presence."

Cori watched as a group of men walked to a nearby table. None of them glanced in their direction.

"Always best to use that one after your food has been delivered to the table," Alfie nodded.

Pru folded her hands and sat up straight. "Well then, let's get down to business. Have you asked the Elemental family if we can camp on their property?"

"Seth spoke to them yesterday. The whole family should be aware by now—what I am, what I predicted, how it puts me in danger..." She sighed with the heaviness of it. It was going to take a lot of adjustment. Being so exposed.

Alfie arched an eyebrow. "Do you think they were shocked?"

Cori swirled the wine in her glass, contemplating the question. "I'm sure they were." The sting of guilt marred the sweet gulp of her wine.

"Don't feel too bad." Pru patted her hand. "Sometimes we have to lie to protect ourselves."

"Yes, of course. Sometimes we even have to kidnap people to protect ourselves," Alfie said with a shrug, stabbing his tomato with a fork.

"Can you let it go already?" Pru shot back at him, rolling her eyes. "How many times do I need to tell you? You were right, Alfie. I was wrong about the kidnapping idea. When we get back to California, I'll get it engraved on a trophy for you."

He smiled wryly, leaning back. "What about a nice gold medallion? I can wear it around my neck every day."

"I'm about to put my hands around your neck every day," Pru muttered under her breath.

Cori coughed. "Well, it's settled. Adrian and Seth trust my judgment with you helping me."

Pru nodded with a smile.

"Of course, they trust your judgment," Alfie drawled. "It's foolish to doubt a Celestial witch, especially one that's *fated* to their brother," he said matter-of-factly.

Cori nearly choked on her french fry. She gulped down some water as Pru patted her on the back. "Excuse me?" She sputtered as she caught her breath.

Pru's eyes widened. "Oh, my Goddess, you didn't know?"

"Of course, I knew!" She was eternally grateful for the veiling stone now. "I just didn't think it would be so obvious to everyone else. Hell, I don't even know if *he* knows..."

"Oh, darling," Alfie said pityingly. "He knows."

Cori put her head in her hands. The connection between her and Adrian was playing out in front of everyone. She had hoped it would be less obvious. If a human like Jordan could sense the tension between them, it should not have shocked her that other witches could sense it, too.

"How else would he know where to find you on the island?" Pru asked, her mouth full of salad greens.

"Actually, he knew because I sent him a message." Cori explained how she had found the piece of paper and the pen on the back seat, allowing her to send Adrian the S.O.S. with her mother's spell. Her heart jumped as a forgotten event clicked in her mind. "That was the same spell my brother used to send me a message this weekend."

Pru and Alfie exchanged a dark look. "Yes, we know about that message," Pru said slowly.

Cori narrowed her eyes on her. Until that moment, the pentagram had been pushed to the back of her mind. "I know you know about it. I *saw* you. You were in my cottage and found it. What did you want with my brother's note, anyway?"

Pru's aura darkened and contracted. "Cori…" she started.

"I'm listening." Cori's fist clenched her fork. There was no mirror nearby, but she could see her reflection in Alfie's glasses. Her eyes pulsed a deep gold as she let her Eye reach out to them, reading them for any sign of deception. Alfie shivered as Prudence shrank back. "This arrangement will never work if you hold information back from me."

Alfie shook his head. "We were in your cottage that night to banish something," he explained. "We had been following you that day, and we could sense something dark was in your cottage. It's common, you know. Sometimes humans own things that are dark…a trinket from a pawn shop, a piece of art. We break into houses all the time, actually. When you were out, we followed it. The note was in your drawer, and we used the pentagram to banish the magic that was on the paper."

Her heart pounded, and her stomach twisted into a knot with the truth that she already knew. "My brother sent me that note."

Pru twisted her face sympathetically trying to formulate words, but she gave Alfie a pleading look instead.

"We have some intelligence on your brother, if that is what you're asking," Alfie carefully replied.

Cori raised her eyebrows expectantly. "What intelligence?" She was still unsure if she was strong enough to share what her father had revealed to her when he visited from the spirit realm.

Pru sucked in a deep breath, biting her lip. "Dark magic was all over that note because Enzo was the one who sent it."

"What are you trying to say?" Cori knew what they were trying to say, but to hear it aloud meant that she could keep what her father had told her to herself. No, she wasn't ready to tell them about her father's prophecy, but if they already knew about Enzo, that made the matter a lot less complicated.

Alfie and Pru exchanged a look.

Alfie cleared his throat. "We have intelligence on Enzo that suggests he has been working with a dark magic coven."

Cori blinked back at them. "Why? How?" She had so many questions. What exactly did they know?

"For the past two years, he has been traveling to LA once or twice a month," Prudence explained. "Each time he goes, he stays with a friend who's well-known for being—a reformationist. They believe the Covenant has robbed witches of their true power. According to them, magic should be strengthened by a combination of light and dark forces."

Her mouth felt dry. She wished she could summon Carl over to refill her empty glass. Alfie pulled out a thick leather binder and opened to the first page divider. He turned it toward Cori.

The binder was full of pictures of her brother. As she slowly turned the pages, each photo captured Enzo doing seemingly mundane things. Enzo walking into the airport. Enzo exchanging a bag with another man in the park. Enzo with his arm around a woman's shoulders as they walked down the street.

Her breath caught in her chest as she turned the page and spotted a picture of Enzo holding the hand of a small girl. The photo was snapped from a distance, but Cori could make out the girl's golden-brown hair reflecting the sunlight. She stared at the picture, her mouth agape, lost in the image of the little girl, who could be only five or six years old. She felt her hand move to the photo, the electric energy of her magic connecting with the image. Her Eye flashed open.

A child's laughter echoed. The smell of candy and the sound of little feet running away.

"Cori," she heard Prudence whisper as she snapped back to attention. "That's Enzo's daughter. Based on what we know from the address, the girl's mother is registered in the Sonoma County Charms Coven. She has no marriage record..." her voice trailed off. "That's the only picture we have."

The lump in Cori's throat expanded as she trailed her hand over the picture. The sound of her laughter was so familiar, like something out of a forgotten dream.

The implications of her years in exile never felt more real than it did in that moment. She had missed so much time she could never get back, and here was the living proof that her heart would never be the same. There were parts of her brother's life she had become so displaced from, it was impossible to really know him in the same way she once had.

Her heart ached for her brother, someone who had tried to fill the void of her father's absence in her life with every fiber of his being and every shred of his soul, even though he was only this little girl's age when Cori had been born. And yet—this little girl was another lie. Another secret. She couldn't bring herself to ask what the little girl's name was.

She fractured as she turned the heavy pages of the binder. There were dozens of pictures of Enzo. Walking up to the door of their town house, carrying a bag of what appeared to be takeout, out to dinner with a few friends. When she turned to a picture of him at a restaurant, she immediately recognized the face of one friend at the table. "Calvin."

Alfie and Prudence exchanged another dark look. "Calvin

Hanson. High priest of the Los Angeles Reform Coven. You recognize him?" Prudence asked with surprise.

Cori nodded, a lump in her throat. "Cal was in my coven growing up. He and Enzo were best friends. His family moved to LA when they were in high school. I think they moved right before the prophecy."

Calvin was leaning his arm over the back of the booth with a satisfied smile on his face. Enzo and the woman sitting with them appeared to be laughing, perhaps at one of his jokes.

Cori shook her head. All this time, Enzo had not been trying to stop them, he had been conspiring with them. "My mother had recently sent me a cutout from a pamphlet. Calvin is holding a meeting about the prophecy next week."

"The LARC. They have a nefarious reputation. Calvin is the reason we think Enzo got tangled in dark magic," Prudence said, her eyes darkening, as she leafed through the photos in the binder.

Each turn of the page revealed a chapter in his life that she had not been a part of, and each image shaved off a piece of her heart, left bleeding and withering on the floor at her feet.

"Listen, Cori," Pru said gently. "I know this is hard news to hear. We don't have the full story behind Enzo yet, and we don't know how deep he's gotten or what his motives are. Your brother has a reputation around town, and a lot of witches have become scared of him."

That didn't surprise her. Her brother always had a temper and a rebellious edge to him.

"It feels like a betrayal to tell anyone anything about him," she explained. "Ever since the prophecy, Enzo and my mom have been the only ones who have really protected me. The coven always had an attitude that it wasn't *their problem*. It was always family business." And until last night, she had believed that to be true.

Prudence and Alfie were aware of Enzo's truth the whole time she was in the dark about it. They had an entire task force dedicated to him, and she had been oblivious.

"I wonder how much of a *problem* you truly were to some of them, Cori," Alfie said darkly. "Maybe it wasn't an unwillingness to help protect you, but a willingness to put an end to the problem by other means."

A shiver danced over her skin. Her mother had always feared this. After the prophecy, she had broken ties with many old friends for this very reason.

Her mother. Her blood ran cold. "Do you have a binder like this for my mother?"

"If we did, it wouldn't have much material," Prudence said, shaking her head.

Cori's eyebrows knitted together. "What do you mean?"

"Your mother doesn't get out much these days," Alfie said sadly.

Her eyes widened as she bit her lip. All this time, her mother had been isolated, too. She tried to picture her mother—her lively, bubbly, extroverted mother—as a shut-in.

"People have been in to see her," Prudence explained. "Enzo brings her a lot of food, and she accepts visitors, but the only glimpses we get of her are from the front window as she waves hello or goodbye."

Cori closed her eyes and cradled her head in her hands as she recalled the vision of her mother on the phone in her kitchen. "They argued." Alfie and Pru returned baffled looks at her. "A few days ago, I saw Mama in a vision. She was on the phone talking to my brother, and the conversation was tense. He was asking her to go somewhere with him."

Prudence pulled out her phone, her expression fierce as the glow of the screen illuminated her dainty features. "I'm telling my dad to get a safety detail on Astrid. ASAP. We need to figure out where Enzo wanted to take her."

ADRIAN

The motor of his truck whirred to a halt as they came to a stop in the driveway.

"Do you really think everything about your brother and this Calvin guy is true?" Adrian leaned back in the driver's seat, rubbing his temples. He had picked Cori up from Carl's after another abysmal weigh-in at the dock. On his way to get her, his stomach had twisted into a knot, and he knew she was upset before she even got into the car.

Her face was pale, as though she had seen a ghost. She had filled him in on what she learned from the Grays on their way back to the farm.

"There was no sign of deception that came from them when they were telling me. My Eye sensed nothing but sincerity." She sighed. "As much as I don't want to believe it, and I hope to the Goddess there's more to the story, what they're telling me matches up with the visions I've been having lately."

She told him about the argument between Enzo and her mother.

He leaned back, studying her. "Can you tune in to what they're doing right now?"

She shrugged. "It doesn't work that way. I can only get snippets of information, and it comes to me at unexpected times."

"Like when you had the vision about the electrical cord."

"Exactly. Some visions come in my dreams. Sometimes they're connected to strong emotions." She closed her eyes, shaking her head. "Delivering the prophecy was completely unexpected. It came out of nowhere. I can't control it. According to my nonna, it's not meant to be controlled. Visions and prophecies are gifted to us from the Giver."

He crossed his arms and shook his head heavily. "Some gift," he said with resignation. He reached across the armrest, grazing his fingers along her charm bracelet.

"Nonna always said I wouldn't get information that I wasn't meant to know," she mused aloud.

The passenger door of the trunk clicked heavily behind them as they made their way up the gravel path to the farmhouse. Adrian and Seth had collected her buoys—or as Seth liked to call them, sea doughnuts—while they were out on the water earlier. They could accomplish more in a day than Cori would have gotten done by herself in a week.

"Anne and Jordan should be back by the end of the week. Anne emailed me this morning. Thanks to Jordan's powers of persuasion, they negotiated a deal. I appreciate you collecting my samples today." Her voice was wary. "Did you tell your parents about...everything?"

He nodded. "Everyone except Ariel, but I expect she heard by now." His speculation was short-lived. As they opened the door to the house, Ariel practically bombarded them in the foyer.

"Cori, when I heard you were Celestial—I nearly died. Literally—almost had a *heart attack*. Do you think you can read people through photographs? There are at least three guys on the lacrosse team that have said some things to me in the past few months that made me say *hmm*, was that flirtation, friendship, or am I just imagining things?"

Seth stood in her way at the top of the staircase. "Ariel, what the hell is wrong with you?" he asked.

"Seth, get out of our way right now!" There was a steady

billow of steam coming from the top of Ariel's head, and the flames of candles in the window surged as she spoke.

Adrian crossed his arms as he shot his little sister a warning look. "Cori is not your personal tarot card reader."

Cori bit back a laugh as Ariel gasped. "Do you read tarot?!" she asked excitedly.

Cori shrugged. "I mean I can, but I don't make a habit of it. It's not nearly as accurate as reading palms."

Ariel's eyes widened. "Shut *up!*" Within a few seconds, she had set Seth's pants on fire, causing him to leap out of the way as Ariel pulled Cori by the arm up the steps into her bedroom.

Ariel held Cori in her room for a while, and by the time she was free, the table was already set for dinner. Seth, wearing a fresh pair of pants without burn marks, had a surly, sour look on his face. He glared at his little sister as she and Cori joined them on the back deck, but Ariel smiled devilishly at him in return.

Adrian leaped from his seat to pull out Cori's chair.

"Whoa, such a gentleman all of a sudden," Ariel teased him. "Where did you learn that move?"

David's deep voice echoed from the doorway as he balanced a salad bowl and a water pitcher in his arms. "I know where he learned it—from his dear old dad."

Adrian groaned. David put down the salad bowl and placed his hands on Cori's shoulders. "Glad to see you in one piece." He smiled down at her. His voice turned serious. "I've never been prouder of my sons as I was when I heard how they rescued you."

He pulled her into a hug, and blood rushed to her cheeks. Adrian had been dreading how his father would respond to Cori, but he puffed out a sigh of relief. David could be brash sometimes, but at his core he was a loyal person.

"So, what's the deal with the Gray witches coming to live here?" Ariel asked abruptly, her mouth full of pasta.

"Ariel," Hannah warned. "Cori has had a long day, and she doesn't need to rehash everything for the hundredth time."

"No...it's OK." To Adrian's surprise, Cori told them everything. About her meeting at Carl's, what she saw in her reading of

Prudence on the island, how she moved to Yale, all the way back to the day she delivered the prophecy itself.

"I'm still having a hard time with this *weakness through the Other* part." Seth furrowed his brow.

Adrian nodded. "I've been having trouble understanding that part, too."

"It's simple," Hannah explained, folding her napkin into a neat square. "Magic comes from a lot of different sources. Different *Others*. Charms witches pull their energy from other witches. Gray witches pull from light and dark magic, Celestial witches from the stars, and Elementals from the elements. The *Other* is different depending on what kind of witch you are."

"Why did you never tell us about the prophecy?" Ariel asked. "You had to have known about it."

"You know what," David said, crossing his arms. "I remember hearing about it, but I had completely forgotten about it until now. I think I got word through your grandmother. She had a few friends who were Charms witches. It was never something that worried us—being Elemental and all."

Hannah nodded in agreement.

"This prophecy is supposed to come true on the winter solstice of this year?" Ariel shivered as she spoke.

"Ninety-seven days," Cori said ominously.

"What are you going to do about your brother?" Seth asked.

Adrian's anger swelled at the mention of Enzo. He would rather die than hurt his family. Enzo had betrayed his sister, and that told Adrian everything he needed to know about him. Cori locked wide eyes with him, her face pale. He diverted his gaze to his plate, his jaw clenched.

She let out a heavy breath. "I think we need to get more information. Prudence and Alfie hope that the combination of my visions and the intelligence in the San Francisco Gray Coven might give us a better idea of what is actually going on."

"So what? Prudence and Alfie have a bunch of special-agent, private-eye Gray witches just roaming around the city?" Ariel asked as she stabbed a noodle with her fork.

Cori laughed at the description. "It sure sounds like it." She told them about the binder full of Enzo's pictures. "It sounds like they have a task force just for my brother and my mother. The group that's here in Maine was protecting me all this time."

"They also police whatever area they're living in. Banishing dark magic, witches that fall out of line, and evil objects," Adrian explained.

Ariel leaned back, crossing her arms. "I always just thought Grays were quirky freaks. I had no idea they had all that responsibility."

Cori told them how hurt Prudence had been when she had shown the same ignorance about Gray witches and what their roles were.

"Prudence explained that when the Covenant was formed, the dark witches of the day went in two directions—those who would abuse dark magic and those who would protect it," Cori explained. "The reason dark magic had to be banished in the first place was because humans had grown so fearful of it."

"Which is why the Covenant was put into place after the Salem trials," David chimed in.

"So, you mean to tell me that for the past four hundred years, the Gray witches have been in charge of keeping all the dark magic under control?" Ariel asked.

Cori nodded. "That's why they were so excited about the prophecy."

"I still don't get how they can pull energy from dark magic and not use it," Seth said.

"I've seen them do a few spells and charms," Cori said with a shrug. "None of it seemed dark at all to me. Today they used something called a veiling stone at the restaurant to muffle our voices."

David choked on his drink. "Are you serious?" he asked, clearing his throat.

"Yeah, totally serious." Cori raised her eyebrows. "It seemed innocent enough, just a piece of rock and some gems."

"A veiling stone is a magical object that is pulled from the grave of a witch," he explained. "It's considered very dark to take from the dead."

Hannah laughed at his explanation. "It makes perfect sense, though, doesn't it? They're taking a dark object and using it for good, right?" She paused, sensing the minds turning around the table. "That's what makes it *Gray*. Who knows? Maybe they even had permission from the witch who they took it from before they died."

"Dark objects like veiling stones are really powerful," David said.

"And why humans were so terrified of us," Hannah added.

"Well then, we know one thing for certain," Seth said standing. "At least we have a bunch of badasses on our team now."

Our team. They laughed in agreement at his rationalization as they all stood to clear the table. Adrian's heart swelled. His family had fully embraced protecting Cori, and he knew they were doing it for him. Even though she had been in his life for only a few short days, they embraced her without question.

Meanwhile, in California, Cori's own brother was plotting against her. Cori bit her lip as she twirled the charm bracelet around her wrist. Anger gripped Adrian's heart, squeezing until blood laced with hatred buzzed through his veins.

CORI

Humidity lingered in the air as she rested her head on his shoulder. The heaving of his chest slowed as she chased the shimmering water droplets on his shoulder with her fingers. Tracing the tattooed wave that crested over his ribs, his skin twitched in response to her touch.

He let out a contented groan as he pulled her closer to him.

"I can't move," he stated simply.

"Same," she agreed.

"Damn it, Cori. What are you doing to me? You know, you can't keep me up late like this every night. I wake up early, you know."

"Adrian, it's not even nine o'clock."

She felt him grab her by the hips, hoisting her on top of him. "In that case..." He pulled her into a kiss as his hand slid back between her thighs. She gasped against his mouth before he bit her on the neck, trailing kisses to the peak of her breast.

"I thought you said you couldn't move," she said coyly as she felt him growing hard against her thigh. She ran her fingers over his chest, still slick with sweat and vapor.

She felt his lip curl up against her skin. "There's a part of me that disagrees."

She kissed him again, biting down on his lower lip. He groaned impatiently as he swelled against her. His hands moved from her breasts down onto her hips as she slid slowly onto him. She stilled for a moment, savoring the intensity of the connection between them, before she leaned back, rocking her hips.

She watched him at first, enjoying the way his body responded to her as she rode him—his muscles tensing as his head leaned back. Water clung to his body, streaming down his chest and arms in shimmering beads of moisture.

She closed her eyes, reaching out for his magic, and it was almost too intense for her to bear. As her magic became interwoven with his, she drank in his pleasure like a drug.

When she felt his grip tighten around her hips, she leaned forward deepening her thrusts and intensifying the friction between them. His hands let go of her hips, pulling the back of her head down into a kiss as he came.

She slowed for a moment before his hand landed on the small of her back, urging her on. He ran his hands up and down her back as the heat rose and fell within her. He was still inside her as they collapsed in a heap of wet, exhausted limbs.

"I'm sorry, I didn't mean to keep you awake so late."

He smiled sleepily. "I'm not complaining. But I'm starving. And exhausted. And my back hurts."

She pushed herself up to a standing position. "That's three complaints in a row, actually." She caught him staring at her for a moment before she pulled on her shirt and shorts.

"Fair."

"I'm going to grab a quick shower. I'll rub your aching back when I'm done." He smirked at her mischievously as she retreated into the bathroom.

She hadn't told Adrian yet about the visit from her father. Anxiety had consumed her all day over how the Huxleys would react to the truth about her past.

While her own family had cast her away, these strangers had opened their arms to her. Bitterness rose in her throat. She knew she had to tell him, but she had seen the fury rise from Adrian's aura anytime Enzo's name was mentioned at dinner. How would he respond to the news that it was now up to Cori to save her brother from his own fate?

How was she even going to accomplish that?

It took a few moments for the water to heat, and as she stepped into the steamy spray, she savored the feeling of the heat washing away her tension. She was halfway through washing up when she noticed the pressure change slightly from the water falling from the showerhead.

A thick stream fell down her shoulder, thicker and more powerful than the rest of the spray. The water fell down her arm and jutted down her neck, before curling forward between her breasts and down her abdomen. There was something supernatural about the way the water was moving around her body.

Water encircled her nipples, making her gasp before an even stronger jet trailed down her abdomen and down between her thighs. She was about to yell out to Adrian to stop teasing her, as she felt the sinful warmth of the water trace tight circles around some of her most sensitive spots.

She gave in, leaning against the cool tile with one hand for a few moments as the water licked her in all the right places. It didn't take long before she cried out, climaxing again as the water continued to trace slow circles. The pressure returned to normal as she caught her breath. She rinsed off and hastily wrapped a towel around herself.

He was whistling in the kitchen, cutting a peanut butter sandwich in half. "How was your shower?"

"It was fine."

"Sounded like it was more than fine." The corner of his mouth crept up.

"I feel very clean."

"I don't know, that sounded a little dirty to me." He bit into his sandwich, pleased with himself.

She raised her eyebrow and dropped her towel. The smug

expression melted from his face as she slowly stalked toward him. She hoisted herself onto the countertop, pulling him to her as she wrapped her legs around his waist, allowing herself to escape into his magic as she kept him awake far too late into the night.

ADRIAN

H e awoke with a start. Had he fallen asleep? He couldn't
even remember who had drifted off first. He squinted in
the darkness. *Oh Goddess, what time is it?*

After a few moments of searching, he found his cell phone on
the bedside table. Four thirty. Thankful to his internal alarm
clock, he slid out of bed and showered off, savoring the hot water.
He riffled through the kitchen carefully to avoid making too
much noise. After brewing a pot of coffee, he scrambled some
eggs and buttered a few pieces of toast, setting aside some for Cori
on a separate plate. He zipped up his jacket over his coveralls and
covered her eggs with foil.

His phone lit up as a text alert from Seth flashed on the screen.

> Want me to pick you up?

Sure, thanks

> Want to tell me where the fuck you are?

I'll walk

> Stop being a baby. Be there in five

Adrian rolled his eyes in at his brother's teasing as he shrugged his jacket over his shoulder. He locked the door behind him, lingering for a moment to seal it with the protective charm Cori had taught him, as the wheels of the truck rolled to a stop on the gravel.

He settled onto the warm leather of the passenger seat after tossing his bag into the truck bed. An extra green juice was perched in the center console, and The Decemberists were playing on the stereo.

Seth handed the juice to his brother as he shifted into drive. "Just in case you were feeling tired this morning. Made an extra for you."

"Thank you." Adrian took the tumbler happily. Despite his annoyance at Seth's teasing, he appreciated the kind gesture. He closed his eyes, taking a large swig. "Ugh, didn't expect the celery." He coughed, forcing down another large swig.

Seth shrugged. "Gotta get the toxins out."

As the truck crept down the slope of the cliffside, Adrian craned his neck to watch the sky. The moon was setting over the trees, casting an eerie glow over the water as the sun opposed it to the east. He squinted hard at the moon, trying to sense its magic. The drum of the tide seemed to beat through his veins.

No matter how far away from the ocean he was (and he admittedly had never strayed too far away from it in his life), he could feel it around him. He could feel the hum of the magic in the vapor of the clouds and in the groundwater under his feet.

He looked up again at the moon and beyond it to the stars peppering the morning sky, trying to sense the same hum, the same pull of magic.

Unlike the ocean, which felt full and deep and alive, the sky seemed immense and cold in its magic. How was it for her? When she looked up to the sky, was she overwhelmed by the magnitude of the magic there? A magic he was sensing despite its vast occupancy in the surrounding universe.

He shivered as he pictured her face gazing up, her delicate features soaking up the magic in the moon's glow as her eyes emitted the gold of Celestial magic. Magic from stars occupying a place in the universe light-years away.

If the magic in the surrounding water was infinite, what was it like to tap in to a power that was infinite?

The jolt of the truck shifting into park startled him, and he shivered again as he unbuckled his seat belt. Seth was pulling his jacket around his shoulders as they unpacked their gear from the truck bed and made their way to the dock. They weren't alone.

"Rise is 6:14 a.m. today, we can be on the water in fifteen minutes." Seth started prepping the rig as Adrian warmed up the engine and mapped out their route. The heavy clomping of boots announced David's presence on the boat.

"Your mother packed up soup and sandwiches for lunch," he declared as he set down a large cooler and thermos. "Feeling more like winter every morning this week." He pulled his hat over his head and turned up his collar to cover his scruffy neck.

He looked out over the tops of the trees, already turning gold. He took a deep breath of cool, crisp morning air. The chill traveled down his throat and permeated his bones as the boat pulled away from the dock.

As they crested over the waves and the shoreline thinned behind them, he could not help but feel like he was swimming toward something that was frightening and immense.

CORI

The muscles in her shoulders and back cramped with tension as she craned her neck over her laptop. Data points from her metallic deposit samples had been entered meticulously into the spreadsheet, and all there was left to do was run the preliminary statistics.

She stretched her arms over her head as she rubbed her sore shoulders with satisfaction. This was precisely what she had been brought here to do, and it felt good.

The next phase of Anne's project—and the essential funding she had secured—hedged on the fact that they would get a publication out of this data. They would show the impact of dumping into the local waterways to the EPA.

Anne had been lobbying politicians in Maine for the past few years to strengthen their laws and fines, and now she would have the data to back up her claims.

A soft knock sounded on the door frame as Jordan peered around the corner arching his eyebrow expectantly.

"Well?" he asked.

She smiled up, raising her brows. "I'm running the stats now."

He sipped his coffee, trying to conceal his excitement with a casual act, but the restless drumming of his fingers on the mug gave him away.

She smirked at him. "You want to help?"

He beelined to the seat next to her as she pulled her laptop between them. "Of course, I want to help. Move the hell over." He took another excited sip as he squinted at the thousands of data points on the spreadsheet.

Cori sighed. She had never met anyone with so much energy in her life. It probably had something to do with the endless stream of caffeine the man ingested through the day.

"I promise I won't tell anyone that you've been stalking me all morning over this spreadsheet," she assured him.

"I love math, Cori. It's not my fault I'm a big nerd trapped in this sexy body." She snorted, and he punched her on the arm. "Just run the numbers, and stop being a buzzkill."

She tallied the columns carefully and plugged the data into a series of statistical formulas. With the samples she had collected, she could build on Anne's original data and make it into something worth trending. She and Jordan had worked late the past couple of nights, and it all led up to this moment.

Cori leaned back on her chair as she made her final calculations. Her head turned toward Jordan, who had his hand clasped to his mouth with excitement. "Is that the final p-value?" he asked with a wide grin.

She blew out a satisfied breath. "My friend, you are looking at genuine, bona fide statistical significance." They both sprang to their feet, hugging each other as they jumped and squealed like a couple of teenage girls at a K-pop concert.

In their excitement, they did not notice the man leaning on the door frame watching them with crossed arms.

"Holy hell!" Jordan yelled as he spotted him in the doorway. "You cannot sneak up on people like that. Are you trying to give us a heart attack with your Michael Myers impression over there? Halloween was almost two weeks ago."

Adrian raised an eyebrow, trying to stifle a laugh. "I tried to say hello, but I was overwhelmed by the squealing." He strode over to Cori and planted a kiss on the top of her head. "I left my ski mask at home today, anyway. Ready to head out?"

"Michael Myers does not wear a ski mask." Jordan huffed, shuffling his papers into folders on the desk. He angrily scooped up a pile of paper clips. "You just waltz in here with your tight T-shirt and—party over." Dull green jealousy radiated from his aura. "This is one of the biggest moments our organization has had in the past two years. There is no way in hell you're just going to head home with your hot boyfriend and not celebrate this."

He pulled out a disinfecting wipe, clicked the cover shut emphatically, and began vigorously wiping the surface of her desk.

"Oh God," Cori said cautiously, glancing expectantly at Adrian. "He's starting to rage clean. He means business. Carl's?"

"Obviously." Jordan smiled easily, his jealousy melting away as he pulled out his phone. "I'm sending a text to Jess and Anne to meet us there." He rolled his eyes. "I'll tell Anne she might as well bring Geoff."

Jordan and Geoff had not been on good terms recently after a heated argument over who Rory Gilmore's preferred boyfriend had been. Geoff was team Dean, and according to Jordan that was *the biggest red flag he had ever seen.*

"I'll ask Prudence to meet up with us," Cori suggested, pulling out her own phone.

Jordan arched his brow.

"Make sure she brings those hotties she's been camping with." Jordan had liked Prudence immediately when he met her. Everyone had. The more Cori got to know her over the past two months, the more she knew it was incredibly hard *not* to like Pru. She had an infectious, bubbly charm that seemed to win over everyone she met.

Pru was spending almost all her time with the Huxleys when she wasn't taking a turn guarding Cori or patrolling town for signs of dark magic. She had helped Hannah with a complicated series of charms to defend the farm, and she had won over Ariel when she gifted her a crystal that glowed warm in her hand when someone nearby had sinister intentions.

For the first time since she was a young child, perhaps for the first time in her life, Cori felt like she had a genuine friend.

Someone who knew the real her and accepted her for what she was. Death threats, sinister prophecies, and all.

Despite Pru's sweet and genuine likeability, Jordan seemed even more drawn to Alfie. It was easy to imagine why.

Alfie had a casual confidence and a sharp, sarcastic tongue that was incredibly seductive, if not a bit grating. Most of his clothes were sleek black and high fashion. With the contrast of his platinum blond hair, black leather jacket, and tall, muscular frame, he looked like he stepped right off the pages of *British Vogue*. Although Alfie tried to play it cool, Cori could sense the satisfaction oozing from him any time Jordan entered the room and started drooling.

"I'll meet you guys there," Jordan said as he gathered up his things. "Jess said I should drive home first so I can have as many drinks as I want, and she can drive me back to our place later. Plus, I need to grab a heavier coat." He winked at them as he grabbed his car keys. The days had become shorter and the nights bitterly cold as November weather settled on the coast.

Cori gathered her own things at her desk, noting the sun was dipping low on the horizon over the trees. The tops of the pines stood out in dark contrast against the amber glow of the sunset.

Her tattered notebook was tucked into her bag, and she realized with a pang of guilt that she had forgotten to mark down the day. November 10th. Forty-one days until the solstice.

She felt Adrian slip his arms around her, and she leaned into him. "Congratulations, Cor." His voice rumbled through her chest as she stared out the window over the bay.

These past few months had felt like a blur. It was inconceivable to her how she could feel so at ease with someone she had known for such a short period. Everything about him—the feel of his hair between her fingers, the curve of his shoulder, the muscular fortress of his arms around her—felt like home.

She knew why. And she had a feeling he knew, too, even though they had not spoken about it.

Part of her magic was sensing the emotions of others, but she was starting to sense Adrian even when she was not physically near him. He had jumped into the water yesterday when the line on one of their traps had broken, and although he was nearly a mile offshore when it happened, Cori had felt a flush of ice dance on her skin the moment his body hit the water. She shivered when he told her about it later.

Adrian's magic was...it felt like home. There was something comfortable about him she had not felt since she had left San Francisco. As she felt his arms around her, she let his magic penetrate her skin. Her body surged with a salty, cool mist of the ocean beyond her window, and the air became heavy with the smell of pine. Cool mint danced on her tongue as his magic washed over her all her senses.

She pulled away after a moment and took his hand. "It's a Friday night," she reasoned with a mischievous shrug of her shoulder. "Might as well go get a little sloppy at the bar."

He smirked back at her. "As long as you promise to let me get sloppy with you later."

Her lip curled as she let her imagination run wild with heat, and she knew he could feel her desire at the thought. His gaze narrowed on her as she closed her eyes and sucked in a breath. "Deal."

They set out on the path into town as leaves drifted down from the trees. The air was pleasantly crisp, and the spiced aromas wafting from the bakery filled the atmosphere with the smells of autumn.

The equinox had come and gone uneventfully, but an unease stirred within Cori with the realization that the seasons had changed a final time before the impending winter solstice. A chill rippled across her skin.

Despite their closeness. Despite feeling the bond take root, stronger with each breath, there was one thing she didn't have the courage to share with him. With anyone.

The secret of her father's prophecy remained locked in her heart.

Whenever Enzo's name was mentioned in conversation, powerful hatred surged from Adrian, his aura a bright crimson with angry swirls churning around him like a hurricane. He felt that Enzo's involvement in the LARC was the ultimate betrayal, and he was more than happy to keep her safe and hidden for the next forty-one days.

Cori had been secretly tracking Enzo's and Calvin's whereabouts through the LARC's social media. Prudence's father had planted some wiretaps in their boardroom. Paolo was right. They were planning to kill her at the site of the formation of the Covenant.

But nobody knew that she planned to leave for Salem to meet them there.

Adrian dropped her hand and put his arm over her shoulder as they walked up the path to Carl's. "You OK?"

She sighed. "I'm OK," she assured him as she tipped her eyes up to the sky. The half-moon allowed the stars to surface with bright radiance.

"There's the woman of the hour." Seth's booming voice grounded them back to reality as he set up the steps, his arm wrapped around Jess as Jordan trailed behind them, scrolling on his phone. "Jordan tried to explain something about a chi-square..."

"Seth learned that a chi-square and a chai latte are not the same thing," Jordan scoffed.

Jess stifled a laugh.

"Whatever. It seems like a super impressive thing that only smart people would understand. But I'm always down for drinking to celebrate."

When they entered Carl's, Anne and Geoff had already secured them a large booth in the back in the direct line of sight of the television airing the Patriots game. Seth and Geoff immediately became invested in the game as Jess and Jordan ordered a round for the table.

Cori felt the air become heavy with magic as Prudence and Alfie sauntered in. Prudence wore a fashionable cashmere sweater with a neat, pleated skirt that hit just above the knee and navy tights. She pulled her Chanel lipstick out of her designer handbag and used her phone camera as a mirror to reapply. Alfie, as usual, looked like he stepped right off the runway, even though he was wearing a plain black T-shirt and strategically ripped jeans.

Alfie and Pru tried to fit in around town these past couple of weeks, but they always turned heads wherever they showed up. The dangerously cool vibe they gave off was in stark contrast to the rugged and laid-back attitude embraced by the locals.

Prudence gave Carl a warm smile and a hug when she spotted him coming near their table. "Carl! Did you try that snickerdoodle recipe I gave you?" she asked him excitedly, wrinkling her nose.

"I did, honey," he replied. "I would have never thought to add cardamom, but you were right again." She winked at him as he ushered her into the booth. "Cori, I heard you had a major scientific breakthrough today. Should I pour you a glass of that nice Riesling we got last week?"

"Carl, you're the best."

The barkeep blushed for a moment as he wiped down their table. "My pleasure, kiddo. Adrian, I'll grab you a nice, dark ale," he said, clapping him on the shoulder. Carl hurried away to the bar as Pru settled into the booth next to Cori.

"Fern is here, too," Prudence informed Cori in a low voice. "She's doing a perimeter check." With her nose ring, multiple tattoos, and electric blue hair, Fern would fit right in at any biker bar. Cori smiled to herself as she pictured the Mainer locals gawking at Fern as she stalked around the bar. Unlike the other Gray witches, Fern was quiet, sullen, and introverted. She was all business. Calculated and cunning.

Cori watched Fern slide into the booth like a ghost, nodding at them. "Everyone checks out," she reported to Pru as she pulled out her phone and started scrolling. Even though she appeared to be absent-mindedly scanning through social media, Cori knew she was watching the door as she turned over a crimson red crystal in her palm.

Shortly after their second round of drinks, the conversation got heated.

"You mean to tell me you're fine with what he did?" Jordan asked with disgust.

"What did she expect him to do? Shut down his life for her?" Geoff replied heatedly.

"The guy claimed to love her, and she was out of the picture for less than a fucking day before he did her dirty!" Jordan fired back.

"*They were on a break!*" Geoff argued, throwing up his hands.

Anne shook her head as she took a long sip of her beer. "Are we still arguing about Ross and Rachel twenty years later?" she asked in disbelief.

Jordan put his hand on her arm gently. "I am saying this because I love you. If you need the name of a good divorce lawyer, I know a guy. And you can stay with me anytime, right, Jess?"

Jess laughed, shaking her head. "Absolutely, Anne, we got your back."

Cori smiled, letting the warmth of wine and friendship wash over her. She leaned back into the booth, sighing deeply and savoring the feeling of being comfortable and a little tipsy.

But the peaceful feeling was fleeting. She had just finished her second glass of wine when the sharp edges of a folded piece of paper materialized in her hand. Her stomach turned and her heart pounded like a hammer as she unfolded the paper under the table. She recognized the curling lilt of her mother's handwriting immediately.

351-555-1221

Just a phone number.

She looked down at her hands as all the blood drained from her face. Her friends continued chatting heartily around the table, undeterred and unaware of what she had just received. When she met Adrian's eyes however, he was fixed on her, worry etched into his face.

He knew. *He felt it, too.*

She shot him a pleading look, and he rose from the seat casually. "Yawn...early day tomorrow," he announced. "Cor, you want to walk home with me?"

Seth arched a suspicious brow at him. Tomorrow was Saturday.

"Sure, I'm exhausted anyway after all that number crunching." She rose from her seat as well, kissing Jordan good-night before they hurried out the door, hearts pounding in tandem.

ADRIAN

"Cori, what's wrong?" Adrian walked briskly behind her as they hiked up the dirt road that led to the cliffside. She was hyperventilating, and her legs moved in short frantic steps over the road. The beat of her heart drummed through him, even though he was not physically touching her. Adrenaline in her veins fueled his own.

"I'm scared to say it out loud," she said, out of breath. They turned the corner onto her street as the cottage came into view ahead of them.

As they rounded the path, she held out her arms, willing the front door open magically with a hushed spell. She waited until he was inside before she walked through the house, locking the windows and doors, carefully spreading magical reinforcements over them.

When she finally stopped moving, she held out her shaking hand to him, revealing the note.

He drew in a breath. "Who is it from?"

"My mother."

He took a step back. "What does it say?"

She opened it and presented it to him.

"Just a phone number?" His brow furrowed as he turned the

paper over in his hand. Anxious tension bubbled over in Cori as she turned the charm bracelet on her arm.

She paced. "I need to call her," Cori said.

"Are you nuts?" he bit out, perhaps a bit hastily. "What if this is a trap?"

"It's her handwriting, Adrian," she said quickly, growing irritated at his hesitation.

"What if your brother..." He took a steadying breath, his shoulders tightening as the thought of Enzo sent rage through him. "What if your brother forged her handwriting?"

"It's from her," she said simply.

"OK, fine. Maybe it is from her. What if someone forced her to write it. What if they're trying to get your phone number? Or worse, your location?"

His words bounced off her. Her eyes widened as though possessed, her pupils dilating, transforming her already dark eyes into black voids. "I'll call her now." She made her way to her purse and searched for her cell phone.

Adrian grabbed it from her.

"Cori, stop!" Her eyes were completely opaque. Something wasn't right. "At least let Prudence and Alfie look at this note first. Please," he pleaded with her. "Don't do anything yet."

She slammed her hand down on the table, glaring at him. A shiver of fear ran across his skin. "We don't have that kind of time!" she shouted at him. Despite the stern tone of her voice, her expression was empty. A blank void. "I'm sorry, Adrian," she said in an otherworldly voice. A whispered incantation escaped her lips.

An intense pressure built on his arms.

He reached for her but, before he could touch her, ropes materialized from thin air, binding his arms to his sides. They coiled and spread over his legs, tightening around him with magic that was so fierce his heart hammered with dread.

The tension of the ropes bore down on him, and his chest became tight as it became harder and harder to draw in a breath. Rough fibers scratched his skin, coiling onto his neck.

Cori turned slowly, as if she were sleepwalking, and headed toward the old rotary phone on the wall.

"Please," he called out with a strangled breath. Ropes were squeezing the air from his lungs while they cut off his air supply at his throat. Her hand drifted up as though she were suspended by strings. Her fingers turned the numbers on the dial, releasing them one by one.

The phone rang once, twice. The blank look on Cori's face was replaced with one of confusion, her eyes widening as the color returned to them. Adrian gasped for breath when the ropes released him. He untangled the coils, now loose around his limbs. Before he could make his way to her, a click sounded in the air followed by a soft, panicked voice.

"Hello?" someone whispered quickly. A flash of recognition echoed in her eyes.

"Mama?" she breathed.

"Cordelia, listen to me." The voice on the phone echoed over the receiver, loud enough to be heard across the room. "You need to hide. Now. They're trying to use me to get to you, but I won't let them do it. The coven is corrupted. Your brother—" A deep, baritone voice called her mother's name from a distance on the other side of the receiver.

The muffled sounds of raised voices on the other end of the line were washed in static as there was a struggle for the phone. A definitive click reverberated through the cottage as the phone went dead in her hands and the call dropped.

She froze, staring at the rotary phone in shock.

Dread shrouded him. It didn't matter what Astrid had done. She was Cori's only family, and now she was in trouble.

"Take a breath," he said.

"Your arms." She traced her fingers over the ligature marks the ropes had branded on his skin.

"That wasn't you, and you know it." Her eyes met his, brow furrowed. "It was almost like you were possessed or something."

She glanced back down at the note, now crumpled in her hand. "I don't recognize the number. Or the area code."

She had been bewitched somehow, and she had not been in control of her body when she summoned the ropes. Someone was using her as an extension of their magic. Dark magic.

The feeling of panic deepened as he inhaled the sting of burning wood. His eyes watered, and he turned toward the source of the smell. The old rotary telephone on the wall was being enveloped in wispy tendrils of smoke.

The smoke poured into the room as eerie blue flames curled from the wall. Adrian walked to the sink, attempting to summon water, but none would come.

"This has never happened to me before," he said through gritted teeth, his chest heaving as he used all his energy. Still, nothing came.

"We need to get out of here!" she yelled through the hiss of the smoke as the wall set ablaze. The fire curled and cracked through everything it touched with an unnatural speed.

They ran toward the front door and turned the handle, but it didn't budge. The magic of her earlier charm was heavy on the door, sealing it closed. She tried to reverse the spell, touching the door, yelling the incantation into the air, but again, nothing happened.

Adrian looked around in a panic. "The fire is keeping us from using our magic somehow." He ran through the room trying every window that he could. Every single one of them was sealed tight. "Cori, is there any part of the house you didn't use a security charm on?"

She spun on her heel, racking her brain for a solution. "The window over the kitchen sink!" The antique, wavy glass didn't open the way a traditional window did, and she had never sealed it because there was no way to physically get through it.

"We have to break it," he said to her.

She nodded, pulling her shirt over her mouth. They made their way through the building smoke to the window in the kitchen, pulling open drawers. "We won't be able to use magic to get out of here," he said, grabbing a rusty hammer out of the top drawer. "We're going to have to do this the old-fashioned way. Stand back!"

She shielded her eyes as he drew his arm back, thrusting the hammer at the window. Glass shattered onto the countertop. He grabbed a towel, coughing into the smoke, and cleared the glass quickly before he hoisted her toward the now open window.

She leaped out of the window, a large boxwood on the other side breaking her fall, as she slid into the sharp, waxy leaves and brambles. Adrian followed behind her, blood dripping down his arm from where the glass had shattered against his hands, leaving red splatters on the green leaves that broke his fall.

They scrambled to the path that led away from the house as they saw the smoke rising above them. The roof was completely engulfed in the eerie blue flames now as a thick column of black smoke snaked up into the sky.

Adrian pulled out his phone as he heard a yell from the path.

Hannah and David were running toward them. Hannah ran to Cori, embracing her as David approached the house. "Are you OK? We saw the smoke." David looked for signs of life from up and down the road. The neighboring houses were dark and quiet.

"Adrian, over here! Help me with the hydrant." The cap of the hydrant popped off magically as a gush of water came pouring out. David concentrated his force onto the water, diverting it to the house as Adrian directed the spray to the roof. Despite the intensity of the spray, the fire grew.

"What the hell kind of fire is this?" David yelled to them through gritted teeth.

Adrian's concentration over the water faltered at the sound of his mother's panicked voice. "Oh Goddess. What is she doing here?"

The dark figure of a young woman was walking toward them. As she came closer, Ariel was drawn to the fire like a moth to a flame, curiosity etched into her features.

As she approached them on the path, power and intensity pulsed from her as she regarded the fire with a look of amusement. It was jarring to see her walking so calmly toward something so chaotic.

"Ariel, no!" Hannah called to her.

If Ariel heard her mother's voice, she didn't acknowledge it as she stopped in front of the house. She planted her feet on the ground and raised her hands high into the air, cocking her head slightly to the side. A small smile curled from her lips as she lowered her hands slowly.

She moved. The fire responded. Like a stove burner that had been turned down to a simmer, it died. A smile spread on Ariel's face as a deep, red glow burned in her eyes. She bent her knees slowly, pulling her body to the ground as the fire was muted to a smolder.

By the time her hands reached the gravel below, the once ferocious fire had been extinguished completely. A sizzle of electric energy intermingled with the charred smell of wood in the air as thin wisps of smoke dissipated.

Hannah was frozen in space as she watched her youngest child rise slowly off the ground. After a few moments of stunned silence, Ariel laughed—a slow, deep cackle that turned somewhat maniacal after a few moments. But Ariel silenced, her eyes blank.

The last thing Adrian heard before his sister's lifeless body collapsed to the ground was a scream from his mother's throat.

CORI

Alfie walked Cori back to the Huxleys. The electric ash in the air burned her nose, fueling the acidity in her throat. Her body was so numb, she floated into the house without realizing where her limbs were taking her.

She slumped into the kitchen chair as the kettle whistled on the stove. Prudence poured hot water over tea bags, but the herbal aromas that wafted from their mugs indicated there was more than just tea in those cups. Pru bounded up the stairs to Ariel's room with the tea and a tray of vials filled with mysterious substances.

David paced the kitchen as Seth cleaned Adrian's wounds. The sound of Hannah's sobs echoed down the stairs as Cori fought the rise of vomit in her throat.

This. This was exactly what she feared, playing out and coming to life all at once. The cottage that Anne had graciously let her live in was destroyed. She had nearly strangled Adrian. His arms—the vomit was rising into her throat.

Ariel. She had almost died extinguishing that fire. There was no guarantee that she would make it. The murmur of Alfie's voice broke through the buzzing in her ear, reassuring her that Prudence would heal her, but it didn't matter. She could have died. She still might die.

Because of me. Because of my prophecy.

She had allowed herself to get close to this man. *This family.* All because of some horrible twist of fate from the Giver. She cursed at every ounce of magic within her, her Eye shriveling in her inner contempt.

I don't want it anymore, she prayed to the Giver. *Take it back. Take back my magic. Take back the bond of fate.*

The smoothness of Alfie's voice broke through her thoughts. "We got the story straight with Anne and Geoff," he explained as he rubbed his temples. "I told her that the two of you discovered the house on fire when you returned from the bar. Geoff went on and on about some electrical issue they had there right before you moved in and seems to be convinced that was the source. Poor guy feels dreadful about the whole thing."

"How did you explain that the fire extinguished itself?" David asked with a raised brow. He and Seth exchanged a worried look before diverting their eyes up the staircase.

Alfie shook his head heavily. "Wasn't too hard. When the fire department got there and started asking us questions, I modified their memories. The crew at the fire department now believes they put out the fire. The chief also told Geoff he found some faulty wires behind the old rotary phone."

"How do you modify their memories and not use dark magic?" Adrian asked curiously.

Alfie shrugged. "It's not too hard. Before you say the spell, you need to cast away the dark element. Only a Gray witch would be able to do it without projecting dark magic through the spell. When you cast out the dark element, you can use the spell only for pure purposes. If you try to use it for personal gain, it won't work."

Cori's head spun. The more she learned about Gray magic, the more awestruck she was with it.

Prudence appeared in the stairwell, her face pale and her shoulder slumped. Cori's heart dropped as every face in the room angled expectantly toward the stairs.

"Ariel is going to be OK," she said with a shaky voice. "She's awake, but she's exhausted."

The Huxley men let out a collective sigh of relief. Cori allowed herself to breathe deeply, sucking in air, pushing away the nausea. Adrian looked toward Cori, but she diverted her eyes.

"Now on to my next patient," Pru said, setting down her bag and pulling out a large jar of salve. She settled in the chair next to Adrian, scrunching her face up as he exposed his lacerations to her.

Cori put her head in her hands. His arms looked like meat that had gone through a grinder. The same voice whispered to her. *Because of me.*

Adrian flinched as Prudence dabbed a thick, tarry liquid from an amber bottle onto a cotton ball. As it contacted his skin, he winced in pain at the burn but watched in wonder as the thick goo bubbled over his wounds and they faded into his skin. By the time she was finished, the lacerations looked like they were old, healed, and mildly scarred. She rubbed a thick salve over his skin with a cotton ball.

He leaned back in the kitchen chair, regarding his wounds. "What is that stuff?"

"It's Sanitatem," she replied as she wrapped gauze around his skin. "An ancient healing potion."

"Prudence is quite gifted in potion-making, especially for healing arts," Alfie said warmly. It was rare for him to give a compliment like that, and it made her blush a little.

"My grandmother was a *Saludadore*," she explained. "A Gray witch with healing powers. She taught me some of her best potions when I was little."

Cori's Eye flashed into Prudence's past.

A tiny girl, no older than six or seven years old, stood on a kitchen chair next to a farmhouse sink. The woman next to her was petite, her skin wrinkled yet smooth. Smile lines encircled her eyes. Herbs were ground with a mortar and pestle as the little girl pulled petals off a flower.

The woman reached over and tucked a blossom into the little girl's hair as she tickled her side. The girl giggled as she dropped the petals into a heavy, ancient-looking cauldron.

As Cori returned to herself, she found the entire table was staring at her intently.

"You had a vision?" Adrian asked, worry etched into his face.

Cori nodded, disgusted with her Eye for not listening to her prayers. "Your grandmother reminds me a lot of you, Pru."

"You saw Gram?" Pru asked dreamily. "Was she here in the room? Like a spirit?"

Cori shook her head. "No, I saw you standing at a big sink with her." As she explained what she saw in the vision, she noticed tears well in Prudence's eyes. Even Alfie seemed a little choked up.

"She was a sweet little lady," Alfie smiled.

From across the table, David rubbed his face in thought. "Cori, you get these visions randomly?"

She shifted uncomfortably in her seat. "Yes. They usually come to me when someone near me is experiencing a strong feeling. When Pru mentioned about her grandmother—it was a powerful emotion of nostalgia. The emotion leads to the vision."

"You can't choose what you see and don't see?" he asked.

"Well, I can choose to see into someone's life if they allow me to read them. Like the day Prudence let me read her on the island. I need to be physically touching someone, and they choose what I see."

"What about spirits?"

"What do you mean?" She knew exactly what he meant, but she was hoping she was wrong.

"Can you summon a spirit?"

There it was. The connection between Celestials and the spirit realm was a mystery. Despite her connection, she did not know what the afterlife was like. Nonna had warned her about talking too much about the spirit realm with other witches. The Giver did not give them information they were not supposed to have. And what happened in the spirit realm was the biggest mystery of the universe.

She sighed deep, her shoulders tensing as she diverted her eyes to the table. "No."

The last time she had seen a spirit, her father had appeared to her in the middle of the night. The garden bench where he had sat with her was now burned to a crisp. Now was not the right time to mention her visit from her father. *Would it ever be the right time?*

She felt Adrian squeeze her shoulder, and she swallowed the lump of guilt down into her chest. Her Eye blinked a warning. *He deserves to know.*

She pushed her Eye down into her gut where it belonged, silencing it.

"It's a shame you can't just turn on what's happening like a news show," David continued shaking his head. "You must be terrified about what's going on with your mother right now."

Alfie and Prudence exchanged a serious look. "Speaking of that, we need to talk about what happened tonight," Pru said in a serious tone. "We looked at the note your mother sent you, and there were two serious dark magic charms connected to it."

A chill ran down her spine. "How?" she asked.

Alfie pulled the note out of his pocket. "Don't worry, all the magic has been banished from it," he explained with a furrowed brow. "Whoever cast this has a deep understanding of dark magic."

Pru nodded in agreement. "Not a casual dark magic user," she interjected.

"Quite," Alfie agreed. "The first spell was a *compulsion*. Cori, did you feel drawn to call the phone number on the paper? Pulled to do it no matter the cost?"

Her head throbbed as she recalled the feeling of panic and drive that had washed over her as she had held the paper. She nodded.

"When you were walking to the phone," Adrian chimed in, "It was like you were possessed. I tried to stop you, but you..."

Her blood turned to ice as she remembered the ropes that she had summoned. "I cast a *rope bind* on you," she replied. Her eyes flitted to the ligature marks on his arm as she felt tears well. Prudence's hand gripped hers with a comforting squeeze.

Prudence frowned deeply. "Compulsion forces you to complete a task at all costs. It drives you to strike out against anyone who tried to stop you. It's a truly evil way for a witch to force their hand."

"As soon as I finished dialing the number, I felt the spell lift," Cori explained.

Alfie rubbed his temples, processing the information. "The second charm was a *conduction*," he explained. "By itself, conduction is not dark. In fact, your mother's clever note-passing charm is conduction." He raised an eyebrow. "When you use conduction to transfer harm to another witch however, dark elements become embedded into the spell."

"Whoever tied the charms to the note sent fire to us with a conduction spell?" Adrian asked, his jaw tightening.

Alfie nodded, crossing his arms. "Through the phone. It was not just any fire they sent you. It was *Byzantine fire*."

"What the hell is that?" David asked anxiously, bracing himself to process exactly what his daughter had taken on.

"Zion is looking into it," Prudence explained.

Zion was a brilliant magical historian, a witch who specialized in the history of magic and how it pertained to the modern practices. He spent most of his time back at their camp doing research.

"I knew it was something really rare and powerful when you described it, David," Pru said.

"It grew when we tried to put it out with water," David explained, anger edging his words.

"That's because Byzantine fire is an ancient form of warfare. It's a magically enhanced fire that the Greek witches used against the Romans. Water cannot put it out," Pru said darkly. "It also seals anything near it that's been touched with magic."

Cori shivered. They had been trapped in the house by her own protective spells. Whoever sent the fire knew that the house would have been warded. Grief washed over her. There were only two people in the world that knew the routine that Cori would use to seal her house.

Enzo.

Adrian tensed in his chair, and Cori knew he had gleaned the same thought. "What kind of sick fuck would try to use something like that on another person?" he asked through a tightened jaw.

"A sick fuck who wanted to kill you," Alfie explained, his eyes narrowing.

Adrian's shoulders tensed, red tendrils painted in black rolling off his aura as the humidity in the room grew.

"Whoever summoned the Byzantine fire had one flaw in their plan," Prudence explained, a mischievous smirk tugging at her lip. "They didn't count on the fact that a Fire Elemental would be nearby. Only a Fire witch can extinguish it."

David went pale. "Does that mean only a Fire witch could have summoned it?" he asked.

Prudence nodded. A chill ran down Cori's spine. Ariel had almost died extinguishing that fire. Just how many witches out there were involved in the plot of her murder?

Alfie and Prudence exchanged a serious look. "We've been thinking. I think we should leave. Soon. We need to come up with a plan to go into hiding. Pru and I think the safest place to go right now will be to the campsite. It's highly fortified with protective spells."

Cori's eyes widened in panic. This was not part of the plan. If they whisked her away to some remote location, it would make it infinitely harder for her to sneak off to Salem in December. Adrian grabbed her hand. When she looked up at him, his eyes were fixed on her, as though sending her an unspoken message.

The group discussed a preliminary plan for a few moments, but Cori could only hear the muffle of their voices over the churning of her mind.

Waves of bitter remorse whipped through her like the ocean

in the eye of a hurricane. She nodded back at Adrian as they rose from the table together, the feel of his magic a comfort to her, despite her internal unrest. As the screen door squeaked behind them, her hand still clasped around his, she felt as though they were walking directly into the path of the storm.

CORI

Cori awoke alone in the tent the next morning to the sound of the ocean's roar. The cliffside campsite on the periphery of Huxley Farm was adjacent to a cluster of greenhouses, and as she peered through the tent flap, the late morning light danced off the glass and metal frames in the distance.

She squinted as her eyes adjusted to the gleam.

Adrian had agreed to accompany the Gray witches when they left town with Cori. Even though his sister was still unconscious. Even though Cori was the reason they were all in danger. Despite the rope bind that she had cast on him. With no regard for the lacerations that marred his arms. He was willing to risk everything for her.

And it made her sick.

The remnants of hot tears stung her eyes as she examined the sky, the fading moon low on the horizon. Stars tumbled above her, whispering despite the light of the sun drowning them out.

She desperately needed to tell Adrian about her father's prophecy. A large part of her wanted to run. Hiding was always comfortable for her, but Adrian had made it clear—he was ready to follow her.

She took a breath, her heart cracking with the bite of Enzo's betrayal. Somehow, power had won over love. She knew her brother had to still love her. Love is not something you can turn off, like a switch.

As she approached the steps of the Airstream, Adrian and Zion spoke in hushed whispers through the door. She halted, gripping the cold metal of the door frame.

"Wherever you plan to take her, I'm coming with you," Adrian explained matter-of-factly. "I already told my dad that I wouldn't be getting on the boat again until after the solstice."

"I figured," Zion's deep voice replied.

Cori peeked into the trailer. Zion was hunched over his laptop at the dinette with Adrian. He reached back to his record player and grabbed a Marvin Gaye record from the stack. The Gray witch was constantly researching, even in the middle of a conversation.

Like Cori, Zion had received a conventional education in addition to a magical one, earning his doctorate in Medieval Studies from Harvard last year before joining Prudence's team.

He typed feverishly as he conjured a flame to his incense, washing the campsite with the scent of patchouli. His uncanny ability to multitask truly baffled Cori.

"I haven't found the person I'm fated to yet...if there is one." Zion shook his head. "But if I were in your position, I wouldn't let her out of my sight. I don't know how you two are handling it."

Cori held her breath in the shadow of the door as she waited for Adrian to respond. They had still not spoken of the bond, even though his magic wound itself more tightly around her with every passing day.

Adrian sucked in a breath, and it felt as though time were standing still. She tamped her magic down as she waited for his response.

"I've never been more terrified in my life," he replied with a ragged sigh. Even though she couldn't physically see him from her position in the doorway, she sensed him dragging his hands through his thick chestnut hair. "If something happened to her, I don't know if I could make it."

She let go of her breath. He had not denied being fated to her. She had a feeling he must know as strongly as she did, even though it had not been brought up in their conversation. But what he said in response to Zion made her stomach turn. This was exactly what she had feared when she first saw him, walking toward her on the beach with the impending tide rolling toward her.

How could she drag another witch into her cursed destiny? Especially now. Especially *him*. After all he has already gone through. Adrian may be fated to her, but the entire Huxley family had been at risk because of her. She closed her eyes and let her Eye bubble forward.

You love him.

She had never let herself think so freely of it before this moment. He had become a part of her, something that was interwoven into her existence. She bit back tears when she realized what her death would do to him. The bond was already too strong. Maybe Enzo wouldn't kill her on the solstice, thanks to her father's sacrifice.

But someone else in the LARC might step up and finish the job. Adrian would never be capable of loving anyone else in his life if she was killed.

You need to tell him what you plan to do.

She had never felt so on the brink of death. The experience in the fire made it seem more real. Death threats were always a part of her future, something she had been preparing for over the past nearly ten years. Adrian was recently thrust into this. Her guilt was immense and all-consuming.

If she tried to run away, she knew he would stop at nothing until he found her and assured her safety.

Her hand tightened on the handle of the door as she hoisted herself up on the metal stair.

"Good morning," she said nonchalantly as she slid into the dinette seat next to Zion.

Across the table, Adrian's face flushed and his heart quickened, the blue pools of his eyes swirling.

"Zion and I were researching the best places to go into hiding," he said hastily. He slid his long leg across the table brushing it against her calf. Her cheeks brightened as she leaned toward the laptop to get a better look at the map on the screen.

"Acadia?" she questioned. A northern territory of Maine's national park was highlighted.

"Acadia is protected natural land. There are several areas north of the park that are rich in iron ore. The Brits used to mine the area before it became protected. Hiding there is a good idea if you are fleeing dark magic," Zion explained.

"What do iron mines have anything to do with dark magic?" Cori asked, an eyebrow arched inquisitively.

Zion stretched his arms and smiled excitedly. As a magical historian, he never missed an opportunity for a history lesson, and he got a gleeful glint in his dark brown eyes whenever he was asked to delve into the past.

He tied his braids into a neat ponytail as he dug under the seat, producing an ancient-looking book with a thick brown leather binding that gleamed in the light of the overhead lamp. He casually gestured toward the coffeepot that floated to Cori magically. She greedily filled her cup.

"It's documented well into the Middle Ages that the element of iron has been used by humans to ward off evil. It's the reason horseshoes were used as good luck charms and hung over the doors of ancient dwellings. People believed that iron repelled darkness. Magical historians have traced it back to witches in antiquity setting out three iron stakes in a triangle around their homes to repel those who practiced dark arts."

Zion and Adrian exchanged a look before Adrian spoke again. "My family owns a cabin up north of Bar Harbor near some of the old mines. My grandfather passed it to my dad. It's a great fishing spot. Right near the Devil's Oven."

"Devil's Oven?" she asked incredulously.

Adrian smirked at her as he took a deep swig from his own mug.

"Terrible name for a place to hide out from evil. The irony is real. But—it's a very protected place," Zion explained, the subtle Caribbean accent blooming in his voice. "The rangers in the park won't even speak of it. Many humans who have tried to explore the area have gotten injured or killed."

"It's a place that can only be safely inhabited by a Water elemental," Adrian chimed in with a wink.

Her pulse quickened. They planned to hide out in a dangerous camp near a cursed cave. She spun her charm bracelet as she sipped her coffee. Adrian's eyes swept over her face, and she knew he sensed her anxiety.

His large hand clasped over her own, squeezing. When she looked up into his eyes, his amusement had melted away. "Cori, I would never bring you somewhere I thought you were going to be in danger," Adrian assured her. She locked her eyes on his face, feeling the sincerity of his words wash over her. Electric bites of his magic charged his touch.

Guilt washed over her again. If it was hard for dark witches to find her there, it would be even harder for her to escape.

"It would be extremely unlikely for a dark witch to get to us out there. Between the iron under the earth and the protection of the ocean," Zion paused dramatically. "It would be a death sentence. It's a perfect place to wait it out until the solstice."

She let out a tenuous sigh and shrugged. "Forty more days. I guess this is our only option."

"It's a good option, though," Zion assured her. "Prudence, Lionel, and I are coming with you. We're going to park the Airstream near the cabin away from the danger of the ocean so we can sense if anyone is coming. Alfie is going to stay here to guard the Huxleys and Anne's place. Prudence's dad put together a task force in California to try to track what happened to your mother after the fire. Fern is going to be in charge. She took the first flight out this morning."

A chill ran down her spine and her lips tightened into a thin line as she digested the plan. If anyone could find her mother, it was Fern. The Gray witch moved like an angry ghost and tackled every task without fear.

"I already wrote to Anne last night and told her I had a family emergency back in California and would need to be out of work for the foreseeable future," Cori chimed in.

It had been difficult to lie to Anne and even more difficult to ask for time away from her work. The more time she spent at her new job, the more she fell in love with the research. She would miss out on submitting her data and the rough draft of her paper to the EPA.

"I'm sorry you have to miss out on your data submission," Zion said sympathetically, shaking his head. If anyone would understand, it was him. "Before you know it, this will all be behind us. You won't have this prophecy hanging over your head, and all of us Gray witches can practice magic peacefully, without having to patrol and police everyone else." A determined look flashed in his eyes as they grew quiet.

"Then life can really begin," Adrian said, breaking the silence. Her attention snapped to his face, and he smiled back at her.

She couldn't stop the flush rising to her face as she soaked in his smile, because she knew exactly what he meant by those words. Their life really could begin—together. If they made it.

ADRIAN

The light was a muted rose gold as dusk approached. Adrian steered the truck through the familiar, spruce-lined side roads with ease but slowed to assure he could keep the truck trailing him in his sight line. Lionel was driving his own truck behind them. The Gray witch was skilled at guiding the large camper trailer, but these roads were winding and steep in some places.

After turning down a hidden driveway, Adrian pulled to the side of the property, stopping to help them park on the grassy embankment at the edge of the grounds overlooking the sea.

Adrian took Cori's hand, guiding her to the rocky trail that led to the cabin. He had warned her on the ride that the rocks could be slippery and jagged as he steered her down the path between two roughly hewn cliffs. The path was so narrow in some places that they had to turn sideways as they walked.

Adrian stayed ahead, making sure the rock was free of any moisture that would cause her to lose her footing.

The water was already snaking near the path as high tide approached. Within the hour, the path to the cabin would be covered in water, and there would be no way to get to the little cabin on the top of the embankment.

He knew this path like the back of his hand. His family had

spent countless weekends here through the years. After David's father had passed, it became a somewhat more somber place to visit, but Adrian held nothing but warm memories of the place.

As they reached the clearing on the rocky outlet where the cabin was perched, Cori gasped. The cliffside around them sparkled with sea glass and the waves below billowed onto the shore. Despite the cold autumn air, some wildflowers danced in the wind, coaxed to adapt to this unwelcoming climate with Hannah's magic.

"It's beautiful," she said as she took in the view. Beautiful and remote. A perfect place for them to hide. No electricity. No address. No paved roads. Impossible to find unless you knew where it was. He wanted to scoop her up and fold his arms around her, concealing her here forever.

When she wasn't near him, it was as if a part of his heart was outside his body. A part of his heart that was in danger and not guaranteed.

Her face angled up to the sky, like it always did, and the glow of the setting sun settled on the curve of her cheekbones and the golden streaks in her hair that blew in messy waves around her face.

He traced the light with his eyes, down her face and over the curve of her neck. He walked ahead of her into the cabin, trying hard to conceal from her how much he wanted to run his hands over her skin, but he knew she could sense it.

Once inside, he uncovered the furniture and set the wood-stove alight with a match. She waved her hands over a few candles, coaxing them aglow. He smiled to himself as he recalled how Ariel had made Cori promise to never teach Adrian a candle-lighting spell.

His sister had woken up this afternoon. She had opened her eyes, focused on her mother's face, and asked, "Did you see me put out that fire? I'm a badass bitch, Ma."

At that moment, they knew Ariel was going to make a full recovery. Adrian knew Cori felt incredibly guilty that Ariel had been hurt, but what happened wasn't her fault.

She was one of them now. Her own family might have cast her away, but that wasn't how he was raised.

The cabin had only one room. A stove in the center, bunk beds in the corner, and a Murphy bed on the far end that was pulled down. The wood-paneled walls were stained a reddish brown, reflecting the firelight in amber waves that crested over the walls like waves. His heart swelled as Cori noticed his grandmother's paintings on the walls. She was a talented artist, and seascapes were her favorite scenes to capture in oils and watercolor.

He watched Cori from the corner of his eye as she arranged some of her things, mostly borrowed from Prudence and Anne, and unpacked her sparse belongings. Hannah and David had not been to the cabin since the summer, but the dwelling still felt warm and lived-in. The beds were still made with fresh, flannel duvets.

She bent down over her duffel bag and pulled out a thick, cozy sweater. His pulse quickened as she pulled it over her head and the fabric slid over the swell of her breasts.

She met his gaze and flashed him an exhausted smile as she pulled her hair into a loose knot. "Come outside. I want to show you something," she said.

He grabbed a blanket and followed her out the door.

The sky had darkened fully now, and the stars were radiant and countless above them. The tide had indeed swallowed the path below them, surrounding the cliffs. She leaned into him as they took in the dazzling night sky above them.

He wrapped his arms around her, one of his favorite flannel quilts around his shoulders, as she pointed to the sky.

"Look to the south." She gestured over the roar of the ocean. "Tonight is the peak of the Leonid meteor shower," she explained. "It will be perfect conditions to see them in the new moon with such a clear sky, and if what I feel is right, there will be a meteor storm in the first hour of nightfall."

They stood there for a little while in silence as they gazed up. He rested his chin against her ear, counting her breaths as his arms rose and fell over her shoulders. A gasp fell from her lips.

The sky was suddenly alight with several sparkling streaks, falling soundlessly into the atmosphere. Her magic swelled to life, as though the falling meteors were charging her battery. He dipped his gaze down to her eyes, alight with a bright golden hue as they reflected the sky above her.

The meteors fell, dancing through the sky with glowing light for a few moments before they slowed. She sighed and leaned her head back against his chest. "That was lucky," she sighed contentedly. "Meteor storms in a new moon are rare."

He tightened his arms around her and kissed her neck. "I'm simply lucky to be here with you," he whispered into her ear.

Her shoulder stiffened before she turned toward him suddenly, startling him. "How can you say that?" she asked him with wide eyes.

He was speechless for a moment, taken aback. "I'm happy to be here with you," he said slowly and emphatically.

"You're happy that we had to escape here? You're OK with the fact that, until a couple of months ago, you were safe, and your life was easy? Now you're stuck here with me, someone with a death sentence. My prophecy completely disrupted your life."

Tears welled up in her eyes and spilled down her face as the words tumbled out, as if they had been hanging on the edge of her mind. She took a step back, her body shivering with the cold of the night and her guilt.

"Your sister almost died because of me, Adrian. I can never forgive myself for that. Your parents risked their lives to stop that fire. A fire that was sent for me. Seth accompanied you to the island when I was kidnapped. Who knows what could have happened to the two of you if I had been kidnapped by someone who wanted me dead."

His brows knitted together as he took in what she was saying. "Stop." His voice quaked as he searched for the words. "Stop acting like you're a burden to me somehow. I don't really care that you disrupted my life. I don't even care that someone tried to kill us yesterday." He slowed his words and shook his head. "It wasn't because of *you* that any of those things happened, Cori. It was because of the fuckers who are trying to kill you. This was their fault. Not yours."

She shook her head. "I'm not worth any of that."

He couldn't believe what she was saying. She had been so brainwashed to think that she was the problem. She was the one that needed to hide. A hollow sense of dread drilled through his abdomen. Maybe she didn't realize what he had known from the beginning.

"My life might have been disrupted, but that's only because I didn't know what it was to live before I met you," he said with a strained voice.

Her eyes widened.

He swallowed thickly. "I'm lucky to be here, with you, and I will do anything for you. *Anything*. Because I love you. You have to know that. You can read everything I feel, but I can also read you." Her lips parted as tears fell down her cheeks. "Because we're bonded. I'm fated to you, Cori."

Her eyes were wide and brimming with tears as she took in a breath. She opened her mouth to speak but was unable to make a sound as he tipped his head down and brought his lips to hers.

Through the bond, her sadness and tension melted away, replaced by a fire that sparked under her skin and ignited him. He kissed her deeply, parting her lips with his tongue. Her back arched as she leaned into the kiss. Fire spread into his blood. When her hand grazed his cheek, he broke free to catch his breath.

Every part of him tensed and hardened as he grabbed her hips and hoisted her up, his heart hammering as her legs wrapped around his waist.

He carried her into the cabin, nudging the door open with his shoulder, his erection already straining against his pants, as she kissed down the column of his neck. Her breaths were unsteady and frantic, and his heart pounded as she tightened her legs around him.

He crossed the room to the bed and lowered her carefully. She pulled him toward her, his arms braced on either side of her, as he kissed her again, slowly this time. Savoring the taste of her, pulling on her lips with his teeth as she let out a moan. Her hands grazed his chest, and his muscles tensed in response to her skin on his. He pulled off his shirt hastily, craving the feeling of her breasts pressed against him.

Within a few seconds, they were bare to each other, his body suspended over hers. Her frantic breaths danced over the skin of his neck as she wrapped her legs tighter, pressing his length between her thighs where a deliciously wet heat built for him. She arched her hips, igniting friction between her soft thighs and the hardness of his erection.

She stilled, despite their hammering hearts and the heavy humidity building on their skin. Her eyes met his before she brushed her face up against his and whispered into his ear.

"Adrian." His heart faltered at the sound of his name on her lips. "I love you, too."

He pulled back for a moment and found her eyes before their lips came together again. He let out a deep, ragged moan as he felt her hands dip lower on his abdomen before encircling him, working him in firm strokes.

He reached his hand down to meet hers and trailed his fingers up her thighs before sliding them inside her. Her body arched closer to him as he felt her bite gently at the skin on his neck. "I need you," she breathed into his ear.

He steadied himself and braced his arms over her shoulders as she guided him inside her. Inch by inch, he slid himself deeper until he was lost in her.

His thrusts were slow and methodical until she let out a pleading groan, angling her hips toward him, deepening him. His thrusts became urgent as her muscles tightened around him and pulsed around his length with her release. She let out a cry as she came, her fingers curling into his hair, as he continued to swell inside her.

A wave of her magic coursed through his veins.

Breathless, he reached under her thighs, tipping her hips up as he buried himself deeper. She cried out, and he felt her contract around him a second time as they came together, his release filling her in the depths of his last thrusts.

He dipped his head against hers as they reeled in the shock waves of what they had just shared. They were still joined as he shifted to his side and pulled her close to him. She fell asleep in his arms as he traced the lines of her body with his fingers. He let exhaustion wash over him before he succumbed to the warmth of the fire and her body. That night he dreamed of a thousand streaks of light in the sky.

CORI

They awoke the next morning with the sunrise, their limbs tangled together in the stillness of a peaceful night's sleep. Cori did not dream of anything, and her mind felt clear and peaceful. She could tell Adrian felt the same way as she opened her Eye to his aura, deep blue and serene. The surrounding mist morphed into smoky red when he realized she was staring at him.

"I can't hide anything from you, can I?" he asked as he pulled her toward him.

She laughed, shaking her head before he claimed her with a kiss. Their bodies moved in tandem all morning, unrushed and slow. By the early afternoon, she was finally hungry enough to get out of bed. Adrian heated water for coffee over the stove as he peered out the window.

"Tide is coming out. We should probably go check in on everyone when the path is passable," he said.

She shrugged at him. "That would mean you would have to put on a shirt."

He winked back at her. "Not if you don't want me to," he said, taking a sip of coffee.

"It's cold out there." She arched her brow mischievously at him. "Did you know there's a rumor going around town that you have nipple piercings?" she asked him.

246

"What!" he laughed, nearly choking on his coffee. "Who told you that?"

"Jordan," she said with a matter-of-fact shrug.

He rolled his eyes. "Sounds like the kind of stupid rumor Seth would start," he said, shaking his head.

"Or maybe there are just a bunch of people in Farley who fantasize about what you look like with your shirt off," she reasoned with a teasing smile. Her eyes swept over the muscles of his torso and the tattoos that curved over his wide shoulders and powerful arms. She couldn't blame anyone for fantasizing about him.

He raised his eyebrows skeptically at her.

The little cabin felt more and more like home as the hours passed into days. Days that went by with the secret of her father's prophecy still locked away in her heart.

She was more terrified than ever to tell him about it now that she knew the bond had fully taken root. They spent most of their time up at the campsite. Adrian began helping Zion with his research, focusing on a few cases of Celestial witches in the past who had been put into danger after delivering a controversial prophecy.

A Celestial witch named Margot had foretold that the food shortages in France in the 1780s would lead to the revolution and downfall of Louis VXI. When the king's consort found out about her prophecy, there was a bounty put on her head.

Of course, these were times that witch-hunts were part of societal norms. When a group of revolutionaries found out that her death would put the revolution into jeopardy, they smuggled her to England until the monarchy was overthrown.

The more Cori learned about the Celestials that came before her, the happier she was that she had agreed to go into hiding—at least for now. There were countless prophecies made through the ages, but it was difficult to find any that were related to the fate of the magical community.

It was also difficult to tell if there was any truth to the widely held belief that a prophecy would not come to be if the witch who delivered it was killed. Zion had poured all his energy into this. According to him, if they could find a case of someone who had escaped a murder, it would give them more information about how to protect her with magic.

"Do you believe it's true?" Adrian had asked her one night. They were huddled under the warmth of the quilts, protected from the December night air, and the warmth of his body had nearly lured her to sleep when he asked.

"Humph?" She turned toward him at the sound of his voice and buried her head into his shoulder. "Do I believe what is true?"

"Do you believe it won't come true if they kill you?"

She was silent for a moment as grief washed over her. Her father had believed it. So strongly that he had made the ultimate sacrifice. When her nonna had lived with her, she had asked her the same thing. Nonna's answer had always haunted her.

"I believe it's true," she sighed. "Can I show you why?" She held out her hand to him, a shiver of anticipation radiating from his skin with her contact.

He nodded. She placed her hand, skin to skin, over his chest and opened her Eye to him, connecting him to a memory.

Nonna sat in the big armchair in the living room, a crocheted afghan draped over her legs as she pulled the needle in and out of her cross-stitch. Her arthritic fingers shook slightly, but the needles hit true with each tiny X she stitched on the thin fabric.

On the television, the local news started. She watched with sadness as the scenes of a house fire flash to the screen.

"Two young children are dead in Nob Hill this morning after a four-alarm fire. The fire commissioner believes faulty electrical work ignited the blaze. The mother of the children, a thirty-four-year-old woman, is in critical condition at Highland Hospital."

She watched Nonna's heavily lidded eyes shift to the screen with a sad look. She shook her head morosely as she returned to her work, muttering a prayer in Italian.

"Nonna?" Cordelia asked tentatively. Her grandmother's

eyebrow arched in interest, but she continued to work on her stitches. "Have you ever had a vision about something terrible that was going to happen?"

Her fingers stopped moving as she pursed her lips. "No, Stellina." She put down her needlework, an introspective look gathering in her glassy eyes. "I have seen my deal of misfortune, but never something so horrible as that." She gestured to the television.

"Have you ever given a prophecy?" Cordelia asked her.

Nonna's face scrunched as she put down her stitching. "Si, but not every prophecy is as profound as yours. When I was a young woman, I delivered a prophecy. It was during the war and the Fascists had taken over everything. Our school and our town were under their complete control. I was just a girl. I foretold a general would come to our town and his presence would usher in the end of the war."

Cordelia listened aptly to the story, her eyes wide. The coming of the general had led to the eventual arrest of Mussolini and the liberation of her country.

"Nonna, you changed the world," she said in awe.

The wrinkles on her grandmother's forehead deepened at her response.

"No, Cordelia. Il Duce would have been arrested no matter what I prophesied. I was only the messenger. I believe the message needed to be delivered to give the people some hope. Those were desperate times."

Cordelia's wide smile faded. "Your prophecy gave hope to the people in your village. Mine struck fear in the hearts of witches everywhere.

"The Giver has a reason for you, too. The Covenant has been betrayed for too long, and many have suffered because of it. No magical law can hold forever if it is not obeyed. Magic is a gift, and every time someone breaks the law of the Covenant, they put the gift in jeopardy. This would happen whether you foretold it or not."

Cordelia had heard this so many times, but it did little to lessen the heaviness of her burden.

"I think there is an important reason you delivered this information to the world," Nonna continued, squeezing her hand. "It will give witches time to repent if they have broken the Covenant, to right a wrong. And those who have suffered at the hands of dark magic will have hope. It's a chance to save what we have."

Cordelia nodded her head. She knew there was truth in this explanation, but for every witch who is hopeful, there is one that is resentful and fearful. She shivered at the thought.

"Weren't you scared the Fascists would try to kill you?" Cordelia asked.

Nonna shrugged. "The Italians are superstitious people. I'm sure if the Fascist government had found out, they would have had me punished. But I delivered this prophecy to my coven, and we were not sympathetic to the regime. We were overjoyed. We only shared it with people who shared the same view."

Cordelia cast down her eyes. Her coven had not responded to her prophecy with joy.

Nonna's shoulders sagged. "If I have told you once, I have told you one hundred times. The Giver chose you to deliver this news because you are blessed by the Mother with great powers. You are strong. The Giver never gives us what we are not strong enough to bear."

Cori's eyes diverted to the window. "Have you ever known someone who died because of something they foretold, Nonna?"

Nonna's wrinkled face contracted, the lines deepening around her eyes. She breathed deep, her hand resting peacefully on her heart. "Si, Stellina." Her wrinkled hand wandered to the charm bracelet she wore on her arm, her fingers running over the smooth gold of charms. "If your life is taken with the intention to kill the prophecy, the prophecy dies with you."

Deep furrows appeared on Cordelia's forehead as she digested the disturbing information. "So, if someone kills you, and the reason they kill you is to reverse the fate of the prophecy, will it work?"

"If that is the intention," Nonna sighed. "Then yes. When you die, your magic dies with you. So does anything tied to it." Her deep-set eyes drifted to the moon as she spun the bracelet around her wrist.

"The intention is everything, Cordelia. You must always remember. Your intention hangs on every spell you cast with your magic."

"So, if I died in an accident, like Papa did," Cori reasoned. *"My prophecy would live on?"*

Nonna's eyes widened, her shoulders still. Her next words come slowly, deliberately. "If there is no intention, your magic will not die with you." She paused; her eyes also fixed on the sky. *"Regardless of the hand that takes you."* She rose slowly from her seat and folded the blanket with weary hands.

Her face softened as she bent to kiss her granddaughter goodnight. Before she walked out of the room, she dropped the charm bracelet into her hand. "This has always comforted me, Cordelia. Keep it close when your heart darkens." She slipped it onto Cordelia's wrist before walking out of the room.

She looked down at the little charms, the gold smooth and worn. She rubbed her own fingers on the metal, still warm from her grandmother's touch.

Cori shivered, pushing the vision away as they returned to the warmth of the present.

"Your grandmother knew someone who was killed to reverse a prophecy?" he asked.

She sat up in bed suddenly. "Adrian, there's something I need to tell you."

ADRIAN

Worry flashed in her eyes as she stood up and walked toward the window. "I should have told you a long time ago, but—I wasn't sure if I should."

He cocked his head at her, raising a curious brow. "If there's something you need to tell me, then tell me."

She squared her shoulders and sucked in a breath. "My father visited me. In spirit form, and he told me something that—" she choked on her words. "Something that changes everything."

His heart dropped as he sat up in bed. "When did he come to you?"

She stared at him for a long moment. "In the middle of the night. On the day that I was kidnapped."

He shook his head in disbelief. "That was months ago," he said, dumbfounded. Heat curled over the surface of his skin. How could she have not told him about this?

She twirled her bracelet around her wrist as she paced the floor. "I meant to tell you. I was so shocked by what he told me that night. I'm still processing it."

Adrian stood, closing the distance between them. "What did he tell you?"

She met his gaze, her eyes wide. Her voice shook. "My father gave a prophecy of his own. Before I was born. He predicted Enzo would kill me, and to assure that it never happened, he killed himself."

Sound sucked out of the room, replaced by a deafening buzz in his ears. Adrian scrubbed a hand over his forehead in disbelief. "Fuck. Cori..."

She took a deep breath, her brow knotted. "Because of my father, Enzo can't kill me, but Calvin can kill him. And my mother. I need to stop the LARC. I need to be present with Enzo on the night of the solstice."

A heavy beat of silence passed between them as the buzzing became deafening. He ran his hand through his hair as if he was pressing the weight of her words into his head. "Are you serious? Your brother betrayed you, and you want to run directly into the line of fire to save him?"

Her lip trembled as though the words were begging to break free. "If my brother and my mother die on the solstice, my father's death would have been for nothing." Desperation edged her words.

Heat built in his chest. How could she have kept this from him? "Did your mother know about your father's prophecy?"

She nodded, and the fire spread through his veins.

More lies. Another secret. He thought he had done enough to earn her trust. "That's why she sent you away. Not to save you from dark witches but to save you from Enzo. Your own flesh and blood."

She stepped closer to him, closing the distance in the thick air between them. Golden embers flared in her eyes. "Why is it so difficult for you to understand that I need to save them? I haven't seen them in almost ten years. I know you have your opinions about my family, but they're all I have."

Her words twisted into his chest like a knife. "How can you say that? They aren't all you have. You have a family that will do anything they can to protect you. Here."

"And the sacrifice they made for me eats away at me every day,

Adrian." She spun away from him, letting out an exasperated breath. "Your sister almost died. For what? I shouldn't even be here."

His words tightened in his throat. "We've been through this a thousand times, Cori. What can I do to make you realize that you're worth protecting?"

She spun back around toward him, her eyes glowing with all the light of the sky, amplified by welling tears. "You can support me. I need to face this. I have a chance to save my family. My father died to give my brother a second chance. He sacrificed everything for me—for all of us—and the least I can do is try."

He took a steadying breath. "Enzo can't kill you. Calvin and the LARC can. You can't put yourself in that kind of danger."

Her face softened. "I would never ask you to come with me, I'm just asking you to understand. This is why I was so scared to tell you." A single tear fell down her cheek.

Scared to tell him? Through her whole adult life, she had been conditioned to hide, but he thought he might be immune to that instinct. The last thing he wanted was for her to feel compelled to hide from him. His hand lifted instinctively, this thumb brushing away the teardrop. "Because you thought I wouldn't want you to go?"

She whispered. "Yes."

"Of course, I don't want you to go. If you got hurt—if you died, Cori—it would rip me to shreds."

"I know." Her voice was a whisper as she cast her eyes down to the floor.

He hooked his thumb under her chin, tilting her head toward him until she was forced to meet his stare. "I'm not going to let you go alone."

"I'm not asking you to come with me."

He shook his head. "If you need to do this, then I'm coming with you. Because if one of them tries to kill you, I will rip them to pieces," he said in a low voice.

"This is exactly what I was afraid of."

"You were afraid that I would want to protect you? Damn it, Cori, let me feel the way I need to feel about this."

She considered his request, her chest rising and falling in the silence. "What about how I feel?"

His voice was a rough whisper. "Tell me."

She shifted her body toward him, pulling him into a kiss, pressing her lips to him with such urgency he nearly lost his balance. His magic connected to her with the power of waves on the ocean, urged on by the storm building inside him. As his hands grazed over her body, his tension melted.

A rush of heat washed over them, the cool air in the cabin becoming thick and humid. She traced the edges of his tattoos with her fingers as though she had memorized them, trailing over the muscles of his back and arms.

After so many years of trying to hide herself—conceal who she really was—his greatest wish was that she would hold nothing back from him again. He wanted all of her. All the messy visions, the messages from ghosts.

The feeling of the moon pulling him into the sky. The magic of the stars raining on them with the speed of their light.

Hands, rough and thick against the smoothness of her skin, slid up her back as he undressed her. Her bare skin brushed up against his chest, and she gasped, calling out his name.

Claiming him.

Electricity danced over his fingertips, and the surrounding air fractured into a million droplets of water, swelling with the weight of his magic.

His fingers tangled in her hair as she pulled him closer. "Cori, please."

A whispered plea—to let him in, to allow him to worry, to understand what she was worth, to allow him to love her with everything she deserved.

Her magic washed over him, and continued to course through his veins as their bodies moved together, his arms braced on both sides of her. Water clung to his skin, shimmering in the muted glow of the moonlight.

They were still for a while, connected as their breaths steadied and their hearts slowed in tandem with one another. She turned and nestled herself beside him as he tucked her into the blanket and pulled his arms around her.

He fell asleep, his face buried in her hair.

When he awoke in the morning, the tide around the cove was low. And she was gone.

PART THREE
MOON IN SAGITTARIUS

"Sagittarius is where freedom lives, Cordelia. Always trust yourself when the archer holds the moon."
-Nonna

CORI

Stealing his car was never part of the plan, but desperate times called for desperate measures. She had awoken in a cold sweat, still naked and entwined in his limbs. When she slipped away from him, her mind had churned with the nightmare that had awoken her.

With panic in her heart, she pulled out the tattered notebook and opened to the back cover where the picture of her father had been safely tucked inside.

Still there.

In her dream, the photograph had been drifting on the wind, down the side of the rocky cliff toward the sea below. She hugged the picture to her heart.

She tucked the photograph back into the safety of the book's binding, as she turned to her most recent tally mark. Her eyes blinked in the candlelight as she read the date on the page, pulling out her phone to look at her calendar to compare.

She hadn't made a tally mark in over a week. For the first time in over three thousand days, she had forgotten to count. Her pen scratched the marks on the page as guilt washed over her. Somehow, she had gotten so swept away in this place, that she had forgotten to count the days.

Days until she would be reunited with her family and the prophecy could be considered a memory. *Ten days.*

Her hand stilled, the pen frozen over the hash marks. What would her life look like at the end of those ten days? Would she be leaving Maine and moving back to California? Reuniting with her mother and her brother? One person who had lied to her, another who had tried to kill her.

Adrian's tall body was too long for the sofa, but his arms and legs draped over the sides limply, as if he was fully at peace. She gripped the notebook in her hand, a countdown to the moment she would leave him.

She swallowed hard, pushing down guilt. Her bags were packed before she realized she was packing them. Low tide rolled away at six in the morning, allowing her to pass through the cove. The Airstream was quiet, the lights quelled, as she turned the engine of the truck over. She didn't know where she was planning to go, but she started driving south.

She drove for about an hour before she realized Lionel's truck had been trailing her. Her fingers drummed against the steering wheel as she devised a plan. She turned sharply off the road at the next exit.

One turn. Two.

No car trailed her as she pulled into the parking lot of the gas station. She pulled the truck into the farthest parking spot from the road and turned off the engine. She twirled the string of her sweatshirt in her fingers as the air in the truck grew colder. Adrian's coat was draped over the back seat. She pulled it over her shoulders, shrugging her arms into it.

Damn, it smelled like him.

Another pang dripped down her throat as she breathed deeply, inhaling his scent.

A sudden rapping on the glass of the window stopped her heart as she nearly jumped out of the seat.

Prudence glared at her, her hands on her hips, shivering in the cold outside of the car. She arched her eyebrows expectantly at her. Cori rolled down the window. "You're not wearing a coat."

"I'm not. I had to jump out of bed and chase you frantically down the highway," Prudence returned, her lips drawn into an angry scowl.

"You didn't have to chase me anywhere." Cori shrugged innocently.

Prudence narrowed her eyes, "Where exactly are you trying to go, Cordelia?"

Pru had used her full name. Like she had been a teenager sneaking out of the house. Cori winced. "Salem."

Pru pursed her lips before an exasperated sigh escaped them. "By yourself?"

Now that Prudence was saying it aloud, she had to admit it sounded reckless.

"Do you want to explain what happened that made you want to run off to the scene where an entire team of dark witches is actively trying to kill you? Alone."

Cori didn't want to explain. "Adrian and I had a fight." It was a simpler answer, but it was the truth.

"Adrian loves you," Prudence said simply, arching her brow at her. "He's fated to you for Goddess's sake. He will not want you to be anything but happy. For the rest of his life."

She swallowed deeply. "I feel like I'm being pulled in so many directions, Pru."

"I've been following you for a long time, Cori."

"Creepy."

Pru's face was serious as she crossed her arms. "You need to let people in. You were at Yale for four years of undergrad. Two years of grad school. It took you three years to complete your doctorate. I never saw you make one friend."

Her words stung. "I let him in. I've been dreaming about his face since I was a child. He gets so worked up over Enzo. It's like I can't have Adrian and my family at the same time."

"Come back to the campsite, Cori. The solstice is ten days away. We can figure this out."

She shrugged. "I doubt it. But I'll try."

"Good. I didn't really feel like driving all the way to Massachusetts."

Cori had convinced Prudence to find a place to eat breakfast before they drove back to the campsite. She ignored the frantic text messages from Adrian, turning her phone upside down as they ate eggs and hash browns at a small diner on the side of the highway, as though they were two old friends simply meeting up for brunch.

Adrian was pacing on the outside of the Airstream when they returned. She pressed the keys to the truck into his hands as through she had had simply been out to run an errand, avoiding his eyes.

It was even more difficult for Cori to recount her father's prophecy to Pru and Zion than it had been to tell Adrian. Pru shook her head heavily when she learned that Paolo had committed suicide to save his children. Zion listened patiently, his hands rubbing his temples as he digested and processed this new piece of the puzzle.

"Makes you wonder how many other Celestials have had to do the unspeakable," he said heavily.

Cori swallowed hard. She had wondered the same thing. If she ever foretold the death of someone she loved, she could not overcome that.

Nonna had told her so many times. *The Giver only shows us what we are strong enough to handle.* After what she learned about her father's sacrifice, she did not doubt his strength.

"Cori," Pru asked nervously, picking at her fingernails. "Do you think Enzo knows about your father's prophecy?" She raised her eyebrow, a thoughtful look on her face.

"He doesn't know," she replied. "Why do you ask?"

"What your father did not only saved you, Cor, but it makes you completely untouchable," she explained, thumbing through one of Zion's books. "To Enzo at least."

Adrian raked his hand through his hair. "But it doesn't prevent one of the other scumbags in the LARC from trying to kill her," he said, seething anger in his voice.

"That's true, but Calvin wants Enzo to be the one to kill Cori," Zion explained hastily, jotting down a few notes.

"What makes you think that?" she asked. Her stomach turned over.

Prudence flipped the pages of an old book with a thick leather cover and turned to an illustrated page. "Aha, found it!" she said triumphantly. "Remember when my father went to the meeting about the prophecy the LARC hosted in September?" she asked, jabbing her finger onto the page and turning it toward Cori.

The page was illustrated with the picture of a hanged man, his blood dripping grotesquely to the floor as another man, the wielder of the rope also bled into the same puddle. Bile rose in Cori's throat as she read the caption. "The Blood Bond of Death?" She pushed the disturbing illustration away.

"Way to be sensitive, Pru," Zion said, rolling his eyes. Pru shrugged apologetically at her. "This is a medieval text of dark magic. I'll read what was presented at the meeting to you," Zion cleared his throat. "*If life is to be taken from another witch by means to end their magic, their magic will be returned to the Other if taken by thine own blood. If the blood of the dead and that which took life were to mix in the Earth, the magic of the dead will be erased and restored to the Other by their death.*"

"So, if you are killed by someone who shares your blood, your magic doesn't just die with you. It gets transferred to the Other?" Adrian asked.

"Exactly." Prudence nodded. "They want to kill you, Cori. But they also want to make sure that your prophecy dies with you. If Enzo is the one who kills you, your magic—and your prophecy — will return to the Other. Everyone who takes part in the ritual will be strengthened by your magic. When you make the prophecy part of the Other, it can never come true. Not now. Never. It's an extremely dark way to kill another witch."

Cori remembered what Nonna said. If their intention was to

kill her magic, her prophecy would die with her. Calvin wanted to leave nothing to chance in her death. She realized that this must have been the reason they recruited Enzo in the first place. All the pieces of her father's prophecy fell into place, and at the end of the line was her murder.

"We think this is why Calvin Hanson asked your brother to be the one to kill you. This book is studied heavily by the LARC." Zion explained, as though reading her mind. "If the magic of your prophecy returned to the Other, it would seal fate. The prophecy could never come true."

"So, killing me would end the prophecy, but Enzo killing me is like an insurance policy that it could never come to be," she rationalized.

Prudence and Zion nodded solemnly.

Adrian stood, his hands clenched to fists. "If this is how they wanted to kill her all along, why send her that fire?" he asked angrily.

"We don't think the fire was meant to kill her, just injure her, and locate her so she could be captured. We intercepted two witches snooping around the fire right after it happened. The fire made it possible for them to locate you with magic. I think they expected to find you, injured and weak. Instead, they found Fern," Zion explained, the corner of his mouth tipping up. "After she was done with them, they didn't even remember their names. She tied them up and tortured them. Then she put them on a bus headed for Canada after convincing them they were escaping a cult."

Cori couldn't help but laugh. "Lesson learned. If you don't want to be tortured or brainwashed, don't mess with Fern."

"Or her friends," Pru agreed, fighting back a smile.

Fern was possibly the scariest witch Cori had ever known. She had no pity for those who were on the receiving end of her wrath. Thanks to her, her location was still a mystery, and all the witches in Farley were safe because of it. Cori made a mental note to give Fern an enormous hug the next time she saw her but had second thoughts when she remembered Fern wasn't a huge fan of physical contact.

"On to the next order of business," Prudence said with authority as she rose from the dinette. "Lionel needs to pack us up and get the Airstream ready. I need to call Alfie and tell him to rally the troops."

Cori ran her fingers over the grotesque images in the book. She would be there, looking Enzo in the eye when the moment of the solstice passed. She would get her life back, but so would he. Thick leather creaked under her fingers as she slammed the book closed. "We need to get to Salem."

CORI

Cori's eyes adjusted to the dim light of the early morning, peeking through the heavy curtains. Adrian was still asleep beside her, wrapped in the stiff sheets, his chest rising and falling heavily and peacefully. From across the room, Seth snored softly from his bed. Alfie shifted around restlessly from the floor.

Seth and Alfie had arm-wrestled the night before over who would win the bed, as had become the custom, and Seth had won for the first time since they arrived three days ago. Although she was glad Seth was catching up on much needed rest, Cori was sure that they would all pay the price for Alfie's lack of sleep.

Prudence and Zion had stayed back with Lionel in the Airstream at a campsite on the outskirts of town while the rest of their group had found a decent motel near Salem Harbor. It was central to town so the Gray witches could patrol the city without being noticed.

Cori wasn't sure what to expect from the town of Salem. After all, this was the place where the Covenant was made, a previous hub of witchcraft, and home to several of the largest covens in the country. She felt connected to this place, even though she had never physically stepped foot in the town itself.

They had headed straight for the motel upon arrival. Cori had decided to stay hidden from the LARC until the moment was right. She could glean from the others that the town was mostly touristy and full of fake witchcraft shops and character actors. There were so many witches—true and false alike—wandering around, it was easy to blend in.

Alfie and Prudence determined that several members of Calvin's coven had been spotted in town. The local Charms coven was large and active in the community, but Zion had wisely connected with the local Gray coven before their arrival. Per report, there was plenty of dark magic to worry about in this town.

Most of it was attributed to history and the fact that many dark relics were hidden in and around Salem. It was common that the Gray coven would end up policing witches traveling from out of town, drawn to the history of the witch trials.

Despite being stuck in the motel, one thing she could sense beyond the walls of their room was an incredible amount of spiritual energy in the town. On the drive to the motel, she had seen more spirits from the road than she had ever seen in one place before. Cold magic lingered on her breath and clung to the hairs on her skin, reminiscent of the chill she usually felt from spirits roaming the Earth.

Light grew brighter behind the curtain, and a shiver ran through her at the thought of how many witches had died here. And for what?

Fear. Power that was out of control.

So many humans had become fearful of the dark elements of witchcraft that even those who had not practiced dark magic were burned. Innocent witches and many humans who were falsely accused. If magic was shared through the Other—like she had always been taught—what had happened while so many witches were being burned through Europe and the colonies? What was magic like before it became vilified? What would it be like after the solstice?

On the ride to Salem, she had asked Zion about the Other and how it was differently interpreted between the sects of magic. Of course, he had studied it extensively. She replayed their conversation in her mind.

"It wasn't until I met Adrian that I realized Elemental witches don't think about the Other the same way Charms witches do," she had explained to him.

"Of course, they don't," he shrugged matter-of-factly. "Elemental witches don't rely on other witches like a Charms witch does. As Charms witches, your mom and Enzo rely on the members of the coven for unique skills. To them, the Other is the community that strengthens their magic."

"What do Gray witches consider the Other to be?" she had asked with curiosity.

"Gray witches consider magic to have multiple layers. There is magic, and then there is the Other. The Other is all things that have the potential to have magic."

Her head spun as she recalled his explanation. "So, you consider the Other to be the lack of magic?"

"No." He shook his head. "Not the lack of it, but the potential for it. That's why Gray witches use so many magical relics." He pulled out the veiling stone from his bag. She recalled how her skin had tingled as he placed the stone in her hand. "This once was an ordinary object, but it carried energy. Gray witches know how to use this energy and channel it into magic.

Before the Covenant, Charms witches used to do the same thing, but they used a combination of the dark and light element from the object. It was much more powerful." He shook his head. "But it was much more dangerous. Our ability to control dark and light energy makes us Gray witches. The energy we channel the magic through is the Other."

After their conversation, Cori had felt dizzy. She wanted to learn more about how different witches interpreted magic. Zion had given her a few of his favorite books on magical theory.

During her time in the motel room, she had studied them with Adrian. They had learned that most witches differed little on how they viewed the Mother and the Giver. The Other was up to interpretation.

The solstice was only two days away, but she still did not know what her words meant.

All those who have borrowed from the betrayal will weaken through the Other.

How would they weaken? Would it depend on how they interpreted the Other? Maybe a Water Elemental who used dark magic would be less connected to the magic of the water. Maybe a Gray witch who used the dark elements in making their relics could not connect to the magic in objects. Would her connection to the spirit realm be weakened? If a Celestial could read emotions through the aura, would her connection become clouded?

The more she read, the more she realized the Charms witches had the most to lose from her prophecy. She remembered how her mother had been the go-to person for healing charms in their coven. She had shared so much magic with her fellow witches. What would happen if those witches could no longer share? It was no wonder that most of the witches who were trying to stop her were from Charms covens, and that her own coven had betrayed her in the end.

She squeezed her eyes shut and tried to slow the turning cogwheels in her mind. Sleep had been evading her since leaving the cottage on the cliffside. Thinking of the cottage made her heart ache. She had never felt so at peace as she did there.

With Adrian.

She let her mind swim into the memory of what it felt like to wake up in Adrian's arms, warm and skin to skin under the thick blankets. They had not been in a rush to wake in the mornings, feeling as though they were tucked away from the rest of the world. No lobster to catch. No data to collect.

She would awaken to his touch before the sun fully rose and they would get lost in each other before she even fully opened her eyes. The room was cold and dry each morning but became warm and humid with Adrian's magic as their bodies joined.

She smiled to herself at the memory of hot, thick air around her. He claimed he couldn't control the way his body reacted to the surrounding atmosphere.

In the cottage's isolation, surrounded by the sea and protected by the rocky cliff, Cori had felt blissfully free to give in without restraint and make the air heavy all day long. Her skin flushed, wishing she could relive those mornings again.

She wasn't sure she would ever feel that free again—or that she could ever return to the little cottage where she had told Adrian that she loved him. The place where their bond had been irrevocably woven.

Adrian shifted on his side and wrapped his arm around her, as though he was drawn to the quickening of her pulse. She draped her leg over his hip, leaning against the hardness of him as she drew him closer. He moaned a bit in his sleep, and she kissed him silently. She felt his lips curve upward against her own as he slid his hand to her thighs, grazing her skin as he pressed closer. She gasped at the contact, only to hear Alfie's agitated voice from the floor.

"If you guys are going to fuck, at least have the decency to warn the other people sleeping in the room," he gritted out.

"Shh, Cori I think they can hear us," Adrian whispered loudly.

"Don't worry," she reassured Alfie. "That's not my kind of thing."

"What's not your kind of thing?" Seth asked as he stretched luxuriously on his bed.

"Exhibitionism," she said as she reluctantly pushed Adrian's hand from straying up her thigh.

Seth stretched as he sat up in bed. "Alfie, damn. Nobody likes a cockblocker."

Her skin flushed with embarrassment. "He's not being a cockblocker." She sat up and swung her legs over the side of the bed.

"I disagree," Adrian said grumpily as he pulled the covers back over his head.

"Alfie's just jealous," Seth teased. "He misses his boyfriend."

Alfie groaned. "I cannot believe I was naïve enough to tell either of you any information about my love life," he said, rolling his eyes. Jordan and Alfie had been spending more time together before they were called away to Salem. Alfie had finally admitted they officially started dating.

"I think you forget sometimes. You've been hanging out with a Celestial witch for the past couple of months," Adrian said, raising his brow. "I'm pretty sure we would have figured it out eventually."

Cori nodded in agreement as she pulled on her wool socks and fleece sweater. "Yeah, I saw that relationship coming from a mile away."

"I thought you didn't like exhibitionism," Alfie retorted.

"More like voyeurism. It's not my fault I can sense your aura." She shrugged, pulling on her thick fleece sweater.

"What does my aura look like right now?" he asked her, frowning.

She opened her mouth to answer, but Seth beat her to it. "Your aura looks permanently pissed off to me."

"Agreed," Adrian said. "I'm also picking up a strong 'superior British douche' vibe."

Alfie glared at them as he pulled on his sweater. Two nipple rings adorned his heavily muscled chest. She bit back a laugh, wondering if Jordan knew this piece of information about his new boyfriend, but made a mental note to tease him about it the next time she saw him.

"Not my fault I'm surrounded by a bunch of American assholes all day," he retorted.

Cori rolled her eyes. It was very early in the day for this kind of bickering. "I'm starving," she said, changing the subject.

Seth stood up. "I thought I saw hunger in your aura," he said, raising his hand. "I volunteer to fetch the bagels."

"As much as I would love to accompany you, I just got instructions from Prudence," Alfie said, scrolling through his phone. "The local Gray coven has decided to hold an emergency meeting about the increased dark activity in town expected in the few days before the prophecy."

Cori shivered. She was sure that Calvin was not the only

witch who practiced dark magic that was making a pilgrimage to the birthplace of the Covenant this week.

Alfie and Seth hastily got dressed and left for their various tasks as Cori sat perched on the edge of the bed. She absent-mindedly twirled her charm bracelet and bit her lip as she considered the reality that droves of witches in this town likely wanted her dead.

The click of the door snapped her back to reality. She turned her head and saw Adrian stretching as he rose from the bed. Her anxiety melted away at the sight of him, her eyes trailing over the swell of his shoulders, the black ink of his tattoos that seemed to curve perfectly around the muscles of his back. A strand of dark chestnut hair, mussed from sleep, fell in front of his face as he bent to pull on his shirt.

"Looks like we're alone for a few minutes," she mused, tipping up her shoulder. She tossed her hair to one side, tilting her head up expectantly.

He dragged his thumb over her lower lip. "What I want to do with you would take more than a few minutes," he replied. Smoky red heat rose in the surrounding air, and she knew he was thinking about exactly what he wanted to do.

Her cheeks flushed as she rose to her knees. He stood next to the bed as she reached for his waist and pulled him to her. "What does that mean?" She trailed kisses down his collarbone. His muscles tensed in response to her touch as a frustrated groan escaped his lips.

He wrapped his hands in her hair, tilting her head back. His lips grazed hers as he spoke, "It's been days since I was last inside you, and it would take time to make up for how much I missed you."

The evidence of just how much he missed her pressed up against her abdomen, and she couldn't stop her hand from tracing the muscles of his chest. A deep breath of annoyance puffed out of his lips as his phone illuminated on the bedside table.

"Who is it?" Cori asked as he glanced down at the screen.

His lip curled with a smile as he read the text message. "It's from Seth."

He tilted the phone to her so she could read the message.

> Bagels obtained. I'm going to take the long route back and then sit in the lobby. You guys come find me when you're ready.

The promise of borrowed time flashed in his eyes. "Come to think of it, I'm not all that hungry," she said with a shrug.

"Speak for yourself," he laughed, as he lifted her off the bed.

It had been only a few days, but what he said was true, and she felt it, too. She felt empty without him, without the feeling of his body moving inside her, like the tide pulled by the force of the moon. Their magic was desperate for a connection, and the air around them thickened with humidity.

She angled her head against his, grazing his ear with her mouth as she whispered to him. "I just want to lie next to you for a little while."

What she needed, more than anything, was to feel that peace again. The way it felt to lie in his arms with no agenda and no ticking clock, the way it had been at the cottage.

He nodded, the muscles in his shoulders relaxing. She laid down and he pulled the blanket around them. He settled behind her, curling his arm over her waist. Cori listened to Adrian's breaths as the surrounding air morphed into cool blue contentment.

He scooped the hair away from her back, the humidity dissipating as he willed the water out of the surrounding atmosphere. She shivered, the cold air stark against her skin. If she died, he would never feel that connection with her—with anyone—ever again.

ADRIAN

He had made peace with Cori's need to confront her brother, but he had not made peace with the possibility that she could get hurt—or worse—in her attempt. Cori pulled on her clothes, her movements slow and her eyes heavy with thought. He bit his lip.

This will not be the last time you lie beside her, he vowed to himself.

When they had collected themselves and made it out to the motel lobby, they found Seth, who had taken one of Zion's historical texts, reading with a furrowed brow as he sipped his coffee from a paper cup.

He raised his eyebrows at them as they approached but didn't say a word about how long it took them to join him as he handed them some bagels and their cold cups of coffee. Adrian made a mental note to be extra nice to his brother for the rest of the day.

No matter how much Seth teased and beat him up, he always had the interest of his little brother at heart. His chest squeezed as he realized that Seth had dropped everything—fishing, being with Jess, his precious free time—to help Cori. *To help him.*

Adrian felt his phone vibrate at the same time as Cori's and Seth's. They exchanged a dark look. It was a text from Prudence.

Meet @ the coffee shop on Essex Street.
11:00 a.m.

Adrian drummed his fingers on the back of his phone. He had been dreading this moment but knew it was inevitable. Another text flashed across the screen.

Cori—pack a bag.

His stomach lurched. He diverted his gaze to Cori's face, her eyes wide and blinking rapidly. He couldn't read auras, but he *knew* her. She was anxiously twisting her charm bracelet around her dainty wrist as she chewed on her lower lip.

He tried to push down the fear and anger that rose in him as he turned over in his mind all the possibilities of what was to come. He clenched his jaw and tightened his shoulders as he looked up at Seth, still scrolling through his phone as he rubbed his temple.

Suddenly, his brother sighed and stood up purposefully. "If Cori needs to pack a bag, so do we."

Her eyes flooded with tears, before she turned toward Seth and hugged him fiercely. "Thank you," she whispered into his shoulder.

Seth bit back a smile as he shared a confused look with his brother. "I don't know why you're acting surprised by this. We go where you go, kid, that's the deal." He gave her a little kiss on the head. "You're stuck with me, too."

He felt Seth's hand clap him on the shoulder as they walked away. If Pru's plan didn't include him staying with Cori, the plan was going to have to change.

As she wiped her eyes, he recognized the tears for what they truly were. Tears that were weighed down by years of loneliness and resignation of living a life in hiding. A life where the answer was not togetherness, support, or camaraderie against a common goal, but solitude and isolation for the sake of the greater good.

She had spent almost a decade of her life convinced that she was better off alone, and even now he sensed trepidation from her every time someone else volunteered to help her, support her, hold her hand.

The burden of this prophecy had been hers alone for so long, and the thought of her carrying this burden alone was like an iron fist around his heart. He bit down hard on the inside of his lip as he thought of Cori's brother, conspiring against her from afar, despite his knowledge of everything about her. What could have driven him to turn against someone who he was supposed to love and protect?

And at what cost? For the sake of magic?

Fuck magic, he thought. His head was swirling with anger.

If someone told him right now that magic would cease to exist in its entirety if she lived, he would kill anyone who tried to get in her way. He would give up every magical connection in his life if it meant they could be together. If it meant she was safe.

He would rather sink himself to the bottom of the ocean and summon the water to crash through his lungs. He would let his own magic steal his last dying breath before he would let anyone harm her.

Lines of concern shadowed over her brow—he knew what she was sensing from him.

Anger. Disgust. Lust for revenge.

"Let's go pack up," he said, squeezing her hand. He was sure that she was reading him, but he was grateful that she couldn't read his mind. Because at that moment he realized what was going to happen next.

He would find Calvin, and anyone who he worked with. And he would kill them.

CORI

The streets of Salem were dusted with a thin layer of fresh snow that reflected the muted morning sun like starlight as Cori followed Seth and Adrian to the coffeehouse. The Gray witches had been using it as a meeting place since their arrival, but Cori had stayed behind until now, tucked away in the motel room, biding her time.

She felt exposed out in the open, and it made her stomach turn over.

The Huxley brothers were conspicuous as they walked down the street, tall and broad and handsome. Two of them, walking side by side, took up the full breadth of the sidewalk. The corner of her lip curved up despite her unease as she noticed more than one passing woman do a double take as they passed.

She with her black down coat, gray winter cap covering her distinctive golden-brown hair, and a black wool scarf wrapped up to her nose, could have passed as any cold New Englander in a rush to run holiday errands.

A hum of magic bounced around them like electric heat through the cold bitter air. Would the feeling of that energy fade in a few days when the stars finally converged on the solstice? She shivered as an icy wind ripped through her down coat.

She could sense the magic emanating from the Huxley

brothers as they walked a few feet ahead of her. The snow dusting the ground and the flurries swirling through the sky seemed to swirl around them like a halo. Not one flake stuck to their jackets. It was probably killing them they could not simply clear the path ahead of them as they walked, but she knew they were trying not to attract any kind of unwanted attention.

It wasn't clear how much the witches in Calvin's coven knew about her life. If they had any intelligence about her spending time with a bunch of Elementals, now was not the time for the brothers to magically clear a path in the snow.

They entered the coffee shop through a side entrance and walked up a stained, musty cement staircase that led to a set of dimly lit rooms. At the end of a hallway, Seth approached the heavy metal door, his confident knock echoing through the corridor.

An unfamiliar witch opened the door for them as Cori took off her hat. The witch smiled at her from behind the door before diverting her attention to Seth.

She placed her hand on her hip. "Password?" she asked expectantly.

"Borealis," Seth replied quickly, winking.

The witch narrowed her eyes at him, a teasing smile playing at her features. "Sorry, we changed the password this morning. You'll have to come back later."

Seth crossed his arms and cocked his head to the side. "Chloe, do you really want us sitting out here in the cold hallway?" he asked smoothly.

Cori bit her lip as his aura turned smoky red. He was flirting with her.

"You realize I brought precious cargo with me this time, right?" He gestured to Cori who gave a shy wave.

Despite Seth's cool, calm manner, Adrian narrowed his eyes with calculating appraisal. He glanced over at Cori, an unspoken question in his eyes. Even though Cori couldn't read his mind, she could sense his suspicion. She opened her Eye to the witch before her, and all she could read was curiosity and the girlish flirtation bouncing between her and Seth.

She raised her eyebrows at Adrian and subtly nodded her head, his suspicion melting away to relief as the tension in his posture relaxed.

They entered a room that was comfortable and warmly furnished despite the bare hallway that they had walked through to get there. The local Gray coven used this location as their regular meeting place.

The room had several worn yet cozy-looking couches where people casually sat, filling the room with chatter.

Fern stood in the corner, her arms folded around her torso as she silently appraised the other witches in the room with narrowed eyes. Cori considered standing with her for a moment before another young witch caught her attention. He was sitting on a chair not too far away from Fern, bouncing his leg and picking at his cuticles.

He appeared to be young, no older than seventeen or eighteen. His clothes were dirty and worn, and his platinum blond hair was mussed and tousled. She opened her Eye to him, and her heart clenched with the realization that this young man had been through a recent trauma.

"Ahem," Prudence cleared her throat. "I think everyone is here, so we can get started. Is that OK, Chloe?"

Chloe nodded, a steaming cup of coffee balanced in her hands, as she took a seat near Prudence. "Absolutely," Chloe said as she pulled out a clipboard. "I want to call to order this meeting of the Salem Gray Coven," she started with a murmur of assent from the crowd. She hastily took attendance before getting to business. "We welcome our guests from the San Francisco and London Gray Covens today and thank them for their continued help in curbing the rise in dark activity in town. Over the past two days alone, we have disabled several dangerous charms and removed several dark artifacts from the parks and historic sites around town."

Cori shivered as applause rang out around her. *How many of those spells were cast directly because of me?* she wondered.

Chloe continued to the next order of business. "I would also, of course, like to welcome our guest of honor, Cordelia Manganelli." Chloe smiled at her, extending her hand.

The room broke out into more applause, making Cori blush with embarrassment.

Cori smiled and nodded at Chloe as she continued, "We're here today to come up with a plan to keep her safe while we rescue her mother from the LARC. But before we start, I think we can all agree that there is another matter we are most relieved about. With the help of Fern, we've successfully rescued Fintan." She gestured at the young, disheveled witch who waved sheepishly at them amid another yet round of applause.

"To bring some of you up to speed," Pru said toward Cori. "Fintan was recently captured by the LARC and was able to break out just this morning. He's a Fire Elemental who the LARC had been exploiting for his power against his will."

Cori saw Adrian and Seth exchange a shocked look before their mouths fell open in disbelief.

Adrian stood up suddenly. "You..." He pointed at the young man who turned white with fear as he also stood.

"Hold on. I wasn't working for them," he blurted, his hand outstretched. Cori thought she detected a subtle fire in his eyes. "I was forced—"

"You sent the Byzantine fire," Adrian growled at him. The air in the room started to crackle and thicken as water fell from the ceiling. Cori looked up and gasped as a wispy cloud accumulated in the room. He was summoning a storm—*inside.*

"Adrian, calm down." Seth was standing now, too.

"You almost killed us," Adrian hissed. "And your fire hurt our sister."

"They forced me. I didn't even know what I was doing..." the scared young man pleaded with Adrian as he backed slowly away, steam billowing from the growing moisture around him.

The room rumbled, the floor beneath their feet vibrating.

Cori looked up into Adrian's face where rage was replaced with shock. This magic was not coming from him. Fern, standing up from her chair in the corner, released a glowing orb of silvery light.

She walked over to the young man and spread her arms, expanding the protective orb to surround him. She didn't say a word, but if looks could kill, her glance to Adrian would be lethal.

Adrian stumbled back, letting go of his anger. Seth cleared the clouds from the ceiling as Cori slowly got to her feet. She walked across the room to the silvery orb that Fern had summoned.

"Fern, it's OK."

Fern nodded, and the orb dissipated into embers of floating silver that fell to the floor like snow.

"I'm sorry," the Fire Elemental said. "If that fire was meant for you, or if it hurt you." His head hung down between his shoulders as he slumped into the chair. "I didn't even know I could do it—it was like they—" He stumbled on his words, choked with the trauma of his recent captivity.

Cori reached out her hand to him. "I'm a Celestial witch, which means I can sense people's emotions and experiences. If I touch you, you can show me what happened to you with your memories. Can you show me what happened when you were there, Fintan?"

"It's Fin."

"Fin, if you take my hand and allow me to connect to you, you can show me anything you wish, but you will relive it, too. Is that OK? I think it will help me understand what has been going on."

Fin nodded at her, extending his hand. As his aura softened, she was struck by the firm set of his jaw and his platinum white hair. Nausea washed over her when she saw ligature marks around his wrists.

"I'm ready," he said, clenching his jaw.

Cori opened her Eye as she connected with Fin's magic. His aura was a hot, powerful flame. As she was thrust into the memory, she was surrounded by the sweet smell of burning hickory wood as his magic crackled around her.

Fin sat in a small room, appointed in vintage Victorian style— lace curtains and delicate doilies on the furniture. He stared longingly at a fire crackling in the fireplace, his face stricken with frustration. Silvery thread was bound around his arms, connected to an ancient-looking bolt embedded on the wall, glowing ominously like a hot ember. A bed on the opposite end of the room was vacant.

The door cracked open, and a tall man in a neat suit leaned on the frame.

Calvin Hanson smiled smugly down at Fin. "Are you enjoying your new accommodations, Mr. Sullivan?" he asked coolly.

"Why am I here?" Fin snarled up at Calvin with a subtle Irish lilt in his voice. Fire crackled from the bolt on the wall.

Calvin released a soft chuckle. "It's a simple spell, really. Old magic. That's an iron bolt. Has been used in this house in this way for centuries. An ancient relic for sure, but it's nothing complicated. Just spellbinding."

Fin's magic was cut off and tethered to the iron bolt in the wall. He narrowed his eyes at his warden. "That's dark magic."

Calvin stood taller, his jaw hardening. "It's powerful magic," *he spat back with disgust. "You've been force-fed all the false information about so-called dark magic, too." He crossed his arms. "Your reputation led me to believe that you might actually understand what we are trying to accomplish here, Mr. Sullivan." Fin winced at this. "But here we are. We had to capture you. I thought for sure you of all people would come willingly."*

Fin shook head. "I've admittedly done some fucked-up shit, but I've never—"

Calvin narrowed his eyes. "Such a pity. A Fire Elemental. Think of what you could accomplish if you could harness magic to your full potential." He frowned. "Luckily there's more than one way to get what I need from you." He lurched forward, gripping

Fin's shirt with his hand, twisting the fabric. "Give me what I need, or I will be forced to take it from you."

Fin reeled and spat squarely into Calvin's face.

Calvin wiped the saliva off his brow and flung it back in Fin's face before releasing him. "Have it your way, then," Calvin said, smoothing the lines of his suit jacket as he left the room.

Several witches entered the room at once, moving as though they were shadows. The tether connecting him to the bolt tightened as a witch whispered an incantation in his ear.

His eyes became opaquely black as his lips moved in tandem under the influence of their magic, his voice vibrating independently of his mind. Words escaped his lips, foreign and wrong, repetitive and rhythmic. He didn't know what the words meant, but he felt their intention—destroy.

He memorized every syllable before he drifted off to sleep.

———

Fin woke up some time later to the sound of hushed voices.

"Enzo..." a woman pleaded in a whisper. "Let me talk to him."

A man's voice sighed in the darkness. "Fine, but make it quick. We don't have a lot of time."

The face of an older woman with platinum hair swam into his vision. "My name is Astrid. I'm going to help you get out of here," she said with a slow and calming voice. "This is my son, Enzo. He has a key in his left pocket. You're going to steal the key out of his pocket, and then the two of you are going to beat each other up... loudly."

Enzo released a scoffing sound. "Don't worry, I'll let you win,"

Astrid rolled her eyes but continued in a slow, calming tone. "You are not to use fire. You will run into the basement. The door is at the end of the hall, slightly ajar. There's a witch in the hall named Fern who will cause a diversion. You are not to harm her, either. There is a cellar door. You will run to the highway, where a car is waiting for you. Fin, you need to give this key to my daughter, Cordelia. It will unbind you from the bolt, but until she comes back *for me, I will remain bound. Do you understand? There is only one key."*

Fin nodded. Enzo pulled a key from his pocket and detached the bolt. Fin's wrists burned as the fire in his magic returned to him like a wave of volcanic ash. He stood as Enzo noisily knocked over a table. Reeling back, Fin punched Enzo in the nose. A trickle of blood ran over his lip. Enzo shoved Fin hard into the wall, knocking over a portrait from the wallpapered plaster.

"Help!" Astrid yelled convincingly from the other side of the room.

"Go!" Enzo grit out as he shoved him again, knocking down a ceramic bowl from the bedside table as he pushed the key into his hand.

Fin ran down the hall toward a stern-looking witch standing near the basement steps. She fired off an incantation down the hall in the opposite direction. She cocked her head toward the door as shouts and footsteps grew near, as he escaped into the basement where a rush of cool night air hit his cheeks from the open cellar door.

CORI

The connection between them broke, and Cori found herself on her knees, tears falling down her cheeks. It was typical to recover from the exhaustion of a vision and feel emotional, but after reliving the horrors that Fin had gone through, she felt physically sick.

Spellbound. Compulsion. Tied and chained by his own magic.

Fin's eyes were closed as he held his head in his hands. A dry, magical heat that stung her eyes radiated from him.

"You met my family," she whispered.

He nodded, gripping her hand as he slipped an ancient-looking skeleton key into her palm.

She felt cooler hands gripping her arms. Pru and Adrian hoisted her up to her feet on shaky legs. Chloe's voice echoed through the room.

"The LARC continues to operate out of the Sampson homestead just on the outskirts of town. We believe they plan to capture Cordelia today. Fern has been feeding them false information for the past week, and they currently believe that Cordelia is staying in the Whitemarsh Inn. Of course, we have rented a room there to prepare for this and checked in under her name this morning. Enzo was spotted there shortly thereafter."

Zion spoke, concern etched on his face as he watched Cori

from the corner of his eye. "The Sampson house is built on one of the most ancient ritual grounds in the country. Before the witch trials, the Sampson family routinely practiced dark magic in the woods next to the creek where they lived. There is a clearing about two hundred yards from the base of the tree line where it is reported that thousands of human and animal sacrifices have been made over the years."

Fin had stood up and started to pace. "That's where I was held captive?"

"Don't let the floral wallpaper fool you," Fern said darkly as she helped herself to a plateful of food, "That house has seen some fucked-up shit."

Zion nodded in agreement. "The Sampson family were dark witches. During the witch trials, they accused members of their own coven and many innocent humans to divert attention away from their own family. One night a group of witches came to the house and hung all of them to death by the trees in the woods, even their two small children. As a Gray witch, it's difficult to even walk near the clearing in the woods. The dark energy there is overwhelming. We think that's the spot where they plan to kill you, Cori."

"Cal loves tradition," Fern muttered under her breath.

"The death of the Sampson family is considered to be the inciting incident that led to the formation of the Covenant," Zion continued.

A chill crept up Cori's spine as she heard Prudence continue to speak. "The moment of the solstice and stars joining will occur just before midnight tomorrow. If Cori allows herself to be captured today, that should give her enough time to free Astrid so we can get her to safety."

Cori swallowed thickly against the lump developing in her chest. "Why couldn't my mother escape with Fin?"

Prudence shook her head. "We couldn't risk it. Calvin would have suspected Enzo had freed both of them. Thanks to Fern's spying, we have confirmed that the LARC intends for Enzo to kill you. They believe that if you're killed in a blood bond ritual, not only will the prophecy be erased, but it can also never come to be in the future." She turned to the group. "Cori's magic, including the magic of the prophecy, will return to the Other forever. No future witch can bring about the change that Cori foretold."

She heard murmurs vibrate around the room as they reviewed the plan. Adrian's shoulders tensed, and Cori knew why. There was no possibility that he could enter the house with her.

This was something only she could do. *Alone.* She gripped the key in her hand, still hot from the Fire Elemental's pocket.

Alfie turned on a projector machine attached to his laptop, focusing the image of a map on the wall. "The LARC believes Cori is traveling alone. We will position ourselves here"—he pointed to a house at the end of a peripheral street in town—"in the home of a local Gray family that lives close to the Sampson house." The map showed a clearing in the woods. "Just before sunset, we will position ourselves between the creek and the clearing near this woodpile. We have set up a concealment charm just outside the property line that should keep us well hidden. When Enzo cannot fulfill his duty, we will rise from the shadows and take Cori to safety, allowing enough time to pass so that the prophecy is fulfilled."

Seth spoke up, his hands on his temples. "Hold on—" his voice broke through the chatter. "We're letting this entire plan hang on the knowledge that Enzo can't kill Cori—"

"Thanks to your father, Cori. He can't," Pru said softly.

"So, what if he doesn't, but someone else steps up in his place?" Seth asked. He shared an uneasy look with Adrian, who had clearly been thinking the same thing.

Cori spoke this time, her voice raspy and dry. "The conjunction of Saturn and Jupiter begins at 11:55 on December 21. If we make it to midnight, the solstice will have passed, and the prophecy will come to be. Solstice only lasts a moment in time, when the Earth is at the maximum tilt on its axis. The exact time of the solstice this year is 11:53." The pull of the Earth, reeling back to the deepest seat of her axis, tugged on her bones. "I'm sure Calvin has studied this and wants to be exact. They will want my blood to be on the Earth, mixing with Enzo's between 11:53 and 11:55 to assure the prophecy dies with me." Cori swallowed thickly. "My guess is they plan to kill me swiftly so that the timing works perfectly."

"That explains why they've been sharpening the swords," Fern said darkly as she picked the tomatoes out of her salad nonchalantly. Cori gaped at her. No wonder she had been such a successful double agent.

"That means they have two minutes to kill you," Seth continued, exchanging a sympathetic look with Adrian. "By the time they realize Enzo can't be the one to do it, they will have wasted enough time."

Prudence walked to her side. "Cori, are you ready?"

She nodded again as she stood, this time on steady legs. "This feels right," she said with conviction. "The only way I can assure that the prophecy comes to be—and save my family—is by being present for the most critical moment. I've been hiding for nearly a decade, pretending to be someone that I'm not, just for the sake of this prophecy. Too much is at stake to mess it up now, and I can't hide from it anymore."

She locked eyes with Adrian. Despite the fear and trepidation she sensed from him, she sensed something entirely new—a heavy dose of pride.

CORI

Chloe called the meeting to a close, and the room slowly cleared out. Eventually Cori stood alone with Adrian, Seth, and Pru.

Prudence cleared her throat. "Alfie is going to walk you to the hotel. He'll track behind you to make sure it appears like you're alone just in case someone recognizes you." She exchanged a meaningful look with Seth. "We'll give you a few minutes." Seth clapped his hand over Adrian's shoulder sympathetically before following Pru through the heavy industrial door into the hallway.

Cori sat heavily on the metal folding chair, her head in her hands. She had not seen her mother in almost a decade, but she would see her today. To rescue her.

Enzo had helped Fin escape from the Sampson house. A kernel of hope vibrated in her chest. Maybe he wasn't so far gone. Maybe there was still a part of him that wanted her to be protected and safe.

Adrian's hands slid onto her shoulders, kneading the tension out of her muscles. She angled her head up at him, but the worry written on his face was almost too much for her to bear.

"Please be careful," he whispered. "If something happens to you..." his voice trailed off, but she knew what he was about to say. What she had been too terrified to admit, even to herself.

"A few months ago, I was leading a partial life. My entire existence was centered on one goal—stay alive and stay hidden, all for the greater good." Tears welled in her eyes. "Everything I did and every move I made was for this prophecy, and now it's finally time to face the reality of what it means. I don't know what the world is going to look like after the solstice. I don't know if there will even be any magic left. All this time, in the past, when I thought about it, I didn't even care about what happened after. Is that sad? I didn't care if I was alive or dead, or if there was nothing at all. But now I care. I care very much. But there is only one thing I care about when this is all over, and that's you." She felt him fold his arms around her as tears fell down her cheeks. "If the entire world changes, if magic is gone forever and erased from the Earth, it won't matter. The only thing that matters to me now is that we can get past this so we can be together."

He held on to her tightly as the tears shook from her. "Magic won't be erased from the Earth, Cori," he reassured her, "I never doubted that for one minute. And if it is, it won't be your fault."

He took her face in his hands and kissed her. The familiar feel of his magic, the waves moved over her, washing away the feeling of nauseating dread. She broke away from him and studied his face, the perfectly formed constellation of freckles haloing the vivid blue eyes that been a part of her dreams for as long as she could remember.

"I'm really proud of you for doing this," he said sincerely.

She nodded. "I know."

"Of course, you know," he said, the corner of his mouth curling up. "I will not let anything happen to you. I promise you," he choked on his words. "If they actually succeed—if they hurt you, I will kill every single one of them."

Her breath caught in her throat. "Adrian…"

"I don't give a shit about magic or this prophecy," he said, cutting her off. "You are the only thing that matters. I love you, Cori. And if magic as we know it is gone at the end of the solstice, and you are hurt, I will kill whoever harmed you with my bare hands."

A shiver ran up her spine because she knew he meant every word. "I love you, too," she whispered as she pressed her lips to his cheek. She lingered there as long as she could before joining Pru and Seth in the stairwell.

As she followed Alfie in the snow toward the motel, Adrian's magic flowed under her feet like the current under a frozen river. The icy flakes swirled through the surrounding air, the wind caressing the skin of her face.

She savored the feel of each one of them as they clung to her coat and hair, like an icy, familiar kiss.

CORI

The Whitemarsh Inn was a bed-and-breakfast, furnished in a cozy aesthetic. She positioned herself in the great room, a cup of tea balanced in her hands in front of the fireplace. Tea that had been given to her by the concierge.

The scent of juniper berries wafted from her cup. Someone had slipped a sleeping draft into this tea. A sleeping draft that smelled suspiciously like her mother's.

Tapered candles flickered over a holly centerpiece, casting light on a gorgeously appointed Christmas tree. She had been so caught up with the solstice, Christmas had completely slipped her mind this year. She realized she did not even get a present for Adrian before they had abruptly left for Salem.

If we make it to Christmas. She pushed the thought out of her mind and focused instead on surviving.

She reviewed her angle in her mind. Enzo didn't know she was aware of his involvement in LARC. He didn't know that she had been working with a group of Gray witches for the past several months, and he certainly didn't know that those Gray witches had been silently protecting her since she was twelve years old.

How much about her life *did* he know? How much about his own would he be willing to share? If she had intelligence on him, he must have *some* intelligence on her.

He had needed to use dark magic to send her Fin's Byzantine fire, which meant until that moment, he had not known her location. Had they escaped in time before he could track her? She shivered despite the warmth of the fire. She did not doubt that Fern had completely decimated the memories of the witches that had been sent to her, but she sent a silent prayer to the Mother that her friends in Farley were safe and sound.

Would she ever see them again?

Her heart ached. For the first time in her life, she had felt like she belonged somewhere, only to have it ripped away. She wouldn't be able to return to San Francisco, and she could never ask Adrian to leave his family. A family that had become her own.

The light was bright as the door opened into the dimly lit room, reflecting the snow. A tall, dark-haired man entered and shook snow off his jacket, and her heart leaped.

Enzo.

He locked eyes with her, and although she knew that this chance meeting was not by chance at all, his aura radiated genuine shock. "Cor? Is that you?"

She stood, despite her legs feeling like they were made of jelly, and clasped her hand to her mouth. It was really him, standing in front of her. Even though she knew the real reason he was there, she could not stop herself.

Her feet practically glided across the floor as she flew into her brother's arms. Tears fell from her cheeks as he hugged her back.

This man—who had taught her to ride a bike down the steep hill in front of their town house, who had told her silly stories before bed when Mama was late from coven, who had made her grilled cheese every time she was sad because he knew it was her favorite comfort food—was the same man who was charged to take her life tomorrow.

"Enzo?" She looked up at him. He was the same man he was then, though more fearsome and distinguished-looking in his thirties with whispers of smile lines around his eyes. "What are you doing here?"

She knew what he was doing here.

"I should ask you the same thing," he said seriously, falling easily into the role of protector.

"I had a vision," she explained carefully. "It was vague, but it told me to come here." What she said technically wasn't a lie. She continued to choose her words carefully. "Is Mama with you?" she asked hopefully.

He didn't answer her question. "You had a vision to come here, the day before the solstice, and you came?" he asked with exasperation. "What if someone was luring you here?"

He was luring her here. Did he wish she had not come?

"I didn't get that impression," she said carefully. "It felt like I would be safe here. Like it was supposed to happen." Enzo knew that Cori's hunches were never coincidental. He arched a brow at her.

"Mama isn't with me," he lied. "Are you staying here, too?"

She nodded. "Now I know why I had the vision; it was because you were going to be here. I've been so anxious. The closer we get to everything being over, the more worried I've been that something would go wrong."

He clenched his jaw and pain etched his features. It became clear to Cori at that moment that despite his involvement and responsibility, Enzo did not want this to happen. Her eyes fluttered closed. The sleeping draft made her arms and legs feel heavier as she fought to support her weight.

"Cori, let's take a walk. It's not safe to talk out in the open," he said seriously, his eyes darting back and forth.

He led her by the hand down the steps of the inn, snow crunching under her boots as she pulled on her coat.

As they headed down the side street next to the inn, Enzo held her elbow protectively. Suddenly, she was a little girl again, learning how to ice skate as her older brother patiently held on. "Cori, let's walk this way. I have a lot I need to tell you."

As she walked on, the trees seemed to sway unnaturally, and the colors bled together like a watercolor painting in the rain as she stumbled.

Enzo caught her fall as she heard him whisper, "I'm sorry, Cor."

Even as the potion raced through her veins, clouding her mind and blurring her vision, she saw his familiar brown eyes shimmering with gold, and she knew.

He meant it.

CORI

She blinked her eyes open, her vision still out of focus. As she raised her hands to her face, a tug pulled around her arms. Silver threads encircled her wrists, exuding a glow akin to starlight. She traced the threads to their origin at the bolt on the wall that emitted the same silvery sheen.

As she studied the physical manifestation of her magic, tiny specks of light turned as though in orbit around the bolt.

The room was dark, the eerie glow cast from two bolts on the wall the only illumination. The door of the room was slightly ajar. Shadows passed along the corridor—singular shadows not attached to a living being, whispers of a light only she could see. They passed with an eerie sense of calm as the spirits in the hall paced up and down in the ominous quiet of the old home.

She squeezed her eyes shut as she prayed a desperate plea to the Mother.

Please don't show me what happened to them here in this house. Please bless them with peace and silence so they don't notice me.

She watched with a still heart, refusing to breathe, as the spirits passed by, one after another. As time slowly passed by, the spirits dissipated, and the hallway was empty and silent. "Thank you," she whispered into the silent room with relief.

Sheets rustled from across the room in response to her voice in the air. A lamp clicked on from the nightstand of the four-poster bed, illuminating the face of someone Cori had seen only in her dreams for far too long.

"Mama?" she whispered, tears stinging her eyes. "Is that you?"

Astrid practically floated across the room. Her mother's arms wrapped firmly around her. She pulled back and held her daughter's face in her hands, regarding her as if she were made of glass.

"My starlight," she whispered, her eyes wide with awe and fear. "I was beginning to think I would never see you again."

Astrid's voice, once light and airy, felt dense and heavy on her ears. With each syllable, Cori felt the weight of the past decade upon her mother. Her heart broke as she stared into the face of the once effervescent woman who sat next to her.

Her mother had always been petite, but her exuberant personality had made her look stronger, taller. This woman's light had been bled dry, cut down by solitude and worry for her children.

Wrinkles etched her face with a subtle furrow on her brow, and her lips were outlined as though permanently pursed in contemplative thought. Her eyes, pale blue and bright, shone against her porcelain skin like jewels, her head haloed by platinum blond hair that was frosted in pearly white strands.

Somehow her mother looked even more beautiful than she had remembered in the eerie light of their magic, her features a stark contrast to the wisdom of her worry.

Her mother's hand slid over her own and squeezed. "You've been captured as well, then," she said with resignation.

Cori nodded, trying to hide a smile. "What a way to be reunited," she joked. "But I have something for you, Mama." She pulled the skeleton key from the hem of her bra strap, passing it to her mother as a smile tugged at Astrid's mouth.

"Fin is a clever kid," she said, holding the heavy key in her palm. She ran her fingers over the smooth metal. "It was heartbreaking to see what Calvin did to him." Her voice broke. "Now we can get out of here," she said, her blue eyes gleaming.

Cori stilled. "Mama, now *you* can get out of here."

The color drained from Astrid's cheeks. "We need to leave

together," she explained in a panicked whisper. "Cordelia, they're going to kill you."

"I know," Cori whispered back, her words dry on her tongue.

"Your brother—"

Cori held up her hand. "I know about Enzo, Mama." Astrid's eyes widened and her mouth fell open. "Papa came to me. He explained everything." She didn't think her mother could get paler.

"You saw Paolo?" Tears glistened in her eyes. Cori nodded. "What did he tell you?"

"He told me I needed to be present here today."

Tears fell from her mother's eyes as she spoke, and at that moment she realized she was not here to simply set her free from this bolt on the wall. She was here to set her free from the worry, the anxiety, that her daughter would be found.

Free from the gripping dread at the thought that her own son would be the one to take her daughter's life. Tears stung her eyes as she squeezed her mother's hand. "I know Papa died to save me," she continued. "I'm going to make sure his life did not go to waste. I'm going to face Enzo and make sure I save him from his prophecy, too."

Astrid's shoulders shook silently in the darkness of the room as her head fell into her hands. Cori had come here to free her mother of the greatest burden of her life—the truth.

"Your father," she whispered, "loved Enzo more than the Earth and sky. When he delivered his prophecy, it was like the ground had opened and swallowed him whole. He didn't eat for a week." Astrid stood and walked to the window, looking up into the sky as though Paolo himself would be written in the stars. "For a while he seemed OK, like he was learning to cope. He told me about taking the plane out, and I thought nothing of it. He loved to fly; it helped him clear his head." She swallowed her words thickly. "I knew the moment the plane crashed. It felt like someone was ripping my soul in half. My body shook with the vibration of it. I found the note tucked into my dresser drawer."

Tears cascaded down her neck as her mother confessed her worst memory.

"Mama," Cori asked in a whisper. "Does Enzo know?"

Astrid sighed heavily as she wiped her tears. "No," she said, shaking her head. "There were so many times I almost told him. Your brother was in a relationship a few years ago," she said arching her brow. "Did you know?" Cori shook her head, her chest clenching. "Vanessa was so sweet. She brought out the best in him—encouraged him to open his restaurant. Sofia was born soon after."

Cori let go of a breath. The little girl with the golden hair. A giggle whispered in her ear as the smell of cotton candy danced under her nose. "I have a niece." Cori said with affirmation.

Astrid's eyes twinkled now. "You knew, didn't you?"

At this, Cori nodded. She had sensed the familiar presence of the little girl in the photo with Enzo long before she had known the truth.

"Sofia is Celestial, Cori," Astrid said, her eyes glittering knowingly. "I knew when she was a baby. She was just like you—smiling up at the stars and playing with spirits only she could see."

Cori stood up and sucked in air, overcome with simultaneous joy and grief. This little girl shared the same magic that was passed to her from her father and yet—she didn't know her.

They shared everything, yet she was a stranger. She wasn't there to watch the moon with her or teach her about the Little Dipper. She missed her first steps, her first words. And she would never get that time back.

"When his restaurant failed, Enzo got desperate," Astrid continued. "Vanessa had postpartum depression, and they were at risk of losing their home."

If Cori knew anything about Enzo, she knew nothing could hurt him worse than his own pride.

"I offered them a home with me, but Enzo resisted. That's when he reconnected with Calvin." Astrid's lips puckered at the name as though it left a sour taste on her tongue. "He had solutions for Enzo. He fell in step with the wrong ways of doing things. Vanessa didn't know at first, but when she found out, she left. She went back home to live with her mother near Sonoma. Enzo only got to see Sofia on the weekends, and Vanessa only felt comfortable if I was there to watch over him."

"Just like that, he was the bad guy." Cori shook her head.

"Just like that," Astrid agreed, gazing out the window again. "His worst nightmare had come true. He would never be the kind of man his father was."

"Mama, I saw visions of you. You were arguing."

Astrid shook her head with sorrow. "I learned of what the LARC planned to do in September. I sent you that note shortly after I found out about Enzo's involvement. All along, he assured me he was only getting close to Calvin again to try to stop them from getting to you. At first, I believed him."

Cori nodded in understanding. "You wanted to give him the benefit of the doubt."

Astrid nodded, her lips pursed. "I knew he could never harm you, Cordelia. I thought—I hoped—that your father's sacrifice would protect him from the darkness. I did not know it would get this far."

Cori took a deep breath. "I understand now. It needed to get this far. I need to face the reality of my prophecy." She paused, turning her charm bracelet absent-mindedly. "And my brother needs to face the reality of his."

CORI

It took a while, but Cori finally convinced Astrid that she should run to safety without her. After a tear-filled goodbye and multiple back-and-forth arguments about the plan, Cori finally slipped Astrid the key.

It was four in the morning before her mother slunk away, escaping through the cellar door and into the dark night. Cori had explained how to get to the safe house beyond the clearing in the woods, and she knew her friends would be waiting there to help.

She smiled to herself. Now that Astrid was no longer spellbound, Cori had pity for any witch who tried to capture her. The tattered old notebook with the picture of the Golden Gate Bridge was entrusted to Pru before she left. She smiled to herself, wondering what it would have felt like to scrawl the number zero onto the pages.

After all these years apart, this was not the reunion Cori had envisioned. She gazed down at the wispy bonds of silvery light that encircled her wrists and was overcome by resentment.

Her eyes were heavy, but she knew her body would not relax enough to let her sleep. Every twenty years, Saturn and Jupiter pass close enough to each other to be considered a conjunction, but the maximum conjunction had never coincided so perfectly with the solstice before.

She reached out her senses to Saturn, the authority of wisdom and karma in the sky. Nonna taught her that Saturn always delivered wisdom to all she shed light upon. Jupiter is the planet of fortune.

It made perfect sense that, in their conjunction, those who were smart enough to heed to the Covenant would fall on greater fortune than those who cheated the terms. Dark and light may be more powerful in combination than light magic alone, but using the darkness for personal gain or to harm another was about the worst karma she could imagine.

The planets would handle it. They always did.

Footsteps echoed in the hall, and her heart quickened. She sat up straight on the bed, her limbs rigid with fear, as Enzo darkened the bedroom door.

His eyes darted to her in disbelief, then to the empty bed on the other side of the room.

"What happened, Cor?" His whispered voice was stern, but she sensed a hint of desperation there.

"I used the key to free her," Cori explained simply.

Enzo's eyes darted back to the hall, checking to assure they were alone. "I see that," he said through gritted teeth. "I'm confused why you didn't use the same key to free yourself."

"What would've happened to you if I left, Enzo?"

He clenched his jaw and shook his head. His silence confirmed what she already knew. If she had escaped, they would have killed him.

Cori arched an eyebrow at her brother and put her hand on her hip as though they were simply arguing about what game to play on the playground.

"You're the one who brought me here, remember? I may have been knocked out thanks to the potion you slipped me," Enzo visibly winced at her words. "But the last thing I remember was walking away with you."

"You had the key," he said with an exasperated whisper. "I fully expected you to use it. You've always been smart, Cor. Why did you choose this moment to do something stupid for the first time in your life?"

I did it for you.

Cori narrowed her eyes at her brother. She wanted to scream at him, but she reeled her emotions back. "Why did you help Fin escape?"

His shoulders sagged. "I was trying to get Ma out of here. And—" He partially closed the door. "I was trying to give you an out before—"

"Before what?" She stood now, and even though he was a full head taller than her, he seemed to shrink in her presence.

"Do you know what they're going to do?" he asked in a frantic whisper.

"Probably kill me," she said defiantly, gesturing toward her bolt. "This is clearly some dark shit." *He doesn't know you know. It's not time to tell him.* "Why, Enzo?"

He sat on the bed, cradling his head in his hands. "They threatened her, Cori."

Her throat constricted. "Who did they threaten? Mama?"

"No, not Mama." His jaw clenched. "I have a daughter. Her name is Sofia. If I don't help Calvin—" His words got stuck on his fear. "He's going to make sure I never see her again." His defenses were fully down now, despair and grief radiating from his aura. "If her mother found out about all the things I have done over the past few years, she would never let me see her again, anyway. But Calvin would kill both of them. His coven has been using my restaurant as a front to trade in dark objects for the past few years. He blackmailed me."

Nausea rose in her throat. Calvin would kill a *child*? A shiver ran down her back.

"I'm so sorry..." Cori reached her hand toward him, but he pulled away.

"Don't—" He stopped her. "This is my fault. I was failing, and I didn't know any other way. Cal always had a little edge to him, but I didn't know it would be this deep. He helped me get some money, manipulated a few critics with magic, and even used compulsion on a few humans to make them work harder and longer." Cori felt her stomach churn with disgust. "I told him repeatedly that I had no idea where you were, but he knows you are my sister, Cor. I didn't know it would get this deep. Calvin, he's—"

"Go on, Enz. What am I exactly?"

Cori's blood turned to ice at the sound of his voice, cool and silky. Enzo narrowed his eyes as Calvin stalked into the room, calm and confident with a curious expression of arrogance on his face.

Her eyes darted to her brother in desperation. Even though she knew he was fully planning to kill her, her Eye was still convinced that he would let no one harm her. Enzo certainly didn't appear afraid as the gold swirled in his eyes.

All she could see was secret loathing, black and inky, bleeding into his aura like a stain.

"Calvin is cunning. A businessman," Enzo finished his sentence, keeping his expression blank and emotionless.

Calvin laughed and clapped his friend on the shoulder as though he had been given a compliment to his golf swing. He chuckled smoothly. "Thanks, buddy." He shook his head. "So, Astrid finally got out of here, huh?" he asked, almost playfully, as though she had not been chained to the wall on his orders. "Wonder how that happened?"

Cori's cheeks heated as he turned his gaze toward her. "I... um."

"Don't worry, kiddo," he said, punching his best friend's little sister playfully on the arm. Enzo's shoulders tensed, the inky hatred swirling faster. "I figured Fin had gotten the spare key. Makes sense he would have found you." He rubbed his stubbled chin. "Question is—why didn't you join her?"

She was prepared for this question, but Calvin's overt arrogance had surprised her a bit. He asked her the question with amusement, as if he was merely curious how she could have fallen into his trap so perfectly. She looked him in the eye, summoning the best impression of Astrid she could.

"My Eye told me to stay," she replied in a dreamy voice. "I had to listen. Leaving with Mama would have been the wrong thing to do."

Triumph flashed in Calvin's eyes for a fleeting second before he guarded his senses once more with walls of cool confidence.

"Interesting," he replied with a smirk. He would think that her Eye would give her that message. According to him, the right thing to do would be to kill her. The universe was giving her a signal to bend to his will.

Men like Calvin are not rare. They believe that something is owed to them, and the fates will give them what they want eventually. It's natural to think that way when you've spent your entire life being handed your every desire, presented on a golden plate to accept or reject at your whim. It was no surprise to Cori that Calvin felt justified and vindicated in knowing her Eye had led her to stay with him.

To let him kill her. After all, to Calvin, his bad choices were justified by his own self-serving explanation.

He pulled out a little black notebook from his jacket pocket. "I actually came upstairs to welcome you to the Sampson house and get your meal requests for the day," he explained smoothly, a smirk playing on his lips. "Enz, I should have asked you to do this part. You're the restaurant man, after all."

Enzo rolled his eyes. Cori laughed despite herself. He was asking her for her meal requests, knowing they were going to be the last meals of her life. A foul taste arose from her throat, and food was the furthest thing from her mind at that moment. "Why am I here?" she asked boldly, fixing her eyes on her jailer.

Calvin lowered the notebook and considered her from under heavily lidded eyes. He scoffed, "I thought that would be clear."

"Enlighten me," she retorted.

"Well, it's the solstice." He raised an eyebrow, as though her question had an obvious answer. "We must at least try to save magic. We need to keep you safe, Cori."

She felt a tingle work up and down her spine as her Eye hissed a warning at her. She wondered if Calvin thought the bolt on the wall prohibited her ability to read him. But his aura was not a part of her, and her Eye was chained—not blinded. "Safe from what?" she asked innocently.

Calvin's face hardened for a fleeting second, breaking through the charming facade of his face. He pondered his answer for a moment before the handsome smirk returned.

"From the end," he said simply. "Safe from the end."

CORI

C ori watched the sunlight fade behind the yellowed lace curtains of her floral prison. Time moved like molasses down the side of a spoon as the hours of the day ticked by. She had declined breakfast and lunch. When it was near dinnertime, Enzo visited her again, imploring her to eat something.

Suddenly, she was ten years old again, hugging her teddy bear on her bed, telling her big brother about a bad day at school. She nodded slowly and looked up into his sad eyes, golden flecks of light flaring. "Will you make me a grilled cheese, Enz?"

He arranged his lips into a firm, thin line. Unblinking, he nodded and walked out of the room without another word.

It was the best grilled cheese she had ever tasted, and it made her wonder if he used some kind of magic when he cooked it. Just like when she was a little girl, she felt a little lighter with each bite she took. He made it just the way she liked it—with a thin slice of tomato and provolone cheese.

Her eyes had fluttered into intermittent sleep when the dark hours of the day passed by. Spirits sulked past the door of her room all day. Most hung their heads and paced, but none took notice of her. Despite her magic being chained to the bolt in the wall, nothing could keep the energy of the spirits away from her.

She watched the steady march of ghosts through the hall, a

parade only she could see. Just like auras, her connection to the spirit world was not connected to her magic at all, but was external to her, something she could tap into that was not her own.

The Other.

A little girl with plaited blond hair startled Cori as she bounced down the hall. It took her several moments to realize that she was a spirit, as her form was more solid than most of the others that had passed by.

She was dressed in a neat brown dress with floral embroidery, and she floated into the room happily as if on her way to complete a pleasant errand. The air in the room became cool as the little girl plopped herself on the opposite bed with comfortable ease. Cori recalled Zion's story about the Sampson family, and how they had been hanged on the property—even their children.

Was this one of the Sampson children? Was this her old bedroom?

The little girl must have sensed Cori's awareness of her as she lifted her eyes, amusement playing on her pretty oval face. "Can you see me, mistress?"

Cori nodded. "I can." Spirit children were always the most pleasant to talk to, but it still made her ache for them—robbed of life at such an early age.

The girl floated across the room. "Are you Celestial, then? Have you seen my sister?"

"I'm afraid I have seen no other children today." Cori smiled at her warmly. "But yes, I am Celestial."

The girl nodded, smoothing out the wrinkles in her poplin dress. "Aye, I thought it would be so. As am I."

A lump formed in Cori's throat. No wonder this little girl manifested such a clear, solid form. "Are you one of the Sampson children?" she asked her.

"Yes, mistress." Her eyes darkened as her voice fell to a whisper. She peered into the hallway as though expectant. "Are you one of the sacrifices?"

Cool air dried her throat. "I do believe I am."

The girl placed a transparent hand on her forearm. "Do not have fear in your heart, miss." she said with sympathy. "It's not hard at all to cross."

Tears welled in Cori's eyes. This girl was so young to have seen such horrors in her own home. "May I ask a question?" The young girl nodded earnestly. "What does it feel like?"

The little girl closed her eyes. "I don't remember much, but don't worry yourself. It doesn't hurt." The girl crinkled her eyes in a smile, tipping her head up to the sky. "Besides, today is not your day to cross."

Cori had no time to react. She heard a soft knock on the door as she darted her eyes away from the spirit of the little girl. A small middle-aged woman with a stern face appeared at the door. "Ms. Mangianelli, my name is Sue. I will escort you out to the field, dear."

Cori glanced back to where the spirit had been only to find that she had disappeared, dematerialized back to the spirit realm, likely to find her sister and tell her about their conversation.

ADRIAN

B lades of grass broke in frozen fragments as Adrian and Seth crunched their way through the snow to the clearing in the woods. The buzz of the magic hung in the air as they entered the zone where Prudence had cast the protective charms.

Adrian had barely slept last night, and his eyelids were heavy with worry and fatigue, held up only by adrenaline. Alfie motioned toward them silently in position behind a woodpile. He was joined by Prudence, Zion, and Fern.

The Fire Elemental, Fin, was there as well, looking cleaner and less wounded than the last time he had seen him, no doubt thanks to Prudence's healing tonics. The other local Gray witches were back at the safe house tending to Astrid.

It had been surreal for Adrian to meet Astrid. Her mannerisms were so much like Cori's, and she had the same heart-shaped face with delicate features that looked like they were carved out of porcelain.

He closed his eyes and pictured Cori's face, like she was painted permanently in his mind, and his chest clenched.

Ever since Cori had left to meet her brother, he was hollow, made of nothing but bubbles of air. He barely heard anything that Alfie said as he reviewed the plan with them. It wasn't until Seth nudged him hard in the ribs that he snapped back to reality.

"Adrian, did you hear that?" he asked in a whisper.

"No," he said, quickly surveying the surrounding land. He needed to focus. Now was not the time to let his fear get in the way. "Sorry. What did you say?"

Seth thrust a pair of binoculars into his brother's hands. "Look for yourself," Seth said with a small smirk. "That's the sacrificial site on the top of the hill." The woods were dark and bare. No leaves clung to the trees. Adrian shivered at the dead land ahead of him. He wondered if his mother could even coax life from this place. "Do you see what I see?"

Adrian peered into the binoculars and focused on the top of the hill in the clearing woods. There was a tiny stone structure just below the clearing. He lowered the binoculars, focusing on his brother. "Is that a well?"

A smirk spread on Seth's face. "I reckon it is."

Despite the bubbles of anxiety, hope broke through the tension within him. For the first time in days, Adrian smiled back.

CORI

I t took only a few moments to realize why Sue had been tasked with escorting Cori to the field. The woman may have looked plain and unassuming, but from the moment the bolt was released and her hands were untethered, the woman locked her in with an icy stare.

"If you even consider trying to run, I'll gut you," she said simply. Despite the severity of her threat, Sue looked amused, almost as if she wanted Cori to try. "I know about ten different spells that will kill you in your tracks." Cori acknowledged the scary little woman before her with a curt nod. "And if you try to attack me, I know about ten other spells that will dismember you before your lips stop moving," Sue continued, her voice disarmingly sweet.

Cori followed Sue out the front door of the quaint, eerie little house, determined not to let her lips move at all. They approached a clearing in the woods, where the light of a bonfire flickered on the top of the hill. About a hundred people were gathered around the fire, and as she approached it, she realized they were moving in a slow, purposeful circle around it.

She was instructed to stop at the clearing. Calvin was positioned at the top of the hill, standing still, his arms raised toward the fire in his impeccable black suit. Enzo was next to him, holding the hilt of an ancient-looking sword.

His shoulders were slumped in defeat as he stood there, his gaze fixed on her as she approached. Cori did not know what time it was as she walked out onto the clearing, but based on the position of the moon in the sky, she could guess it was almost time.

She tipped her head back, tuning in to the position of the Earth. She was almost completely tipped on her axis as the solstice approached. Wispy clouds dotted the sky, but the stars shone through them.

As she gazed upward, her heart and her Eye opened to the heavens above her. Saturn and Jupiter were about to touch, whispering at her urgently as she planted her feet in the barren ground of the wood.

The time is near, Cordelia. Have faith in your purpose.

Sue ushered her over to Calvin, and she was shocked to realize his gaze was fixed on the same stars in the sky.

"Beautiful, isn't it?" he said, genuine wonder in his voice.

"I'm inclined to agree," she answered him.

His eyes shifted to focus on her, startling her, pulling her away from the heavens.

"How does it feel to hold such power, Cori?" Calvin asked her, his voice raspy, desperate.

"What do you mean?" she asked innocently. But she knew what he meant.

"What can you see when you look at me?" His question was pleading, urgent despite the relaxed posture in which he stood.

She hesitated, biting her lip. "Are you asking me to read you?"

"I'm asking you to read my future," he said, the nervous curl of his lip succumbing to the charm of his smile for a fleeting second.

She gestured to his arm. "May I?" she asked. He nodded in affirmation. She took his forearm in her hands and opened her Eye to him.

. . .

A young boy ran through a handsomely appointed living room. An impeccably dressed woman sat on a sofa, thumbing through a magazine as an older woman watched the boy with interest as he repeatedly attempted to shoot a basketball through a tiny toy hoop.

"Calvin," the older woman commanded.

The boy trotted promptly to her elbow.

"Yes, Grammy?" The boy was gap-toothed and bright-eyed, eager for the explanation of her summons.

"What does Grammy always say?" she asked, a keen smile pulling at her lip.

The little boy's eye twinkled. "Hansons never quit."

The old woman's eyes crinkled in a smile. She kissed him, staining his cheek with a smear of bloodred lipstick, before he went back to his game.

Cori reentered the present, her eyes bleary from the vision.

Calvin's eyes were wide. "What did you see?" His question was raw. Urgent.

She swallowed hard. "Hansons never quit."

His smile deepened, his eyes glittering with the reflection of the bonfire. "Right. They don't, do they?" Calvin smoothed out the front of his suit, adjusting the cuff links. He clapped his hands three times. "May I have your attention, everyone?"

The dancers around the bonfire stopped at the commanding presence of his voice.

They sat on the ground immediately, as though they were children listening for the next instruction from their school-teacher. Cori imagined how many times the same people in the crowd had listened to him in coven meetings, letting the commanding timbre of his voice brainwash them.

Calvin cleared his throat. "Today is an important day. As you all know, hundreds of years ago, on this very land, our elders made a decision."

The aura of the crowd contracted with fear and anger, a

dangerous combination of emotions. Cori scanned the crowd for Enzo who was the only person beside herself still standing, clutching a sword in his hand like an unwanted appendage. Calvin lectured on.

"For hundreds of years, dark magic has been vilified by humans." A collective wave of disdain erupted from the crowd. "So, in the Covenant, our elders banished dark magic, preventing it from ever coming together with the light. Preventing magic from ever reaching its full potential. That ends—today."

Cori's ears became numb to the sound of Calvin's voice. She knew how this speech would go. First, he would vilify the Covenant to his followers. He would follow that up by vilifying the prophecy that she delivered, but there would be a twist. At the climax of his speech, he would acknowledge how her Eye had willed her to come.

Twist it into the fate of the future being foreseen by the witch who had given the prophecy, justifying the reason for her death. The reason she should die, to cancel out everything. Not just her prophecy, but the Covenant itself.

Cori's chest tightened as bubbles of air surfaced from her abdomen. Saturn and Jupiter reached out to each other in the sky as Calvin's voice repeated her words.

Words that had haunted her and terrified her for so many years. Words that had caused her to wonder what it would be like to be killed.

"The Gray Covenant has been betrayed, weakening the Giver, as was foretold by those whose oath was made. When the great conjunction of Saturn and Jupiter occurs on the winter solstice, the Mother will collect the debt of three hundred years of stolen darkness. All those who have betrayed the Covenant will receive no more, and all those who have borrowed from the betrayal will weaken through the Other."

His words—her words—reverberated through her ears as her heart pounded. Enzo's grip tightened on the sword. Reflexively, her hand traveled to the little charm bracelet Nonna had given her. She felt her fingers glide over the smooth metal, worn over so many years by her touch. By Nonna's touch before her.

She felt the metal electrify under the pads of her fingers as she thought about what her brother must be feeling right now. She was terrified to die, but she knew she would feel much more terrified in his position.

Why at this moment, did it have to be Enzo?

The man who had once wiped her tears. Who had taken her to the wharf and bought her ramen and ice cream. The man who had filled the void in her heart, who had stepped into the shoes of her father after he had died for her.

Died for them.

A voice whispered in her ear, a voice so familiar, it reverberated through her chest. *Stellina.* Nonna's voice crackled through her as though she was listening through the old rotary phone line.

The Giver only gives us what we are strong enough to see, Stellina. Do you know why I gave you that bracelet?

Cori shook her head slightly, scared to clue in those near her to her secret conversation.

I held on to that bracelet for my whole life, but it always belonged to you. Only someone who is strong enough to summon the spirit realm can use that bracelet the way it is supposed to be used. Use it now. Show your brother what he needs to see.

She opened her eyes, but she did not realize until that moment that they had been closed. Her hand was already moving over the smooth gold of the bracelet, as if her fingers had walked themselves there on their own accord. As she looked up into Enzo's face, she was shocked to see that his gaze was not focused on her at all, but on something just beyond her, his eyes wide with wonder.

Cori turned on her heel. "Papa?" Her voice was ice on water, delicate crystals, nearly broken with the tension of the air. She turned back to Enzo. He saw him, too. She knew he did. The way he looked at him with wide, golden eyes, his mouth agape as though about to ask a question.

She had called her father here. Presented him to her brother, tapping into a power she never knew she had.

Paolo glided toward them until he was standing between his children.

Daughter of sea and sky. Son of darkness and light.

In the distance, she heard Calvin's speech ending. Cheers intensified from the crowd around her through the buzzing in her ears.

The axis of the Earth deepened as the true moment of the solstice approached. Saturn winked at her with comfort as Jupiter gripped her shoulder, squeezing tight.

Paolo reached his hand out to his son, placing it on his shoulder. "Enzo. It's me."

"Papa, I—"

Paolo held up his hand. "Do you remember our last trip to the wharf?" Enzo nodded back at him. "Enzo, nothing is more beautiful than the light on the ocean at dusk. Do you remember why?"

"Yes." Enzo's stunned face was dotted with tears as his grip on the sword tightened.

Cori's mouth moved, but no sound came out as another round of cheers and applause erupted from the surrounding crowd. Paolo embraced his son in a hug, and Enzo's eyes widened as his father whispered something in his ear. Her father glided to her, his hand brushing her cheek with nothing but the light of his spirit. The whisper of his words was a cool kiss of light. "My star, be bright."

With the final breath of his words, he was gone, and she stood before the impassioned crowd with her brother. Her eyes connected with Calvin's—triumphant and confident as the stars intensified in their orbit above her. The earth was breaths away from the moment of her deepest axis. Calvin nodded at Enzo, his knuckles white on the hilt of the sword.

In the eerie light cast between the bare limbs of the trees, a flurry of snow fell around her brother as he raised the sword over his head. She squeezed her eyes shut, as adrenaline surged through her, readying herself for the pain of the blade as she heard the scrape of metal against bone.

When she opened her eyes, Calvin's severed head was at her feet, the same look of triumph etched into his face as his head rolled away, staining the forest floor with the sacrifice of his death.

ADRIAN

A drian's legs tingled as he crouched with his brother behind the woodpile. Prudence had set up a timer on her phone to make sure they did not miss the window that the conjunction and the solstice coincided, and she had propped her phone beside her as she gazed through the binoculars.

Alfie readjusted the position of the veiling stones that had been set up to shield them as the time ticked down.

The pang of nausea grew in his gut as he watched a large group of people assembled on the hill. The clock ticked down, so slowly it felt as though time were moving in reverse. They had some idea that there would be a gathering, but based on the shadows moving around in the clearing they were significantly outnumbered.

The shadows of two men stood at the top of the hill. Seth nudged him as the figures of two women appeared from the house. He could tell by her rigid steps that Cori was terrified as she walked up the hill. He glanced down again at the clock.

Five minutes.

Heat flushed his cheeks despite the cold air.

He was going to be sick.

One shadow clapped his hands and spoke. *Four minutes.* The air around Adrian thickened as each second that elapsed shaved off a piece of his patience. Fat flakes of snow flurried down around them.

Alfie looked back at him, compassion in his eyes. "Is that you, mate?" he asked, gesturing to the snow. Adrian nodded, the lump in his throat preventing him from articulating words. He expected Alfie to tell him to calm down, reel it in, but the Gray witch clapped him hard on the shoulder.

Two minutes. Prudence stood, her stance catlike and ready to strike as she handed the binoculars to Alfie.

Through the silence of the woods, he heard the deafening clang of metal followed by a terrified scream.

"Holy. Fuck." Alfie sprang to his feet, shoving the binoculars in his bag.

Adrian's eyes darted to the hill in a panic as he sensed Cori's heart quickening, even from a distance. The snow was falling thickly around the clearing now, swirling in a frantic wind.

"Enzo just killed Calvin," Prudence's voice echoed urgently in his ear. "We have to move! *Now!*"

CORI

S now swirled around Enzo as he lifted the sword again and stabbed Calvin's headless body through the heart.

Her voice was frozen in her throat as the crowd of people around them jumped to their feet, yelling to one another. Someone screamed, followed by the angry voice of a man.

"Kill her!"

Enzo's eyes darted back toward the crowd as he yelled into the wind. "Cori, get behind me," he commanded. He raised the sword again with his right hand as an orb of red light encircled his left.

The crowd advanced upon them as Enzo struck back, using the magic from his left hand to stun those who came near them and the sword in his right to strike them down. Cori racked her brain for the defensive spells she had been taught as a young girl.

She shouted the incantations as she directed a stream of magic at the angry mob moving toward her, knocking them onto their backs with the force of the spell.

They were helplessly outnumbered, and panic gripped her as she and Enzo became separated. She spotted a small stone structure not far behind them, and her Eye practically pleaded her to run toward it.

An urgent voice whispered in her ear. *Use your gift, Stellina.*

"Enzo, this way!" she yelled as she started to run to the structure.

She stilled midstride as the ground under her feet rumbled. Enzo had caught up to her, his white shirt tainted with blood and his eyes glowing fiercely.

"Do you feel that?" he asked her.

Just as she was about to answer, a torrent of water erupted from the stone structure beside them, gushing into the air forcefully like a geyser.

A well.

She searched the darkness of the surrounding wood, looking for Adrian. She saw him running, accompanied by Seth, their faces with matching expressions of focus as they ran toward the well.

"Cori, get down!" she heard him yell through the rush of water. Through the darkness, she saw his eyes flash, striking blue orbs glowing through the thick night, as he raised his hands, focusing his energy into the sky.

High above them, a cracking sound echoed through the air as the soaring water turned to ice, glistening like crystals from the light of the stars.

"Now!" Seth bellowed from the base of the well.

Light pulsed from Adrian with the intensity of his magic as the ice crystals, sharpened into enormous arrows in the sky, directed themselves down on the advancing crowd, spearing them violently.

Cori screamed as she watched several witches, not more than a few yards away, fall to the ground, impaled by the ice, their blood staining the sparkling snow beneath their feet.

"Who the fuck is that?" Enzo asked her, his eyes wide with shock.

Cori opened her mouth to respond before freezing in fear, her eyes fixed on the house at the bottom of the hill. Dozens of witches had emerged from the house, and they all appeared to be armed.

Not with magical relics but with *guns.*

Fear gripped her as she watched them pass around rifles as they shouted back and forth, gesturing to where they stood at the top of the hill.

"They need to use human weapons," she said aloud to herself. "The prophecy has come to be." Her heart leaped as she checked in with the Earth, her axis already tilting back toward the sun as the moment of the true solstice came and went.

A collective desperation rolled off the angry mob at the bottom of the hill as they marched up to the clearing.

She stood on the top of the hill, rubbing the smooth gold on her bracelet as she focused on the dead ground below her feet. Ground that had seen thousands of human sacrifices. Souls that still walked these grounds. Souls that would now be called to do her bidding.

The surrounding air turned a shimmering gold as magic tore through her, urging the souls from the spirit realm. She felt her mouth moving, but she did not recognize the voice that came out.

"Here on this ground, you were betrayed by the darkness. *All those who have betrayed the Covenant will receive no more, and all those who have borrowed from the betrayal will weaken through the Other.*"

The *Celestial* Other.

The magic in the spirit realm. An army of thousands of forms, wisps of light cast upon the shadows of the trees, rose from the ground. The legion of souls advanced upon the Sampson house amid the sounds of screams. They could see them.

Enzo stilled beside her, his face pale. *He could see them, too.*

In that moment, she understood. She understood why Nonna had saved that bracelet for her. Knew what her father had meant when he had said Enzo was not the only one she could save tonight. Both of them must have seen this moment, must have seen that within her she had this power.

The power to summon the spirits back to this realm.

Prudence's mouth was agape as she ran to her side, crimson blood smeared on her face. "You did that?"

Cori nodded as the army of spirits walked slowly toward the

Samson house. "The ghosts of every sacrifice killed on these grounds. I've been watching them since I came here."

Prudence held her head in her hands in disbelief. "Do you think they can hold them back?"

Enzo shook his head. "They won't hold for long before they break through and hunt us all down. There's nowhere to run. According to them, you just stole their magic after I killed their idol. I know these witches. They won't stop until we're hanging from these trees."

The spirits had encircled the crowd, forcing them to retreat into the house. Screams pierced through cool air as the spirits began to advance on the windows and doors.

Cori's breath caught in her throat as a tall, thin figure approached them from near the well. Fin's eyes were glowing as an amber wave of passionate fury rolled from his aura. The corner of his lip ticked up with a wicked grin as he ambled toward the bottom of the hill. She called to him, begging him to come back as he trudged into the line of fire.

It was as though he was possessed, pulled by the spirits that had advanced on the house. He stopped midway down the hill, crouching low, touching the ground with his hands as the air crackled with electricity around them. He laughed, the sound hot and menacing in her ear before his lips moved.

Her mouth fell open as tendrils of white-hot flame licked around the foundation of the Sampson house. The Byzantine fire spread with unnatural ease, enveloping the windows and doors of the ancient structure.

Muted screams of the people who were trapped inside echoed through the wood. Along the perimeter of the house, the army of spirits moved in tandem, encircling and trapping the members of the LARC inside.

The trees swayed in a ghostly dance above them as Fin's hands lifted from the snowy grass. He rose slowly to his feet, cocking his head and raising his arms as the flames intensified. The fire engulfed the wood beneath him as though he were simply turning up the burner of a stove.

Cold air raced through Cori's chest as the collective energy of the spirits she had summoned in the surrounding woods fled to the spirit realm, finally freed from the sacrificial land where they had been murdered.

Someone urgently grabbed her hand. She looked up at her brother, his eyes wide with shock as the Byzantine fire reflected in them. The fire spread with fury over the floor of the wood, engulfing every structure, tree, and person it encountered.

Sirens wailed in the distance as the Sampson house crumpled into a pile of ash and twisted bone.

CORI

A pristine Christmas tree adorned the corner of the living room at Huxley Farm, glittering with heirloom ornaments and twinkling white lights. Cori breathed in the aroma of fresh pine as Hannah buzzed into the room, straightening picture frames, and dusting off the mantle.

"Hannah, it's OK. You don't have to fuss like this," she explained, fiddling nervously with her charm bracelet. The same bracelet that had somehow summoned her father's spirit. A connection between realms. It was little wonder to her now why her fingers reflexively rose to the bracelet whenever she felt unsettled.

Hannah peered up from her perch on the floor where she had started to magically sweep pine needles off the tree skirt. "Are you kidding me?" she asked with a squeak in her voice. "Your family is coming here to meet us, and you think I'm not going to clean up?" She smoothed her apron down with irritation.

"At least let me help you," Cori offered, lighting some candles on the coffee table.

"Absolutely not!" Hannah snapped at her. "In fact, get out of this house immediately. I'm sure your boyfriend misses you. Go check and see if he's up in the apartment. And make sure he doesn't look disgusting." Hannah shooed her out the front door and slammed the screen shut with finality.

She eased her coat over her shoulders and pulled the zipper up to her neck, wondering if she would ever get used to the chill of Maine winters. The sun was setting over the forest to the west, lighting the sky over the ocean with an amber glow. The wispy clouds were frosted in bright pink as Saturn peeked out over the horizon.

She closed her eyes and filled her lungs with the salty air. For the first time in nearly a decade, she felt light. The prophecy was now behind her, no longer an ominous part of her future but a part of magical history. She said a prayer to the Mother that she could feel this light for the rest of her life.

Cori's magic did not weaken after the solstice, but she would always remember her brother's blank eyes on the car ride away from the fire. His magic, the flame living in his soul that defined who he was, was reduced to a mere ember.

In the days following the solstice, Cori and Adrian continued to use their magic tentatively. Cori could still see auras and spirits. When she kissed him, she still felt the force of the ocean rippling through her. She tried each spell and incantation gingerly, and everything seemed to be as it was. Just as Adrian had predicted, their magic was untouched.

Astrid was weakened. She and Enzo had checked into the Whitemarsh Inn after the fire. Her eyes were sad when she explained to Cori how she had been. "All of my old spells work just the same. I don't feel any different, but"—her eyes crinkled with sadness. "I tried to conjure a new spell today, and I could not seem to create anything new." She shrugged. "I guess an old lady like me won't have much use for new magic, anyway."

Cori heaved a sigh. "But what will it be like for all the new Charms witches who have not yet come of age?" she asked with worry.

"I expect it will take time. The Other needs to be restored," she explained wistfully. "Until then, Charms witches will be limited in what they can do."

After the prophecy, the mystery of the Other made more sense to Cori than it ever had. Charms witches pulled energy from each other, and there used to be a strength in numbers. After so many witches lost their power, it made sense that the ability to create new spells would be hindered.

It was almost as if the Other had been cleansed of the darkness, but the past had left a stain.

The Celestial Other was different. It was so immense that the magic of the stars and spirit realm could not be touched by the evil actions of witches. Adrian's magic also seemed untouched, solidifying his belief that the Elemental Other was much bigger than the witches that pulled energy from it.

As she made her way up the wooden steps to Adrian and Seth's apartment, she heard excited chatter coming from upstairs. She entered to find Seth and Adrian sitting on their couch while entertaining Jordan and Jess.

As soon as they had arrived home from Salem, Seth had proposed to Jess. He had been unusually quiet on the way home, and as soon as he parked the truck, he left abruptly, saying there was something he had to do.

Jess had accepted his proposal (to nobody's surprise) and Seth had spent the past few days explaining everything to her.

Much to Seth's amazement, Jess was not at all surprised to learn he was a witch. Apparently, Seth had a hard time keeping his powers hidden from her in certain situations. Jess convinced Seth to tell Jordan, as well. She simply didn't keep secrets from her best friend. Jordan, on the other hand, was shocked and angry that the Huxley's and Cori had been keeping such a colossal secret from him all this time.

When he found out about Alfie, his stance on the subject morphed from anger to intrigue. It was one thing to find out a bunch of your friends were witches, but it was completely different to find out the man you have been sleeping with had been one all along.

"I feel like Bella from *Twilight*," he had explained to Cori.

"Except we aren't vampires, Jordan."

He had promptly told her to shut up and stop raining on his parade.

As she entered the room, Seth was replaying the events of the fire for what seemed like the hundredth time.

"Cori, if you ever summon a ghost in front of me, I will divorce you as my friend," Jordan warned her.

"What did you tell the police when they got there?" Jess asked, her attention focused on her fiancé as though he were the only person in the room.

"Prudence and Alfie helped with that," Seth explained. "They can modify people's memories." Jordan's eyes widened. "They constructed a story that we were out hiking when we saw a forest fire. Even though Fin was the one who put out the fire, all the firemen remember heroically fighting it."

"Did they find the bodies of all the evil witches that died?" she asked.

Cori shivered. "The Byzantine fire didn't leave any trace of their bodies. All the humans at the scene were relieved that the house had been abandoned. Or so they thought."

"What happened to the Fire witch?" Jordan asked with a shudder.

"Fin went back to his mother's house in Boston. He and his family are originally from Ireland, and he said he had some business to attend to there," Adrian said darkly.

"Did you tell Ariel about him?" Jess asked, her eyebrows raised high.

Seth chuckled. "Are you kidding me? Mom and Dad would kill us. Not sure how great of an influence he would be on her."

Cori shrugged, remembering how Fin had shown her a part of himself when he was trapped in the Sampson house. He may have a poor reputation, but her Eye told her that his intentions were good.

She wondered what kind of business he had to attend to in Ireland. "I don't think he would be too much of a bad influence. He helped us, after all."

"Nah, if he hadn't shown up, Adrian would have just killed them all with his ice weapons," Seth joked.

Cori smirked at Adrian, who had blushed.

"Can all Water Elementals turn water to ice?" Jess asked, raising her eyebrows at Seth.

"Nope. Dad and I can't. That's one of my brother's special talents," Seth explained, nudging Adrian on the arm.

"Wow, Adrian. You're just like Elsa," Jordan reasoned.

Adrian glared at him through Seth's roar of laughter.

A flash of headlights beamed into the room as Seth looked down at his watch. "Shit. Cori, that must be your family. Sorry to cut this short, we have strict instructions from Ma that we have to look presentable." Seth was still wearing his coveralls that were smeared with what looked like some kind of bait.

Adrian and Cori walked Jess and Jordan out and headed toward the door of the farmhouse.

"You're nervous." He put his arm around her and squeezed her shoulders with a knowing smile.

"I can't believe I have a niece," she said, shaking her head.

"She's going to love you." He kissed the top of her forehead. "You didn't have any feelings or visions about her?"

"You know what? I think I did. I had sensed her, but I didn't know who she was." She sighed heavily. It had not been long ago that she had known Adrian in the same way, familiar in her dreams but a stranger to her reality. "I wonder if she knew about me." She had been so disconnected from her brother's life, but Sofia was Celestial. "Are you nervous to officially meet my brother?"

Adrian stopped in his tracks on the garden path, his face stern. "I know he's your brother. I know he did the right thing in the end. He saved your life, Cor. For that I will always be grateful to him." His mouth was a straight line as the muscle in his jaw twitched. "I will always respect him," he said, carefully choosing his words. "But I don't know if I'll ever be able to trust him."

Cori nodded in understanding. Respect is a gift, but trust is earned.

Adrian shoved his hand in his pocket and climbed the steps to the farmhouse. Inside excited chatter from Hannah and Ariel echoed her mother's dreamy voice as Adrian entered through the creaky front door.

She looked over the side of the cliff, watching the silver beams of starlight glittering on the crests of the waves below. Cori whispered a message of thanks to the sky.

EPILOGUE

PAOLO

SAN FRANCISCO, 1996

The heavy clang of a bell echoed in the distance, reverberating through the salty mist. On the corner of Hyde and Beach Street, a man looked down at the tiny boy who gripped his hand, tighter now in anticipation of the trolley coming up the hill.

The young boy's hair was tossed from the breeze off the bay, and smears of finger paint stained the front of his crisp, white tee shirt.

"Do you hear the bell, *Piccolo*?" Paolo asked.

His son's face turned up, the familiar golden shimmer in his eyes twinkling as he nodded earnestly.

The trolley scraped along, a group of tourists clicking their camera flashes. Usually, when Enzo asked to ride the trolley, Paolo would playfully scoff at him.

"The trolley is for tourists," he would say, Americanizing his Italian accent. "You, my boy, are a native San Franciscan."

Enzo gripped his father's palm with one hand and the leather strap tied to the rail with his other. He insisted he ride while standing, "like a real rider." The boy pointed excitedly every time he saw someone pull the chain for a stop, wondering who would get off.

They arrived at the wharf just before the sun dipped down into the bay, as the sunlight bent through the settling fog. Paolo scooped his son up by the arms, perching him atop his shoulders to afford him a better view of the boats.

"When I'm growed up, I'm going to drive the boats, Papa."

Paolo took in a heavy breath, pushing back a bitter ache. The boy had such innocent wonder for a future that was so cursed. He swung his son's legs over his shoulder, resting the boy on a nearby bench.

"Enzo, I wanted to have a special night together, just you and me. Because tomorrow, I'm going on a trip."

"But Papa, tomorrow is the first-grade concert!" His little fists clenched up, tears welling in his eyes.

"*Certo, Picolino!*" He gripped his son's shoulder. "I wouldn't miss that for the world. I'll leave tomorrow afternoon, after the concert. Tonight, we eat ramen, and tomorrow we'll have ice cream to celebrate before I leave."

Enzo smiled through his tears, his grin punctuated by a gap from a lost tooth. "Are you taking a trip in your airplane?"

"*Si, volare,*" his father nodded. "I'm flying because I'm going very far away this time."

The boy nodded back in understanding before resting his head on the rail, gazing out at the boats. Dusk was settling upon them as the foghorn beckoned the last sailors to shore.

"When the sun is going down to the ocean, it's bright on the top and dark on the bottom. I can't tell if the water is blue or black," the boy mused.

The man gripped the rail. "*Si,* there is energy all around us. The energy from the sun warms the water, but the energy from the water is heavy and deep. The light can't reach all of it. At the bottom of the ocean, there's no light at all, even at the height of the day."

Enzo squinted down at the water, as if trying to see whatever light was left. "Just like the sky with nighttime," he said, trailing his fingers along the rail.

Paolo chuckled. "Exactly," he continued. "It's like that with the water and the sky, but it's that way with everything. Everyone and everything, deep inside of them, has darkness and light. Even people," he said slowly and carefully. "Do you understand? All of us have the power to choose what we are, son. We can choose to be illuminated by the light, or we can choose to be swallowed by the darkness."

The young boy tilted his head. "Papa, it kind of looks the most beautiful at this time of day. You know? When it's both."

"Both like what?"

"Both light and dark."

He nodded at his son, agreeing with him as he looked out over the water. The little boy was right, after all. A chill ran over his skin as the wind picked up from the bay, chasing away the last wisps of fog.

"Are you ready for ramen, *mio caro?*" The boy nodded excitedly, leaping up from the bench. As he ran ahead, he spread out his arms as though he were an airplane, tipping them from side to side as he soared through an imaginary sky.

———

Enzo's story is just beginning! Stay tuned for *A Vision of Lights*, coming soon.

ACKNOWLEDGMENTS

Dearest Reader,

Thank you for coming along with me on Cori's journey. Even though this story took only a few years to come to fruition, it's rooted in a lifetime of wishing.

I want to thank my brilliant editors, Kate Angelella and Anne-Marie Rutella. You have managed to guide me and cheer me on at the same time.

Thank you to my beta readers Christina, Christina, Anne, Mickey, Diana, and Veronica. Huge thanks to John, my writing partner extraordinaire. Special thanks to Kristin and Tami for helping me ensure the spice is right.

My children have been my biggest supporters, my main characters always.

Lastly, and most importantly, I want to thank Matt, my fated mate. Thank you for encouraging me and being my anchor.

ABOUT THE AUTHOR

Maria A. Eden is an emerging author of paranormal fantasy romance. Follow on social media for updates. Join my newsletter with the QR code above for exclusive content, updates, and more!

Leave a review:

https://www.goodreads.com/book/show/209777502-the-gray-prophecy

https://mariaedenbooks.com/

instagram.com/maria.a.eden.author

Sneak Peak

A Vision of Lights: Book Two in the Elemental Realm Series

Astrid peered up at her son with heavily lidded eyes as the door swung closed. Now that they were well and truly alone, the dishes began to quietly and methodically load themselves into the industrial dishwasher as her magic filled the room.

Enzo fixed his gaze on the rag he was using to wipe the counter as glass after glass glided to the washing machine.

"You can use magic, you know." Her words were firm, but her voice was soft.

"Don't want to drop something." Enzo's jaw clenched as picked up a wine glass.

"It's not completely gone, Enzo."

He sighed. "It's mostly gone, Ma."

"How will you know, if you never try?"

"Because I'm not supposed to try." He set down one of the glasses a bit too firmly, and the stem broke in his hand, slicing into the meaty part of his thumb.

Silverware froze in midair as Enzo grabbed a rag to wrap around the laceration. Spells for mending broken glass weren't hard to weave, and he had a good one in his Grimoire.

But what good was a book full of clever spells to someone who had lost their ability to wield them? Cori's prophecy foretold that all witches who used dark magic would lose their powers, and he was paying the price for his old decisions.

"It's gone, and it's my fault. I need to own that," he said. He didn't look up, but Astrid's stare was palpable.

Forks and knives resumed their dance through the air. Several long moments passed before she broke the silence. "Will you please come to dinner with me tonight? Hannah has been nice enough to invite us every week. It's the least we can do. After everything they did for your sister."

Enzo rubbed his temples. The thought of eating dinner while Adrian fantasized about drowning him in the ocean seemed less than appealing.

He wiped the countertop with vigorous circles. "I'll go."

The smile lines around Astrid's mouth peeked out as she held back a grin. "Really?"

"I actually need to ask Cori something. It's a big deal. I should ask her in person."

The rest of the dishes whizzed into place as Astrid grabbed her coat and keys. She didn't give him a chance to change his mind as she made a beeline for his car, singing a song under her breath.

It was rare that Enzo had good news to share, and what he was about to tell Cori was the best news he could imagine. He grabbed his coat and squared his shoulders, readying himself for the lion's den.

-

Printed in Great Britain
by Amazon